——————— ★ ———————

We skidded over gravel and under the belly of the terminal, through the parking lot. The Staten Island Ferry was just pulling away from the slip. The boat was too far out for us to make it. We were almost out of skating surface, trapped at the end of Manhattan.

Another volley of bullets tore into a concrete pillar on my left, sending showers of dust and tiny scraps of debris flying into my face.

"Hang on, Abby," Ike warbled, and I could hear her terror. She squeezed my right hand, gave it a tug, and we put on a final burst of speed, sailing up into the air off the pavement, up and over dark water, over eight feet of open space, and landed on the back of the boat, our skates screaming on the steel deck.

"Duck!" she yelled, and we slid under the chain and into the bowels of the ferry.

——————— ★ ———————

"There's real wit and ingenuity in this debut mystery..."   —*Washington Post Book World*

"Draws you into the world of TV news, the soaps, and the ego-driven world of big-time broadcasting."   —*The Honolulu Advertiser*

"This book is a gem—a good mystery with fair clues, some believable action, and one hell of a sleuthing duo...a terrific debut."
    —*The Drood Review of Mystery*

Forthcoming from Worldwide Mystery by
POLLY WHITNEY

UNTIL THE END OF TIME

Polly Whitney

UNTIL
DEATH

TORONTO • NEW YORK • LONDON
AMSTERDAM • PARIS • SYDNEY • HAMBURG
STOCKHOLM • ATHENS • TOKYO • MILAN
MADRID • WARSAW • BUDAPEST • AUCKLAND

This book is for my husband, Michael, for everything; and for Richard H. Brodhead, Dean of Yale College, for encouraging my antics.

UNTIL DEATH

A Worldwide Mystery/November 1996

First published by St. Martin's Press, Incorporated.

ISBN 0-373-26219-1

Here they come, the couple plighted—
On life's journey gaily start them.
Soon to be for aye united,
Till divorce or death shall part them.
                         —Gilbert and Sullivan
                              The Grand Duke

AUTHOR'S NOTE

ONE

EVERY TIME I tried to tell her the story of the three umpires, something interrupted me—usually her. I'd been trying to tell her the story since the divorce.

It's a good story, but it's one of those that really depend on context, so you sort of have to work it into the conversation when you see an opening. The story works best when the conversation turns to disputed ways of looking at things. As it turned out, I had stumbled into a perfect context that particular night because we were about to find ourselves involved in a baffling set-piece murder, although I didn't know that when I tried once again to foist the story on her.

"You know, Ike," I said, "I've been thinking, and this divorce thing may turn out to be the smartest idea you ever had. I'm a happy man tonight. It reminds me of the story of the three umpires...."

"I wish you'd give it a rest," she responded, not cordially. "I've got more serious things to think about than your dopey umpires." She frowned up at the swirling fog that occasionally parted to reveal an impenetrable black sky, and she impatiently pushed those wild blond curls away from her temples.

I glanced at the curls.

It was the kind of wet night she complains that her naturally curly hair might as well be "a possum with a cheap permanent." Her ninety-five-dollar haircut had become what I call "weather head," not that I would mention such a thing when I was trying to tell her a story. She hadn't divorced me for tactless weather behavior.

The heavy rains had moved east, trailing a warm blanket of humidity. A thick and shiny mist was rapidly rolling in from the west off the Hudson River, behind the storm, carrying with it the metallic scent of dirty salt water and reflecting the soft neon pastels of the city at street level.

That kind of mist hugs the streets, obscuring the scale and softening the raunchiness of the city, and makes New York look like the set of a 1940s musical, a brooding but beautiful cardboard town produced by a resourceful imagination and a low budget. I could almost hear a mournful clarinet straining behind the blue notes of the taxis splashing by on West 72nd Street. I felt like stepping into the street and executing my half of a tortured, lonely tango. And I was dressed for it: black tie, tails, pleated shirtfront, shiny patent leather shoes. A cardboard man on display in a shamelessly sentimental, two-dimensional town.

But you can't tango alone, or tell stories alone, not unless you're really wacko, which I'm not. Merely recently divorced. And all I wanted was five minutes of Ike's time to prove that she didn't know everything. Fat chance. She had told me more than once that men who need to tell stories are narcissistic. Maybe. The way I look at it, a man has to find some love somewhere.

And when his supply has been cut off in reality, the imaginative impulse takes over to fill the vacuum. Divorce makes a man a little prone to romantic fantasy starring himself, makes him temporarily unable to resist seeing and examining the legally diminished new spectacle that is himself, and that's especially true in a mirror-rich place like Manhattan, which surrounds its cast with reflecting surfaces that redouble the random urban choreography of its streets. In the three weeks since the divorce was finalized, I'd been encountering myself practically everywhere I looked—in windows, in thousands of mirrored sunglasses, in cocktail glasses, in brass doors, and on the silver surface of my imagination. The cardboard man was everywhere.

That rainy Monday night wasn't the first time I'd imagined myself in the middle of a movie set. New York is a city that cooperates with a lonely man's fantasies, if he limits them to two dimensions. A man gets in trouble only when he starts to confuse the bright illusion with battered reality, when he misinterprets the reflected figure as a companion, when the landmarks of his dreamscape take on the authority of the waking world as his shadow passes them in the night.

And nothing alters a man's grip on his landmarks quite like being on the receiving end of a divorce, because, when it comes to the short end of the stick, most men have been taught that it's much more blessed to give than to receive.

When Ike handed me my head on my way to the door, she changed the way I look at a lot of things, myself included. A lot of things. That's what I was trying to tell her, because the way you look at things can change your life.

Take that big plastic top hat mounted above the entrance to Playtime-in-Brazil, the dance club on 72nd Street. That night—while Ike was refusing to listen to the story of the three umpires—was the first time I really looked at the hat.

It's a revolving hat, a silly architectural ornament, like that replica of Lady Liberty on the roof of the Statue of Liberty Warehouse on West 64th, or the rear end of the black '59 Cadillac sticking out of the front of the Hard Rock Cafe—a kind of benign structural growth, typical of the Upper West Side of Manhattan. That soggy Monday night in late June the mist was collecting along the blue neon brim of the hat, sparkling along the gas tubes with wet reflections of headlights, of the traffic signal at the corner, and of the foggy yellow candlelight in the windows of the All-Souls Cafe next door. The top hat—which, when I was a married man, I had always thought was a lazy cartoon of New York cultural stereotypes by the club's Argentinean owner—was now almost pretty in the mist. My point of view had changed.

The hat's about four feet tall and sits at an angle on the brick face of the building above the door, sort of rakish, and it sports a blinking silver-sequined high heel on its rotating neon brim. I had never noticed before, but the big hat provides almost no protection against even the lightest rain; in fact, I saw that water was somehow gathering on what seemed to be the flat brim and dumping out with impersonal regularity at measured intervals, in pint-size waterfalls, onto couples sheltering briefly in the doorway before they stepped down to the sidewalk to flag cabs or hurry across 72nd Street.

I studied the contraption and discovered that it was the large silver shoe that was filling slowly with water as the hat revolved and, at the top of the hat's rotation, the shoe spilled water down in a straight line, like a dainty fountain with one jet, or like one of those vulgar garden statues of little boys that I think are slightly amusing and that Ike once said are "perfect models of the sum total of male ingenuity." But we were having an argument at the time, so I'm not convinced she really didn't like the statues.

That particular night, the top hat was occasionally lit from beneath as the door opened and the dancers and the audience left the club. But the way I was looking at that hat for the first time—really seeing it fresh—it was turning with fairy grace and sparkling wet colors from Oberon's forest, and the rainwater it spilled looked like it was full of good luck. And Ike had stepped out into the night from the club's foyer, spread out her yellow plastic slicker on the steps, placed our pewter trophy beside the slicker, and sat down directly under the hat.

She and I had been among the last to leave the club, as usual because we were arguing, although that night was anything but usual for us. It was our first dance contest since the divorce. A dance partner is even harder to find than a life partner, so we had decided to keep that baby when Ike threw out the bathwater.

Perennial fourth-place finishers (losers) in all dance contests, that night we had stunned ourselves—and the other couples and the judges and the audience—by taking first place for artistry in the tango. I had passed up complimentary tickets to the Tony Awards over at the St. James Theater in order to dance in this tango competition, and it was nice to be accepting a trophy in a minor show starring myself instead of watching a bunch of people I didn't know accept theirs in a big theater before a television audience of millions. A man who's been handed his head is pretty grateful to be handed something else for a change.

The hot-argument-of-the-minute was about how Ike and I would split the tango winnings. If things went the way the divorce had gone, Ike would get the $500 check and I'd end up with the pewter trophy.

I sat down next to my little ex-wife on the wide stairs under the revolving top hat, taking care to position myself off to one side. I was looking at the hat and noticing how pretty it was and how it was loading up with fresh ammo. We were changing out of our dancing shoes, which we had to do outside the club because Playtime-in-Brazil does not allow skates anywhere near its polished wood floors. We don't mind when we're exiled outdoors to get equipped, which happens a lot. Rollerblades are purely functional for both Ike and me; they're transportation, not toys.

We were sitting there, getting out our wheels and absorbing the dampness, and the dull first-place trophy on the steps between us was glinting with lights reflected from the passing taxis and from the top hat. The blue neon brim cast arcs of twinkling reflections on the trophy, the useless pewter man bending over the useless pewter woman in a stylized dip—a metal couple caught forever in a metal dance with about the same level of real intimacy as Ike and I had left between us.

"I repeat—getting a divorce was a major brainstorm, Ike," I said, stuffing my shoes in my backpack and casting my eyes up at the hat. "We never danced like that when we were enjoying wedded bliss, or whatever the hell it was. It's like the three umpires...."

"That's *so* typical, Abagnarro." My former spouse dropped her ruby red high heels into her backpack and tugged a white in-line skate over her right ankle, pulling the laces tight. "You just don't get it, do you? Now you're equating the divorce with winning a dance contest. God! You always need to find some outside validation for your simplest decisions. It's like you have to have a report card on everything you do, some way of seeing things so it looks like you won."

"I *did* win. First place for artistry."

"I was talking about the divorce, Abagnarro."

I was too interested in the top hat to get really worked up, so I merely said, "I wouldn't be so free with the fine old name of Abagnarro, if I were you. It's not your name anymore, and I'll thank you to have some respect. *And* the divorce wasn't my decision, simple or otherwise, so that's two mistakes you've made already with your loose, flapping lips. *And* if dancing the most artistic tango in New York is merely a 'report card' for you, I must have been dancing with some other blond hussy, her breasts pressed invitingly against my shirtfront." Ike gave me a heated look and opened her mouth, but I put up a hand and went on. *"Invitingly,"* I repeated. "The woman I held in my arms a few moments ago was a creature of molten passion and sinuous, dusky fantasy—not the little shrew seated here on a cheap yellow slicker yapping about my faults and gazing with rare goodwill at a set of pink polyurethane wheels." I looked up at the hat, just to see where it was in its little cycle of irrigation.

"I wasn't yapping," she snapped.

"It sounded like yapping. What would you call it?"

"I wouldn't call it yapping."

"It was yapping. I know yapping when I hear it."

"You're the one who's yapping. Molten passion, my eye. Sinuous, dusky...whatever you said. You wish! That was quite a speech. I've heard shorter filibusters on the floor of the Senate. Do you think you're done yet, Abby?"

"I'm only pausing for breath."

"Well, hold your breath until you turn purple," she said, pulling on her other skate and yanking the laces tight. "I've got to go to work, and I'm ready to roll." The heavy mist had really started working on her hair, and it was frizzing into a blond cloud. Bad hair. While she finished tying her laces, she gestured with her elbow at the pewter figures twined around each other on the base of the trophy. "Do you want to keep that doorstop? It'll match all the other metal junk in your new apartment, or should I say your new swamp?"

I sneaked a look at the top hat. "How nice of you to make that fantastically generous offer. I wonder what's behind door number two." I patted the trophy. "Why don't you keep the pewter heirloom?'' I held out my open hand. "I'll take the five-hundred-dollar check, Ike, if you don't mind.''

I had bestowed the nickname Ike on the recently divorced woman by my side several years earlier, when she was a more reasonable and fun-loving person, naming her after the overalls she was wearing when we met. The sturdy denim garment was part of what I called "the farming loot" she had brought, along with some rigid morals, from Missouri when she graduated from college. New York had softened the morals a little, but the overalls were made of sterner stuff. They were a brand of overalls with the name of the maker stitched on the back pockets with what looked like baling wire. "Ike" is the logo for those stiff, unattractive unisex garments that come from the nearly dead creative juices of ninety-year-old Ike Mason, the only millionaire Booneville, Missouri, ever produced. The overalls were cute on Ike, but they look like poured concrete on everyone else, so Mason's Missouri millions are a mystery to me.

Ike, ignoring my outstretched manly hand, shrugged on her backpack, grabbed the railing, got her skates under her, and stood. Since the check from Playtime-in-Brazil was safely tucked into the pocket of her backpack, she only curled her lip at me and gave me a dirty look. Ike should have been on the stage, which is where she wishes she was, so I hadn't told her about my passes to the Tonys. She really would have been mad if she'd known about those tickets. Complimentary passes to the Tony Awards do not come along every day, but then neither does a chance to get my former spouse into my arms without her scratching and kicking.

When she's not scratching and kicking or yapping, Ike's a born actress, a fantastic look-giver. She can pack quite a bit of narration into a look. The one she was giving me at that moment was the kind you'd give a plausible panhandler who'd just successfully used a crowbar on your conscience and then you spotted your own wallet in his pocket. The look was fastidious, disgusted, disappointed, and ever so hurt by humanity's cheesy side—meaning me.

If you think that was a lot of information from one little glance, it helps if you've seen Ike's eyes. Nobody looks at my ex-wife without a quick feeling of sensory overload. Her left eye is a Caribbean dark blue, her right eye is a Sherwood Forest green, and her eyebrows are dark and full. Now, my theory is that many women are pretty, but for a woman to rate being called beautiful, there has to be some striking flaw, like Lauren Hutton's split teeth or Maria Shriver's wandering jawline or Cindy Crawford's mole—something that relieves the face from ordinary good looks. With Ike, it's those weird eyes.

I glanced up past her lovely face and wildly curling hair, and saw that the silver shoe was reaching the top of its rotation, and it looked very pretty at the point over the door to the dance club.

Playtime-in-Brazil is not as fabled as Roseland, and not as fussily upscale as Le Salon, but it draws the most expert young ballroom dancers in New York City (or, as Ike calls it, "the world as we know it"—transplanted midwesterners invented that snotty New York insularity, and now the real New Yorkers, like me, get blamed for it). Anyway, Playtime's finances are rock solid, and a check drawn by the club on its Chase Manhattan account was not to be trusted to me, the biggest spendthrift who ever collected credit cards, which is probably what Ike was thinking, not that I'm really like that.

"Fat chance you'll get your paws on this check, Diamond Jim," she said. "I'll drop off your share at your mother's. I've got to be down in that neighborhood tomorrow anyway." She turned her head slightly to the left, and that wonderful top hat, its blue neon brim looking like a halo over her head, ground out another inch in its slow revolution, and the silver high heel dumped its stream of collected rainwater onto Ike's shiny blond hair and down the back of her red dress. It was a great dress for dancing the tango, because it left her back bare so she could feel the subtle pressures of my hand as I led her through the *medio corte,* the sexiest part of the tango. And it left her wide open for the waterfall.

She squawked and lost her balance for a second, her skates sliding out of control. She grabbed the railing. When she regained control, she gave me another look with those eyes, as though I had just left a meeting with the hat and had sent out the memo to douse her. She jerked her yellow plastic slicker off the stairs, slipped it on over the red dress and the backpack, and glided across the sidewalk into the street, circling behind a splashing taxi, the frothy scalloped hem of her dress swirling around her legs.

"Hey, Ike!"

When she had navigated the traffic on her skates, she executed a neat speed-stop and turned, standing in the sparkling mist in the middle of 72nd Street. "What?" She snatched the hem of her dress up in handfuls, tying a crude but efficient knot in it to lift the skirt away from the puddles.

"You're a much better dancer now that we're apart!" I shouted over a couple of cars. "Maybe doing without sex has made you appreciate my guidance more on the ballroom floor!" A couple of people had stopped on the sidewalk to listen in. "What are you, spy school graduates?" I demanded. "Go home and watch CNN if you're so nosy."

Ike, ignoring the strangers, took a quick breath and fired back without delay, "What makes you think I don't have a sex life now, Abby? Your ego is the size of the World Trade Center, and just as full of weird bullshit." She turned, cruising gracefully around another couple walking along under an umbrella, and skated east toward Broadway, disappearing into the thick, swirling fog.

Getting the last word in by vamoosing is an unfair tactic. All I could do was give the hat a silent gesture of thanks for the timely cascade and finish putting my blades on. That was one of the troubles between us, although not THE BIG ONE. Ike was always dressed and ready to go long before I was, and she won't tolerate standing around. Even a simple thing like going to a neighborhood movie would turn into a logistical headache, often with her at the box office holding the tickets in her hand as I came strolling around the corner to meet her. Our inner clocks were set differently or something, ticking at different rates, or in different universes. But now, I was thinking, maybe something completely magical had happened to our previously perverse and afflicted timing: our tango had been smooth as glass; there had been no daylight between our bodies; the rhythm had been so locked between us that I might have been dancing with my image in a mirror. Plus, in a sweet dividend of timing, the top hat had entered the argument on the steps of Playtime just like the cavalry coming over the hill. I was thinking my luck had changed.

I should have knocked on wood.

I picked up the trophy and headed for Broadway. I finally caught up with Ike as she was skating into the western curve of Columbus Circle. She may get off to a faster start than I do, but I've got the power moves, and she doesn't stay ahead of me for long. I never missed the opening of any movie I really wanted to see.

TWO

TOGETHER WE rolled up in front of the stingiest revolving door in New York. The O. Armitage Broadcast Center (which most people call—not lovingly—"the Emerald City") is blessed with those giant two-story sea green glass doors with the steel hardware and the famous etchings of news anchors past and present, but those doors have been locked as long as I can remember. I've never seen anyone use them. As far as I can tell, their only function is to look nice for the hundreds of tourists who photograph their green splendor every day. Everyone who actually gets into the building has to be funneled through the midget revolving door and checked by security, although at that time of night traffic through the door is spotty at best, with only us overnight news types up and about. We're pretty much on the same schedule as vampires, those other pale professionals who sleep by day and feed on the public body by night.

I let Ike go in first, pointedly being a gentleman, which really ticks her off because she says it's sexist, which it is. *Better a rat to the cause than a nonentity,* I thought, and I followed her in, the fog threading in through the door with us.

Aside from its great and photogenic green doors, the Emerald City is ugly, a dark and dirty thirty-story mosaic of green marble and rough gray granite. So the thick, rolling mist that night was something of a cosmetic relief. The ugly building houses the flagship news operations of NTB, both radio and television, as well as the Entertainment Division, and the storied green marble penthouse office of Othello Armitage.

Ike had met the almost legendarily elusive Othello Armitage, the man who owns the building and pays our salaries. She said he was something of a cross between P. T.

Barnum and the Tin Man. Armitage believed, according to
Ike, that there might indeed be a sucker born every minute,
but when the sucker grew up to be an advertiser he wouldn't
pay you a nickel for telling the unvarnished facts. The real
money was in telling the news with plenty of heart. Ike
claimed that Armitage was a paradox: a steely idealist who
had a vision of informing the electorate with raw doses of
sturdy American values like honesty and hard work, while
ruthlessly screwing our advertisers for what we could get.

I gazed over Ike's shoulder as she showed her NTB ID
card and signed the logbook, along with the time, which was
11:56 p.m. Under a few other names, Ike had written:
"Mary Tygart." She'd gone back to her maiden name, and
I wasn't used to it yet after two years of calling her something different and easier for me to spell. I signed in under
her name, and we skated in silence across the dark green
marble floor and down the hall together toward the open
doors of one of the elevators. A good job is even harder to
find than a dance partner; we both work for the network, so
we were still stuck with each other overnight, which is another one of our problems.

The elevator doors closed. Ike pushed the button for the
twenty-seventh floor and pulled her slicker up and over her
head, shaking the raindrops off onto the elevator's green tile
floor. That was quite a dress she was wearing. Cleavage
doesn't earn you any marks for artistry from tango judges,
but it's on my scorecard.

"You got some decent clothes in your office to change
into?" I asked, purely requesting information.

"What's it to you, Abby? You're not my husband anymore, and you're not my mother."

"It's not my maternal urges that just made the temperature in this elevator shoot up about ten degrees."

She surprised me then. She blushed. Just like she used to
do when I made a pass.

It was really cute. So, mistaking (I swear) the blush for an
invitation I was very happy to receive, I leaned over to give
her a little grope, and she slapped my face so hard I thought
I could hear the midnight *Radio News Roundup,* and the

lead story seemed to be about a car bomb in my head or in Northern Ireland or some other war zone.

"God, can't you even behave yourself at work, Abby?" Her Missouri twang didn't sound like the angel of death, so I guess I was coming out of it.

I moved my head tenderly, to see if I could still turn it without outside help or a prosthesis. "That was a strictly Pavlovian response, Ike. Just a lingering bad habit. You rang the bell and I salivated. I didn't actually want to touch you on a conscious level." I put my hand up to feel my cheek. "Not that I'm sure I'm conscious."

The elevator door opened. She tried to paralyze me with a look that said she thought I was a Bob Packwood wannabe and skated off down the hall toward her office. I watched her for a minute as she cruised along the green linoleum and rounded the curving wall, her flowing red skirt brushing the ultrasmooth plum-colored plaster as she disappeared from view. Then I glanced at the guy in the black tie and damp penguin suit staring at me from the mirrored wall of the elevator. He had a vivid red mark on his cheek. "What are you staring at?" I demanded, and left the elevator.

The hall was quiet; I couldn't even hear the whir of Ike's skates, so she must have reached her office while I was conversing with the mirror. Her office was a focal point at that hour, especially since the *big changes* at the network.

Ike's the broadcast producer of *Morning Watch,* the two-hour news/talk show whose mondo-bizarro promotional campaign you've probably seen. I guess Othello Armitage finally decided that our paltry 2.5 million viewer slice of the morning audience needed some company, so he had gone to the NTB vault with some blasting powder to get a few advertising dollars. The result was those awful ads on buses and in the newspapers and on the air: There's a picture of a couple of bloodshot eyeball-like fried eggs and a smiling strip of bacon, and the slogan says: "Watch us: We'll jump-start your head." This was the first major-league advertising budget the show has had in its thirty-five-year history, and it was supposed to be geared to the new co-anchor, trying to break the show out of its image as the creaking, wheezing geriatric patient of the morning news shows. That was the public background for the hot currents of new energy—both benign and malign—that had jolted *Morning Watch*, and if the hall was now quiet, it was only because much of the complicated dirty work had already been done behind closed doors, and anybody who had anything to say about it had already said it.

The private background, some of which was deliberately leaked into the public arena, had been smoldering long before the buses rolled with those new ads. Hannah Van Stone, after almost thirty years on the air, had just left the show. Old Hannah—and I mean *old*—had been co-anchor of *Morning Watch* back when television sets were still made in the United States. When her contract had come up a week earlier, the network, in a surprise public move, "promoted" her to UN correspondent and assigned the anchor spot Hannah had lavished on herself for decades to Concepción Candela, a twenty-six-year-old Mexican-American. Since Hannah's co-anchor, Noel Heavener, was also a dusty war-horse and had not been put out to pasture on a dead assignment, the message from the network was loud and clear.

Never one for conducting her business behind closed doors, no matter how hard the network tried to contain her, Hannah had inaugurated her public retaliation by calling every reporter she knew and giving great, nasty interviews to *Newsweek* and *Time* and *Spy*, all about sexual discrimination at NTB News, about how you could keep an ugly old man on the air but *God-forbid-a-woman-should-show-one-wrinkle*. Actually, Hannah had a few more than one, but you see her point. Armitage must have gone out, broken the padlock on his wallet, and bought himself a dozen roses when he read those interviews, because, as everyone knows, bad publicity is still publicity.

Then, Armitage had fanned the flames of bad press by opening his closed door and granting a rare interview to the *Daily News*, in which he was quoted as saying, "A younger, more attractive woman co-anchor will make Noel Heavener look better."

Hannah had answered that one physically, but not publicly. I guess she thought she'd sabotage the new anchor, or Noel, or the show, or all of us, and she went nuts one morning after we got off the air. That was her last contract day as co-host of *Morning Watch,* or, as it is now known at NTB, "Black Friday." The damage to the news block set in Studio 57—we called that set "the aquarium" because it was bounded on two sides by freestanding panels of clear Plexiglas—was so extensive that the whole thing had to be struck and rebuilt over the weekend. Quite a tantrum, but at least it was confined behind the massive closed doors of Studio 57.

And Hannah had another trick up her sleeve. She had been obstinately slow to vacate her palatial suite of offices on the twenty-seventh floor, flaunting a fierce and controlled and nasty-tempered inertia at the network. From my point of view, it was like watching a rhino sink knee-deep into mud—you have another rhino coming in who wants to use the mud, but who wants to relocate the first rhino?

So the situation forced Hannah's young replacement to share space in the Green Room until Hannah could be budged, which most of us thought would be sometime before doomsday, maybe, depending on the rumored lawsuit—the NTB grapevine was floating the speculation that the lawsuit would make the budget for *Terminator 2: Judgment Day* look like a shoestring. If the rumors were correct, or even close, there was a lot riding on which direction the fan was pointing when the legal shit started to fly.

The new anchor was outwardly pleasant about it all, but a roll of computer-designed bunting had been clandestinely tacked up over Hannah's office door, and I thought Connie Candela was the secret artist. On the river of paper, huge block letters spelled out: "Here lies Hannah Van Stone. Forgotten, but not gone." Hannah smiled grimly whenever she passed under it through her door, but the only change she made was to underline the last two words with thick black Magic Marker. So, I guess you could say that some of the dirty work was conducted *above* closed doors.

I didn't really blame Hannah. She was a good anchor, and no one who's as big an air hog as Hannah wants to go to the UN. She might as well have tried to get on the air from the grave, or Central America.

But Ike blamed Hannah. Ike was breaking in the new anchor and trying to go along with the "Jump-start" promotional campaign by producing a full week of timely theme shows for the boomer audience, all the while keeping an eye out over her shoulder in case Hannah launched some new offensive. This week, *Morning Watch* was spotlighting the work of artists combating the spread of AIDS through awareness and philanthropy. When Hannah had been ensconced in the anchor chair, we used to do shows that probably appealed to serious-minded farm children and retirement communities for Alzheimer's patients and people who'd been living in isolation for twenty years, so Ike was a little edgy about having some real material to work with. Excited, but edgy.

Ike had started the week by bringing in an exhibit and the young curator from the Museum of the Surreal that had just opened down in the Financial District. The museum houses the world's largest collection of Salvador Dalí's works, as well as a small group of surviving artifacts from the Dada movement, and 5 percent of their admission price is going to AIDS research, which was generous, because that would put the museum's finances at break-even. The Museum of Modern Art had thought so much of this charitable approach that they had supported the new museum's opening by lending a couple of really famous Dalí paintings from their own permanent collection, and those paintings had made it, under heavy guard, over to the Emerald City for our show.

We've had plenty of valuable stuff on *Morning Watch*— crown jewels, plutonium, a ton of cocaine, fertilized human eggs—but Ike had several nerve fits about having the Dalí paintings in the studio with our newly created UN correspondent on the loose. Everything had gone smoothly and the paintings were safely back in the new museum, along with that fur-lined teacup and the battery-operated hammer and all the other leftovers from memorable nightmares that told me I had a lot to learn about art.

However, I do know a lot about music, and Ike had scheduled Heinous Face for this morning. I didn't think she'd be stressing out about anything they brought to the studio, not even the much-ballyhooed Tama drums. It's funny how Ike's mind works: scheduling the hottest rock band in the country after letting a high-brow museum for hallucination enthusiasts kick off the week. Frankly, I'd rather have a Face album in my apartment than fur-lined crockery or a painting of limp watches, but that's another difference between Ike and me. I doubted she'd ever even listened to a Face album. She was only interested in their twenty-city AIDS tour.

Thinking about the public and private shenanigans of NTB's morning show wasn't helping my headache. I went down to my office and took off my skates, stuck the dance trophy up on the shelf next to my one and only Emmy, did a quick read of my computer mail, helped myself to aspirin for my ringing car-bomb head, and took a major-league nap on the couch.

I usually don't come in as early as Ike does, and that tango had taken something out of me. When I woke up, it was already 4:45 a.m. I sat at my terminal screen and dialed into Use-News, the database that NTB operates. I read the news wires for a while and checked the lineup that Ike had mailed into my electronic queue. Everything appeared to be on schedule, so I combed my hair, straightened my black tie, put on a pair of sneakers, and started the hike over to the control room, which is where I spend most of my time as the show's director. I was going to check in there before going to the studio. The technical crew had rehearsed with Heinous Face the day before, but we still needed a run-through in the studio with all their sound gadgets and our own.

The twenty-seventh floor is laid out pretty much like a wagon wheel. The outer rim consists of a huge circle of small offices, like mine, that have sharp angles on the exterior window wall and smooth, rounded inner walls that open onto what we call "the tube." That's the continuous plumcolored hallway that rings the spokes of the wheel. There are only four spokes, the thinner corridors that run from the tube to the center of the wheel and meet at the hub, which is Control Room #1. Between the spokes are studios and large offices (like Hannah's) and smaller control rooms, and they all open from the tube. Most of NTB's broadcasts— except the sitcoms and the game shows, of course, which are made in Hollywood—come out of the Emerald City, from the twenty-seventh floor and the twenty-eighth, where the soap operas are taped, but only the News Division's facilities have that distinctive wheel layout.

The tube was quiet and empty when I left my office. As I walked, I looked up at the portraits on the plum-colored inner wall of the tube, the wall opposite the little offices. They were high-quality oils, done over the years by Samantha Harris. She had been retained by Othello Armitage almost forty years ago, when he started NTB News at a clear radio station in Carteret, New Jersey. Those first portraits of NTB radio anchors were now at the head of the long arc of oil paintings in the circular corridor—the tube—of the twenty-seventh floor of Armitage's New York headquarters.

The two ends of the line of paintings don't meet yet; there's still plenty of room in the tube for future anchors. Harris has kept the commission, and she's done the face of every anchor NTB has ever had. Ike says that her painting some of the world's most commercially exploited and recognizable faces is hideously ironic because Harris was one of the pioneers of *non*-representational art.

The pictures adorning the network's hallway were not the usual Harris bedsheet-size explosions of squiggles and slashes and blotches that you see in the same museums that feature hot pink light bulbs and bicycle seats supposedly representing the heads of bulls. Instead, these paintings were modest images that actually looked like something—the TV people whose names were on the frames. The portraits were now worth a fortune, according to Ike, an almost incalculable treasure, because Samantha Harris, of course, has far surpassed NTB in both fame and critical approval, which even I can tell because her stuff's in the Guggenheim Museum and our stuff isn't. But whatever tie she had to Armitage was apparently strong, because she had made herself available to paint every new anchor who took up the spotlight in the Emerald City, including the new oil of Concepción Candela that was hung at the more recent end of the august, curved, unbroken line of broadcast history I was now walking beside.

Noel and Hannah's portraits were there, and even one of "Hippie," the handsome sheepdog that had spent a year as mascot of *Morning Watch* back in the late sixties. I stopped for a moment under the portrait of Concepción Candela. The artist had captured the glow of the new anchorwoman's clear, dark skin, and the luster of her thick, shoulder-length hair, and the softness of her rounded lips, and the hardness of her brown eyes, the prematurely calculating look in what should have been a still-innocent twenty-six-year-old face. I took a closer look at the brush strokes that gave the impression of three-dimensionality to Connie's high cheekbones. It was a beautiful painting: beckoning, intimate, almost as though a curtain had been lifted from a small private window onto the talents of both women, artist and subject, represented on its canvas.

I had to give myself a shake to break contact with the painting. For my money, Samantha Harris was a better painter than Salvador Dalí.

As I continued along the hall, I looked down at the green linoleum, to see if I could trace the path of Ike's Rollerblades to her office, but the floor was pretty badly marked up from all the equipment that gets moved around the twenty-seventh floor, and I struck out.

The light was on in Noel Heavener's office, and I glanced in as I passed. For an anchorman who'd occupied the same office for thirty years, Noel kept his digs on the Spartan side, with little accumulation of souvenirs and newsjunk. Most other offices on the twenty-seventh floor are personal museums of the planet's late history, with pieces of the Berlin Wall, paraphernalia from political conventions, Iraqi army helmets, dried lava from Mount Etna, and so on. Newsjunk is a kind of coin among the media; we bring back from our travels these fragments of history and trade them or give them to each other. They're also a kind of combination diary and crystal ball as we approach the millennium: they show us where we've been and hint at where we might be assigned next. But there was no personal record of that kind in Noel's office. Only a few framed pictures of horses on the wall, a couple of photos on his desk, a freestanding tie rack that was empty. Neat stacks of magazines on a Parsons table. A clean coffee mug. His computer.

As I continued along the tube, I could smell the heavy perfume issuing from Hannah Van Stone's suite. And hair spray. And cigarette butts. Her door was closed and I couldn't see any light under the door, but there was fresh cigarette smoke in the air, a wisp of gray floating out above her door. The computer banner over her door was already starting to turn yellow along the bottom edge from the two-pack-a-day habit of the new UN correspondent.

The door to the Green Room was wide open, and I could see the lead singer of Heinous Face sitting in an overstuffed chair, his dark head bent over an acoustic guitar as he strummed a few chords. He did not look up as I passed, and since there was no sign of the talented young drummer I was eager to meet, I didn't interrupt the guitar solo. But I could smell fresh coffee brewing, and I was tempted. I hesitated.

Connie Candela's red eelskin briefcase was shoved under the makeup table, and her reading glasses were standing on their lenses, up against the mirror. Those glasses never got much use, because of her contact lenses, and she was careless with them. Her computer and printer were set up in the middle of the makeup table, and the terminal screen was dark. There wasn't any other sign of life in the Green Room but the guitarist, so I passed the chance for coffee and moved on.

At the corner of the Green Room, I turned down one of the spokes leading from the tube toward the central control room.

Ike was already in Control Room #1, along with the show's technical director and a writer and a few technicians. She was seated at her terminal screen, apparently having a frantic electronic conversation with the Moscow Bureau about a piece on the mechanical trouble they were having in Russia downsizing their nuclear stockpile. That was all I could tell when I looked over her shoulder, that and the fact that she had changed into a pink sweater and black slacks and that her hair was especially curly in the back.

At that time of night, a couple hours before we go on the air, Ike is usually fine-tuning the news segments of the show. She's already got the studio guests tucked away, thinking about whatever book or new movie or cause they're plugging. I'm rarely starstruck, because I see so many big names come through the studio, but Leonardo Brown, the Face drummer, was a personal hero of mine, a real musician, and I was looking forward to rehearsing with him. I hadn't taken anything but cynical notice of all the well-publicized and loud lust he aroused in his female fans, who were listening to Brown with their hormones, not their ears. What I cared about was his musicianship. It was Brown's musicianship that had earned him his nickname—Satan.

That three-and-a-half-minute drum solo on "Voyage to the Underworld," which had been the group's first number-one song, had given rise to the legend/story that Brown had made a pact with the devil in order to tap into an infernal power source that gave his drumming hands a magic speed. I pay attention to all legends/stories about drummers. People who spend as much energy as I do dancing tend to be suckers for the mythology of drummers; they're the timekeepers, and dancers hear them. Satan Brown was probably the best drummer since Buddy Rich, another pop artist Ike probably only recognizes from crossword puzzles, which she leaves all over the control room.

Control Room #1 looks like the cockpit of a large, state-of-galactic-art UFO. It's twenty-three feet long, ten feet deep, and full of switches, electronic boards, little yellow or red lights, levels, phones, microphones, computers, people when we're close to airtime, and a bank of sixty-six monitor screens on one wall. Everyone who works in the control room faces that wall.

Two rows of consoles run parallel to the wall of monitors. Ike's console is next to the sound engineer's, and their row is farther back from the bank of monitors and elevated above the other boards by about three feet. I stood by her side for a couple of seconds, trying to read her mood, and then, tired of being ignored, I sauntered down the two broad, carpeted stairs toward the well of electronic boards around my station directly under the monitors. I sat down at the director's console, put on my headset, and flipped hastily through the script handed to me by a production assistant. I made a mental note to stop by the Graphics Department to check the electronic supers we were using, and so on. I hadn't seen the floor manager around anywhere, but I knew he'd probably already moved the studio cameras into place for the news set, which is the first one we use.

I leaned back in my chair and, swiveling toward the technical director next to me on my right, I asked him to start a camera check. He flipped several switches, and monitors in the bank of sixty-six color screens above our consoles sprang to life, most of them showing color bars, but three of them flickering with the dim outlines of the news set. I squinted to get a look at the camera angles and see what changes I needed to make so the pictures would work with the script, wondering why it was so dark in the studio.

Studio 57 has four Hitachi studio cameras. We don't use robot cameras on *Morning Watch* because those run on tracks and the studio has so many sets spread around for the program that we'd always be tripping over the tracks.

The sets include the aquarium, the kitchen, the living room, and the den. After the opening news segment in the aquarium, we were going to take Heinous Face from the living room set, with them performing their number-one single "Heart on the Stairs," and then Connie would move over to interview them around their instruments because, of course, everyone wanted to see Satan Brown with his custom Tama drums, which, unlike most rock drummers' kits, were jazz drums. Interviewing him there with his kit had been my suggestion.

From the monitors, I saw that the cameras were set up at the news desk in about their usual positions. Connie was already in makeup and seated in one of the big upholstered anchor chairs at the desk. That was a little early for the talent to be in the studio. I looked at the clock over the line monitor, which showed *Early Watch,* the program actually going out over the network at that hour.

It was 5:21. I figured Connie still had first-week nerves and was dealing with them by making herself crazy sitting out there alone on the set.

The monitor for camera two was showing an awkward low angle, giving me a shot of Connie's shoulder, a very nice shoulder in a forest green jacket with black piping that would bleed electronically and play hell with the weatherman's chromakey—the device that allows us to display electronic maps and other graphics as if they were suspended behind the weatherman—as the chromakey works on its own green background. For the three or four times Connie would be interacting with the weatherman over on his set beside the anchor desk, we didn't want it to look like Connie's head was floating in Lake Michigan—if she wore that green jacket, her torso would seem to disappear against the chromakey screen, leaving her head and hands drifting like limp helium balloons.

I booted my computer and sent a quick note to her personal assistant, alerting her we'd need a change and telling her to scratch all shades of green off her list of anchor fashions. I wrote it in Spanish, because I didn't want to hear back later that Lourdes Ramirez "no can spik Ingliss."

The monitor for camera three gave me a better shot of Connie. She was leaning back against the chair, her head to one side.

"Ike, take a look at monitor three," I said, turning around in my chair and pointing at the screen.

Ike looked up impatiently from the bright yellow text on her blue computer screen and glanced at the bank of monitors on the wall of the control room above my station.

"Holy cow," she said. I guess Ike forgot she had her headset on, with the mike built into the mouthpiece, because she leaned forward and pushed the lever on her console for Connie's telex and spoke into the gooseneck microphone that connected the control room to the anchor's ear. "Wake up, Connie. Are you okay?"

Connie didn't move. I looked back at monitor two. From that shot I could see that Connie didn't have her telex on.

"She's not wired," I said.

Ike ripped off her headset and flew out of the control room. I kept my eyes on the monitors and within a minute I saw Ike appear behind Connie, which meant that Ike had run all the way, because the door to Studio 57 opens on the tube, down one of the spokes and on the opposite side of the wagon wheel from the Green Room.

On the monitor I saw Ike put her hand on Connie's shoulder. When Ike touched her, Connie slumped to the side and her elbow slipped off the armrest. That's when I ripped off my headset and raced for Studio 57.

Most of the studio was dark when I pushed open the door. Lighting the place adequately for television is no sinecure, with what amounts to four independent sets in the architectural equivalent of the Bat Cave. There's more than four hundred powerful lights suspended from the ceiling, but the studio's big enough to park a jumbo jet in, with plenty of room left over for a couple of troop-transport helicopters and the Batmobile.

Even without any lights on over the living room set, which is closest to the studio door, Satan Brown's Tama drum kit sparkled in the gloom.

Across the studio, I could see Ike kneeling by one of the two anchor chairs inside the clear walls of the aquarium, with her hand on Connie's arm. The news set is the one farthest from the door where I was standing, with the kitchen and den off to the sides. I saw that only a few of the lights over the news set were on, and that accounted for the muddy quality of the shots I'd been getting on the monitors in the control room. The only other light in the whole place was the glow from the TV screen recessed down into the top of the anchor desk. When I heard Ike's voice, it sounded like a little girl calling out across a canyon.

"Is that you, Abby?"

"Yeah. What's the deal?"

Ike lifted her hand over her eyes and looked over toward me, and I realized she couldn't see me in the darkness by the door, so I crossed the living room, veering around the drums, and hurried over to the desk.

Ike gave me a look that told another one of those long stories. "She's dead, Abby."

THREE

I DIDN'T ASK Ike if she was sure of her facts.

Concepción Candela looked dead.

And Ike wouldn't have said Connie was dead if there was any other option on the menu. Journalists who have seen colleagues and soldiers and mere bystanders fall on battlefields are maybe even more reluctant to believe in the finality of death than people with safer jobs. The paradox of war zones is that they never encourage you to grow accustomed to death.

Ike and I were both fairly new to the control room end of *Morning Watch*. Before we had achieved our current eminence, she and I had, in different capacities, covered the Gulf War, and Operation Just Cause in Panama, and the LA riots, as well as various other military and civilian three-dimensional games of chance where the score is kept in bodies, and we'd seen dead people before. But as much as Connie looked dead, she looked different-from-dead, too. Her hair was perfect, and her makeup was perfect, and her clothing was perfect, and she was sitting propped up in the anchor chair just like she was ready to go on the air. She looked poised-and-perfect-dead.

"This is awful," Ike whispered.

It was worse than awful. Connie looked like somebody's idea of a pretend death. A TV death—the kind that doesn't really hurt, and you get to be on a different show next week.

There wasn't a mark or a murder prop on her that I could see: no gunshot wound, no dripping Spanish knife protruding from her chest, no frayed and dirty rope around her lovely throat, no depression left from the brutal force of a blunt instrument. She simply looked lifeless, like an anchor doll. A big, dead, beautiful, young Mexican-American anchor doll. Her telex was on the anchor desk, and the wire was laid out neatly, the way the floor manager leaves it, ready for Connie to put it on. It looked like she'd never touched it.

I know why murder was the first thing that occurred to me: Connie was too young to die of natural causes. But after my first glance took in the absence of—well, the absence of anything—I wondered if Connie had suffered a heart attack. I don't know anything about strokes, but surely, I thought, she was too young for that. I moved closer and gazed at her face. Something looked wrong to me. Some slight flaw in her looks. Concepción Candela didn't have flaws, I thought. Ike has flaws; Connie had a perfect TV face. I couldn't place what was bothering me, couldn't give it a name.

Ike cleared her throat. "We're supposed to do something, Abby. It's weird, but I want to shout for the medics. I tried for a pulse. No luck."

"Doesn't she look wrong to you, Ike?"

Ike focused her green and blue eyes on Connie's face and studied her for a total of three seconds. "Wrong? She looks dead. I'd call that plenty wrong."

"I don't mean that, dummy," I said. "I mean wrong. There's something wrong about the way she looks. I can't explain it. Like a mirror angled wrong or something."

Ike rocked back on her heels and looked at me. "Do you feel all right?"

"What's that supposed to mean?"

"Nothing. Just what I said. You sound like you need to sit down and put your head between your knees."

"If I thought you cared, I'd get down *on* my knees."

She made a noise and reached into the well of the anchor desk and pulled out the telephone. I noticed her hand was shaking.

"Who are you calling?"

"Nine-one-one." She paused to think. "And Warren Greenburg, if he's in the building. And Little Joe."

Warren was the show's health correspondent and a medical doctor, and Joe Ayles was the executive producer of *Morning Watch*. Ike must have been thinking faster than I was, because until she mentioned Little Joe, it hadn't sunk in that we still had to go on the air at 7:00 with a news program and here was the lead story sitting in the anchor chair.

In the ordinary course of events, Ike would never invite the network dayside brass to bigfoot her on a judgment call, but I didn't blame her for getting Little Joe out of his nice, warm bed in his nice, warm Park Avenue apartment and kicking this particular nice, warm news item upstairs. That's what TV executives are for: taking the heat. That's how they get so nice and warm.

I thought I should do something while Ike was phoning, so I went and shut off the cameras. We didn't want everybody back in the control room to come running like a pack of nosy gazelles into Studio 57, and I hoped they'd been too busy or too bored or too cynical—or the control room monitors too dark, the pictures too muddy—for them to realize what was happening out here. I hoped it looked like we were having a conference with Connie if anybody was paying attention. I was kicking myself for leaving the monitors on.

I strolled over to the studio door and turned on a couple more lights, selecting switches carefully from the many complex combinations available on the double bank of controls for the studio lights. Ike put her hand over the receiver and hissed at me across the acre or so of concrete floor.

"We're not supposed to touch anything, Abby."

"Well, you touched the phone."

"That's different, you ding-a-ling. I'm supposed to use the phone. It's my duty as a citizen to use this phone. It's practically a constitutional mandate for me to use this phone. My use of this phone has been ordained by every statute the city council ever wrote. My use of this phone—"

"Okay, okay. Get a grip. I only touched a couple switches. You're acting like this is murder."

At least I hadn't been dumb enough to cover my hand with a handkerchief when I shut off the cameras and touched the light switches, the way they do on TV mysteries. I may have contributed some of my fingerprints to the studio hardware, but I hadn't wiped anybody else's off. Besides, I don't carry a handkerchief.

Ike hung up the phone.

"I've got to do something drastic about the show," she said, and she was talking way too fast, the words tumbling out like quarters from a hyperactive slot machine. "Noel will have to do it alone, unless we can drag someone out of bed. I know Hannah's in the building, because I smelled her awful cigarette smoke, but I'll be damned if I'll go crawling to her. If anybody's gonna crawl, Little Joe can do it himself when he gets here. If I reach him before the show. I got his stupid answering machine."

I elevated an eyebrow. That was certainly an odd time of the night for Little Joe to be away from his nice, warm apartment. He always answered his phone himself when he was there. Like most of us in the business, he suffers from newscolepsy, a sleeping disorder that makes you answer the phone even in your deepest dreams. Some people call it newsomnia.

"What about his beeper?"

"I tried that." Ike swept her hand through her curly hair, and more words tumbled out of her mouth at lightning speed. "Abby, you stay here with Connie and wait for the cops and the medical types."

"Hold on just a minute there, little woman." Ike's verbal motor was still stuck in hyper-speed, and I thought I could help out by giving her adrenaline pump an anger adjustment, so she'd have more reliable interior chemical assistance in the crisis. She looked and sounded pretty shaken, so I said, "I'm not staying in here with Connie. This place is like the tombs of the pharaohs, and I don't relish hanging around like a tourist who hasn't used up his Kodak film. Call security."

"Don't be such a sissy." She stamped her foot. Adrenaline. "I'll call them from the control room. Just don't let anybody in here until they show up."

I started to walk out, like a sissy, and she got one of those looks in her eyes, like the queen's stableboy had found a dirty pebble on the royal path.

"Dammit, Abby, I outrank you on the show."

I stopped. "Yeah, well, this isn't the show. This is real life. Ask me nicely." I crossed my arms and looked at her, which, of course, is not all that easy when she's got her eyes at full intensity.

"You're so impossible, Abby. Just do this." She took a breath and made a sour face, like the word she was about to say had an unpleasant taste: "Please."

"Ah, the magic word. All right, all right. But I'm doing it for Connie."

"God!" Ike gave her blond hair a couple of vigorous pulls. "God forbid you should do the teensiest little thing for me."

She took another deep breath. She bent over Connie and touched her cheek. Then she ran out of the studio.

I stood there wishing I'd asked Ike if she had reached Dr. Warren Greenburg chez the Emerald City, not that I thought there was any hope for Connie, because there clearly wasn't. But it would have been nice to have an official person say the word so I could stop feeling guilty about not knowing mouth-to-mouth or even the Heimlich maneuver.

By now I was freezing. The air-conditioning in Studio 57 is always set at subarctic, and that's necessary when we're on the air because the lights are so hot. But I had only turned on a couple of the lights over near the door, the aquarium was only partially lit, and I was shivering. When all the lights are on over the aquarium, the news set is bathed in a huge globe of light so bright, hot, and discrete that it's like a tiny climate of its own, intense and Saharan. The clear Plexiglas wall, that partition with the map of the world on it, which everyone would recognize because it's what you see behind our news anchors when you tune in, helps to hold in the climate bubble. "Desert Wasteland" would have been a better name for it. I don't remember who started calling it the aquarium. Actually, that was probably before my time.

I strolled around, flapping my arms and looking at my watch. If something didn't happen soon, the studio would be swarming with technicians, camera operators, the sound crew, the floor manager. And Heinous Face. God, I was supposed to be rehearsing them. And then I felt guilty about worrying about a rock band when a young and—for all I knew—healthy woman had died in the studio.

I returned to the aquarium, sat down on the edge of the anchor desk, swallowed hard, and studied Connie's face. I was trying to sort out what looked ''wrong.'' I had been giving Ike a hard time to keep her adrenaline flowing, and sitting there so close to the corpse, I realized my own adrenaline level was up in the ozone. My palms were sweating, and I felt like I could run a few miles just for the hell of it and then maybe jump rope until I got tired. I could barely sit still. But I forced myself to concentrate on Connie's face. There was something wrong. Something about her pretty face, so composed in death.

But even dead, she looked pretty in green. A pretty newcomer in forest green. I didn't think any of us on the show had known her very well. She'd come out of the NTB affiliate station in Houston, had undergone a three-month grooming period as a general assignment reporter for the abysmally rated weekend news shows, and had not paid anything beyond the first installment of her dues on network television. When someone that young and that pretty makes a major break into the Big Time, the inevitable speculation is about who she slept with to get where she'd gotten. Since Concepción Candela achieved the anchor slot over Hannah's dead body (so to speak), everybody thought the mystery man had to be pretty high up in the NTB slumber party echelons. As far as I'm concerned, the most pernicious and shadowy form of sexism at the network is only a product of the fact that upper management is almost exclusively male: it follows that only women can use mattress politics to advance a set of career ambitions. I'm not blaming the women. This program was, after all, brought to you courtesy of the male of the species.

I hadn't talked to anybody who had the actual goods on Concepción Candela's spectacular rise to the top, and I'd been willing to cut her some slack, on the chance that maybe her Cinderella story was based on goodness and journalistic talent, because that can still happen in this business, but even I admitted that I was taking the short odds. And now the Cinderella story, no matter how she'd managed to get to the ball, wasn't going to have a happy ending.

I realized I was staring at the body and gave myself a little shake. Connie's right arm was hanging down over the side of the chair, and something white was in her hand. I squatted beside her to get a better look. There was a white ribbon tied in a neat little bow around her index finger, and a small piece of paper dangled from the ribbon, puffing out occasionally in a gust of icy air-conditioning skidding under the Plexiglas near the floor. I slid off the desk and knelt beside the chair. It was dark down there, but I've got good eyes. On the piece of paper were some words, in block printing: "I'll be watching for you."

A cold sensation that had nothing to do with the air-conditioning went up my spine.

It was like finding a signature on the corpse. Those were the words Hannah Van Stone had said at the end of every *Morning Watch* for three decades. Her own personal sign-off. And it was then that I knew Connie had not died from a heart attack or any other natural calamity. She hadn't tied that neat little bow on her own index finger without help.

And I knew then why Ike had been acting like there'd been a murder. She has good eyes, too.

I realized Ike hadn't been so insistent that I stay in the studio merely so I'd keep Connie's body company out of respect for the dead, and I had just decided to go stand by the door as a human barricade when it opened suddenly and Noel Heavener walked in, startling the bejesus out of me.

My heart was pounding and I stood up too quickly, trying to block his view of Connie.

Noel had a couple of colorful ties in one hand and a smile on his face. "Good morning, people!" he boomed in his TV voice. "Can't we have some more light in here? Or have I interrupted a love rehearsal? Ha, ha."

That sounded worse than it was. Noel had always been a great guy, a sweet, gentle man, one of the nicest people at NTB News, but there was something wrong with the wiring between his mouth and his brain. He was a terrific reader, but when you let him ad-lib, there was no telling what he'd say. One of the newsmagazines—I think it was *Time*—said that Noel Heavener was the best television anchor in the history of the medium because he was like a ticking bomb: you never knew when he'd go off. Their idea was that the suspense makes for great viewing. You probably saw Noel's live interview with the pope about birth control, or at least read about it the next day. Everybody knows you don't ask the pontiff if onanism wouldn't be a good idea in India.

"It's not a love rehearsal, Noel. Come over here, but don't touch anything."

When Ike told me not to let anyone into the studio, she hadn't meant Noel, and not just because he was a nice guy. Noel made $4 million a year, and he could go wherever he wanted to at NTB. Anchors, especially when they've been around as long as Noel, are not like other people, at least while their contracts are running.

Just because Noel said those strange things on the air, it would be a mistake to think his brain was undernourished. Far from it. He'd read more books than I had, and better ones. He'd met more people than I had, some better ones. And while there may have been a question about his mouth, there was nothing wrong with Noel's eyes, at least not with his contacts in. As soon as he was within fifteen feet of Connie, he had the general idea.

"Bless my soul," he said, running the hand with the ties through his thick, dark (maybe dyed) hair. "Or perhaps I should say 'bless her soul.'"

He stepped around one of the cameras to the front of the desk and took a long look at Connie. He kept his deep brown eyes narrowed at her for a good sixty seconds, but he didn't try for a close-up.

"What happened here, Abby?"

"Not sure yet, Noel. Ike's phoned all the right people. Or at least she tried."

He heaved a sigh and stuffed his ties in the jacket pocket of his brown three-piece suit. "Connie was awfully young. Was it a natural death?"

"I don't think so, Noel."

I didn't want to point out to Noel the neatly tied ribbon on Connie's finger. That little detail would get around the network fast enough. I wouldn't be the only one to haul out a calculator to see what happened when you entered two plus two and pressed the equal key. We'd all get the same answer. We'd shake our heads and think *Hannah might be mean enough to kill her competition, but she probably wasn't stupid enough to sign her work.* Ah, but what if we put away the calculators and did the math in our heads? We'd nod wisely then and think *Hannah could have been trying to blind us with reverse psychology, and using her own patented sign-off might be a ploy to divert suspicion.* But ultimately we'd all let our gut reactions take over. Then we'd think *what the hell, let's suspect her because she's so nasty.* The gossip would be fueled by mass feelings about Hannah (since there's no such thing as mass common-sense in television). Besides, Noel already had a head start on hating Hannah's guts, because she'd been heckling him for years and she was good at it. It wasn't up to me to start indicting Hannah for murder, even formally on the gossip hot line.

"I'd better find Ike," Noel said sadly. "She's going to want my help. At a minimum, I can get her some coffee."

But Noel didn't move away from the aquarium. He hesitated, and seemed to be memorizing the desk.

"Abby?"

"Yeah?"

"Have you seen Hannah?"

"No, but Ike said she's in the building."

"Oh." He swallowed. "I didn't mean anything by that, you know."

"I know."

Still Noel hesitated.

"Any idea what killed her?" he asked.

"Nope. I'm absolutely clueless."

The door was pushed open then and two uniformed cops came in with a pair of green-shirted NTB security guards. One of the cops held out his nightstick to block the guards, and they stayed just inside the door while the uniforms trooped over to the desk.

They both looked Connie over, without touching her at first, but then one of them lifted her wrist, fumbling for a pulse—which had obviously not reappeared since Ike had checked.

The other cop, a black guy wearing big gold-rimmed aviator glasses, asked, "Are you the director guy?"

I nodded.

He pointed at Noel. "You're Noel Heavener, aren't you?"

Noel nodded and the cop turned back to me. "Can you give us some more light here?"

"What about fingerprints?" I asked, remembering Ike's snappy remark and not wanting to be chewed out twice in one night for disappointing Scotland Yard.

The cop stared at my face, as if he were trying to place me. "What? You think I should look for fingerprints in the dark? You think you're Columbo or something?"

"I just don't want anybody saying I destroyed evidence."

"Son, this is the United-States-of-America New York, New York. I can say anything I want. You guys in the media think you're the only ones with rights."

He wasn't really old enough to call me "son," but I let it go and crossed the studio to the bank of switches near the door. I let him have it with all the juice we can shoot into Studio 57. I wasn't going to sass him, but I could put him on to simmer for a while. Four hundred and three thousand, two hundred watts is a lot of heat. And light.

As far as I could tell, Connie's death didn't make any better sense with all the studio lights on.

With the lights on, I experienced this moment of heightened focus, which can happen to people who are used to that many watts while everybody else is still blinking. Everything just stopped for a moment, suspended in the breathtaking shock of the lights. The rights-advocate cop blinked and held his squawk box in the air, squinting over at me. The other cop, the pulse taker, was a guy with such oily skin he almost glowed under the lights; he stood with his feet spread apart, looking stalwart and incandescent and sweaty behind Connie's anchor chair. The security guards looked like they were statues waiting to be picked up by the floor crew. In a way, it was like the top hat at Playtime-in-Brazil. I'd never really looked at a security guard all that closely before, or a cop, not unless they were on some piece of videotape, and that makes a difference.

Maybe I hadn't ever really looked at Noel, either. He stayed over in front of the desk, although there was no chance he was stunned by the lights. He couldn't help looking famous, and he was in full makeup, which always makes a star look more like a star. I was thinking that Studio 57 looked like a TV movie frozen by the VCR pause button, when Hannah Van Stone suddenly blew in past the security guards, breaking the spell, and she looked more like a star than Noel did, maybe because she carried herself with that loose sort of arrogant unconcern that a lioness has when she's rumbling around after a long snooze in the heat of the Serengeti day. Noel would never look that famous, because he actually cared if he broke things or stepped on people, and he watched where he was going.

"Well," she announced, in her throatiest tones, her left hand flat on the heavy studio door she was holding open, "there's more action here this morning than there's been at the UN in twenty years."

She was wearing the same red linen suit over a black turtleneck that she had worn to grace the cover of *Time,* and with her arm flung out like that, the bulge over her waistband showed. She had not posed like that for the magazine.

This was the moment when the rights-advocate cop showed what the rank and file are really made of. He looked at Hannah's famous mane of (definitely dyed) blond hair and her pink makeup and her blue eyes and her stocky figure. With a calculating and malicious gleam in his eyes, he demanded, "Who the hell are you?"

FOUR

WHEN YOU make your living in TV, you take certain things
for granted, things like the working principle that you always have to protect the tender-skinned stars from the
thought that—before they achieved media apotheosis and
the status of American Facts of Life, before they were
turned into huge electronic images flickering into millions
of homes and offices—they arose from the same gene pool
as their less diffusible and slightly messy cousins down on
the street.

But Hannah was something of a special case, and that
morning she needed no buffer between her and the police,
because her hefty ego was on duty, a busy sentinel that
opened doors and peeked around corners for her.

"Are you blind?" she snarled. "As well as stupid?" She
shifted her weight and leaned on the door. "Perhaps you
only watch cartoons."

But Officer Rights-Advocate was a match for her. "Oh,
are you on cartoons?"

I was wishing Ike was there, both because I wanted her to
witness this confrontation and because it was part of her job
to handle the anchors, and just then her voice came over the
studio's PA system from the control room. "Abby, are the
police there yet? Turn camera three back on so I can tell
what's going on. Everybody on the floor knows about
Connie already. I wish you'd turned the monitors off in the
control room before you went loping into the studio like an
adolescent baboon."

She sounded crabby, but she was talking more slowly. The
cops looked around, trying to locate Ike from her voice.

"Abby? Is Noel in there with you? I can't find him. I need
him immediately. The radio desk is reporting a plane coming into Kennedy without any landing gear, and it's less than

an hour before we go on the air. Can you believe that they've cleared the plane to attempt a landing at 7:01? Seven-o-one, of all the impossible times. Where the hell is Noel? He may have to wing it himself if we lead with the plane story.'' There was a pause. "Sorry about the way I phrased that.''

It's true that bad things come in multiples. Hannah had always been the one who talked us through a crisis, because Noel was strictly a reader. A brilliant reader, but that's all he did. Turning Noel loose at the mike was a form of verbal Russian roulette. You knew that, sooner or later, the loaded chamber was going to come around. His famous papal interview had come on the day Hannah had broken three front teeth in an automobile accident, and he had shot *Morning Watch* in the foot. Not to mention the fact that he had probably guaranteed himself a spot in Hell.

I don't know my own face as well as I know Ike's, but I must have shown that Connie's death was now second on NTB News's list of Big Things to Worry About.

The cop studied my face for a second and promptly said, "You can turn on the camera you had on before, like she mentioned. You already touched it, didn't you?''

"Look, I'm sorry. Okay? I'm a director, not a detective.''

"I'm glad you realize that, son.''

I rushed over and turned on camera three and stood close to the news desk so that Ike could hear me as I leaned over and spoke into Connie's telex, not touching it. The PA system is fine, but there's nothing like being right inside Ike's ear.

"Where's the plane coming from?'' I asked.

"Zurich. Three hundred and twenty-four passengers. They're diverting all traffic scheduled for Kennedy to La Guardia and Newark and Hartford. And they've grounded all outbound planes. They're spraying the runway with foam right now, or they soon will be. Seven-o-one, Abby. We'll have to go with it live. I've got a crew on its way out there now. This better not be an instrument failure. I'll bet you anything that goddamn plane just has a hydraulic that's not reading in the cockpit and their landing gear is in peachy shape. But nobody will know if it's merely instrument failure until they lay eyes on the plane.''

"Shit." We got reports like this every couple of months, and it was *always* a bad cockpit reading. But we had to cover them all in case they turned out to be the real thing. I straightened up and looked the cop in the eye. "I hope you got all that. Are you gonna let us use this studio?''

He shook his head. "You must have a million studios in this building.''

Ike's voice came over again. "I heard that. We'll have to use the *Evening Watch* set. Get moving, Abby. Find Noel.''

"He's here with me.''

"Get his butt over to Studio 52. I need you in the control room.''

Of course, it wasn't as simple as Ike was trying to make it. The cops said Noel and I couldn't leave. Apparently, Ike had told them I'd discovered the body. I wasn't sure that was technically true, but this did not seem like a good time to ask for a legal definition of the role of electronic monitors in murder. And Hannah, who had not been invited and was not welcome, was refusing to leave. Like she'd been doing for the past week.

"I'm much better at ad-libbing than Noel," she said, apparently having decided to take a stand. "You can't give him the mike with a crippled plane coming down. Who knows what he'll say?''

Since I don't make decisions about who does what on the air, I tried to ignore Hannah, but Noel had been taking that stuff from her for thirty years.

"Hannah," he said, in his authoritative TV voice, "the anchor usually handles these situations—not the UN correspondent.''

She slapped the studio door and strode across the living room to the news set. On the way, she brushed against one of the cymbals in the drum kit, an apparent clumsiness that was entirely typical of Hannah's overbearing approach to physical objects, and she reacted to the intrusive clashing sound by saying a few words I associate more with subway walls than with television. Correction: subway walls in the Times Square station. By the time she reached Noel's side, she'd skimmed off the top layer of her vocabulary and had worked her way down to the mostly civilized middle contents. God only knows what was at the bottom of Hannah's language tank.

"Noel, not even your biggest fans have any idea why you're on the air. The only reason I got booted off the show instead of you is that at least I can find the UN."

When Noel answered her, he wasn't using his TV voice. He sounded whiny and exasperated: "You don't have to be able to find it. You can just tell any taxi driver in New York where you want to go and he'll get you there. Really, Hannah, why don't you just leave and stop bothering the nice folks at NTB? I don't know what you're doing here anyway."

That was the big question. Hannah had no business in the Emerald City at this hour of the morning, especially since her campaign of harassment against Concepción Candela and the network was obviously over. And maybe Hannah had brought it to a conclusion herself, in a very final move. The younger anchorwoman was out of the way. But if Hannah thought the combination of Connie's death and this plane crisis was going to get her back on the air, she was misjudging the tough little blonde who called the shots on *Morning Watch*.

Ike's voice came over again, and the acoustics are so good in Studio 57 that she seemed to be right by my side: "I just got off the phone with a police captain. He's in the building and on his way to the studio. Can you believe we rate a captain? The power of the media, huh? Are we the cultural elite or what? This captain says we all have to stay in the building, on this floor, but we're free to do what we have to do to get the show on the air. I want Abby in the control room immediately. Noel, you go to the *Evening* studio. Pick up your telex there, and I'll feed you what you have to do. You'll also have to interview that Satan drummer, and I don't know what the hell we'll do about their music. We'll have to drop the background segment Connie taped yesterday. Abby? I need some real leadership from you to get the Heinous Face equipment into the other studio in time. It won't be much of a coup for us if we have a silent band.''

"I'll see what I can do," I said, but I wasn't cocky about the implied compliment from Ike. Some things are harder in TV than others, and, frankly, it would have been easier to get set to cover a riot than to switch studios in the time we had. It wasn't the musical instruments that would be a problem. It was all their sound gear. The show was going to be a mess, in every way it could possibly be a mess: one of our anchors had died in circumstances that looked suspicious, if not worse; a major studio guest was going to go on without a director's rehearsal and in a foreign studio that was set up only for delivering hard news; and we were probably going to go live at the top of the show with a plane crash at Kennedy and with a questionable talent at the microphone, a man who was a face-and-voice mechanic, not a journalist.

There was no sign of the police captain yet. The rights-advocate cop stepped to the desk and leaned over the telex, the little white plug that should have been in Connie's ear, the little white four-inch coil that should have been in place around Connie's neck. "What's the captain's last name?" he asked the telex.

Ike's voice came back over the PA: "Don't you believe me? I've got a lame 747 crawling up my butt and you want to know that guy's name? What's *your* name?"

"What his name, miss?"

Ike's heavy sigh filled the studio. "It sounded like he actually had two names. I didn't really catch it."

The cop nodded to himself over the desk. "That's him." He stood up and pointed to Noel and me. "You two guys can leave the studio, but stay in the building. On this floor."

Noel and I bolted, parting in the hallway and heading our separate ways, Noel struggling to get his tie on as he ran, almost tripping over a cop coming around the hall. The tube was full of uniforms.

I raced back to the control room, slid down the steps, flopped into my chair, grabbed my headset, and started checking the monitors, switching operations to the *Evening Watch* studio. Ike had already been able to light a fire under the technical staff and get them started on the scramble into the other studio, thank God, and I worked with the floor manager and the assistant director and we finally got Heinous Face and their equipment moved. The band members seemed less confused than I would have expected. Maybe they were accustomed to last-minute changes. And it crossed my mind that maybe they also practiced some chemical method of staying loose.

I didn't have much concentration left over to see how Ike was doing with her airport crisis, except to arrange for the remote feed from Kennedy. When I looked up at last, conscious that I was sweating, it was four minutes until seven.

"What's new on the plane, Ike?" I asked, my voice low, showing her how calm I was.

"I don't know yet. Our people on the ground will have eye contact with the plane just before we go on the air, and we'll know if the landing gear is down. Supposedly the plane's low on fuel. It's in a holding pattern over Kennedy until the emergency stuff is ready for it." She glanced at the clock over the line monitor. "Which should be almost now." She flipped a switch on her console and spoke to Noel's telex. "Okay, Noel. Arthur Landau is on the ground at Kennedy. We'll go live to him right after you say maybe ten words, max, about what's happening. Okay? There's a piece of copy to your right on the desk that has everything you'll need. See it?"

I had Noel's mike open for my headset, so I heard him say, "Right you are," and he gave the thumbs-up sign. I hoped he wouldn't do that on the air, but he didn't usually have a problem with his hands. It was his mouth we were worried about. At least he'd managed to get his tie around his neck.

I still had a monitor open on Studio 57, and out of the corner of my eye I could see a lot of people, maybe twenty, moving around. Taking pictures, measuring things, playing with the dust, it looked like. Connie's body was still sitting in the aquarium.

And then, across the top row of monitors, I had the live pictures of the plane coming into Kennedy. "Ike," I yelled, "there it is! Monitors sixteen through twenty! I don't see any wheels down!"

She spoke softly into her mouthpiece. On my cue the technical director threw a switch. And we were on the air. Noel's face and shoulders filled the line monitor.

His magic TV voice said, "Hello, I'm Noel Heavener. This is *Morning Watch,* and we're watching a live picture of..."

I breathed and signaled the video switch from Noel to Kennedy.

Noel continued to voice over the remote pictures now on the screen. "...a plane attempting to land at New York's Kennedy Airport without its landing gear. We go now to NTB's Arthur Landau, who's on the scene. Arthur?"

I don't know what Arthur said because I wasn't listening. The cameraman out at Kennedy was getting superb stuff. Sunlight was bouncing off the wings of the silver and red and white 747 that was low over the end of the runway, and all the foam on the concrete looked like a sea of boiling white soup. The cameraman must've been on his knees. It was a great angle.

The camera was showing the plane straight on. The silver nose of the plane seemed to grow larger in the monitor I was watching, without getting any closer to the ground, and the plane sure as hell didn't have any wheels down.

The 747 kept coming at the camera, like a huge bullet in slow motion. I could see emergency vehicles on the ground behind the plane starting to follow it. I kept saying to myself, "You gotta get down; you gotta put it down; you gotta put it down." I kept waiting to see the plane get lower and slide through the white soup.

I knew it wasn't going to make it. It was still way too far off the ground. The pilot just wasn't getting it down, and, in a split second, I wondered where any pilot would find the courage to slam that giant machine down onto the landing strip.

Then the plane suddenly dropped a few feet and tipped slightly. There was a bright orange flash as the right wing scraped the concrete and sheared off, flying in fragments out of the picture, but the plane kept coming at the camera and, it was strange, but I was aware that I was standing and so was everyone else in the control room. I was holding my breath.

The belly of the plane slid and scorched into the foam, bright red flashes shooting out from the ground like sparklers on the Fourth of July. I heard a huge groan and a wrenching sound, like the plane was tearing the concrete off the ground. I expected the ball of flame, the explosion, but it didn't come. The plane spun to the side, skidding off onto the grass, but still no fire, no explosion. The exit doors popped open, the slides inflated and came down, and people were falling and jumping and pushing down the slides. They ran and looked over their shoulders at the plane, and our cameraman got a great shot of a woman holding onto a child's hand, not seeming to know that the kid's feet weren't even touching the ground. The woman was just doing the running for both of them and holding onto that little hand like crazy.

There never was an explosion. I could see dense white smoke billowing out from a couple of the exit doors near the front of the plane, but the fire trucks were there, spraying arcs and clouds of foam. I guess they were dousing what little fuel was left in the plane.

The entire control room expelled a breath at once. I turned around to look at Ike. Her spectacular eyes were luminous, beautiful wells each containing an unshed tear. She spoke softly into her mouthpiece, but I was close enough to hear her: "Noel, we're going to stay with the Kennedy crew, but Arthur needs to get set for a standup, so he's going to throw it back to you for a question. Ask him if everyone is accounted for. Okay?"

I saw Noel nod, and I cued the switch to camera one on the anchor.

"Arthur," he said, "we've all just seen that dramatic belly landing, and it looked like everyone got out safely. What can you tell us from your vantage point there at Kennedy?"

Not too bad, I thought.

I looked at the clock. 7:04:13. God, we still had almost two more hours to fill. But at least we'd handled the first stage of the emergency as well as anybody could.

We went back to Arthur for another minute and a half of the terrified passengers his producer had managed to grab, but we still didn't have any officials. Without any warning that I could discern, Arthur said, "So that's what we know so far. Back to you in the studio, Noel."

I switched to Noel, and my stomach tightened when I saw the blank look on his face. But then I heard Ike speaking to him, feeding sense into his telex.

"Ask Art about that dramatic drop the pilot did at the last minute. Art's producer says it was about a seven-foot drop. Okay?"

I watched Noel on the monitor. His expression didn't show that he had Ike in his ear telling him what to do and say. He just did and said. The four-million-dollar man.

She kept leading him through it, and between switching back and forth from Noel to Kennedy, I thought it was like a tango. Ike took Noel's hand and led him through the complicated steps, and they both looked like experts. We were all beginning to relax, everyone but Ike. I even got a chance to glance at the monitor for the other studio. Connie's body had been removed, and some of the cops were standing around the news desk, watching our coverage on the little screen the anchors use.

I heard Ike say that we'd go to Noel for "other news," and she spoke into the mouthpiece to tell him to read from his TelePrompTer on camera two. The writer had already prepared a story on Connie, with the few details we had on her death, and all Noel had to do was read it, along with the rest of the script for the news block. Already the original lead from the Moscow Bureau was buried under our top two stories from New York.

While Noel was reading the news, I swiveled around and looked up at Ike. "What about next of kin? Can we go with this? Have the cops called Connie's family?"

"I can't worry about that," Ike said, giving me the kind of disdainful look she'd give a pesky gnat with a broken wing and an eye patch. "If we didn't go with it first, some other network would get it. They probably have it anyway—it's got to be all over the police scanners."

I guess I shouldn't have distracted Ike. I looked at Noel and saw that he was out of copy. And he said, "We'll be back with more coverage of the safe landing of Tell-Air Flight 935, including reaction to that dramatic last-second loss of altitude, when the courageous pilot finally committed the plane to a landing. We all saw the live pictures—a breathtaking seven-foot drop that made all the difference to 324 passengers and the Tell-Air crew. Seven feet. The difference between life and death. That's about the size of a basketball player. Just think. We'll be back after these messages."

My mouth fell open, but I switched to the correct set of commercials.

There was a chorus of groans in the control room.

"*What* did he say?" Ike demanded, flinging up her arms. "Did I hear that right?"

"You heard him," I said, trying to sound cheerful. "A basketball player. It could have been worse. He could have specified race."

She closed her mike and ground her heel into the carpet and made noises, kind of a cross between grunting and whistling, the subdued but insistent cry a baby wolf might make on a particularly cold night in Michigan.

"I could kill him," she finally spat out. "How does he think of those things? What the hell's he got in his head?"

She moved away from her console as far as her headset would allow, and I saw that there was a stranger standing at the door of the control room, holding it slightly ajar and looking in through the glass panel. I did not think it was an especially slick move for Ike to be threatening murder on this particular morning, not with a stranger in our midst, someone who was not clued in to the fine points of the professional treatment of anchors behind their backs.

The stranger was about six feet tall (apparently not a basketball player), his smooth skin was tan, his teeth were white enough to lend out for toothpaste commercials, his eyes were brown, his hair was straight and thick and dark, and I could tell he worked out. I guess Ike could tell, too, because she tugged at her sweater and straightened her hair as well as she could with a headset on.

"You must be the police captain," she said pleasantly, pretending she would have been just as friendly if he'd been ugly.

"I'm the one with the two names," he said, smiling across at her.

"What *is* your name?" she asked, blushing. I didn't like the sight of the color creeping over her high cheekbones. That was the kind of behavior that got her in trouble in elevators.

"Dennis Fillingeri."

For an Italian-American like me, that name wasn't so difficult it should cause all this discussion. Dennis Phil-and-Jerry, I thought. How cute.

"Ike," I said, "we're coming out of commercial. Noel may have some more jokes he wants to tell our viewers."

"Yipe!" she yelped, and jumped into her chair.

With one part of my mind, the part that wasn't switching back to the anchor, I was wondering what the chances were that a homicide captain would turn out to be stupid.

Ike likes her men brainy. Looks are second. Maybe third, after dancing.

FIVE

THE PHONES IN the control room started ringing just as Noel finished up the obit on Connie, and they kept ringing until Ike lost her temper and had a few one-syllable words with the switchboard. Every news outfit and pushy viewer on the East Coast, and beyond into the part of the country that was awake, wanted all the details on Concepción Candela's death, especially details we didn't have.

"Hello, this is Liz Fitzgerald, calling for the *Daily Register* in Clearwater, Florida; was she shot or what?"

Or, from an irate viewer: "You've got your nerve. You think I want to hear about your personal problems while I'm having coffee? You people don't have any sense. But as long as I have you on the phone, was it a drug overdose?"

Or, from a nastier, more cynical, viewer: "Hi, I'm calling from Harrisburg, Pennsylvania; you guys will do anything for ratings, won't you? What'd you do, kill her yourself?"

Or, out of the blue: "Do you have Madonna's phone number?"

I am not exaggerating. Viewers who feel compelled to have a two-way relationship with their televisions manage to say such bizarre things they make Noel's basketball player sound like an apt comparison.

Ike instructed the switchboard to field all the calls about Connie until we were off the air, saying, "If they want to know so bad, they can watch the show. Tell 'em our press office opens at 9:00 a.m., and until then everything we know is coming out of Noel's mouth." Ike paused a moment, an unpleasant light in her eyes. "On second thought, don't mention Noel's mouth."

Even counting Noel's potential amendments and flourishes, what we knew about Connie's death didn't amount to much. All we knew was that she was dead, that we'd found her in one of the anchor chairs, and that the police were in the studio poking around.

As far as I knew, Ike and I were the only NTB staffers who knew about the little white bow neatly tied on Connie's index finger. We'd all been so busy with the scene at Kennedy Airport and with relocating the show into the *Evening* studio that nobody'd had any quality slander time to get the NTB rumor mill greased up, but even so, the note dangling from that ribbon was a hot item, and it would have made the rounds speedily, somehow, if anybody else knew. When it comes to gossip, we're pros at NTB. It's a condition we call "newsitosis," or "news breath," and its major symptom is an inability to keep our mouths closed when we have something smelly to spread around about somebody else. Ike calls it the "news-gathering instink."

The cops certainly weren't waving the note around. Captain Fillingeri stayed in the control room, keeping his mouth shut and his ears open, until we finished with the 7:30 update on Flight 935, and then he was just gone. I didn't see him leave. One minute he was there, and the next he had simply vanished, without leaving a trace of his presence, not even a hiss or a trail of vapor. I did see him appear later on the monitor I was keeping open into Studio 57. I saw him exchange some words with the original cops and take off his jacket. Watching him made me wonder if I should join a gym.

But I didn't wonder about that long enough to make a decision. Grinding out two hours of talk TV with only one anchor to stick in front of the cameras was nerve-racking. There's a good reason why all these long news shows have a pair of talking heads—not even a great anchor can withstand that much scrutiny. That Tuesday morning, Noel was on the air longer than Kevin Costner was on-screen in *Dances with Wolves,* or so it seemed from the control room, and Noel didn't have a horse, a wolf, and friendly Indians to liven up the picture and give it narrative depth. To make matters really dicey, we only had one sizable taped segment that was long enough to give Noel a potty break and to get his makeup de-sweated—a four-minute feature piece on that clean needle program in New Haven, to prevent the spread of AIDS among heroin addicts.

Only two things about the last hour of that Tuesday morning's show stand out for me with any clarity, aside from the frequent updates from our crew at the airport: Noel's interview with Satan Brown of Heinous Face and his sign-off.

By a frantic combination of bent union rules and superior technical talent, the staff was able to rig a miracle and set Heinous Face up to sing "Heart on the Stairs." Ike had stood midwife, coaching necessity as it gave birth to invention, and she had ordered the floor crew to cram the band into a flash studio next to the *Evening Watch* set, and while that was an inspired idea, there were labor pains. In theory, a flash studio is ready to go on the air at any moment, but that's figuring one reader and one camera and one microphone. With all the jerry-rigged wiring we had to do, plus the turmoil surrounding the move, plus all those bodies and all that hardware in the little flash studio, it was a shock and a pleasure to hear how good the band sounded. Congratulations, Mrs. NTB, you have a healthy baby band.

Those guys were real professionals, and I stopped thinking uncharitable thoughts about the probable chemical basis of their cool. Nobody on drugs could have done what they did that morning. At least, not serious drugs.

After "Heart on the Stairs," we went to a two-and-a-half-minute block of commercials; Satan Brown squeezed out from behind his drums in the flash studio and scampered across the *Evening Watch* set to sit beside Noel at the desk for the interview. Brown was wearing a blue denim workshirt with the sleeves rolled up, jeans, and a black vest. His long blond hair was pulled back in a ponytail. In all the confusion, nobody had made him up, so he was a little shiny under the lights, and his slightly crooked nose cast a tiny shadow on his left cheek, but his features were so animated and he was so articulate and he seemed so genuinely evangelistic about their AIDS tour that the interview went over well, especially since Noel was using the questions that had been prepared for Connie.

Ike was listening to Brown's answers from the control room, and she had in front of her the same list of questions Noel was working from, so she was able to nurse him along, but I got the feeling that she wasn't making any special effort, any more than she would have made for any anchor. Noel may not have been familiar with their music, but Brown wasn't promoting the band; instead he was pretty intense about AIDS awareness, and that's a topic Noel was thoroughly briefed on because of the preparation he'd put in for this week of theme shows.

But when Ike cued Noel to wind up the interview, he stumbled a little. "Well, best of luck with your tour and thanks for coming in this morning when we are not at our best. You brought a little ray of sunshine into what is a tragic morning for us at NTB. Live TV, like the threat of AIDS, makes strange bedfellows."

Brown didn't seem to know quite what to make of that, but he was able to cut through the bedfellows part to figure out what Noel was talking about and came through with, "We're all really sorry about Connie, man. She was, like, too young, you know? Uh, Ms. Tygart said she wants us to do another song."

Noel lifted a corner of his script to sneak a look.

Ike took off her headset and let her head fall slowly to her console. She pulled the gooseneck mike down as she went so she could talk Noel into the commercial break before Brown returned to the flash studio to perform "Bonewoman," their latest single, to be heard for the first time anywhere this morning, live, on NTB. We were really breaking ground this morning.

I leaned over the back of my chair to put my hand up on Ike's curls and was pleasantly surprised when she didn't jump. "Noel's just rattled," I said. "We're all rattled. He's done a great job otherwise. He's gotten us through the show by himself. Besides, that was a segment Connie rehearsed, not Noel."

Ike rolled her eyes. There's no way a show producer is going to take a merciful view of an anchor whose jangled nerves allow a guest to take the producer's own personal name in vain on the air. Anchors aren't paid millions to have nerves.

But Noel made it to the end without another gaffe. In fact, he did a great interview with Peter Zydicoff, our movie critic, about restoring classic films, and he actually ad-libbed some decent patter with the weatherman. Hail balls the size of donkeys' knees in Tyndall, South Dakota.

At 8:59:10, Noel signed us off the air. "This is Noel Heavener, for everyone at NTB News, saying good morning to you all and a final farewell to our colleague Concepción Candela. Adios, Connie."

I cued the announcer booth, and the NTB "Jump-start Your Head" slide showed on all but five of the control room monitors: the line monitor with the game show that follows *Morning Watch*, the one still open into Studio 57, plus the three that show what the other networks are up to. And we were dark.

Captain Fillingeri appeared again at the door, peering in through the glass panel, his jacket slung over his shoulder.

"I'm beginning to think you're a decal," I said, "the way you're always showing up on the other side of that door."

"That's funny," he said, not smiling.

"He's a clown, all right," Ike said, not smiling either. "Good old Clarabelle T. Flippant. He keeps us all in stitches."

"I'm at my best when I'm hungry," I said, smiling brightly because somebody had to represent humanity in that gloom. "Ike, I'll treat you to a romantic breakfast at the Museum Cafe—maybe jump-start something other than your head."

Ike turned and looked at me with her eyes narrowed, sort of the way she'd look at a clown who'd just handed her his rubber nose, slightly damp.

"Not so fast," Fillingeri said before Ike could open her mouth to turn down my offer, or to spit on me. "You'll have to delay your breakfast plans." He looked at me like I was

the office pervert, rather than the office clown, and said,
"And any romance plans." Then he pulled a notebook out
of his back pocket, consulted it, and announced, "Mr. and
Mrs. Abagnarro will stay here in this control room. All the
rest of you people are expected over in Room 2718, for fingerprinting and interviews—we may split you up as other
rooms are made available to us. Whatever happens, don't
try to leave this floor. There are police officers in the hall
who'll escort you."

One of our technicians said, "I can find my own way,
thanks," but he was ignored.

Two-seven-one-eight is a conference room, but it's not
very big, so I didn't think the cops were planning a gang interview. I guessed our people would be forming a line for the
privilege of being grilled by the NYPD one by one. There
was some grumbling, not good-natured, but the staff filed
out of the control room, speeding up as it occurred to them
that there were advantages in getting to the head of the line
if they wanted to go home and get some sleep or some
breakfast, or whatever they were planning to get. I sat back
in my chair, linked my hands behind my neck, and yawned.
Since I hadn't gotten anything I was interested in for several months and saw no chance of getting it any time soon,
I could afford to be generous with my time.

When the room was clear, Fillingeri said, "There isn't a
whole lot of grief around here. Are you people as hard-
boiled as you appear?"

"No matter how we feel, we still have to do our jobs," Ike
said, gathering loose script pages from the top of her console. "Nobody on the show knew Connie very well yet.
Naturally we're all appalled and sad, but it's not like she was
a friend."

Fillingeri nodded wisely, like he already knew how many
friends Connie didn't have at the network. "Maybe she
didn't have any friends yet, but somebody here seems to
have been a pretty good enemy."

"I can't even imagine who—are you fingerprinting everyone in the building?" Ike asked, swiveling her chair

slowly from side to side while she stacked the loose script pages on her console and gazed at Fillingeri.

"At least on this floor," he said, "Except for security and the cleaning staff, the other floors have been empty all night."

"Why fingerprint us at all? I can't believe anybody working here doesn't know all about fingerprints. We've even got a couple of people on the staff who could qualify as experts on DNA samples. This place is a raging hotbed of pushy know-it-alls."

"My experience is that people committing crimes sometimes forget their expertise." Fillingeri parked himself on the edge of the console nearest the door. "We're not doing this for the nuisance value, believe me."

"Don't sit on that," I said, strictly for the nuisance value, believe me. He wasn't really hurting anything.

He stood, saw the empty chair next to Ike, took a seat, and got comfortable. So much for my effectiveness as pest.

"I'm sure you both appreciate," he began, in a brand-new tone that said we hadn't been exchanging words already for five minutes—as though he had just walked in and was letting us have both the prepackaged introductory offer from the NYPD and a patronizing, intimate half-smile—"that this situation puts the police on the spot. Concepción Candela came as close as possible to dying on the air in front of an audience of millions without actually doing it. We like to think we're always thorough, but we're doing more than thinking about it now." His chair was facing Ike's, both of them turned sideways to me and up a level, and he started swiveling his chair back and forth in time with hers. "Fingerprints." He shook his head. "You're right." His tone went up a notch to warm-and-friendly. "Killers are pretty sophisticated these days. Still, we have to try everything."

"Killer?" I sat up and stretched. "So it's definitely a killing, like a murder?"

He nodded. "Yeah. Exactly like a murder."

"Why?"

"You discovered the body, didn't you, Mr. Abagnarro?"

"I don't really know how to answer that."

His brown eyes lost some of their calculated warmth. "How about a simple yes or no?"

"Okay. Yes. Or no."

Ike interrupted. "Abby's got Newsheimer's disease."

"What's that?" Fillingeri asked, crossing his ankles under the chair.

"That's what you get when you've been in this business so long you can't remember how to answer a simple question without checking a videotape. Abby's a techno freak."

I leaned back in my chair and frowned up at Ike. "I'm just trying to be exact so nobody can claim that I misled the police. *Some* people don't go around yapping all the time just to hear themselves yap."

"Don't be so paranoid," Ike said, snapping the script together and glaring at me. "Nobody's going to spend time thinking about what you say long enough to misinterpret it."

"Thanks a lot. And I am not paranoid; I'm careful." I turned to Fillingeri. "I don't know if I'm the one who discovered Connie's body. Does it count that I saw her first if I saw her by way of a studio monitor?"

A muscle in Fillingeri's dark, lean cheek twitched. "Why don't you tell me exactly what did happen?"

I explained how I'd seen Connie on the monitor and had told Ike to take a look, and how Ike had gone running to the studio and I'd seen them both on the monitor.

Fillingeri let his eyes roam over the bank of monitors and stopped at the one I still had open into Studio 57. "Is that the one?"

"Yeah, that and the two next to it on the left."

"Turn them on so I can see what they show."

He didn't say please, but I opened the intercom into the studio and, when a voice answered, instructed the voice how to turn on the other cameras. Then I reached across and flipped the switches on the technical director's board. The "Jump-start Your Head" slides were replaced by two different shots of the now-empty anchor chair. I could see cops moving around behind the Plexiglas wall of the aquarium.

Fillingeri watched the monitors and frowned over either what he was seeing or what he was thinking. He turned to Ike.

"So, Mrs. Abagnarro, you were the one who first actually, *physically*, saw the body?" He shook his head impatiently. "God. Television. I mean with your own eyes."

"My name is Tygart, not Abagnarro."

"Oh, you go by your maiden name?" Now there was genuine warmth in his eyes. A lot of warmth.

"Captain, I took my maiden name back legally three weeks ago. Abby and I are divorced."

"Sorry." More warmth. "I must have misunderstood something I was told."

Well, I thought, *now we've got that established. She's available.*

SIX

EVEN AFTER I had accepted the fact of divorce, of never living with Ike again, it was painful to think of her with someone else. So I tried not to think about it, and I certainly had never asked her about it directly. But, in a masochistic sort of way, I wanted to know, and my antennae were activated.

I did not think I was imagining a chemical burst between her and the captain. But Fillingeri did not ask for her phone number immediately. Instead, he said, "Tell me about finding Miss Candela's body. Try to remember any detail you can."

Ike put her fingers on her chin and stared into space over Fillingeri's shoulder. "Well, after I saw Connie on the monitor...she looked like she was, sort of, well, I suppose I thought she was drugged or something. I ran to the studio."

Fillingeri stopped swiveling his chair. "Did Miss Candela use drugs?"

"Not that I know of. Nothing more exotic than aspirin."

"Then why'd you suspect she was drugged?"

"Because of the unnatural way she was sitting. She didn't look normal. She was out, I thought. I'm not trying to malign her character."

Fillingeri nodded. "So then you went into the studio."

"I ran all the way. And most of the studio was dark when I got there. And I ran across to the news set. And then I knelt down beside her and saw that she was dead."

"How'd you know she was dead?"

"I felt for her pulse, and there wasn't any. I felt her chest." Ike held out her right hand, palm up, and looked at it. "Stuck my hand down her blouse. She was not the right temperature and was, you know, unresponsive." Ike shivered. "I've seen dead people before."

He nodded again. "What lights were on when you got there?"

Ike seemed to think. She closed her eyes briefly. "Just several right over the desk. Maybe six, maybe five. Just a few. It was fairly dim in there. There was a little light from the TV that's recessed into the top of the desk."

"Did you see anyone else in there, in the studio?"

"Gosh, I didn't even think to look. I just ran over to the aquarium." Fillingeri cocked his head to one side, and Ike explained, "That's what we call the set where we found her body. What an idiot I am! What if the killer was in there when I found her? I should have looked." Ike glanced at me. "Abby, I must be getting soft from sitting in this chair. I let a major opportunity slip through my fingers."

"You probably did everything you could do." Fillingeri put his left hand over on Ike's console and leaned closer to her. "You wouldn't want to be alone in there with a murderer."

I considered the bank of monitors, and I thought, *Fillingeri doesn't know the way Ike's mind works. She'd love to be closeted with a killer, just to get the story before anyone else could. Maybe even ask him to show her what his favorite position was when he wielded the bloody scimitar studded with emeralds and lurid inscriptions in Latin.*

Fillingeri leaned an inch closer to Ike. "Do you know what time it was when you got to the studio?"

"I think it was almost 5:30." Ike looked at me again. "Is that right, Abby?"

"Almost," I said. "Probably more like 5:25."

She returned the force of her gaze to Fillingeri. He didn't seem to be having any problem looking her straight in the eye, but it looked to me more like he was attempting hypnotism than sizing her up as a witness.

He continued looking at her and then he suddenly sat back, breaking off his attempt to induce a trance, but he kept his left hand on her console. "The floor manager we talked to, a man named Guy Nussbaum, said he and some others took a 'tech five,' which he explained was a coffee break, at 5:10. They all say that when they left Studio 57 there was no one at the anchor desk and all the studio lights were on.'' Fillingeri transferred his gaze to his knuckles as he slowly closed his hand into a fist on the console, like he was used to having a tennis ball there to squeeze for strength exercises—or like he was concealing the shiny gold watch he kept there to dangle before his subjects. ''So, between 5:10 and when Mr. Abagnarro spotted Miss Candela on that monitor, somebody turned out most of the lights, except those few over the desk, and somebody killed her in that chair or put her there already dead.'' He raised his eyes to me. ''Can you remember about what time you first saw Candela on that screen?''

I thought back. I remembered checking the clock above the line monitor at 5:21, when I had first seen Connie on the camera monitor. I had thought it was early for her to be in the studio. And then I had sent that note to her assistant about the green jacket. ''It was 5:21.''

Fillingeri raised his eyebrows. ''Exactly?''

''Exactly. I looked at a clock.''

''His Newsheimer's comes and goes,'' Ike said.

Fillingeri permitted himself a smile and opened his fist, but the smile faded quickly. ''Is it an accurate clock?''

''Very,'' I said, indicating the clock. ''It's reset twice a year, but only because of daylight saving time. If it weren't for that, we wouldn't have to fiddle with the clock more than once every other century—that's how little time it loses or gains. It's got a Cesium 3.58 clock driver that sends an electronic reference to the inner works every two minutes, just to keep things honest. If we're ever off by more than a millionth of a second or so, it's because when we reset for daylight saving, we take the time from the National Bureau of Standards in Washington, D.C.—if they're ever wrong, that's when we'll be wrong.'' I could tell by the way Fillingeri sneaked a glance at his own watch that he was not inclined to doubt the NTB line clock. ''That's how come we never go on the air too early or too late.''

He let out a low whistle and flipped his wrist over so he could study his fingers, giving his watch a rest. "Then it's accurate. Thanks for the lecture."

"You asked."

"Yeah. I did. You don't like plain yes or no answers, do you, Abagnarro?"

"I do when I'm asking the question."

"Very commendable." He didn't look like he wanted to stand up and shake my hand to congratulate me on my standards. "Then we have eleven minutes. Just eleven minutes. Between 5:10, when the floor crew says they took a break and left the studio, and 5:21, when Abagnarro saw Candela." He shook his head. "Eleven minutes. Either to kill her or to plant her in that chair."

"Don't you know what time Connie died?" Ike asked.

"We'll know after the autopsy, sometime late today. But the medical examiner's early guess is that Candela was dead before 5:10. I'm betting those eleven minutes were used for transportation."

"More like setting the stage," I said.

"Why do you say that?"

"Just a feeling I got from looking at her. She was so perfect, and only those few lights over the desk were on. She was spotlighted. Like she was ready to go on the air. A lot depends on how you look at things, Captain. The whole thing reminds me of the story of the three umpires—"

"Save your breath; I already heard it." Fillingeri gave me a bland look. "It's not very funny." He shifted in the chair. "Where were you, Mr. Abagnarro, during that eleven minutes?"

"I know it's not funny; it's *meaningful.* And I was in my office, number 2792. Then I came here." I did not mention that I had been recovering from the effects of a nap. Cops don't need to know everything, even if they did know some unexpected things. I wondered where Fillingeri had heard about the three umpires.

"How about you, Ms. Tygart?" he asked.

"I was in here."

Fillingeri reached for the phone on the console in front of him. "How do I dial in the house?"

"Who do you want to call?" I asked.

"That conference room."

"Just dial 2718."

Fillingeri punched the numbers in. "Mark? This is Dennis. The envelope is smaller than we thought. The crucial time is between 5:10 and 5:21. Eleven minutes. The director says he saw the dead woman on a studio monitor at 5:21. See if anyone who was in the control room can confirm the director—not the clock, the director. Concentrate on that. And I want you to tag anyone who was loose any time during those eleven minutes. That includes Tygart and Abagnarro. Maybe we can start eliminating some of these people and send them home for now. Get their times lined up on your computer. I want this as fast as you can. Do you have enough manpower?" He paused, listening, looking at the clock over the line monitor. "Okay. No, I'll get that later." He held the phone and listened again, still studying the clock. "Look, they're just people, Mark. Don't let them pull any richer-and-holier-than-thou television attitude stuff. I hate that media crap." He hung up. So Fillingeri had a dark side. Or he thought we did.

There was a long silence in the control room, with all three of us gazing up at the screens on the wall. The kind of charged, crackling silence that registers as black noise at the electromagnetic level.

Richer and holier I didn't know about, especially the holier part, but I did have one thing the cops didn't have, and I wasn't feeling smug about it. I was wondering if I should tell the captain that Connie had looked "wrong" to me, her appearance somehow "off," beyond the fact of death, and I was weighing the pros and cons of volunteering such a fuzzy detail and was just voting no because I didn't like the captain's poorer-and-naughtier-than-thou attitude when I realized he was staring at me.

"Something, Mr. Abagnarro?"

"No. Not really. I was just wondering why you've ruled out a natural death. What killed her?"

"We don't know yet. But let's just say there's a circumstance that makes a natural death seem very unlikely."

"The thing tied on her finger?"

"Oh. You know about that."

"Yeah. I saw it."

"Well, the NYPD watches morning TV sometimes, especially when business is slow, and some of us recognized that calling card. That's how Hannah Van Stone ended the show every day. Her very words." He shifted in his chair. "I read she was fired. Some magazine with her picture. That true? That's all there was to it?"

"Something like that. You should really talk to Joe Ayles or Othello Armitage or somebody. Somebody who can speak for the program. I don't get into that contract stuff. Besides, somebody other than Hannah Van Stone could have put that note on Connie's finger. There were a lot of people around this morning. There always are."

"Yeah, I thought of that." Fillingeri tapped the edge of his open hand on Ike's console. "But you both know about the feuding, don't you?" He tracked Ike's line of sight, checking what she was staring at on the floor.

She seemed to have gone mute, so I answered his question. "There wasn't any real feuding, not between Connie and Hannah. It takes two to feud. Connie was pretty nice about all the shit Hannah's pulled. If you've seen that banner over Hannah's office door, that was just meant to be funny, whoever did it. Playfulness. Not like breaking furniture or bringing a lawsuit."

"One of those women broke furniture?"

I nodded. "Hannah. Somebody leaked, and the story made the gossip columns around town."

Fillingeri had a look on his face that seemed to say that TV people sure did the nastiest things. Then he used his right hand to rub his chin and included both Ike and me in a different look. "Did either one of you touch that note on Candela's finger?"

"I didn't," I said. "I just read it."

Ike shook her head.

She stood up and stretched. It's really impossible to be in a room with a woman who's doing that and refrain from giving her the once-over, even when she isn't as pretty as Ike. I saw Fillingeri trying to look like he wasn't looking at her. He cleared his throat and pretended he was thinking police thoughts.

"Let's get back to this 'tech five' business," he said gruffly. "Do they always take their break at 5:10?"

"Depends what else is going on," I said. "But usually about then."

"How many people know that?"

"Everybody who works on the show overnight. Probably a lot more people. And the executive producer knows, too, of course, but he's not around on the overnight. That's Joe Ayles. By the way, Ike, did you ever reach him?"

She shook her head.

"What's this?" Fillingeri asked.

"Nothing," she said. "It's just that when I found Connie. I called several people. One of them was Joe. I got his machine. I left a message, but I haven't heard back yet." She didn't mention that she had also beeped his pocket pager.

"What's an executive producer?" Fillingeri asked. "I thought you were the producer."

"He's in charge of everything," she said. "I'm just in charge of getting the show on the air."

"So he schedules the guests? What I'm after is who got Heinous Face here? And whose idea was it? How did that happen?"

Interesting, I thought. Heinous Face. The captain was including America's rock darlings in his dark, ugly suspicions. I glanced up at Ike as she flung herself back into her chair.

The look on Ike's face told me that she was completely caught up with the captain, and I was betting that she'd been thinking about Heinous Face when she went into that stare. I wondered what she knew about the band that I didn't know.

She answered readily, but her answer sounded like she'd been working it out ahead of time. "Just before Hannah was reassigned to the UN, there was a meeting about what we were going to do to move the show forward. To make a real, substantive change from sixties-style anchor-heavy hard news stories to nineties graphics-driven, softer packages with 'younger' topics. This was two Tuesdays ago, before Hannah got the word she was out. Joe Ayles and Concepción Candela and Noel Heavener and I were at the meeting." This was news to me, that Hannah's ouster had been known in advance by more people than just Othello Armitage and Joe Ayles. It sounded like a palace coup. Ike went on without glancing at me, which was just as well, because I'm sure my eyes carried at least a little speculation and accusation. "The reason Abby wasn't at the meeting was that it was mostly about editorial content, not technical stuff. Anyway, we talked about a lot of things, but mainly about creating theme shows or theme weeks. We were hammering out the details of this Artists and AIDS Activism Week, and I suggested the new Museum of the Surreal. And some other ideas were mentioned. And then Heinous Face came up, which was because they're just launching this AIDS Awareness mega-tour, 50 percent of the profits from which are going to research to find a cure and to promote education."

Fillingeri seemed to think that was quite a speech from Ike. He cocked his head at her. "Who actually brought the name of the band up? Who introduced the idea?"

"Connie."

"Concepción Candela brought it up?"

"Yeah."

"Everybody like the idea?"

"Of course. How could we not? We'd kill to get the hottest band in the U.S. on *Morning Watch,* on any terms, for any cause. Whoops. I didn't mean that. You know what I mean."

"I know what you mean. Just a manner of speaking. So everybody liked the idea?"

"Of course."

"Miss Candela didn't have to sell the idea then?"

"No, but..." Ike took a breath. "But when I said we'd tried to get them on the show several times before without any luck, she said something like, 'Don't worry about it. I can reach them.'"

"What did she mean by that?"

"I don't know."

"What did you think she meant? You must have thought something."

Ike didn't hesitate. "That she either knew someone in the band or her agent did. After all, this was going to be her first week on the program, so she wanted the ratings to show that she could cut it. Getting Heinous Face would pad our ratings and make her look terrific."

Fillingeri finally withdrew his hand from Ike's console. "Where can I find this Joe Ayles, the executive producer?"

"I don't know. He must be in the building by now, dealing with Connie's death at every ghastly level."

"He didn't answer his phone when you called him? That was his home number? What time was that?"

"Just after 5:25, or whenever we found Connie. If Abby says we found her at 5:25, that's when we found her. I told you he's a techno freak, and he always knows stuff like that. Then I called Joe from the studio and got his machine at home. Maybe he just slept through it."

"Maybe." He produced a smile, allowing it to spread across his face, slow and deliberate, and I thought it was just as genuine as the warmth he could turn on and off in his brown eyes. "Well, I'm going to have to talk with both of you again, but now we need your fingerprints. I can take you into the studio for personal attention on that. You won't have to wait in line."

"Captain Fillingeri," I said, "are you just going through the motions? Everybody you're printing could have his or her fingerprints all over the studio for a good reason. Including Heinous Face. Their equipment was in there."

He gave me a hard look. "We're interested in that note. It's got a nice set of prints."

"Oh," I said.

Ike and I accompanied Fillingeri to Studio 57. As we walked down the hall, Fillingeri tried to make conversation with us, commenting on those Samantha Harris portraits of the NTB anchors spanning our broadcast history. "I've often wondered," he said. "What does *NTB* stand for?"

Ike grinned wearily. "Not-The-Best."

Fillingeri smiled. "You're Not-That-Bad," he said, touching her elbow cozily, like they were a couple of pals out for a stroll in the park. I thought that was a trifle friendlier-than-thou for a police captain, and I was wishing he'd make up his mind whether he liked us TV types or not. I had already made up my mind about him.

We passed Conference Room 2718 and the line of staffers still waiting for their interviews. The line was not long, and it looked like the cops were sorting and rerouting the staff with admirable efficiency, especially given the number of smart mouths I knew were among them. I'm all for having a smart mouth; in fact, I sometimes insist on it. But there's no doubt that snappy rhetoric plays hell with bureaucratic machinery. That's part of the reason most of us had developed speedy oral reflexes, for the monkey wrench effect. But, in this case, I guess most of the staff had applied brakes to their mouths so they could go home before they had to come back and put another show on the air.

We left them to their misery and continued along the tube, brushing past more blue uniforms than you'd see in Washington Heights on a Friday night.

It was so warm in Studio 57 that all the cops and crime-scene technicians were working without their jackets. Despite Fillingeri's promise that we'd get some kind of special treatment, we had to wait almost half an hour before anybody got interested in us again. Ike spent the time on the phone in a corner of the living room set, finally making contact with Little Joe and the rest of the dayside. I eavesdropped while they discussed pulling in the weekend anchor to help Noel out in the morning, and I took the phone briefly to discuss the setup for the next day, which was going to include a live remote from London—the Symphony Orchestra Against AIDS.

We were finally fingerprinted by and gave our names and addresses and work titles to a woman who looked like a well-adjusted vampire temporarily low on fuel. Her skin was so white she couldn't have been outdoors since she was put in her tomb about five years back, but she was smiling, and there was more genuine warmth in her pale smile than in ten of Fillingeri's more robust attempts. Her fingernails were so long I didn't see how she could work with other people's fingers without drawing blood. But she was quick and enthusiastic with the ink and surprisingly strong, and when she bent my left thumb down on the cardboard I heard the joint crack. I asked her for her job title, just to pass the time, and she said she was a ''forensic chiropractor.'' If I decided I needed to brush up on my own routine with a few clown lessons, she was my woman.

I stood there having my hand yanked around, and I was halfheartedly watching Fillingeri stalk around the studio with another guy in plainclothes, heads together in a heavy consultation over a computer printout. Fillingeri looked back at me once, and I didn't think he was checking to make sure the happy vampire wasn't breaking my fingers.

Ike was finished with her calls. She got up and trailed after Fillingeri, asking him if we'd have the studio back in our control by the next morning's show.

''You'll have it back in a couple of hours,'' he said. ''As far as I'm concerned, you can leave, Ms. Tygart. But, like I said, we'll be needing you again.'' He winked at her. ''You'll be happy to know you've been alibied by at least four people for those crucial eleven minutes.''

That's nice, I thought. Nobody suspected my beautiful ex-wife of murder. What a breakthrough.

''What about Abby?'' she asked.

Fillingeri frowned slightly. ''That's a different story. So far we can't find anyone who can place him during those eleven minutes." He stuck his left hand into his pants pocket up to his wristwatch—I could hear his change jingling and see his fingers moving behind the fabric—and he gave her a warm, sympathetic, intimate gaze. "We've been told Abagnarro's got a hasty temper. Somebody said it's a very bad idea to cross him."

SEVEN

STANDING THERE with ink on my fingers in Studio 57 and hearing a cop tell my former wife that I was both a murder suspect and a sociopath, I had to appreciate the cop's strategy, having used it many times myself. You don't have to work for a trash tabloid to get good at gossip. You just call it something different at the network level: information pooling.

It's a tried-and-true system for getting people talking: he would offer a titillating piece of information, with a tacit hint of more to come; it would then be Ike's turn to come back with some information of her own; and pretty soon he'd have started a regular gabfest, with everyone contributing, a sort of potluck symposium on NTB's dirty laundry. I've been around the highest levels of data trading long enough to know how the whole thing works. Gossip may be a filthy little marketplace with bogus goods, but that never stopped anyone from browsing there to see what they could pick up cheap.

At NTB News, our own intricate information shop is so institutionalized that we've named it: the Great Hudson and Harlem Used Teabag Company. When you want the inside dope on a coworker, you start the conversation by saying, "What's new at the H & H?"

And if anyone has the inside dope on yours truly, as well as an ax to grind, that person is Ike. I could just picture all of my sins being trotted out like so many rusted canned goods, especially with the cozy, sympathetic audience she now had. I don't know what the clinical term would be for the emotion that had me in its clutches—mere embarrassment, guilt, paranoia, fear—but I was no longer looking for ways to amuse myself at Fillingeri's expense or for easy ways to get Ike's attention. Being singled out by Fillingeri as a murder suspect rocked me out of that unreal overnight world full of purely fantastic retributions and rewards, where impossible things turned out to be true—first place in a dance contest or the miraculously safe landing of a crippled jet—and even death confined itself to the temporary gilded realities of a television studio.

Connie's death was real; her killer was real; those eleven minutes represented an actual pathway across public space, between a private confrontation and a private farewell, a dangerous pathway through open territory. Eleven prosaic, safe minutes when I had been waking up from a nap, combing my hair, putting on shoes, traveling to the control room. Traveling.

At precisely the same time the killer was traveling to Studio 57 with Connie's dead body. Now I saw myself on a parallel course with the killer, both of us making our way through the wagon wheel layout of the twenty-seventh floor, both of us silent and unobserved. And now Fillingeri was merging my identity with the killer's. I asked myself if I had heard anything, seen anything, during those eleven minutes that would separate those identities.

Nothing came to me. I had merely walked to the control room, like I do every night of the week. Nothing special, nothing different. I had done nothing I didn't always do, nothing to elevate the trip out of the routine, to make it memorable. Except stop to look at the portraits on the wall. Mainly Connie's portrait by Samantha Harris.

A visual memory stirred. The surreal dissolved to the mundane, the overnight fog lifted from Manhattan, and I suddenly found myself jolted two steps ahead of the police. First, of course, I knew I didn't belong on that computer list of suspects Fillingeri was carrying around; second, I knew what was "wrong" with Connie's appearance when we found her in the chair. I had been thrown off by the perfection of her placement on the aquarium set, by the perfection of her death without any outer mark of violence, by the simple picture of what I had expected to see: a pretty woman presented in her own setting.

And in someone else's makeup. That's what had been wrong.

It was thinking about the portrait, recalling the smooth colors of Harris's rendering of the lovely new anchor, that jolted me into seeing the dead woman's face the way I should have seen it when I first walked into Studio 57 and confronted that perfect picture of death. Maybe I would have realized sooner if the lights over the aquarium had all been on. In death, Connie had been wearing the rather flat, pink-based makeup worn by our pale northern anchors—like Noel and Hannah—not the darker shade Connie should have worn, with its much longer gold spectrum, its tropical warmth.

Those eleven minutes may have been crucial for Fillingeri—and for me—but I now knew that eleven minutes was nothing for the killer's agenda. It takes time to put makeup on right, and it had been applied perfectly to Connie's face and neck. And someone other than herself or a makeup artist had put that makeup on Connie; I knew she wouldn't have sat still for the wrong makeup if she'd been in any condition to object.

And I also realized that I didn't have an alibi for any part of that night—not after Ike and I had parted in the elevator around midnight—when the killer had needed enough time to work on Connie's face. But those eleven minutes between 5:10 and 5:21 were inviolate, the only window open on the killer's movements.

I don't know how long I stood there in Studio 57—I wouldn't call it *lost* in thought, but *found* in thought. When I tuned myself back into the buzz of studio activity, Ike was standing in front of me, with Fillingeri at her shoulder.

"Abby, tell him where the hell you were. I think he's serious about this."

"I already told him. I was in my office and then on my way to the control room. Nobody can back me up on that, because I was alone." I dragged my eyes away from hers and looked at Fillingeri. "I gotta talk to you."

He seemed surprised. Apparently he had thought it would take more time and energy to wring a confession from me.

Ike was surprised, too. "What do you mean, you have to talk to him? This is really creepy, Abby. I don't like this."

The studio was still full of NYPD crime scene specialists, but the energy was less purposeful than I'd noticed earlier on the monitor. They were winding down, packing up, getting ready to vacate.

Fillingeri glanced around. "Let's find someplace to sit down where we won't be trampled," he said.

"How about taking a walk down the hall?" I suggested. "I want to show you something."

Ike plucked at my sleeve impatiently. "Will you just spill it, Abby? What's all the mystery about? If you know something about Connie's death, I *order* you to tell me."

I ignored that and started to lead the way out of the studio, but I felt the fingerprinting vampire's nails on my forearm and stopped.

"You want a towel?" she asked.

I wiped my fingers, thanked her, and was tempted to deposit a dollar on her table. I left the studio, with Fillingeri and Ike beside me. We walked along the tube in silence for a while. Fillingeri seemed inclined to pretend he wasn't holding my leash and that we were just out for another pleasant stroll. Pals.

As we passed Conference Room 2718, I saw that the line of *Morning* staffers had departed, probably for more interviews in other parts of the building. When we were a few feet past the partially open door, it opened all the way and one of Fillingeri's cohorts stepped into the hall. He had what appeared to be a twin of Fillingeri's computer printout in his hand and signaled to the captain with it.

Fillingeri went to his side, and together they looked at the paper and exchanged a few words in low tones that I couldn't hear. Then Fillingeri said, louder, "Abagnarro's had an inspiration. If it's any good, maybe we can take him off the list."

If that was supposed to be an incentive, a not-so-subtle nudge for me to get busy and produce my surprise alibi with a dramatic flourish, I was genuinely sorry that I wasn't going to be able to oblige.

I was standing so close to Ike I could smell her perfume. Chanel No. 5. Classic fragrance. I'd bought it for her. At least I hoped I'd been the one who bought it, since she never buys perfume for herself. She pinched my elbow gently, cast a glance at the computer list, and sidled up to Fillingeri.

"I have to go to the john," she said. "I'll be back in a jiffy."

Fillingeri smiled at her warmly, stepped aside, and she walked between him and his partner, glancing sweetly at the captain—treating him to her remarkable mismatched eyes—and brushing his cohort's arm. *If she didn't get a good look at that printout,* I thought, *she's lost her news instincts.* Before she came to *Morning Watch,* Ike was the hottest producer in the NTB Investigative Unit. She doesn't miss many opportunities to snoop, and she's good at it. Among the newsjunk in her office, interlaced with her other souvenirs of life in TV journalism, are three of those golden statuettes from the Academy of Television Arts and Sciences. No wonder she didn't want the crummy tango trophy.

Fillingeri handed the printout back to his colleague, who folded it over once and returned to 2718, and we continued along the tube. Before we'd gone another ten feet, I could hear Hannah Van Stone's melodious tones pouring through the partially open door of one of the production offices.

"This is an absolute triumph of thickheadedness," she said snidely, in that famous deep and throaty voice, and I could almost hear her sneering. "Absolutely unparalleled for purity in the history of denseness. I don't have a witness, you toad. Perhaps the next time you wish me to produce an alibi, you'll be good enough to phone ahead and warn me. I'll have my secretary schedule something. In the meantime, I'm due at the United Nations. Even you must have heard of them. They're a little outfit over on the East River, and if you show them your handicapped ID, they can arrange a special tour for you."

Another, exasperated, voice said, "I'm not handicapped."

"That's the tragedy of it all," Hannah returned. "But when you can finally bring yourself to admit it, then and only then will modern science be able to help you. Goodbye, Sergeant. I wish you luck in your search for a cure.''

"Just a minute, Miss Van Stone. You can't leave.''

"Watch me.'' That was the aging lioness snarling.

I glanced at Fillingeri. A frown was fighting with a grin on his face. He put out his hand to let me know he was pulling in my leash. I stopped. He pushed the production office door open just as Hannah was pulling it from her side, and there was an awkward moment when neither one of them was in perfect touch with their centers of gravity.

"Goodness, Captain,'' Hannah said, and the fire in her blue eyes seemed to crackle. I hadn't seen her so mad since she first heard the word about her new job over at the East River. She was so angry her face was red under her makeup, and she lashed her smooth blond hair around her shoulders. "Are you trying to hurt me? Is this an example of police brutality?''

"That was an example of unfortunate timing,'' Fillingeri snapped, giving her back the fiery stare. "May I ask if your behavior right now is an example of media arrogance?''

My, my, I thought, *two fully ripe examples of rampant stereotyping.* I was used to the painful things Hannah could think up to say, most of which she really meant. In addition to actually meaning the nasty things she came out with, she enjoyed saying the words best calculated to get a rise or get her way. But I wasn't such an expert on Fillingeri's motivations, whatever they were. So far, that was two things he'd said to indicate he had it in for television people. I was beginning to wonder if his mother had abandoned him at a tender age in Phil Donahue's garbage can, which was not an image I wanted to dwell on.

"*My* behavior?'' Hannah said, her left eyebrow rising at least an inch. "What about the behavior of the New York City Police Department?'' She hitched the sleeves of her red linen jacket up over her elbows. "Apparently I'm being detained here simply because I lacked the foresight to hire someone to watch my every move last night. Believe me, I won't make that mistake again. I intend to start advertising for someone suitable the minute I leave this building.''

"Miss Van Stone," Fillingeri said, his jaw tight, "we're not out to inconvenience you. You must realize that we have to speak with everyone who had the opportunity to move Miss Candela's body into Studio 57."

"Well, you are inconveniencing me," she said. "I didn't move her body, which I have already told this ignorant bullfrog passing himself off as an ignorant detective." She glanced with loathing at the poor guy. "I have, in fact, already told three different police toads that I did not move her body. I went even further. I have told all three amphibian representatives of your office that I also did not murder Miss Candela. Why the hell would I kill her? Not even my worst enemy has ever called me stupid. And it would have been extremely stupid for me to attempt that little floozy's murder. Everybody on the planet knows I was having a very public fight over the anchor job she took from me with every once of strength she had in her thighs."

Fillingeri's eyes opened wide, but the other cop just looked pained. Apparently, he'd had sufficient exposure to Hannah to get himself acclimated and wasn't shocked.

Fillingeri pointed at the tape recorder on the table and stared at Hannah like he wasn't sure of what he was seeing. "Are you aware—Jesus, you must be aware—that everything you're saying is going on tape?"

"Of course. And because I happen to have eyes in my head, I'm also aware that I'm speaking before witnesses, as opposed to, say, phantoms. If you want to hold a press conference, I'll repeat what I said. I'm not ashamed of speaking sense. Use your brains, Captain." She drew in a deep breath, but for a fifty-eight-year-old woman on two packs of Virginia Slims a day, she was going strong. "If I were going to content myself with a cheap thrill on the order of Connie Candela's murder, would I have provided myself with a motive you can find if you exert yourself sufficiently to pick up any supermarket tabloid?"

"I don't know what you'd do," he said, narrowing his eyes at her. "Frankly, you're something of a surprise to me."

"That is hardly my fault. Now you'll be wishing that I hire someone to keep the police posted on my quirks and foibles, my likes and dislikes. Perhaps you'll be satisfied if I merely keep a journal and mail it in every week or so? With the expense of the professional alibi I'm expecting to add to my staff, I don't think I can afford more than that."

I didn't like finding myself on the side of the evil anchor-woman—excuse me, *UN correspondent*—but since I was apparently in pretty much the same position as Hannah, I was admiring her delivery. Snappy. Good pacing. I leaned against the edge of the door and folded my arms across my chest, wishing for the second time that morning that Ike was around to catch Hannah's act.

Fillingeri didn't share my way of looking at Hannah's attitude. "Why don't we shelve all this cleverness? That's all it is, cleverness. Just expensive words strung together." He hunched a shoulder at her and turned to the other cop. "Where does she say she was from 5:10 to 5:21?"

"She doesn't," the cop replied.

"She's refusing?" Fillingeri asked.

"Yep."

Hannah snorted. "I'm not refusing. I'm simply saying I don't know."

"Is there something wrong with your memory?" Fillingeri asked, a nasty edge to his voice.

"No," she said, a hint of a satisfied smile in hers. "There's something wrong with my watch." She held out her fleshy wrist to him. "It stopped at 4:07. This unfortunate circumstance, however, I'm happy to say, will not necessitate enlarging my staff by yet another person. The alibi expert can also serve in the capacity of timekeeper, should I ever be so unfortunate again as to wear a defective watch." She smiled at him, showing her teeth. "Feel free to inspect my watch. You may also help yourself to my expensive words. Consider them a donation to the needy."

Fillingeri barely glanced at her watch. He put his hand down on the table in front of the other cop and said, "Get someone to look at that watch." He straightened up and left the room without glancing at Hannah again.

As we started down the hall, I heard Hannah start on the toad: "Don't even think of touching it unless you have a jeweler's license. This watch cost me two thousand dollars, you slimy bully."

"Me?" That was the toad's voice. "I'm the bully?"

Fillingeri shook his head a couple of times and then flipped his hand at me. "Let's go. I forget where the hell we're going."

"I was going to show you something down the hall."

He shook his head again. "Is she for real?" he asked.

"Oh, I don't know, Captain. I sort of admire her."

"You do?"

"Yeah. She's got real balls."

Fillingeri laughed out loud. "I'd say she has several pairs."

"The saying around the show is that she's got enough to supply the cast of *A Chorus Line*."

Fillingeri laughed again. "Jesus. I feel sorry for the UN."

EIGHT

FILLINGERI AND I reached the newer end of the row of Samantha Harris paintings, and I stopped.

"This is what I wanted to show you," I said, tapping the frame of the portrait of Concepción Candela. "It was finished and hung up last week. It's a really good likeness. The artist must be around seventy by now, but she hasn't lost her sure touch. Connie almost seems alive, doesn't she?"

Fillingeri gave it a good once-over. "She was pretty. Nice picture."

"Yeah, but what I wanted to show you is the color. This painting shows Connie's dark skin, with all those great gold tones. Because her complexion was so different from most of our anchors—we've been a little retarded about filling our minority quotas—she had to wear different makeup, very different makeup."

"So?"

"So, when I saw her in the chair this morning, I thought there was something wrong with the way she looked, other than the fact that she was dead, of course. And I just realized what it was. Connie's got the wrong makeup on. Other people from the show might have realized it, too, but the light wasn't good in the studio, and then you guys kept us out of there. I saw Connie up close, and so did Ms. Tygart. But I think Ike was probably so concerned with seeing if Connie was still alive, and with calling 911 and everything, that she didn't really look at the face the way I did. Or for as long as I did."

Fillingeri took a deep breath and expelled it slowly. "Nobody has said a word about this. Anybody else from the show see her up close like you did? Anybody else who'd know about the makeup?"

I didn't have to think back. I'd already worked on this in the studio when I was holding hands with the vampire. "Noel Heavener. But he didn't get as close as I did. And Hannah. But same for her. She wasn't as close as I was. I'm sure a lot of people in the control room saw Connie, too, on the monitor, after I put all the studio lights on, but we were so busy with that airplane and with all the other stuff, it's not surprising if nobody else noticed Connie's makeup."

"I'm not sure I get this. Are you saying she put the wrong makeup on?"

"No. Connie would never do that. None of the talent would make a mistake like that, not even an inexperienced anchor. They all really care about their appearance, which is a huge understatement on my part. I'll give you an example. During the Gulf War, the control room was standing by here in New York, taking in a live satellite feed from Arthur Landau. Before they put him on the air, they had him in their monitors, and the show producer was talking to him. Arthur was on a rooftop in Dhahran, Saudi Arabia. Up to the last minute before he was cued to go on the air, with Scud missiles screaming in behind him, he was combing his hair. Combing his goddamn hair with Scud missiles incoming. He combed his hair for four or five minutes, while the satellite was holding his signal and he was waiting for New York to cue him. I know, because I was with him. Only, I wasn't combing my hair. I was cowering beside a wall on the roof."

"Jesus, and you guys expect us to think you're bringing us the truth on these news shows."

"Hold on a minute there, Captain. All he did was comb his hair. He didn't tell any lies."

"You know what I mean. It's all phony. NTB didn't show the pretty boy combing his hair."

"Yeah? Maybe you wouldn't think it was so phony if you'd been up on that roof. Saddam wasn't using fake Scuds." I was starting to bake a little under the collar. "And we don't get hazardous duty pay for stuff like that. It's just part of the job."

"Calm down, Abagnarro. I'm sorry I said that." He stuffed his hands in the pockets of his slacks and studied the portrait of Connie again. "So, somebody else did her makeup. Is that what you're saying?"

"Yes. Somebody who knows how to do makeup, because she looked almost perfect."

"But somebody who didn't know she used special makeup?"

"I don't know about that. Maybe it was somebody who couldn't get access to the stuff Connie wears."

"Where is the makeup kept? Is there a special room?"

"We have makeup rooms, but there isn't any makeup lying around this place, not to speak of. All our makeup artists are freelancers, and they bring the stuff with them in their kits. The anchors probably have enough in their desks to get on the air in an emergency, but it's not much and that rarely happens; the women anchors have some little things, you know, mascara and lipstick."

"What about Candela's personal assistant?"

"She'd have only as much access as Connie. But Lourdes does not do makeup, and anyway, why put the wrong color on if she did?"

"Why would anybody make her up wrong?" Fillingeri tilted his head and stepped back from the portrait. "What kind of makeup was used? What kind is on the corpse now?"

"I don't know for sure. Lighter colors than she uses. Used."

Fillingeri abruptly turned on his heel and strolled along the curving line of portraits, giving each one a quick scan and stopping briefly near the other end of the line to look at the early portraits of Noel and Hannah. He strolled back, repeating his scrutiny of the faces. When he reached my side, he slipped his computer printout from a pocket and consulted it, running his finger down a column, but he was careful not to hold the paper so I could read over his shoulder.

"All your makeup artists—we talked to three—are accounted for during those eleven minutes when the body had to have been moved," he said. "How long does it take to put that stuff on?"

"To put it on perfect, the way it looked on Connie, without getting it on the hair or the clothes, I'd say at least eleven minutes."

"Eleven minutes? Are you trying to be funny?"

"No," I said. "I'm trying to show you that the eleven minutes you're concentrating on don't tell the whole story. I'm giving you something else to look for. Connie had to have been made up before 5:10. What you're supposed to do now is say, 'Thanks.'"

"Thanks," he said gruffly. "But this doesn't change the importance of those eleven minutes when the studio was untended. No matter who put that makeup on Candela, or how long it took them, the body still had to be moved to Studio 57. And there's only eleven minutes for that activity. It's like a little tunnel of time, straight and narrow, and I've got to find out who moved through that tunnel. And you're still on my list. You were loose, Abagnarro."

"Okay, but I had no reason to kill Connie Candela. I hardly knew the woman."

He leaned his shoulder against the wall, next to Connie's portrait. "You're a recently divorced man, Abagnarro. Mind telling me what was behind the breakup?"

"I do mind. That's none of your business."

"Did it involve another woman?"

"None of your business."

"Maybe not. Tell me what it is about guys like you, Abagnarro. You wouldn't think it to look at you, but sometimes you TV types get laid by some great-looking women." A slow smile touched his lips. "Maybe you got Concepción Candela after you took care of the little blonde."

I was tempted to hit him, partly for what he said, partly for the snide way he said it, like he was enjoying himself. I guess he could read my face, because he turned his smile cold and said, "I wouldn't try it. I've got at least thirty-five pounds on you, and it's in all the right places."

Out of the corner of my eye, I saw Ike hurrying along the tube toward us. I wanted to change the topic, pronto. I lowered my voice.

"I don't know what it is about guys like you, Fillingeri—doing all that thinking about who guys like me are getting laid by. You ought to go scrub your mind. I will tell you now that I never lusted after Connie Candela, she never lusted after me, and we didn't have anything but a cordial working relationship. She wasn't my type, either to fuck or to kill. My type is coming down the hall."

Fillingeri pushed himself off the wall with his shoulder, not using his hands at all. Showing some of those thirty-five pounds hard at work. "Take a damper, Abagnarro. I just took a jab to see where you were tender. I should tell you one thing: the technical director says that you're right about the 5:21 end of the tunnel. He looked at his watch when you asked for the camera check. You've been honest with us about a couple of important things, and we're grateful. More than grateful. Without you, we'd still be back at square one. But you haven't said anything that tempts me to take you off my short list of possibles."

"When you get the autopsy results," I said, "I think I'll be off that list. I have no knowledge of poisons and no way to get any. That, with no motive, and I'm no longer a candidate."

"What makes you think it was poison?"

"The only other thing I've been able to come up with is maybe it was a natural death after all. Maybe somebody just found her dead and put her in the chair with that note, with the wrong makeup, for some reason I can't even guess." Fillingeri gave me a dirty look and I went on. "Or she was poisoned. What else could it be?"

"You tell me. All of a sudden, you seem to have the inside track on this killing."

Ike bore down on us. "Tell me what I missed. What's Abby's secret info?"

Fillingeri didn't waste any time. "Ms. Tygart, did you notice anything unusual about Miss Candela's makeup when you found her?"

"What?" Ike looked lost. "What about her makeup?"

"I guess you didn't," he said.

"I don't know what you're talking about," Ike said, glancing over at me. "Is this one of Abby's ideas?" She paused and looked sharply at me. "Is that what you meant when you said something looked 'wrong' to you? Was there something wrong with her makeup? Is that all? Who cares about Connie's stupid makeup?"

"Ike," I said, "Captain Fillingeri thinks I have a lot of potential as the chief suspect. So I care about Connie's stupid makeup."

But Fillingeri raised a hand. "Nobody said you were the chief suspect. We're just interested in your whereabouts during those eleven minutes. You said you were walking, from your office, right?"

"Right."

"There's gotta be more to it than that. You saw no one else? Didn't stop in the john? Didn't stop at a soda machine?"

I reiterated my journey, starting from my office, leading past the Candela portrait and past the set of suites housing Hannah, Noel, and the Green Room. "I guess the only person I saw was the lead guitarist of Heinous Face, but he didn't see me. If you know his itinerary, that at least ought to corroborate what I say."

Fillingeri pursed his lips and nodded. "It would if he'd left that room any time between four and six. He didn't. You could have seen him in there some time outside of the eleven minutes."

"How do you know he was there the whole time?"

"He had the phone in there off the hook, playing love songs to his girl in Seattle. She backs him up on that." Fillingeri shook his head in disbelief. "What a way to spend the night. I'll bet her ear hurts."

Ike rubbed her own ear, perhaps in sympathy, and looked up at Fillingeri. "I still don't get this makeup baloney."

Fillingeri looked at his watch. "I'll let your husband— sorry, ex-husband—fill you in. I'm late for a meeting with your executive producer." He shot me a look over his wrist. His muscular wrist. "Don't go anywhere, Abagnarro."

"Am I under arrest?" I asked, rubbing my eyes.

"Not yet. You'll know when we arrest you. The NYPD's not subtle about stuff like that."

"Then I'm going home. I've got to walk my dog." I looked at my watch. "Jeez, it's past eleven o'clock."

Fillingeri seemed to go into conference with himself. "You can go home after your statement is dictated, typed, and signed. You'll do the dictating and signing in your office in five minutes; the NYPD will handle the typing. I'll send someone down there. Then you can go home, but I'll expect you to answer your phone yourself. All day. Be there." He walked off down the hall the way we had come.

I leaned back against the wall and slid down into a sitting position. Ike sat down in front of me with her legs crossed.

"Who else is on his list?" I asked.

"I only got the quickest, dinkiest, tiniest little peek as I went by," she said. "But"—she held up her fingers to count off the names—"you, Hannah, Noel, Satan Brown, Fred Loring from Graphics, Brad Washington. He's that security guard from Alabama; remember him?" When I nodded, she continued, bending down another finger, "And Lourdes Ramirez, who, although she may be hot-tempered and the biggest tyrant I've ever met, I now feel sorry for. She cannot go up against the U.S. Immigration and Naturalization Service now that her sponsor is dead. I'm not sure about how green cards work, but don't you have to have a job?"

"I think so."

"Well, Lourdes ain't got one now. Connie won't be needing a personal assistant anymore—not that I mean anything theological by that." Ike seemed to lose herself in thought for a moment. "Of course, being on Fillingeri's list will keep Lourdes in this country for a while."

"Probably." Suddenly I was struck by Ike's research methods and laughed out loud. "That was a dinky peek?" Then I was struck by the results of her methods and sat up straight. "Noel?"

"Noel Hubert Heavener, king of the flaming non sequitur. Himself in all his glory. Really, Abby, if Noel killed Connie, he must have thought he was doing something else."

"Like what?"

"Oh, who knows how his mind works? Like washing his hands or learning rock climbing."

"You're just pissed because of what he said on the air today. Noel's only dopey with a microphone in front of his face. And then only when he's unscripted."

"Yeah, well, picture him scripting a murder for himself." She put her hands behind her on the dirty green linoleum and leaned back. "Besides, I was only pissed for a little while. You gotta love Noel. I hope the cops aren't making him cuckoo. Cuckooer. More cuckoo." She shook her head, her blond curls bouncing. "Abby, have you ever noticed that all the strange things Noel comes out with happen to be true?"

"I never thought about it."

"Well, they are. Basketball players *are* about seven feet tall. Live TV *does* make strange bedfellows. It's not like Noel says strange untrue things. That might be worse."

"Speaking of strange bedfellows, the captain was asking me about NTB's sexual schedule."

She looked up. "What'd you tell him?"

"That I wasn't sleeping with Connie."

She snorted. "Connie wouldn't sleep with you."

"For God's sake, Ike, have a heart. My self-esteem is already black-and-blue."

"Oh, I didn't mean it like that." She leaned her curly blond head back again and rolled her shoulders, the soft wool of her pink sweater sliding to reveal the straight line of her collarbone. "Next to Little Joe, you're the most important person on the show. You're the one who takes what the rest of us do and turns it into television." A couple of technicians passed us in the hall, stepping around Ike's outstretched hands. "What I meant was that you don't have the kind of influence that interested Connie. Oh, you could light her wrong or make the TelePrompTer roll out of sync or do a thousand things to make her look good or bad. You're the make-or-break man, Abby, when it comes to success in this business. Noel, for example, knows enough to suck up to you. But I think Connie was too new to network television to realize just how important you are." Ike raised her head and looked at me. "She isn't interested in you that way. Wasn't. Didn't. You know what I mean—past tense. The only reason she'd have for sleeping with you is that you're fantastic in bed, and it's common knowledge that Concepción Candela did not waste her time in bed having fun."

I was bereft of speech. I wondered if Ike could hear my jaw crack when my mouth fell open.

"What was that stuff about the makeup?" she asked offhandedly, just as though she hadn't applied jumper cables to my stalled ego. "I was so relieved when I found out that's what you were talking about. I thought at first you were bringing Fillingeri down the hall so you could confess to the murder."

"Why would you think such a thing? What motive could I possibly have for killing Connie?"

"Maybe it was the other way around," she said unconcernedly. "Maybe you asked her to go to bed and she said no. How do I know what you're up to these days?"

"I wasn't up to Concepción Candela—who, by the way, not that I'm changing the subject, was not wearing the right makeup when we found her, to answer your original question. She was wearing a much lighter number than she usually wears. That's what Fillingeri was asking you about." I leaned my head back against the wall, hard, wishing I had some control over Ike's opinion of me. "Listen, Ike," I said. "I don't go around asking women to go to bed with me like I was taking a poll."

She ignored the part where I spoke in my own defense and concentrated on the one nugget of news in my speech. "Well, well, well," she said, biting her lower lip for emphasis and nodding her head. "I knew it was murder from the first minute I saw her in that chair this morning, but this proves it. I still have great news instincts."

"Yeah," I said, closing my eyes and involuntarily thinking about some of her other instincts.

"Don't patronize me, Abby."

"I wouldn't dream of it."

"You're doing it. You are patronizing me. I'm one of the best journalists in America, and I plan to break Connie's murder in . . . well, faster than Fillingeri. I don't mean to criticize the NYPD unduly—New York is a rough city—but remember that last piece I produced for *Crime Watch?* Forty-point-one percent of the murders in this town go unsolved. Out of 2,166 homicides reported in the city last year, 868 were unsolved. Eight hundred sixty-eight! That statistic does not inspire me with awe. But you know what I think?" She put her head to one side and gazed at the portrait wall. "I think the ones that get away are the ones that just pull a gun, blow the victim away, and head for the hills. Simple murders. Quick and dirty. But Connie's murder, well, that's so full of window dressing that it's probably a detective's dream murder. I wonder, though, if Fillingeri might not be a little burned-out? He surprised me with all this indiscriminate fingerprinting and waving secret computer lists around so that anybody can wander along and take a peek."

"I wouldn't say he's burned-out. The way it strikes me, he's simply nasty." I tried to read the smug look on her face. "Ike, I'm getting the idea that you despise Fillingeri."

"Don't be silly. He's very cute. My point is that my investigative skills are still pretty hot. *I'm* not burned-out." She pantomimed her own earlier actions in stealing a look at Fillingeri's list. "It's nice to know I haven't lost my touch by sitting around on my duff putting television on the air." She winked at me. "Remember, pal, you're looking at the woman who brought down Senator Joseph F. (as in Frisky) Bartel for hitting on his female staffers—and sexual harassment is one of the most difficult of all charges to prove." She smiled reminiscently. "Plus, it wasn't exactly peanuts when I nailed the IDF's assassination training camp in the Negev."

Ike was referring to a piece she had produced for *Around the Watch* when she had been the ranking producer in the NTB Investigative Unit stationed in Israel during Desert Storm. To get the story, Ike had worked on the premise that if Saddam had nerve gas, the Israelis almost certainly had it, too. *The Israelis always have state-of-the-military-art toys,* she reasoned, *so why not nerve gas?* She had almost single-handedly traced the top-secret, ultra-elite Israeli army units called "Sayerets." Each division or brigade has one, and the elite of the elite is called "Sayeret Matkal," which is attached directly to the Israeli Defense Ministry. Ike had located documents and one source willing to speak off-the-record concerning the fact that the Sayeret Matkal had been trained by the Mossad to inject themselves with atropine (the antidote to nerve gas), sneak into facilities containing Muslim fanatics, spray nerve gas, and slip away into the night.

Ike's smile faded slightly, leaving a wistful, dreamy expression. "Of course, I've never investigated a murder, but it's got to be easier to get the goods on a killer than on an elected office pervert or on Israeli intelligence, both of which I have done. I wouldn't feel so cocky if this were a hit-and-run murder. You know, the bang-you're-dead kind. But Connie's murder isn't one of those. Solving it will be a matter of pure news gathering and being intensely alert and actually hearing what people say. I do that every night, plus put a television show together."

I opened one eye to see if she was serious. I couldn't tell. "You're not serious, are you? You're going to go after this like a news story?"

"It *is* a news story."

"True, but are you going after it yourself?" If Ike decided to go after the story herself, as opposed to parceling it out to her staff, it was time to warn the poor hornets that she'd be sticking her pretty nose right into their nest. Ike has an unorthodox style for a journalist who ranks as high as she does. She's not bad at delegating authority, but she likes to get her own hands on the scene of the action as well. She's very tactile, I guess. She did not get her industrywide reputation for nailing down the tough stories by looking under conventional stones and asking conventional questions, or by letting her staff do those things for her. She likes to touch things, literally feel her way through a story. There was the now-celebrated collection of weird sexual aids in the hidden drawer of the oak table in Senator Bartel's office, which Ike found with only a screwdriver and excellent timing—and Minnesota had to find a new senator. There was the night Ike crawled under the barbed-wire fence in the Negev, accompanied only by a camerawoman equipped with infrared film and camouflage gear—and *Around the Watch* had the Sayeret Matkal story.

"I don't know. Maybe I am serious." She fixed me with an intense scrutiny, running her eyes over my face as though she were looking for a clue to what made it work. "There was a time, Abby, when the least hint of suspicion directed at you would have sent me to the wall like a tiger."

I swallowed hard.

She glanced at her watch and got to her feet. "Well, I gotta run. Some of us fortunate few will not have to live out the rest of our days under a cloud of suspicion like you, and there's an open casting call over at the Circle Rep. I have to change my clothes, and I'm already late. Wish me luck."

"You can't possibly do all that—audition for a play and produce a daily two-hour television program, plus produce an investigative report, not with your crazy idea of investigating like a commando. And what if you audition and actually get the part?" I shook my head sadly and said, "Although why this audition would be different from the legions of others eludes me." She tossed me a nasty look, but I went on, because one of us had to remember that we were a prize-winning dance team. "And when will we ever get a chance to rehearse at Playtime-in-Brazil? The waltz competition is next week. Ike, you can't do everything."

"Pooh. Watch my dust."

I put up a hand in defeat. "You win. Do what you want to do. Don't listen to me."

"*And* maybe I'll take French lessons, too," she said musingly, as if she hadn't heard me. "I've always wanted to speak French. I have a whole new life now as a divorced

woman, and I mean to use my free time pleasing myself."
She bent to brush floor dust from her slacks. "If you end up
in jail, it will be because you're actually guilty. I'm not pro-
posing some shoddy, slanted tabloid journalism." She
started down the hall. *"Au revoir."* She gave me a sidelong
glance but kept walking. "By the way, Abby, you don't own
a dog. Tsk, tsk. Lying to the big, handsome police detective."

NINE

FORTY-POINT-ONE PERCENT of New York's murders unsolved.

Ike's statistics did nothing to increase my affection for Capt. Dennis Fillingeri. I wanted to get out of the Emerald City and do some serious thinking about the little walk I had taken while the murderer was taking his. Or hers.

And aside from the fact that I was eager to perform a quick exit from Fillingeri's list of suspects, there was a weird atmosphere on the twenty-seventh floor among the staff of *Morning Watch* as they got ready to leave for the day and filtered downstairs—an everyone's-talking-about-everyone-else-and-none-of-it's-good mentality—and that climate was not conducive to productive thinking or brotherhood among broadcasters. It probably wouldn't be all that terrific for the show either, if we were all watching our backs instead of our monitors.

Despite Fillingeri's kind permission to go home and walk my dog, I didn't get out of the building until almost one o'clock. I had to repeat my statement about strolling in the tube to a cop who did shorthand. He borrowed my computer, typed what I had said, and printed it for my signature. He kept the disk, which was NTB property, and didn't even offer me a receipt. Not that I don't steal disks from NTB, too, but at least I work for the network that I victimize. For an officer of the law, his grasp of the principles of petty thievery was pretty shaky.

By the time the cop walked out of my office with his booty, the twenty-seventh floor was crowded with *Evening Watch* personnel, and since they have five times our audience, as well as serious pretensions to being the "program of record"—the jewel in the NTB News crown—they had arrived with the attitude that *Morning* had not only con-

doned a murder, but was also acting weird, and that it was
our obligation to rectify matters by immediately giving them
the full story for use on their broadcast. And because I was
the one who had discovered the body and fixed the outside
limit of the eleven minutes at 5:21, it was like having twenty
Fillingeris after me at once, and while all of them were richer
and maybe holier than him, they had nothing on Capt.
Dennis Fillingeri in terms of those thirty-five pounds, so I
was more tired and annoyed than in any danger from the
pushy, self-serving, irresponsible electronic media. The
bums.

Noel, who was smart enough to suck up to his program's
director, because he'd been working in television long
enough to know how important I am, sought me out and
tried to absorb some of the static, but the friction that day
between the evening and morning shows was almost too
much even for someone as nice as Noel. When the hounds
from *Evening Watch* were sick of looking at my tonsils while
I yawned, they tried to get Noel to agree to a live interview
that evening, which really shows how arrogant they are on
that show, thinking either that they could corral his mouth
or that their prestige was so great it didn't matter what goofy
thing he said. Or, in fairness to them, maybe they genuinely did not know what a risk they'd have been taking. I've
never been convinced anyone on the evening show watches
us. Although you'd think the interview with the pope, which
everyone knew about, would have clued them in to Noel's
Lady-or-the-Tiger mouth.

But Noel graciously declined to appear on *Evening Watch*,
on the score that he thought NTB News would be better
served by downplaying the story of Concepción Candela's
death. And, about 12:30, a memo came down from Othello Armitage, himself, that said NTB should tell the story and
tell it well, but with the smallest number of bells and whis-
tles, so Noel won his point.

I still have my copy of that memo. I saved it because it was
the only memo I ever got from Armitage that carried his
personal signature, instead of a computer facsimile:

Surely I speak for the entire NTB family when I say that
I am deeply shocked and saddened by the tragedy that
unfolded on the twenty-seventh floor of the O. Armitage Broadcast Center in the early hours of this morning. Concepción Candela was a talented young
journalist, who had much to contribute to our programs and to the journalism community as a whole.

But our grief and our understandable dismay should
not be allowed to intrude on either our ability to help
the New York City Police Department or our ability to
put the highest-caliber television news on the air. I feel
certain that you will cover this story as you would cover
the death of any national figure: with thoroughness and
dignity, but without any of the sensational and/or personal elements that will be the staple of lesser news
outlets. Get it accurate; keep it short.

O. Armitage

I suppose that Armitage had decided that *a certain type* of
bad publicity could actually be worse than no publicity, and,
in sharp contrast to the treatment of his stinging, colorful,
and well-publicized disagreement with Hannah Van Stone,
the Concepción Candela story was to be made as invisible
as possible for a television event that the rest of the media
would no doubt hump royally, like minks in mating season.
The way I translated the memo was "Don't bury the story,
because that would cause comment and ugly speculation,
which we don't want and can't afford; but don't feature the
story, because that will help people to forget it as quickly as
possible, which we do want."

A subtranslation I read into the memo was that Ike's
plans for an investigative report would have to be tossed into
the same file we use for our candy wrappers and Chinese
takeout cartons.

When the memo made the rounds on the twenty-seventh
floor, Noel was in my office, helping me fend off the *Evening* tribe. The memo defused them, and they left. It was
that simple. You don't argue news ethics with the man who

owns the microphone. Noel folded his copy of the directive, slipped it into the inside pocket of his brown jacket, and sat down on my Danish Modern excuse-for-a-couch, loosening his tie.

As the last of the *Evening* pests cleared out of my office, I spun my chair around to face Noel, took off my sneakers, and reached for my skates.

"You go everywhere on those things, don't you, Abby?" he asked.

"Everywhere I can. Safer than the subway, cheaper than a cab, faster than walking, better exercise than sex—not that I'm claiming to remember that last one. At least I've *entered* a cab in the last six months."

"You miss Ike terribly, don't you?"

It was still difficult for me to talk about Ike, and most people who worked on *Morning Watch* knew that, but this was Noel. I kept it light. "I certainly miss the sex. I can't exactly miss Ike, seeing her every night."

"You still dancing together?"

"I almost forgot about that, too. Look up on the shelf behind you. We won that trophy last night, although now it seems months ago. First place in the tango."

"I've never been dancing. Isn't that odd?" He smoothed the crease in his trousers with expensively manicured hands—hands tend to look older on TV, and anchors pay plenty to keep their mitts in shape. "Well, the dance contest explains your black tie, then. One of those police officers asked me about the way you're dressed."

I tugged my laces. "They did? What'd they say?"

"That you were dressed to kill. Ha, ha. He thought that was funny. Wondered if you dressed this way every night."

"I hope you told him I usually carry a bloody ax and a flamethrower."

He laughed. "I wish I had said that. I can never think of clever things like that on the spot. Not unless I'm on the air. Being on television does something to my inhibitions."

I bent over my skates, keeping my eyes on the laces so I wouldn't have to arrange my face. I didn't want to hurt his feelings.

"Abby?"

"Yeah?"

"Do you think I killed Connie?"

"Of course not." I looked up. "Nobody really thinks that. You're just trapped by those rapidly becoming sacred eleven minutes. Same as me. Why would you kill Connie?"

"Abby, I was afraid of Connie. Because of her, Hannah got kicked off the show. I can't allow myself to feel profoundly over what happens to Hannah, because she's such a brute to everyone, but I care about what happens to me. I can't do anything besides anchor. It's all I've ever done."

"We're all afraid of something, Noel."

While I tied my skates, he stood up and wandered around my little office, looking at the toys and junk on my shelves, spinning the cut-glass globe I'd bought in Argentina and keep on my desk. He reminded me of a little boy waiting his turn in the dentist's office, all restless energy and an anxious frown.

When I had both skates tied, I sat back in my chair and folded my hands over my middle. I wanted to get on my wheels and roll, but I could hardly kick Noel out of my office.

"Noel, what were you doing then?"

"You mean *then?*"

"Yeah, *then.*"

"This is so embarrassing."

"Then forget I asked." I stood up and rolled over to get my tuxedo jacket from behind the door. "I'm not trying to be a junior Dennis Fillingeri."

"Abby," Noel said, picking up the little globe and holding it between his hands like a basketball, "he says I'm a suspect."

"Me, too."

"You are?"

"At least we're in good company, huh, Noel? You and me."

"Did he tell you if anyone else was unaccounted for during those eleven minutes?"

I considered rapidly while I shrugged myself into my jacket. There didn't seem to be any reason to clutter up Noel's mind with the list Ike had seen. On the other hand, it didn't seem fair to let Noel go on thinking he and I were the only nominees at this convention gathered to elect a killer. But after a quick review, and borrowing some reasoning from O. Armitage, I decided that Noel would be better served if I got it accurate and kept it short.

"No," I said, "Fillingeri didn't tell me who else he suspects."

"Darn. He wouldn't tell me either."

"He's a louse, Noel."

He returned the globe to my desk. "Well, I guess you want to get going." He started for the door, which I held open for him. As he crossed the threshold, he turned back to face me. "I was in the bathroom, Abby. I don't want you to think I'm a louse, just because I wouldn't tell you where I was."

He trailed off down the hall, his shoulders drooping and his step far from springy. I felt sorry for him. Noel Hubert Heavener did not have the kind of ego that most anchors—Hannah Van Stone, for example—can lay claim to: swollen into a tough bubble around the self, a durable coating that protects them from real criticism and imagined slights, as well as allowing them to think highly enough of their abilities so that they can go on the air without fear. Ego is probably the most important quality for an anchor to have; otherwise, they'd never step under those lights and take the chance of blowing it in front of millions of people. If you think, even for a second, that you're going to be rotten, you will be. If you're the kind of person who ever wondered if you've got what it takes to be a television anchor, you'd better not apply for a job reading the news. You haven't got it.

Noel's ego was adequate to get him on the air with a script rolling on the TelePrompTer in front of him, but it was not adequate for him to ward off the tender ministrations of Dennis Fillingeri and company the way Hannah had done. As I watched Noel go down the hall, he looked like what he was: a tired, gentle old man who had just learned that some very unpleasant people thought he was capable of murder.

I pulled my door closed and locked it. I skated down the hall toward the elevators. I punched the button and waited. The doors slid open, and Little Joe walked out, surrounded by his yes-people. I tried to slip around the edges of his crowd into the elevator. I could just see the shiny top of his bald head as I sneaked by.

"Abagnarro," he said, standing on his toes so he could see over the ring of yes-heads. "Just the man I want to see. Where have you been?"

"Not hiding out," I said, surprised at his rough tone. "I've been in my office for the last hour. And my telephone works, Joe. You could have called me."

"I didn't want to climb over Othello's desk and sit in his lap."

"You were up there? Did you ask him if he killed Connie?"

"Yeah. I wanted to see what it felt like when he chewed my hide into bloody shreds. I'm masochistic like that." Little Joe eyed me through an opening created when a couple of his people broke ranks to let a janitor in lime green coveralls slink out of the back of the elevator. "Abby, step down the hall a minute; I want to talk to you." His pale green eyes swept the shoulders of his herd of sycophants. "Alone."

The sea parted, and he led the way while I tried to skate beside him. It was more like mincing. Rollerblades usually give me a sense of freedom; I can do any move on blades that I can do on ice skates. But now I was hampered. Have you ever tried to ice-skate slowly? I didn't have much choice, because Little Joe always took little steps. I could have kept pace with him by skating circles around him, but that would have seemed a little pointed. So I minced.

To keep my mind off my skates, I started making conversation. "How were the Tonys? Good seats?" I figured that whatever was eating him, I'd at least remind him of my recent generosity regarding certain tickets.

"Fine. That's not what I wanted to see you about, to give you my review." Joe didn't make me wait long to find out what was eating him. "What the hell was the big idea telling that police captain who thinks he's an Alec Baldwin clone that I wasn't answering my home phone last night?" he demanded in a low voice.

"Alec Baldwin has blue eyes," I said, by way of offering simple information. "Fillingeri's are more of a cowshit brown."

"I didn't say *I* thought he looked like Baldwin. I said *he* thinks he does. Don't change the subject."

I put my hand on the wall to keep my balance. "Joe, if you want to vent your spleen at me, okay. But don't pretend you're the only one who's had a difficult morning. I discovered Connie's corpse before I tattled on you, so that puts me one up in the bad morning category."

He chewed his lower lip and scowled up at me. *His* eyes looked babyshit green, and they were bloodshot. "So why'd you give Fillingeri that guff about my answering machine? He acts like he thinks I was out on the town with unspeakable companions or, worse, somewhere killing Connie. Jesus, Abby, it's not a crime to sleep. You guys on the overnight must think I do nothing but sit by my phone waiting for it to ring, hoping it's some prying lunatic from NTB who wants to see what I'm doing at the crack of dawn."

"Gee, I'm sorry I didn't make up a story about you instead, Joe. I just wasn't thinking, or I would have told Fillingeri that Ike called you after she called 911, that you answered in a groggy voice, and that you and she then had a long talk about Shakespeare's plays. That way, when you got to the Emerald City, he could have asked you which play was her favorite, just to check and make sure I'm not a liar. By the way, her favorite is *A Midsummer Night's Dream*, in case this ever happens to you again. It won't do to get your stories crossed."

"You don't have to get snotty, Abby. I just wondered why you thought you had to say anything at all about that phone call."

"Because it came up, that's all. I didn't have a master plan. Besides, what do you care what Fillingeri thinks? You weren't even in the building. Do you know about that eleven-minute business?"

"Yeah. So does the Japanese prime minister and every microbe in Antarctica." He shook his head. "Sometimes I hate this place. Jesus Christ, this building has leaked like a sieve, and everybody knows."

"Well, then, you already know you're off the hook. You're not even on Fillingeri's list of NTB assassins. If he gets curious about why you didn't answer your phone, he's just taking a survey. Blow him off."

"I did. I've been around, Abby. Longer than you have."

"Then why are you busting my chops? Need practice?"

He took a step back, broke off eye contact, and changed the angle of his gaze to take in my pleated shirtfront and black tie. "I'm just wondering about your loyalties, Abby."

"Kiss my ass. You didn't wonder about my loyalties when I was dodging Scuds in Saudi Arabia or when I was taking baths with commie cockroaches in that world-class fleabag across from the Kremlin."

"Listen." He put his little hand on the sleeve of my jacket. I glanced down and he withdrew it. "We need a staff meeting. I guess we're all a little edgy."

"If by 'staff' you mean the overnight people, you'd better not call a meeting until well past midnight. You wake anybody up, Joe, after the night and morning we had, your staff meeting will make the Alamo look like an ecstasy convention."

"Jesus, Abby, go home and get some sleep. I'm sorry I said that about loyalty."

"I'm sorry you did, too."

I pushed off angrily and skated down the hall and into the elevator, which was thoughtfully being held by a yes-hand attached to a yes-arm. "Thanks," I said. I reached into my jacket pocket for a quarter to toss at him, but I came up empty. "I guess your reward will have to come from knowing your loyalties are appreciated." The doors slid together and the car went down.

TEN

IF I DIDN'T HAVE a quick temper, I guess I'd be the first Italian-American of my acquaintance to veer away from the stereotype. Or maybe it's not an ethnic thing; maybe it's geographic. Certainly all the role models in my large family over in Queens have spent half their lives blowing their tops first and asking questions later. But I'll say this for my own temper: the quickness works in both directions, and by the time the elevator reached the ground floor, I was back to whatever level of serenity is normal for me. *Joe Ayles had just been blowing off steam,* I thought. As executive producer of the Morning Murder Show, he was sitting on top of the geyser.

The elevator doors opened, and I saw the most recent of my Italian-American acquaintances at the security desk, the logbook open in his hands and a uniformed cop by his side taking notes.

"I thought you had to walk your dog, Abagnarro," Fillingeri said.

"I'm gonna be honest with you, Captain. If I don't make it home by noon, my dog takes himself out for a walk."

"Smart dog. Does he keep his watch accurate? What kind of watch does a television director's dog wear—a Rolex?"

"Why? You interested in his jewelry or his alibi?"

"You never know." Suddenly he smiled, and it looked like a real smile, the kind you can't help rather than the kind you help along. "Will you answer a question for me?"

"That's why I came downstairs."

He nodded thoughtfully. I guess he did look sort of like Alec Baldwin. "This place is really strange. There's a copy of *The Wizard of Oz* on a chain in one of the men's room stalls up on your floor."

I thought, *maybe Noel was reading up on the Munchkins during those eleven minutes.*

"That's NTB News for you, Captain. We're always up on the latest. The lead story on *Evening Watch* tonight is going to be about the Wicked Witch's most recent act of terrorism. She's going to blow up some poppy fields if Dorothy isn't surrendered."

"No kidding." He passed a hand over his forehead and through his dense hair. "Abagnarro, give your sense of humor a rest and tell me something. According to security, there's an informal rule that anchors don't have to sign this book when they arrive at the building. Why's that?"

I shrugged. "I suppose it's because everybody's supposed to recognize them instantly. If you want an autograph, you usually slip them a piece of paper, not a security log. What's the problem?"

"Well, for one thing, we have no way of knowing what time Miss Candela got here last night."

"Gee, you're going to end up not liking us, Captain."

"I'm trying to keep an open mind. But why you'd have security without enforcing it, that bothers me. I'm not paid enough to exert myself giving you people a hard time just for the hell of it. These little details make a difference, you know. If Candela came in too late for the killer to put the wrong makeup on her, or if she came in at any time later than about five o'clock, the whole thing doesn't make sense. Think about it, Abagnarro. This was your contribution, after all. If she got here later than five, Candela'd only have time enough to get herself upstairs and get killed before she was taken to the studio. Her personal assistant said she never saw Candela last night."

"Are you saying Connie might have been killed somewhere else? Or made up somewhere else?"

He hesitated a fraction of a second. "I don't think that's very likely. I'm just saying I wish you people had better records of who comes in that revolving door."

"It's only the anchors who don't sign the book. And the guards at least look at their famous faces. You couldn't sneak through that little door on your belly and crawl past the guards unless you were made out of putty.''

''You also couldn't get Heinous Face's drums through there. They're not made out of putty.''

''The Face drums and the rest of their equipment came up through the back, sometime overnight, from our loading dock. A lot of hardware goes in and out of this building.'' The wheels were turning, and I could feel a tiny smile starting at the corners of my mouth. ''Somebody could have come up the back way last night, somebody not on your list. The killer didn't have to be someone who works on the twenty-seventh floor. You know, Captain, your little list of nonalibied personnel doesn't look so airtight anymore.''

''Yeah, I'm crushed.'' He didn't look crushed. ''So I've done some checking. The one department in this asylum that seems to play the game by the rules is the Operations Division. Their records are impeccable. Those drums came up last night from the loading dock out in back of this building, in the company of their owner. A big star like Satan Brown, using the service entrance.''

''His drums are special. Everybody knows that.''

''Yeah. Even me. I know a couple other things, too. NTB carried the Tony Awards last evening from the St. James Theater. I happened to catch the last hour. And, Mr. Abagnarro, I figure you guys had to move some cameras over to the theater. No cameras, no TV pictures, right? So I asked your vice president for operations about his system, and he gave me a personal tour. The back door to this place has been factored into the equation.''

''So that little computer list that has my name on it is still your roadside atlas to the murder?''

''I haven't found any reason to change my mind or my map. The Tonys were over by midnight, and everybody who escorted those cameras back here came in through the NTB loading dock and left again well before 3:00 a.m. Brown came up at 4:05, with a security escort. Nobody, not even a rock star, gets past your security out there without showing ID and signing the book, both when they enter and when they leave. The operations VP says he keeps a tight grip on his expensive toys. I guess you folks are more fastidious with your gear than you are with your people.''

Since that was more or less true—the kind of big, computerized Hitachi cameras we had used to broadcast the Tony Awards late Monday night cost more than $120,000 apiece, which meant we had taken well over half a million dollars in camera equipment alone from the Emerald City to the Theater District on NTB trucks—I didn't argue. The total cost of the Tony broadcast equipment, with the mobile control room, the sound system, the lights, etc., put NTB's fastidiousness cost at well over a million dollars.

It would have been nice to find an alternate route inside Fillingeri's eleven-minute time tunnel, and right out our back door would have been convenient. But Fillingeri was correct about how NTB treats its equipment, and security on our loading dock would have gone over well at Fort Knox. You don't take chances with a million dollars' worth of Othello Armitage's hardware. If anyone had sneaked into the building through the back, he or she had done so under a cloak of absolute silence and utter invisibility, like a colorless, odorless gas. Some deadly gas, like carbon monoxide.

That was an arresting thought. Gas. Gas doesn't leave marks on a corpse. But I refrained from making that bright suggestion to Fillingeri, because if it turned out to be right, I didn't want to be the man with the fascinating ability to predict autopsy results.

''Well, Fillingeri.'' I watched him close the logbook over his hand. ''I'm not going to stand here and defend NTB policy regarding its people or its doors or its gear. I'm pretty tired of defending, period. In fact, I'm tired. Good-bye.'' I skated toward the revolving door but turned my progress into a circle and rolled back to the desk. ''What time are you going to bed?''

He blinked. ''I don't know. Why?''

''I'm just hoping that you're sound asleep at home in your little police bed when I get back here tonight.'' I shrugged. ''It's just a warm fellow-feeling. You look tired.''

"Stay by your phone, Abagnarro," he growled. "And don't lose any sleep about me losing sleep."

I let him have the last word, just to show that I could. The midday sun was streaming through the great sea green glass doors with the etched faces, casting hazy, distorted shadows of famous mugs on the darker green marble floor. I skated across the shadows and left through the revolving door.

I was skating into Columbus Circle, clockwise against the traffic, when a thought occurred to me. Colorless, odorless gas. If anybody had sneaked into the Emerald City through the loading dock, he or she must have been cloaked in invisibility. Colorless, odorless gas. Like fog. The fog embracing Manhattan's streets the night before like smoke from dry ice.

I nearly skated into the front fender of a cab.

It squealed to a halt, throwing the passenger in the back seat up against the plastic panel. The driver leaned over and cranked down the window. "Hey, asshole!" he yelled. "Why the hell don't you stay in the rink where you belong? You're makin' it a nightmare out here. Goddamn freak show."

"What's the matter with you?" I demanded, slapping the heel of my hand down on the hood of his cab. "Haven't you ever seen anyone do something stupid before? Get a life, for God's sake."

I skated back to the curb and braked, surveying the street down to the alley that runs east and west beside the Emerald City. I cruised along the curb until I came to the delta of the alley, threaded my way among the herd of pedestrians on the sidewalk, and headed into the shadows between the buildings.

The alley was about what you'd expect, with Dumpsters and litter and a couple of homeless people sitting well apart from each other on the same set of greasy concrete steps. No companionship in that despairing fraternity. I felt my usual pang of guilt and skated past them, but their eyes did not follow me in an accusing stare. They weren't blaming me.

I rolled through a narrow urban mine field that could send a skater flying, picking my way around bottle caps and broken glass and rotting vegetable matter, staggering my skates so I could stay upright as I sailed through a yellow puddle of spilled popcorn. At the other end of the alley, I rolled out into the sunshine again onto Columbus Avenue.

The NTB loading dock is a stark rectangle of concrete that juts out over the sidewalk on Columbus at about my shoulder height. Three white NTB trucks were backed up to the dock, leaving one space at the curb for another truck. A set of concrete steps, about three feet from where I stood at the end of the alley and painted a rusty-looking green, gave access to the dock from the sidewalk and to a small green door directly above the steps. Two uniformed cops and a man I took to be another cop in plainclothes were standing up on the dock, chatting with a short, dark-haired, brick-shaped woman in jade green NTB coveralls. The presence of the cops told me that Fillingeri might not be as light-hearted about this back entrance as he had indicated. He may have factored it into the equation, but that didn't mean he liked the answer.

As I stood there at the corner of the alley, watching the cops and the forewoman exchanging secrets about the security industry, the big overhead door to the cargo bay started sliding up and away from the concrete floor, rolling silently on well-oiled runners, and a yellow forklift swung out into the sunshine on the dock, accompanied by a man wearing a business suit and speaking into a cellular phone. I recognized him from seeing him around the building, and I thought he was probably an operations manager. He walked to the edge of the dock, and a fourth NTB truck rumbled down Columbus, executed a neat K-turn, and backed smoothly into the last parking slot. The suited man punched a button on his phone and stuck the instrument into his jacket pocket.

The door of the truck opened, several men jumped off onto the dock, and the forklift rolled forward. About twenty rolls of carpeting were taken off the truck, followed by a refrigerator, a wine rack, a super-flashy Art Deco jukebox,

what looked like the bar from one of the older saloons in
Manhattan—complete with scuffed and dented brass foot
rail—and parts from a gigantic brass bed.

Soap operas, I thought. A new location must have been
written into the story line—maybe two new locations, because I couldn't think of any tavern scene that would require a brass bed—and here were the locations coming off
the trucks. NTB has the two granddaddies of all soap operas, *Monday Always Comes* and *Meg's Children,* and while
I am not a fan of either show and can't distinguish between
a lovable bitch and a nasty goddess, I thought it was a reasonable bet that the citizens of television's most venerable
sin-towns occasionally frequent taverns and/or brass beds.

A couple of green canvas hampers on wheels were trun-
dled out to the truck, and the rolled carpets were dumped
into them and taken inside to the cargo bay. The forewoman gave each piece a good going-over with her eyes,
and, by golly, she made each worker sign the book on her
clipboard—each time he went inside and each time he came
out. They signed, but I could tell they thought it was a nuisance and a waste of time, although nobody gave her any
unnecessary lip.

The cops observed the entire operation, the plainclothes
officer standing back off to the side of the dock. I'd seen
similar operations several times. But what I was looking for
this time involved looking at the scene differently, looking
for possibilities, for what *could* happen.

What I was trying to do was paint over this bright picture, turning it darker on the surface of my imagination,
blurring those sharp shadows and shading that bright sunlight to the muted, hazy grays and blacks of Manhattan at
night, and then coloring them over with a thick, rolling
fog—the same dense fog whose acquaintance I had made
outside the dance club the night before. Into my mental
picture I inserted a stealthy figure, approaching the green
steps from the alley through the dense, smoky wall of mist,
his (or her) clothing dark, waiting for an opportunity while
the tired NTB crew concentrated their energies on a million
dollars' worth of gear they were bringing home from the

Theater District. It would have been a desperate gamble for someone intent on murder. But I already knew that Connie Candela's killer was a desperate gambler. He (or she) had moved Connie's dead body through the tube on the twenty-seventh floor, using part of an eleven-minute chunk of time when some other person could easily have been using the same eleven minutes in the same set of halls. Me, in fact.

If there was a glimmer of a silver lining for me about this picture I had constructed on the canvas of an extremely willing imagination, there was a lowering dark cloud for Fillingeri, and I did not think he had written off the back entrance to the Emerald City. Judging only from the questions he had asked me about my relationship with Connie Candela, there didn't seem to be anything lukewarm about his imagination.

ELEVEN

THE ONLY EXPERIENCE I'd had investigating murder was from a bar stool at the All-Souls Cafe, next to the dance club on 72nd Street, where they have the TV on every Sunday night for Jessica Fletcher. There's usually a pool on among the bar regulars to see who can get the solution before Mrs. Fletcher has one of her "hunches." I do not believe in hunches, and I usually bet pretty heavily. Ike says I'm as bad as the viewers who phone the network to hassle us about our program. "It's just as useless to bet on fiction as it is to complain about news," she says.

I didn't know if Fillingeri believed in hunches any more than I do. But I did not doubt that Fillingeri had taken a good look at the NTB loading dock, or that he had understood just how significant it was that Connie's corpse had been discovered wearing the wrong makeup, or that he would investigate the currents of bad feeling associated with the recent changes on *Morning Watch*—although I did wonder if those eleven minutes were a kind of security blanket for him. They were impregnable, so certain, so airtight, that he might latch onto them as the single key to unlock the secret of Connie's death. But since I had actually traveled through that eleven-minute tunnel on a parallel course with the killer and I had seen nothing that provided the slightest clue to the killer's identity, I wasn't as keen on those eleven minutes as Fillingeri apparently was. And at least two things, in addition to the actual murder (if the medical examiner's early guess was right), had happened before the 5:10 starting line in Fillingeri's desperate little eleven-minute race. The killer had coated Connie's face with pale makeup and had fashioned the note that appeared on her index finger. The problem was, Where? Nobody seemed to know where Connie had been overnight before I spotted her on the monitor from the control room.

If nobody knew where Connie had been overnight, everyone would soon know where she had been for the rest of her short life. I did not doubt that Fillingèri would do an expert job on Connie's background, as far as that job could be done by going through files and pulling out pieces of paper and interviewing bureaucrats. Cops and reporters cover a lot of the same ground in bureaucracies, and I knew the drill he'd be following.

But I thought I had just discovered a different approach, and I wanted to make sure that my starting point made sense, that I was not blinded by the foreground of the picture that was Concepción Candela's death. It *was* a picture, the way she had been placed in that anchor chair. A carefully wrought and thoughtfully presented display. Artifice. Showmanship.

Television. Television is nothing if not physical. It depends less on the imagination than any other medium. Everything is supplied for you. If you want to make television, you have to have all the supplies.

Like Connie's death: the star, the makeup, the props, the studio, the cameras, the lights, even a little script—"I'll be watching for you"—supplied in neat block letters on a little piece of white notepaper tied by a white ribbon on the corpse's finger. Television. What paid my salary and kept the Emerald City from being turned into condos.

Television. After checking out the loading dock, I thought I might be on the right track, but I wasn't sure where the track was taking me. I needed to have a question answered by an expert who was on my side. I started skating, which I can do on automatic pilot—almost.

Some people in the Big Burg are not thrilled by those of us who have taken to speed skating on the sidewalks and streets, but I look at it this way: I'm not polluting the air, I'm not sawing holes in the ozone layer, I'm not wearing out the infrastructure, and I'm not contributing to the parking problem. Occasionally, I admit, I do scare a pedestrian (or

a cabdriver), but people who don't want to be scared from
time to time should go live in some other city.

The lunch crowds were out on the streets when I left the
loading dock and headed downtown on Columbus (which
becomes 9th Avenue), skating the fourteen blocks to 46th
Street in less than two minutes. There isn't a lot of margin
for error at that speed on that obstacle course, and the best
advice I can give the person (either the skater or the pedestrian) experiencing it for the first time is to keep your knees
flexed and your eyes open, don't deviate suddenly from your
course, and never watch your feet. And hope for the best.

The 300 block of 46th is known in the Theater District as
"Restaurant Row" and is home to Gypsy's, the restaurant
my family has owned since 1952 and where all the theater
crowd hangs out sooner or later. My parents had befriended just about every struggling actor and actress and
director and playwright who ever went on to make it in the
Big Time, and a lot more who didn't.

My mother started running Gypsy's by herself after my
dad passed away eight years ago, and she's transformed it
from a starchy old bore with a huge overhead into a three-
star hot spot that's minting money. That's not saying anything against my dad's abilities, but Carole Abagnarro certainly seems to have found her métier. And it doesn't hurt
the cash register that all the people my parents befriended on
their way up still treat Gypsy's like a second home.

My dad never met Ike. She came on the Abagnarro scene
after he died, but ever since the separation and divorce I've
been hearing about what my dad would have thought of my
shocking failure as a husband. That's one of the iron shib-
boleths in the extended Italian family that populates the old
neighborhood in Queens: it's always the man's fault when
a marriage dies, no matter whose fault it was; and the
woman gets all the credit when a marriage succeeds, no
matter who's been supplying the heftiest percentage of the
bliss. I've been trying to tell my mother—who says she has
become a feminist since being in business on her own—that
this belief system actually does disservice to women by pre-
serving the stereotypes of woman as domestic angel and man

as barely housebroken animal, but she just says, "Spoken like a man, Abby. Always living inside your head. You'd rather argue philosophy than take responsibility for your emotional life."

And I say, "I don't have an emotional life, Ma; I'm divorced."

And she says, "That's your own fault."

So, I hadn't been around at Gypsy's much in the past few months. But this afternoon, with the shadow of Concepción Candela's death and official suspicion both touching me, and no wife to go home to and no dog to walk, and a question for an expert, I found myself tearing down to 46th Street with real anticipation of some unconditional sympathy and fettuccine, and an answer. The only shibboleth in my family regarding murder has always been the one that begins "Thou shalt not," and since I hadn't and wouldn't, I thought I'd be welcome at the Abagnarro eatery.

I rounded the corner to the east and pulled a speed-stop in front of the silver-and-gold door of Gypsy's. My mother considers Rollerblading to be an example of the bad manners creeping into New York *proper* from its sprawling exurban detritus—"Hey, you're acting like you're from New Jersey; you wanna do that, go to a shopping mall"—as well as a threat to her hardwood floors. Gypsy's is her turf, so I parked myself on a fire hydrant, changed into sneakers, and tucked my skates into my backpack.

The difference between real life and television is that although they often overlap in your space, television can't follow you around. From my perch on the fire hydrant, I caught my reflection in the sparkling clean glass of the big bay window of Gypsy's, right next to the menu. *There he is,* I thought, *that tall guy who follows me around wherever I go. That strange, lonely, two-dimensional guy who's been trying to skate so fast his mistakes won't catch up with him. Skating away from the mistake that cost him his marriage.*

I sighed, blowing breath out through my mouth audibly, and shrugged, and stood, and the man in the window mocked me, move by move. I pulled the silver-and-gold door open and went inside, hoping to leave him out on the street.

My mother caught sight of me across her crowded dining room from where she stood behind the Formica-and-chrome bar, where she was talking to a few customers and watching *Meg's Children* on the TV above the wine racks. Working for a television network is a little like working in a spider web—it's hard to shake your job when you knock off for the day—and here was another reminder of NTB, but this was one I welcomed. I had a question about Meg and her brood, and behind the bar was my expert. My mother started watching the soap about seven years ago, out of loyalty she said, when I was hired at NTB as a production assistant, and she's been hooked ever since.

She waved to me, reached under the bar, came up with a Heineken, popped off its top, and stepped around the end of the bar. I met her halfway and she handed over the cold beer.

"You look rotten, Abby," she said, giving the maternal ogle to my face and my tuxedo. "I heard about Miss Candela."

"I feel pretty rotten. Connie was only twenty-six, you know." I gave her a kiss on the cheek, and she took my hand, leading me over to her favorite booth against the wall. She likes that one during the lunch wave because she can still see the TV. She doesn't seat people there unless that's the only booth left. "Ma, the detective in charge of the whole thing thinks I may have had something to do with it."

We slid onto the red leather benches. She reached across and patted my hand. "I know. Ike called me this morning so I'd hear it from her instead of from CNN or the radio or something. You should have called me, Abby."

"I'm sorry, Ma. I was tied up with the police captain and then Noel Heavener and the *Evening* spies. Did Ike tell me everything? That the police are interested in me? This one guy thinks I'm actually a decent candidate for the murder."

"The police are good people, Abby. He's just doing his job."

"Whose side are you on?"

"Yours, of course. You didn't kill her."

"Thanks." I took a sip of the beer, and then tipped the bottle back and drained half of it.

"Have you eaten?"

"I'm empty. Totally, completely, entirely empty."

"I'll be right back."

I watched her as she hurried to the kitchen, her head turning to keep eye contact with the TV until she had to steer through the swinging doors. At fifty, Carole Abagnarro looks forty. She always wears her dark hair in a French braid, and she goes easy on the cosmetics. She works out with Gracie's Gymgirls, doing jazzercize; she runs a couple miles in the park every other day; and she eats her own cooking, which is mostly pasta and vegetables. That's one of the reasons that Gypsy's is so hot now—my mother's kitchen produces healthful food that doesn't taste like freeze-dried oak sawdust the way a lot of health food does.

I cast a glance up at the TV. I knew I wouldn't see the tavern location I had watched them unload up on Columbus Avenue. It takes a couple of hours to build a set like that, and the shows are taped at least an hour ahead of airtime, sometimes even a day ahead—particularly when they have those telephone scenes, because the two halves of the conversation, which of course take place on different sets, need to be edited together. But I wanted to get Carole Abagnarro's expert opinion on the older sets of NTB's afternoon wailers.

All soap operas look alike to me. As I nursed my beer, Meg's offspring seemed to be doing an awful lot of talking about hanky-panky and very little actual hanky or panky. I've been up on the twenty-eighth floor of the Emerald City many times, and I can testify that living room sets outnumber bedroom sets by six to one, so maybe that's a useful barometer of the relatively tame antics of Meg's progeny.

It's difficult to watch a soap opera and keep your mind off being unfaithful to your spouse. Cheating seems to be the rule on the soaps, rather than the exception, and I mean cheating. They talk about it, and plan it, and talk some

more, and do some agonizing, and have several drinks, and
talk about it, and finally agree to meet the next day and talk
it over. I was wishing I could switch the channel when Ike
breezed through the door, her skates dangling by their laces
from her hand. She was wearing my favorite color.

She spotted me immediately and crossed to the booth.

"Oh, hello. I was going to drop this off with Carole, but
I guess now I can just give it to you." She dropped a stack
of money onto the table. "Where's your mother?"

I pointed toward the kitchen and lifted the little stack. I
flipped through it quickly. Two hundred and fifty dollars.
My share of last night's dance triumph. Goody.

"You don't have to count it, Abby," Ike said, giving me
the kind of haughty, unbelieving look an exam proctor once
gave me when he saw me counting on my fingers during the
SATs. "I don't cheat."

There was that word. "It's going to be really hard to hang
onto my appetite with you tossing bombs like that at my
head, Ike. Can't you give it a rest?"

She moved into the booth across from me. "Look, I
stopped at the ATM after I left the audition. I didn't want
to carry all that money with me on the street. If I'd known
you were in here, I'd have skated on by and given that 250
dollars to the first mugger who asked nicely. *You* give it a
rest. I'm tired of how sorry you feel for yourself. You think
everything's a big plan to make you feel bad. I meant 'cheat'
as in 'screw you out of money.'"

I ran my hand through my hair and then stopped myself
in mid-comb, wondering if I was trying to imitate Captain
Fillingeri. "I'm sorry. How'd the audition go?"

"I think I'll get the part."

"What is it?"

"Well, it's practically just a walk-on, with dinky little
lines, but I have to start somewhere. And it *is* Shakespeare."

"Which Shakespeare?"

"The one from England, stupid."

There was no way I could win that day. "I meant which
play."

"*Hamlet*. It's that Donna Steiger all-woman production. You must have heard of it. There was an article in the *Times* on Sunday. I'm going to be Osric, if I get the part." She crossed her fingers. "Frankly, I think we'll shed a lot of psychological truth on all the timeless questions of the play, you know, with just women. Eliminates distractions, I think."

"I'm happy for you," I said, speaking as an eliminated distraction.

She cocked her head and gazed at me. "Are you?"

"Yeah. I really am. Very happy. But it's going to be tough on you, if you get the part, You'll never get any sleep."

"I can sleep in the mornings." Suddenly she smiled. "I've been wanting this for so long."

"You want a beer? To drink to good luck?"

"No thanks. I have to be sober this afternoon."

I signaled the bartender for another Heineken, pointing to my empty bottle, and leaned my elbows on the table so I could get a close look at Ike's lovely eyes. She wasn't my wife anymore, but that didn't mean I couldn't bask like other guys. "Why? What's this afternoon?"

Her smile curved into a mischievous grin. "I've got a date."

"Gee, that's nice," I said, trying not to grind my teeth. "Who with?"

"I'll give you a clue. He's about six feet tall, has dark hair and bulging muscles, and he solves crimes."

I gawked and crashed back against the cushions of the booth.

"And," she added, "if you need another clue, he thinks you're a bad man."

"Well, you two ought to have a grand time. You have so much in common."

"Don't we?" she said sweetly.

"Ike, let's pause the videotape here for a minute." I leaned forward. "I need to talk to you. I've got an idea about Connie's death."

"Why tell me? Why don't you tell the nice captain?"

"Because he liked my other ideas so much that he now thinks they were mere embellishments on my first brainstorm, which was to kill her."

"You're only one of several people Fillingeri suspects. Don't be so self-centered."

"Oh, great. Now I'm an egomaniac because somebody suspects me of murder. Sometimes I wonder about your brain. You know, Ike, I actually thought you'd listen to me. I'm sorry I brought it up."

"I didn't mean to blow you off. I'm listening."

"Is that list the same as when you first saw it? Now that you're such bosom buddies with the captain, maybe you get to look at his computer printouts whenever you want."

"I am not using feminine wiles to outfox the captain, Abby, if that's what you're implying. If I get ahead of him, it will be through sheer brainwork. My brain is working just fine, thanks." She took a deep breath. "And if anyone's using wiles, it's Fillingeri." She glared at me. "But since you ask, the security guard is off the list. The reason nobody on the floor could alibi him for those eleven minutes is that he went home sick at 3:30. The lobby desk checked him out of the Emerald City. That leaves you, Hannah, Noel, Satan Brown, Lourdes Ramirez, and Fred Loring. If we could pry Fred away from his graphics computer, maybe we could get him to marry Lourdes, and that would take care of the green card problem, although he'd have to put up with her temper. That's my matchmaking thought for the day and that's the extent of my inside knowledge of the private business of the New York City Police Department. But I mean to make myself an expert on their business, even if it does take a feminine wile or two. I'm gonna nail this story."

So, I thought, *she hasn't seen the memo from the penthouse.* I slumped farther down on the cushion so I could reach the copy of Othello's memo I had stuffed in my pants pocket. I tossed it across the table to her. "You might want to feast your uncanny eyes on this before you put any mileage on those wiles."

She unfolded the memo but did not lift it off the table. When she saw the letterhead, she reached for my fork and used it to turn the memo around to face her. She read. She raised her eyes to mine.

"Othello can't be serious. He's got major doodoo on his own premises and he takes away the only broom he's got? That's crazy. If ever there was a time to pursue a story aggressively, that time is now." She used the fork to impale the memo and held it up over the table. "Well, you know what I say? I say, 'Pooh.' Let him fire me. I'll get a job waiting tables like a *real* actress." She flipped the fork, memo still attached, onto the table. "Besides, he won't fire me. I've won three Emmys."

"I'm sure everyone on the staff got that memo, Ike. Who're you gonna get to do your legwork?"

"There's nothing wrong with my legs, if it comes to that. Men! First there's you, implying I have to turn into a tart to get information. Then there's Othello, rearing up on his hind legs and roaring, apparently just for the pleasure of making animal noises. Then there's Dennis Fillingeri, who's probably out buying a shirt right now, about one size smaller, so his muscles can pop out over lunch. And then there's you, again, acting like the only thing I'm good for is telling other people what to do. I started in this business at a dinky newspaper that couldn't even afford blue pencils, and I can still do my own legwork."

I did a quick mental survey of her complaints, trying to figure out which one had made her huff and puff. "I didn't mean to make you mad about Fillingeri," I said. "I'm just jealous. I can't help it, Ike."

"You shouldn't be jealous anymore. The most you and I can ever be is friends, Abby." She glanced at her watch. "Oops. I'll call you later, okay?" She smiled suddenly and patted my hand with a sisterly thump, which I guess was progress. It was better than being treated like the Swamp Thing. "I'll just go say hello to Carole and I'll be on my merry way."

She slid out of the booth and I took a good look at her. She was wearing a baby blue miniskirt and a baby blue tank top, with a white sweater tied around her trim little waist.

I cleared my throat. "I can't believe you dressed like that to try out for the part of a Danish courtier. You're not wearing that to see Fillingeri, are you?"

"Well, it's either that or"—she put her arms over her head and tossed her hips in a stripper's bump and grind—"take it all off, baby." Customers were turning around from the TV set to watch Ike, so she smoothed her skirt and the expression on her face got prim. "I'm meeting him in ten minutes by the fountain at Lincoln Center. I don't have time to change."

"Jeez, Ike, you have to be tired. Shouldn't you go to bed instead?"

She grinned at me. "Maybe after lunch with Dennis."

Her steps were light as she waltzed off to the kitchen.

I sat there dazed. Fillingeri. Excuse me, *Dennis*. And Ike.

When she returned, she blew me a kiss as she passed the booth.

"Call me," I said.

The outer door swung inward and she ducked under the arm of the man who was holding it open. His gaze followed her as she strolled toward 9th Avenue.

Another beer appeared on the table. I drank it. My mother emerged from the nether regions of Gypsy's and sat across from me. She pushed a steaming, aromatic plate of thin, flat noodles in *tagliolini carbonara* across the table.

"You look worse than you did when you came in, Abby," she said. Then she eyed my empty beer bottles. "This is what comes of getting soused so early in the day on an empty stomach."

"Yeah, now I'm an alcoholic. Is there anything else about me you don't like?"

"Don't get sarcastic with your mother. I don't like it."

I removed Othello's memo from the fork and ate the pasta in silence. When I finished, the stay-tuned-for-tomorrow's-episode theme music was playing on the TV and the credits were rolling for *Meg's Children*. Two o'clock. *If I was my dog,* I thought, *I'd go find another owner.*

"Ma, your soap opera. Does it have a tavern?"

She nodded. "Roman Nights. Everybody goes there."

"Are they remodeling, or anything like that?"

"What do you mean?"

"I saw some new sets going in the back door at the Emerald City, and I wondered. One of them looked like a new tavern set."

She rubbed her hands together. "Oh, goody. Now I can tell all the bar crowd. We've been wondering because Arnie, who owns Roman Nights, is probably going to jail for assaulting Jake, who was fooling around with Arnie's wife, Jessica, not that anyone blames Arnie, because Jessica practically demanded that Jake hop in her bed. She's so bad." My mother squeezed her hands together in apparent ecstasy. "I love knowing inside information like this." She glanced across to the bar, where the channel had been switched to another network. When she turned back, she said, "You wouldn't happen to know if there's a new hospital room set, would you? I keep thinking Arnie will go after Jessica if he escapes from jail."

"No, Ma, I didn't see anything like that. Let me ask you something else. Are there any Hispanics on *Meg's Children?*"

She shook her head slowly. "There aren't any minorities. Not even African-Americans." She must have been indoctrinated by Ike. My mother always used to say "blacks."

"You don't watch *Monday Always Comes,* do you, Ma?"

"I've only got time for one soap."

"I stirred my fork around in the *carbonara.* "Did you have time to watch our show this morning?"

"Yes. I cried about the airplane. You did a good job."

"Did you happen to notice anything odd about Noel?"

My mother does not like to criticize *Morning Watch,* and I saw an evasive look descend over her features. "Abby, I only saw the first few minutes. I had to go out for my run. I don't want to end up with thighs like Luciano Pavarotti's."

I smiled at the thought. "You can tell me, Ma. What did you think of Noel?"

"What's to think? I went out to run right after he said the plane had landed on a basketball player."

"He didn't say that."

"Yes, he did. I heard him with my own ears. You should get that Hannah back. She didn't make mistakes like that."

"TV news is changing, Ma. You're going to be seeing less and less of the anchors anyway. Soon it won't matter who does the show."

"I'm certainly going to be seeing less of that Candela girl. Such a shame."

"Yeah, I guess that was the killer's plan."

I thanked my mother for the food, went out and put my skates on, and rolled north toward my apartment on West 74th, thinking about how soap sets go in and out of the Emerald City. Sets are not like cameras and electronic equipment. They're big, and an enterprising killer could conceivably hide out inside a piece of furniture or a roll of carpeting, thereby avoiding the front door. The problem was, how could a killer take a chance on getting back out of the building without giving the gimmick away?

I was in bed and asleep by 2:20, a deep, dreamless oblivion, blissfully devoid of stealthy figures emerging from television taverns, and police captains and provocative former spouses, and planes landing on basketball players.

TWELVE

WHEN THE PHONE RANG, I rolled over and opened one eye at the clock. Five-thirty-three. Deciding it was Joe Ayles calling a staff meeting, I almost let my machine do the honors, but I'm a terrible slave to my telephone reflexes, and without my consciously willing it, my arm dragged itself out of the sheets and lifted the receiver.

"What?"

"Abby? It's Ike."

"What's the matter?"

"Nothing. I merely thought you'd be interested in something the captain just told me."

I opened my other eye. "Is it dirty?"

"Don't be disgusting. He's a very polite man." There was a pause, a kind of thoughtful pause with low humming. "Well, mostly polite. But, anyway, he got a call at the restaurant—we had Caesar salad at the Empire Grill; you would have loved it—and the autopsy's finished."

I sat up in bed and the phone slipped off the bedside table, falling to the floor with a jangling metallic clash. "Shit."

"Don't you want to know?"

"Of course I do," I said, grappling with the wire.

"Connie drowned."

"She did not."

"Cross my heart."

"How come the medical examiner didn't say so right away?"

"Apparently the lungs are like sponges. They absorb liquid like crazy, but they're very quiet, and you have to do an autopsy to find out. Isn't that gross? I hate medical hoo-hah."

"They know what time she died?" A sliver of dull light was slipping under the corner of the blackout shade I use so I can sleep during the day, and the idea of man knowing anything about time suddenly struck me as puny and laughable. I knew what time it was on my bedside clock, but my life obviously had nothing to do with the artificial temporal boundaries in place for most New Yorkers. I was some kind of time renegade, a time freak. What difference did it make what time Connie died?

"What'd you say, Abby? You're mumbling."

"What tim did Connie die?"

"Oh. They think 4:30, maybe a little earlier, but not much."

"That's pretty exact. I'm surprised."

"Stomach contents. That guitar guy said she had coffee and a few pretzels at about 4:00. Connie was only in the Green Room a few minutes, and that little detail was buried down in some cop's notes. Dennis was fairly strident on the subject."

I remembered smelling coffee when I passed the Green Room. "Speaking of stomach contents, are you still at the restaurant?"

"No, I'm at home."

"Are you alone?" I asked, crossing my fingers.

"Yep. Just me and the cat."

"I'll be right over."

There was another pause, this one with a distinct chill. "You'd better rephrase that."

"Sorry. May I stop by to discuss a murder matter with you?"

"That's better. Hurry up. Dennis says he may be ready to make an arrest soon. Although it seems that police captains are very macho, and that *may* just be the macho way they talk. Even the way he walked me home was macho, if you can imagine."

I could imagine. I ground my teeth. "If Fillingeri spent the afternoon with you instead of doing his job, how can he possibly make an arrest? Who's he going to arrest—me?"

"Dennis can spend his afternoons how he likes. He's a captain. His minions do the dirty work."

"Sort of like Satan? I mean the one in Hell, not the drummer."

"Abby, are you coming over or not?"

"I'll be right there."

"Brush your teeth. I can smell the beer breath all the way from here."

I not only brushed my teeth; I shaved, showered, and dressed in a shirt and jeans that had just come back from the cleaners. I splashed on Cool Water, which is Ike's favorite cologne. I left my skates parked by the door and summoned the elevator to the ninth floor. When I arrived at the street, I flagged a cab, not an easy task at that time of day. Ike's apartment is only eight blocks from my cell on 74th, but it was a warm evening, the sidewalks were crowded, and I didn't want to break into a sweat from the rush-hour pedestrian wrestling matches and ruin the effect of the Cool Water.

When I got to her building on 82nd, I had to ring the bell. I used to have a key, but that was in the good old days before I turned into a loathsome scum. She buzzed me in, and I took the elevator to the nineteenth floor. I rang the doorbell and waited while she undid the four locks. At that, when she opened up, the door was still on its chain. She looked at me, closed the door to release the chain, and held it open. She was still dressed in baby blue.

"What took you so long?" she demanded.

That hurt. She could at least have noticed the effort I had made to be less loathsome.

"I went back to sleep."

She snorted and stepped away from the door.

That was the first time I'd been in our apartment in several months. There were changes, like new miniblinds and less furniture, but it was the things that hadn't changed that got my attention. Like the way she leaves her clothes on the arm of the rocking chair. Like the smell of baby powder coming from the bedroom. Like the fat orange cat sleeping on my end of the $2,700 green couch.

"He's much fatter," I said, just stating a fact. "I guess he never moves at all now that I'm not here to kick him off the couch. Or have you had him bronzed?"

"The Donald is not fat. He's muscular. It's not his fault he has chromosomes that dictate bigness." She put her fingers on her chin. "Or do I mean largeness?"

"You mean obesity."

"I do not. If I meant obesity, I'd say obesity. What do you think—I don't know how to talk?"

"You know how to talk all right." I caught sight of the cat as he turned in his apparently drugged state and shifted his hindquarters toward the coffee table. "See? It's mutual. Now he's mooning me."

Ike started to give me a nasty look and then suddenly cut it off, replacing it with a resigned sort of superiority. "If you're just going to be vicious, I wish you'd slink back to your swamp."

"Ike," I said, reaching out quickly to take her hand, "truce. Okay?" It sure felt good holding her hand.

She gave me a dose of her eyes before she nodded. "Okay."

I dropped her hand because I could tell she wanted me to. "Can I sit down?" I asked, and my voice suddenly sounded strange and unnaturally loud to me.

"Of course."

She nestled into her end of the couch among a bower of pink pillows (new), tucking her bare feet under her. I hesitated, not wanting to start anything, but I finally gave The Donald a little pat on his rear and he lumbered off onto the floor with a satisfying thud. I glanced at the cushion and nobly sat down without a word of complaint on the orange hair deposit he had left—in jeans that had just come back from the cleaners. The cushion was warm.

Ike wiggled around, scrunching herself into the pillows to get comfortable. "Abby, this is the most bizarre thing. Drowning."

"I still don't believe it. How could she drown? On the twenty-seventh floor of a skyscraper in the middle of the driest concrete wilderness on the planet, she drowned?

There's not even enough water in the toilets to drown in. At least not in the men's room.'' I glanced at Ike's knees as she performed the final pillow scrunch. "Not that I've tried.''

She giggled. "Have you tried the women's?''

"No.'' I smiled. "I thought it might cause comment.''

"I doubt it. In the Emerald City? Anyway, Dennis said that there were no signs of injury to Connie's mouth or nose or any part of her head and no puncture marks on her torso. He said the time of death practically guarantees that she was not drowned somewhere else and then brought to the Emerald City. He said *that* like it was some dire revelation he had read in the entrails of an owl—he reminded me of someone in the *Iliad*. I can't remember if it was a god or one of those crying women.''

"I hope it was a crying woman. But, Ike, you're going too fast for me. Puncture marks? I thought she drowned.''

She wrinkled her nose. "Well, my understanding from what he said is that you could conceivably drown a person by injecting massive quantities of liquid into the lungs. But you'd have to knock out your victim or drug her or something, and he said there was no sign of anything like that.'' Her eyes narrowed at some vista in the distance, her long dark lashes casting small shadows on her cheekbones. "Can you imagine the size of the syringe and needle you'd need to get through the chest and fill the lungs? Or maybe it would be easier to inject her through the back.''

"Yuck.''

"I know. It's so hideous. Heinous.'' She grabbed a pillow from behind her and plumped it on her lap. Lucky pillow. "Speaking of them, Heinous Face is holding a press conference tonight after their Boston concert. We'll have to use part of it on tomorrow's show, about their AIDS tour and all. I'll bet some wily media watchdog will ask them about *The Connie Connection*.''

"Probably. It's interesting that Fillingeri let them leave town.''

"As far as I can tell, he let everyone go. He has no evidence against anyone, except that circumstantial crap about the eleven minutes. I don't know why he's so smug about making an arrest."

"He didn't give you a clue over cappuccino, perhaps while he stroked your delicate little hand?"

"Not even a hint over cheesecake, while he stroked my delicate little thigh." Her eyes sparkled brilliantly as she gave me a challenging look that said, "My cheesecake is my own business."

So, I tried to be bland and businesslike. "Those thighs—I mean those eleven minutes—are pretty tight circumstances. I don't blame him for being impressed." I glanced at her hand where it was resting on her thigh. I looked away. "Ike, this drowning thing. You gotta ask yourself who could be that diabolical. If Connie was drowned, that means she was wet, right?"

"Must have been."

"Then, somebody had to dry her off."

Ike made a face. "And dry her hair and style it. And do her makeup. I hope the murderer does not turn out to be someone I know."

"It probably is. I've been thinking, and it's pretty hard not to believe that it's Hannah. That note. Her anchor throne swiped by Connie Candela while it was still warm." I caught a glimpse of the cat lumbering into the bedroom. "And Hannah'd know how to style hair, wouldn't she?"

"I don't know. She has hers done by Vivaldi."

"Well, what do you think?"

"I have an idea, but it wouldn't be right to say."

"Why not?"

"Bad luck this early in the investigation. Besides, you probably wouldn't agree with my reasons. Or understand them."

"You didn't used to think I was stupid." I sat for a moment and looked around the living room, absorbing now the things that had changed. "You really are studying French, aren't you?" I asked, gesturing at the audiotapes and books she had over on the shelves that had once held my sound system. "How long has this been going on?"

"Il y a quatre semaines. Je voudrais me bonifier, comme un vin bon."

"You don't need improvement," I said, edging closer to her on the couch.

"Don't even think of getting frisky, Abby."

I subsided back onto The Donald's spot, suddenly wishing I'd stayed in the swamp I had slunk out of. This apartment felt so much like my home, with my memories and my wife, that I could hardly stand not to touch her. I don't mean anything like a grab or a grope. I wanted her hand back.

"I shouldn't have come, Ike. Bad idea." I stood up and brushed off the back of my jeans. "I'll see you at work."

"I thought you were so eager to talk to me about something. You invited yourself, remember?"

The autopsy results, combined with being in our apartment, had derailed that train of thought for me. "Oh, yeah. I was thinking. And now that I know how Connie died, this thought gets even more interesting. The makeup."

"Why are you fixated on that? What about it?"

"Just hear me out. Where's the one supply of makeup in the building kept?"

"Women's purses?" She plucked at the pillow she was still hugging. "Here and there? I don't know. In the desks? But that's just some minuscule amounts of Pan-Cake...." Her eyes lit up. "Pan-Cake. Oh. The twenty-eighth floor. The Costume Box."

"The twenty-eighth floor. The soap operas." Now with a nonpetulant excuse to leave the overtones of memory in the apartment, I held out my hand to her across the coffee table and smiled. "You wanna go play dress up, little girl? We could see if the murderer left muddy footprints or his name carved in pancake makeup. And," I said, touching the cool fingertips she extended to me, "Othello's memo only said to limit what we put on the air. He didn't say to limit what we know. I hate being on the receiving end of Fillingeri's rotten, mean suspicions. I've grown accustomed to being on the rotten, mean side that dishes it out."

"That's a male thing," she said, and she put some extra sting in by giving me a superior smile. "It's that thing about wanting to win all the time, like making sure your report card is in order so that when you bring it home your mother will tell you what a good little boy you are. Or what a good little woolly-mammoth hunter you are. Or 'here's your Emmy'—what a good little boy director you are."

"If you don't want to come along, that's okay." I still had her fingertips in mine, and I gave her paw an encouraging squeeze. "But somebody has to slay the woolly mammoth. And I want to satisfy my curiosity."

"Well," she sighed, "never let it be said that I backed away from a woolly mammoth. I've certainly been doing my part to uphold the honor of the media, despite that asinine memo." She unwound herself from the pillows and jumped up. "After all, I'm the one who's plying the police with barrels of anisette. Where's your skates?"

"I'm on foot." I controlled a shudder. "Fillingeri drinks anisette?"

She nodded. "Let me get some shoes on."

She disappeared into the bedroom. It was, of course, what I wanted to believe, but Ike's remark about plying the police with liquor stripped away the veils of romance my jealousy had draped over her tête-à-tête with Fillingeri. I comforted myself with the thought that she was after his information, not that thirty-five-pound layer of brawn he had sculpted onto his frame with barbells.

We took the IRT Seventh Avenue Subway down to 59th Street, which was a mistake because it was the tail end of the rush hour and it felt like most of New York's 3.7 million daily subway riders were going in our direction and most of them had bought auxiliary hands to push with. When we emerged up on the street from the inferno, automobile traffic through Columbus Circle was thick and mean and noisy, and the sidewalk was packed with even more multihanded people in a hurry to descend into the steamy maelstrom of the IRT so they could get in some pushing and shoving exercise before they went home to turn into werewolves.

The lobby of the Emerald City was blessedly quiet and cool. I looked at the clock on the wall. Six-twenty-two. *Evening Watch* would be just about ready to go on the air. We showed IDs, signed our names in the logbook at the security desk, and rode the elevator up to the twenty-eighth floor.

It felt like there was no air-conditioning on the floor when we stepped off the elevator. It was dark and cathedral-quiet. When the elevator doors closed behind us, leaving us in darkness, I groped along the wall and found the light switches. A couple of feeble, naked seventy-five-watt bulbs went on along some tracks suspended from the thirty-foot ceiling. Except for some small corner closets and the flimsy central twenty-five-foot by twenty-five-foot muslin-walled area known as the Costume Box, the twenty-eighth floor is a vast open hall whose outstanding features are the two soundstages, on either side of the Costume Box, each about half a football field in length. The walls and roofs of the soundstages are painted a gleaming white, and in that faint light they looked like sealed dwellings for a race of giants. Outside the stages, cluttered around the open spaces of the floor, there were curtains here and flats there and furniture everywhere and rolls of carpeting in hampers and assorted fake greenery and even a yellow cab, parked outside Soundstage 28-A.

We stepped forward into the silent gloom, hands held out before us to ward off the unknown edges of an alien landscape. I touched the cold metal surface of a forklift that was standing beside the service elevator, next to the one we had used, and felt my way around some empty green canvas hampers on wheels parked along the elevator wall. I knew their color from memory, rather than from the immediate stimulation of my senses. We seemed to be in a blank space of dulled perception, suspended between the bright world of the elevator car and the gleaming white shapes of the soundstages looming up out of the twilight before us like two walled cities left intact in the dry, featureless climate by an ancient advanced civilization that had once flourished in the dense darkling night of a Martian plain.

I did not know the location of the rest of their light switches, so we fumbled around for a while, looking for switches and tripping over rugs and wires. Most of the investment in lights on the twenty-eighth floor would be inside the soundstages, I thought, which wouldn't do us any good out here. Ike finally found a bank of switches on the floor beside the elevator and turned on the power. The hall glowed with about forty pale orange bulbs tucked up into the distant reaches of the ceiling, running on tracks above the stages and the Costume Box, like dull alien moons.

Ike broke the spell, the otherworldly aura of this foreign landscape. "Let's find something to drink," she said. "I'm parched."

I pointed to a water fountain against the outer wall of the soundstage on the left, where the cab was parallel-parked. Ike squeezed in between the soundstage and the cab, pushed the knob on the fountain, and sipped briefly from the slim stream that rushed energetically from the spout. She made a face, wiped her hand across her mouth, and then noticed a dispenser of large plastic tumblers above the fountain. She gave the dispenser a "forget it" gesture and climbed onto the cab's front fender and slid to the floor.

I ran my hand along the smooth wall of Soundstage 28-A as we walked through the silent field of alien shadows. I shoved the double-thick door open, and we entered another landscape. Evidently the switches Ike had found also controlled the hot interior lights of the soundstages. I could see that we were in the brightly lit world of *Meg's Children*. I recognized one of the living rooms they use for agonizing, from a scene I had watched from my mother's favorite booth at Gypsy's. The sets were lined up along the four walls so that it was possible to stroll around the center of the stage and look into each venue of the soap, as though each room had an invisible fourth wall facing us. We peered through the invisible walls like Peeping Toms from another world. Just like television.

We walked past the set of the agonizing room and found ourselves in the ruins of what must have been Roman Nights, the watering hole frequented by Meg's cheating children. The stack of painted flats was low, only about seven feet high, built that short so they wouldn't interfere with lighting and wiring. There was a tangled mat of wiring looped above the dismantled set of Roman Nights. If I'd been directing *Meg's Children,* somebody would have heard about that. If there's one thing you have to be able to depend on in television, it's wiring.

Ike opened a refrigerator tucked behind the bar and handed me a warm bottle. Most refrigerators on sets for television programs are real, meaning fully operational—the art director wants the interior light to go on when the door is opened and wants condensation to form on bottles and glasses when the actors carry them around, because viewers notice details like that, but this appliance was no longer connected to the power, torn loose from its tenuous hold on even television reality.

"Cheers," Ike said, opening another bottle for herself. She tasted the contents. "It's real beer." She dropped the bottle caps in the phony stainless-steel sink leaning against the bar. It's okay for sinks to be phony on TV, as long as you don't plan to wash dishes or bathe the dog. The art director might not like the compromise, but he'd have to take that up with the budget-minded executive producer, who wouldn't mind plugging in a refrigerator but might balk at supplying plumbing.

What was left of Roman Nights looked like spare parts from Any Bar in Any Suburb in Any Town, USA. The walls that had enclosed Roman Nights were the painted canvas flats stacked against each other and ready to be carted away—painted red brocade walls, with phony plastic candle sconces and phony pictures and even phony mirrors (mirrors are tricky on TV, and they certainly didn't want to risk a Hitachi camera showing up over the head of one of Meg's troubled tribe—that would give it away that Meg's children were *not what they seemed*); there were fake potted ferns shoved up against Styrofoam Doric columns, and tables stacked on the bright blue carpet. Microphones on booms hung over the set from above the painted brocade flats.

We strolled through the other sets, drinking our warm beer in the silence, ducking under mike booms, our shoes squeaking on the concrete floor whenever we left the carpeted sets. Their studio cameras, parked and braked on the concrete floor in the center of the soundstage, were also the big Hitachis, similar to the ones we use, but far more plentiful. It looked like the place where the Great Horny Hitachi had come to spawn, and spawn he had, with a cheerful vengeance.

We stopped beside one outdoor scene with a Styrofoam boulder and astroturf grass and bad trees.

"I can't believe this stuff is so cheesy," Ike whispered. "It looks so real on the tube."

I knew why she was whispering. It felt like we were intruding on many lives, that one of the Children would spring from behind a plywood tree or a hunk of Styrofoam, a look of agony on her face and the shoulder of her dress torn.

The silence was full of voices and the clink of ice in glasses and telephones ringing with bad news on the line and doorbells.

When we had walked past the last of the sets, we turned away from the physical shell of *Meg's Children* and left the soundstage through another door, returning to the dimly lit, dry, and hot air of the vast hall of the twenty-eighth floor. Shadows hugged the Costume Box. That design feature is fairly mobile and cheaply built, unlike the soundstages, whose tightly sealed, huge containing walls reflect the latest and best in acoustics and environmental control.

The flimsy Costume Box separates *Meg's Children* from *Monday Always Comes,* which is at the other end of the twenty-eighth floor, but the casts of both soaps use its resources. Perhaps *Meg* even bleeds into the agony of *Monday,* if a dress or a hat or a necklace or a stethoscope travels west from Soundstage 28-A to Soundstage 28-B through the Costume Box.

The Box has four ultracheap-looking but taut muslin walls braced at the corners, no ceiling, and one door, which was locked.

"Damn," I whispered. "Do you know how to fool around with locked doors?"

"Do I look like Mickey Spillane?"

"You mean Mike Hammer."

Ike took a swig of beer and peered at the door through the gloom. "Give me a credit card."

I tugged my wallet from my back pocket, grateful I still had it after that subway ride, and fished out my Amex card. "Don't bend it. I won't be able to eat for the rest of the month if you damage it."

"You'll never learn to budget." She sniffed, which I thought was a derogatory comment, but then she sneezed. It was the dryness and the dust of the twenty-eighth floor. "But there's only a couple of days left in June. If you get hungry, you can always panhandle." She slipped the credit card along the edge of the lock and jiggled it several times. "It doesn't work." She jiggled it some more. "Damn. It always works on TV." She handed my card back to me, and I returned it to my wallet.

"Let me try," I said.

I handed Ike my beer bottle and slipped away into the shadows cast by *Meg's* soundstage. I came back with a seven-foot stepladder. Trust a TV director to know: where there's overhead wiring, there's always a ladder.

I positioned the ladder as close to the muslin wall as possible and climbed. I looked over the top of the Box.

"There's a table right on the other side," I said. I put my hand on the wooden frame and heard something snap.

"What are you going to say if someone finds out you destroyed this place?" she hissed.

"'Easy come, easy go.' If we get caught, I'll put the damages on my Amex card. I make a lot of money; I just never have any in my pockets." I reached out for her hand. "Are you coming?"

She put our beer bottles on the floor and stepped onto the ladder behind me.

I went over the top, with a silent prayer that the wooden frame would hold. I'm no macho stud like Dennis Fillingeri, but even so, those supports were not meant to take my mere 170 pounds. I eased myself down onto the end of a long table, hoping it was sturdy.

"You'll have to do it without my help," I whispered, still reluctant to disturb the Children. "This table will never hold both of us." I jumped down to the floor.

Ike was over so quickly I didn't even have time to glance up her skirt. But I did take her hand to help her down from the table.

"I thought you said you weren't going over the wall for me anymore," I said.

"I said I wasn't going *to* the wall, Abby. Get your news metaphors straight. Besides, I'm not doing this for you. I'm doing it for the integrity of our news broadcast."

There were no lights inside, but the walls were so thin that the one separating us from *Meg's* soundstage looked like a lamp shade over a twenty-five-watt bulb. We stood inside for a moment, getting our bearings, and then Ike dropped my hand and turned to the big table we had used as a landing strip inside the Box, up against the lamp shade wall. The table was covered with makeup, in many shades, many colors, all aromas. The surface of the table was thick with powder, many textures, many thicknesses, all fragrances.

"This is quite a stash," Ike said. "They could make up a lot of different people. But it's politically incorrect. There's nothing here for African-Americans."

I moved to stand beside her and looked down at the messy table. Ike leaned and stretched across the wide expanse of the table, sniffing the jars and studying them. She found a disposable lighter among the cosmetics and flicked it on. She held it on with her thumb and waved it over the table, continuing to examine the foundation and powder and blushes. "I don't see anything dark here, nothing even that would do for Connie Candela."

"We're not looking for something that would do. We're looking for something that wouldn't do. If the killer used this makeup, that explains why Connie was made up wrong. There's no Hispanics on these soaps, at least not on *Meg.*"

"I can see that. But I'm surprised anyway. It's the nineties. Somebody ought to clue these people in." She dropped the lighter on the table, blew on her thumb, and turned to glance around the Costume Box. At least twenty clothing racks on wheels were weighed down with costumes, partially covered with wrinkled canvas sheets, and placed at sporadic intervals around the crowded space of the interior of the Costume Box. There were two couches and an easy chair in the middle of the room, not facing each other, placed there in a random jumble, and a television on a stand. The TV was plugged into a socket on the floor. I guess the actors who play the Children like to check their work.

Ike crossed to one of the couches, knelt on its lumpy brown cushions, and pulled aside the sheet covering a clothing rack beside the couch. Fake furs, evening gowns, suit jackets, ties, shirts, and other agonizing clothes, I thought, for when the Children are dressed up.

"I wonder if Fillingeri knows about this makeup hoard," I whispered.

"I don't know. Probably. He must," Ike said. "He's not stupid." She craned her neck to look at the top of the TV set. "But I bet he doesn't know about this."

She leaned sideways over the back of the brown couch, stretching so that her tank top pulled out of her waistband and revealed her smooth, taut stomach. She lifted a flat green envelope off the top of the TV. It had been lying there in plain sight on a stack of similar envelopes, apparently gathering dust. It was an NTB interoffice envelope, the ubiquitous all-purpose container at the network. They're everywhere. There wouldn't be any reason for most people to notice this envelope. But even from where I stood, even in that dim light, I could see Connie Candela's handwriting across the front in big brown letters. I didn't think anyone working on the soaps would recognize her handwriting. And what she had written in those black, looping, distinctively childish characters—which many of us on the morning staff would recognize from the pronunciation notes she made on her copy of the show's script—consisted of three letters, the letters of another name, a nickname the soap actors would not know: *I, K, E.*

It was a fresh envelope, the standard twenty inches by fifteen, with only Ike's name at the top of the set of blank lines. With interoffice mail, you just cross off your name on the last envelope you got and write in the name of the person you're addressing on the next line. But this envelope had only been used this once.

I joined Ike on the couch, where she continued to kneel and study the face of the envelope, holding it out in front of her and turning her head to gaze at it from different angles. Her name looked like it had been scrawled in haste with a thick, heavy pencil, but it was unquestionably Connie Candela's handwriting.

"You'd better not watch," Ike said. "I'm going to open it, and you're a murder suspect." She opened the flap and pulled out a thick set of art prints, the good kind you can only buy in museums or pricey galleries and have framed so you can pretend you have masterpieces on your walls. "There's seven of them," she said, wriggling around on her knees and bending to fan the prints out on the cushions like a hand of poker, only these cards were big, almost as big as the envelope.

I could see that most of them were prints of Salvador Dalí paintings, and there was one of a photomontage by Max Ernst, I thought, and two of Joan Miró paintings. I'd learned that much from directing the show on Monday morning when we'd had their stuff in the studio—their real stuff.

"Those are all from the promotional kit the Museum of the Surreal sent us," I said. "I saw you give the packet to Connie before the show yesterday. Monday. A couple hours before the show."

"But why was Connie sending it back to me? There's no note inside." She shook the envelope, holding it upside down. "Whoops. Here's something."

A long rectangle of pink paper fluttered onto the couch, the kind of paper the soap actors use to make spills when they're mixing makeup. There was a stack of such paper on the makeup table. Ike snatched the note from the couch and held it up, toward the lamp shade wall of the Costume Box.

The words on the paper had been written in brown eyebrow
pencil, hastily and in Connie's unique script. I read over
Ike's shoulder:

> Keep these safe—most outrageous thing. No art train-
> ing, but I knew instantly when I saw it after today's
> show. Story will make my reputation with your help.

Ike shook the paper and turned it over, apparently to see
if there was anything she had missed. "Jeez, Abby, I wish
Connie could write a decent, straightforward sentence.
What is this gibberish?"

"She seemed to think you'd know."

"Well, I don't. Not by a mile."

"I wonder why she wrote her gibberish up here on the
twenty-eighth floor, with a makeup pencil." I reached for
the paper. "Certainly not to add clarity."

"I wonder if she thought the envelope would get mailed
from up here. Maybe she saw this stack and acted on impulse."

"Whatever she did, she seems to have done it in a hurry."

"But what was she doing up here anyway, Abby? What
would make her snatch a pink makeup spill and a makeup
pencil, instead of doing things the right way, from her office—I mean the Green Room?"

"God, I don't know. Maybe somebody was about to
jump her and stick her head in water." I was just making
noise, but Ike pursed her lips and looked thoughtful.

"Abby," she touched my arm lightly, "if it weren't as dry
as the Mojave Desert up here, that would almost make
sense."

"That's me all over, almost making sense. Maybe we
should turn the envelope over to Fillingeri."

She gave me a fulminating look. "It's addressed to me."

I held up my hands. "Just a suggestion."

"Well, it's a stupid suggestion. You don't think Wood-
ward and Bernstein ever tried to turn Deep Throat over to
the cops, do you? If they had, Richard Nixon would still be
president." She faced the stack of green envelopes behind

the couch on the TV and opened them one by one, shaking them out.

"Not with a limit of two terms, you half-wit. The Twenty-second Amendment."

"Are you sure it's the Twenty-second? I can never remember." The other envelopes were empty, and she tossed them back on the TV. "I confuse that one with prohibition."

"Twenty-second," I said. "Two twos. Two times two equals four. Four-year term. Two four-year terms. The Twenty-second Amendment. Now you'll never have to embarrass yourself again at parties when the subject comes up." I stopped because I thought I heard a sound outside the Costume Box.

"That's pretty tortuous," Ike said loftily. "Besides, you know what I meant."

I grabbed Ike, pulling her onto my lap and clapping my hand over her mouth. The elevator doors were just outside the thin muslin wall of the Costume Box, perpendicular to the makeup table, and I had heard them opening. I held her for a moment, watching her eyes get bigger as she realized what was happening. Just as I was releasing her, all the lights on the twenty-eighth floor went out, and it was completely dark in the Costume Box.

THIRTEEN

NOTHING IS FASTER than the speed of thought. In the time it took me to conclude that building security would not have turned off the lights without first checking around to determine why they were on at that time of night, and for me to conclude that the act of turning off the lights could not be a friendly act no matter who had done it, I also concluded that I might never have a chance again like the one being offered me now by a capricious fate.

Six months of missing Ike and the wretchedness of having no one to blame but myself—everything I had been trying not to confront was suddenly there on my lap, smelling faintly of Chanel No. 5. I removed my hand from her mouth and kissed her before she could move away. I'd almost forgotten how soft and full her lips are. It was a deep and hungry and desperate kiss, and she responded with some desperation of her own, I thought, but it was over quickly.

Whoever had turned out the lights was moving around with a flashlight, and the beam shone through the thin wall of the Costume Box, bouncing along the floor, creating deep shadow pictures on the muslin from the furniture and flats outside. The edge of the beam touched Ike's bare shoulder obliquely through the muslin wall, and we ducked, sliding noiselessly off the couch together and onto the concrete floor.

We crouched there together, and I heard Ike gulp as the stark shadow of a hand holding a gun appeared on the wall, the flashlight beam bobbing behind it so that the barrel's elongated shadow fell against the paper-thin fabric in a sharp but rhythmically moving outline. I heard a shoe squeak on the concrete floor.

The beam swept away and started a circuit around the Costume Box. I thought of the ladder.

I yanked off my shoes, stood quickly, and hurried over to the end of the makeup table. I slid onto its surface, rising to my knees silently, and then, standing, I offered up a silent prayer to the carpentry god that the table would not creak.

I could see the beam of light bounce against the outer walls of the Costume Box, and it continued toward the corner where I stood. I groped in my pocket, grateful that I had no change to jingle, and drew out my pocketknife. What use I thought it would be against a gun I don't know, but it was all I had.

The beam stopped and slid under the door, which was only a foot away from the end of the table. The knob turned. It turned back and forth a couple of times. It rattled, and I could feel the muslin wall pulling outward for a long moment. I held my breath.

The rattling stopped. The beam moved on, away toward Soundstage 28-A. I breathed.

I stayed put for another four minutes, which I happen to know because I was counting the seconds. I heard one of the stage doors open and, about three minutes later, close. I heard shoes squeaking. I heard the elevator doors open again and close. The beam was gone.

I realized that Ike was beside me. I lowered myself to my haunches.

"No more squeaking shoes. Think he's gone?" she whispered, close to my ear.

"I hope so. I'm shaking like a leaf."

"Me, too."

"You? You're scared? You're the girl who crawls around deserts on her belly, spying on the Israeli defense ultra-dirty-tricks squad."

"So? I was terrified doing that shit, too. Be quiet."

We waited another five minutes. Maybe someone had summoned that elevator but had not used it to leave the twenty-eighth floor. My palms were sweating.

"Stay here," I whispered.

"No problem," Ike returned, her breath caressing my ear. "I'll just meditate or do my nails."

I stepped quickly onto a wooden crosspiece, got my elbows over the top of the box, and levered myself up and over to the ladder.

It took me twenty minutes to creep around the dry nooks and crannies of that vast cavern and assure myself that Ike and I were the only human life on the twenty-eighth floor. When I returned to the Costume Box, I was about to climb up and give her the good news when I spotted our beer bottles on the floor beside the door. "Uh-oh."

She responded through the muslin, "What? You were gone for a century."

"I don't think we fooled the gun-packing shadow person. The beer bottles. We left evidence of our carousing."

"Warm beer. It could have been there for days. If that gun person was suspicious, we put on a good act. Why do you think I let you kiss me like that? I was hoping he'd think there was a pair of horny lovebirds up here, getting it on. Besides, our intruder person might not have wanted to be recognized if it wasn't necessary. He was taking a bigger chance than we were."

Well, that explained why he had turned the lights off. And Ike had also explained her passionate response to my kiss. *She ought to do very well on the stage,* I thought.

"I'm not so sure about who was taking what chance, Ike. He, or she, had the gun. And may already have taken that all-important first step toward not giving a damn by taking a life."

"But Connie's killer is a drowner, not a shooter."

"Maybe the killer is versatile," I said.

"I hate talking through this wall. It reminds me of how you used to be whenever you found something fascinating in the newspaper on Sunday mornings and I was in the bathtub doing the crossword puzzle. No matter how many times I told you, you kept reading stuff at me through the door."

Another one of my sins, coming back to haunt me. I sighed and climbed the ladder. She handed me the green envelope and my shoes. I offered her my hand and helped her out of the Costume Box. I put my shoes on and escorted her to the elevator, knuckled the button and waited, allowed her to precede me inside, and pushed the button for the lobby. A perfect gentleman.

She was carrying the green envelope under one arm. We did not speak. The party had ended when she babbled that her only motive for encouraging me in that kiss had been self-preservation, not gratification or even something better.

When we signed out downstairs, we studied the signatures following ours on the top page and flipped it back to see who had signed in earlier than we had and was still in the building. The only name besides mine that was also on Fillingeri's list was Lourdes Ramirez. She had signed in at 6:47.

And while they were not on Fillingeri's list, the big bosses are always interesting to have the poop on, so we noted that Joe Ayles had signed in at 6:05, followed immediately by O. Armitage himself. Ike asked the guard if he'd seen Noel or Hannah, and he nodded.

"Which one?" she asked.

"Both."

I used the house phone to dial Control Room #1. When the show producer of *Evening Watch*—Ike's opposite number—answered, I said, "Tom, are you having a hoedown up there with NTB anchors, past and present?"

"As a matter of fact, we are. And it's your fault, Abagnarro. You shouldn't have killed Candela. It's really messing up our schedules. The anchors are sitting on the floor of Studio 57 in a circle with warpaint on their faces, drawing straws right now to see who gets to help out on your show. The short straw loses and has to sit next to Noel."

"I thought that was all decided this morning."

"*Weekend Watch* had a fit about sharing their anchor. They've got such a weeny audience, they're afraid working even for you *Morning* assholes will go to the anchor's head."

"Nice talking to you, too, Tom. By the way, I put cyanide in your Evian."

"I thought it smelled funny, so I gave it to Othello."

"That's the way my mind works, Tom. If I'd been after you, I'd have poisoned *his* water. This is no ordinary whodunit. It's a to-whom-did-he-do-it. *Au revoir.*"

Outside the Emerald City, I took Ike's elbow and steered for the alley. We went through quickly to Columbus Avenue, without company from any of the homeless. They must have been out for the evening.

The loading dock was shut tight. Nobody could use a credit card or a ladder to breach those doors. *But,* I thought, trying to find the bright side, *there's always keys*.

We walked up to Broadway and 61st. I waved a cab down and gave Ike's address on 82nd. We rode in silence, each of us looking out the windows at the passing scene on Broadway, but on opposite sides of the street, Ike east, me west.

Our next silent elevator ride brought us to the nineteenth floor of her building. Ike undid the bolts on her door, stuck her foot in first to keep The Donald from waddling out into the hall, and flipped a light switch. I followed her in, still being polite.

Deciding one of us had to break the tension stretching between us, I said, "That's what I thought, too. That kiss. It was a perfect scene we created. I bet I came off as a wild man."

"You did."

"Maybe *I* should audition for a play."

"Maybe." She sank onto the couch. She opened the envelope and spread the prints out on the glass coffee table, once again fanning them into an arc.

"Ike," I said, sitting beside her with clinical detachment, merely getting close enough to look at the prints, "these may mean nothing. Maybe Connie thought she was on to something, but like many an inexperienced, over-eager correspondent, she wasn't. It wouldn't be the first time a molehill turned out to be a molehill." I gazed around the living room again. "You can always hang the prints with the other trash on your walls." I said that to keep myself from making a move to clutch her hand.

She has original stuff on her walls, stuff she's bought around the world, framed with good taste and no frills. The

only thing that qualifies as trash in her apartment, besides
the lard cat, is a painting hanging on the outside of the
bathroom door. In lurid, wildly uneven purple letters, it
says: *"El Jefe,"* Spanish for "the boss." A tape editor from
the NTB Miami Bureau brought it back for Ike from the
Philippines, where he was working on an interview with
Imelda Marcos. Apparently, on the back streets of Manila
you can pay prostitutes to paint whatever you want on
poster boards, and the gimmick is that they hold the paintbrushes between the lips of what Ike would call their "love
pets." The painting is only a form of newsjunk, not meant
to suggest anything about the recipient. Just a little souvenir of how things are done in other parts of the global village. Or *with* other parts.

I leaned forward and fanned out the prints in a wider arc
so I could check their edges, to look for any sign that Connie had put some message on them. They had no borders,
no mats, and there was no printed matter anywhere. I
wouldn't have been able to tell them from the real thing unless I turned them over to look at the backs—which were not
canvas. Ike reached across me and touched the prints, examining them, picking them up, replacing them carefully in
the fan.

I turned to face her, to frame a question, and her face was
so close to mine that I could feel the warmth of her breath
on my cheek.

"Is that Cool Water?" she asked, as though she were in-
quiring for the correct time.

"I guess so."

"Don't you know?"

"I can't remember," I whispered, my mouth close to hers.
"You're sitting too close to me. My mind won't work. Ike,
I'd sell my soul right now to take you to bed. It feels like I've
got things crawling all over my skin—nice things. I was lying about that kiss. I meant it with all my heart. It hurts like
hell to love you so much and know that you hate me."

She stood up slowly and walked away into the kitchen.
She started rattling some stuff in the cupboard over the sink,
and The Donald lurched out, from that hidden zone where

cats go to enjoy their stupors, and skidded across the floor, landing at her feet. "Don't trip me, you stupid cat," Ike said.

She fed him and washed her hands. Then she just stood with her wet hands on the edge of the sink and stared out the window. I could hear sirens wailing and horns honking. The usual chorus of nightfall in Manhattan.

"I don't hate you," she said at last. "I used to hate you. I hated you for months."

I sank back against the cushions and gazed blindly at the prints spread out on the table. There wasn't any hope. Her voice sounded hollow and uninterested. I could hear the cat chewing.

"Did Fillingeri make a pass at you?" I asked, more to have something to say than because I thought the answer would have any relevance to my life. It really was over.

"Yes."

"I thought he would." I stood up but continued to gaze down at the prints. The clear lines and colors blurred as I stared at them. "Any chance one of these is the real thing?"

"Not a chance. Don't be so naive. They're just prints. Excellent prints, but just prints."

"When are you going to tell Fillingeri?"

"I'm not sure. Maybe I won't." She was still gazing out over the skyline to the south. That view from the nineteenth floor is one of my favorites. On a clear night, you can see the whole town laid out before you, the whole postcard-familiar island of Manhattan south of the park. "It's my mail, after all, and we don't know it has anything to do with her death."

"Jesus, Ike. At a minimum, it tells us one thing she did yesterday, maybe even overnight. Come to think of it, it must have been last night; she wouldn't have been writing secret stuff about a news story with the soap opera mob around, and they would have been on the twenty-eighth floor all day. She must have left that envelope some time after five o'clock yesterday afternoon, when the soaps go home for the day. She must have done it overnight. These prints may have been the one thing that was on her mind just

before she was killed. And that envelope tells us where she
was when she was thinking that one thing. She had to have
written that note inside the Costume Box, maybe with the
killer around.'' I couldn't tell if Ike was paying attention.
She did not move or shift her gaze from the scene out the
kitchen window, and I continued on helplessly, talking
about Connie because it was so hopeless to talk about us. ''I
don't see how Connie could have been killed up there. In
fact, I don't see how she could have been killed at all, unless somebody took her outside, held her upside down, and
dunked her in a puddle. It rained pretty hard last night.''

''I'll think about it.'' Ike turned away from the window
and abruptly faced me. ''You'd better go.''

She was so cold that I felt like a stranger invading her
apartment. Or worse, not a stranger. The villain who had
wrecked her happy home and then had the nerve to return
to see if he'd missed anything. The past seemed to have
seeped into the apartment with the night air, through the
window, along with the sirens and horns. I took a step toward the kitchen. ''Ike, I'm so sorry. I wish you'd believe
me. I'm not asking you to take me back. I'm asking you to
forgive me. It was the worst mistake of my life. It was a
mistake.''

''No, Abby,'' she said softly. ''It wasn't *a* mistake. It was
the mistake.''

I walked to the door and let myself out. I waited for the
elevator, forcing myself to avoid the almost automatic
glance at the mirror on the wall opposite the apartment
door. I rode down to the lobby and walked out onto 82nd
Street. This time I didn't bother to look for a cab.

FOURTEEN

IT WAS ALL I could do to drag myself to work that night.

Little Joe's original intention may have been benign, but the staff meeting he had called did not give the show a shot in the arm.

More like between the eyes.

In the first place, the director and producer of *Morning Watch* were both crabby and short on sleep.

Second, the executive producer of *Morning Watch* was crabby and short on both sleep and clean clothes. Little Joe had put in a full day at the helm of the Morning Death Ship and then had found it necessary to turn around and steer back to the Emerald City in the early evening for the who's-going-to-fill-in-until-we-replace-Connie anchor sweepstakes. And here he was at midnight, still on board, although it was hard for me to work up any sympathy for him about that since the staff meeting had been assembled at his request, I thought, although it turned out I was wrong about that. But in addition to being short on sleep, I was also short on sympathy in general, and I doubt I would have wasted any on Little Joe in any case, even if he had held the staff meeting at the Four Seasons, over vintage wine and quail breast, and had complimented me on my loyalty. He didn't need sympathy; he needed a valet.

Joe's shirt collar looked gray and rolled, like an uncooked Italian sausage wrapped around his neck, and he had not adhered to whatever his usual shaving schedule was, so his chin and round cheeks were covered with thick black stubble that did nothing to offset the expanse of shiny bald skin on his skull. He was sitting at the end of the conference table, leaning back but keeping his bloodshot green eyes open while we waited for Ike.

That was third. Ike was late. Little Joe had called the meeting for midnight, but she had been busy then because our least favorite (because they don't have even imaginary grievances) terrorist group, the Red Army, had apparently also had a staff meeting, in Tokyo, and they had voted to plant a series of bombs in and around the Japanese stock exchange. Since the NTB Tokyo Bureau is also in that pricey neighborhood, conveniently located across the street from Ginsang's Department Store (nice to know if you forgot to pack your raincoat or your daughter's canopy bed), we were in a position to get excellent pictures of the destruction, as well as a sense of real-life terror, and Ike was arranging for them to lead the first news block of *Morning Watch.*

She finally slid into her chair next to Joe at 12:20, and I thought the chair had all the luck, because she was wearing a pale yellow dress that hugged her hips like a filmy coating of talcum on a baby's... well, never mind—I hadn't slept, but that didn't mean I hadn't dreamed.

I did not know if Ike had slept, much less dreamed, but I could see that her beautiful eyes were shadowed with fatigue. She had twisted her hair into a neat French braid, severely confining her luxuriant blondness, and she managed to look more exotic than ever. Fatigue makes most people look terrible; with Ike, it was simply providing a new light to see her in.

Fourth, Hannah Van Stone had pulled the short straw and was slated to resume her old TV anchor spot beside Noel when we went on the air in about six and a half hours, and she would be doing so in a pink jacket open over a low-cut black-sequined blouse that offered up her puffy chest like a pair of small, downy pillows with liver spots. Since the entire staff now knew about the note that had graced Concepción Candela's index finger, the atmosphere in Conference Room 2718 was not cordial. Putting Hannah back on the air was an example of "spin control" that—since none of the rest of us wanted her anywhere near the set—I had no difficulty in attributing to Othello Armitage: Hannah was not only tried and true and familiar to our viewers, but by putting her back on the air, the network was going to express its heartfelt confidence that none of its anchors could possibly do anything so nakedly self-serving as arranging and carrying out the execution of another anchor.

But we had a piece of fresh evidence around that table that what anchors do officially and in public is not necessarily what they do away from the glare of the limelight. Noel had hissed, "Pig tits," when he sank into the chair next to Hannah's, and even he wouldn't have said that on the air. But Hannah, who is sharp and canny and never oblivious to anything, had been under no illusions about her welcome anyway, so Noel was wasting his hiss. Hannah had what she wanted, if only temporarily, so why care what the rest of us thought?

Fifth, Noel, who was the only person I knew who still drank hard liquor, had obviously stopped off on the way to work to lubricate his hissing muscles with a couple of Rob Roys. He wasn't rip-roaring, but he was fragrant and inclined to be pleased with himself and forthright with others, especially if and when he perceived any resemblance on their part to farmyard animals.

Sixth, Othello Armitage had elected to dignify the meeting with his presence. Everyone else but me had met him before, so I was the only one who broke out into a stare.

O. Armitage stood almost seven feet tall in a gray three-piece suit that must have emptied the vault by a thousand dollars per piece. He had the sinewy, tense musculature of a cobra; he emitted sparks from greenish-brown eyes that made Little Joe's green eyes look like he'd gotten them from the Midtown Lions' Club; his lustrous, tanned skin glowed with vitality and fitness that men who were much younger would have envied, and I knew from various things I'd read that Othello was pushing seventy-five; a brilliant diamond earring flashed from his left earlobe, which surprised me in a man his age; and he was so openly angry that he kept kneading his hands together around a rolled-up copy of *The New York Times*—with visible strength and no sound of creaking joints—which was okay with me, because that was much better than what it appeared he'd rather be doing with them: strangling somebody.

And then there was me, between Ike and Armitage. The undercurrent I contributed was a covert study of everyone in the room, because I wanted to know which one could be carrying a gun without the slightest sign of a bulge.

When Ike was in place, Armitage, who was seated at the end of the table closest to the door, snapped open his newspaper and tossed it out onto the empty table so we could all see what was making him so mad. There it was on the front page: "NTB News Anchor Dies in Studio Murder." It was a neat package, complete with Connie Candela's publicity headshot. And the subhead was worse: "Candela Drowns in Network 'Aquarium.'"

I thought, *That would make me mad if I owned the network, the aquarium, and the drowning victim.*

"At nine o'clock this evening," Armitage said, in a quiet, controlled voice that was chilled with fury, "I reviewed the contracts of each one of you gathered in this room. Not counting stock options and exceedingly generous benefits and unthinkably free-flowing perks, the combined annual salary of the journalism team assembled in this room is $7,455,000." He glared at us collectively, and in turn. I did not take my eyes off him to see if anyone was squirming.

"Earn it," he snarled. He stood and stalked out of the room, leaving the *Times* on the table and a ghastly silence throbbing in his wake.

It was Noel who broke the silence. "Oh, dear. I wonder what he meant by that?"

"He meant," Hannah said, shaking her head slightly, "that NTB stock lost forty-five cents a share on the New York Stock Exchange today."

"He meant," Joe said, patronizing Hannah, "that all of our jobs are in jeopardy. With a shadow like this hanging over the show, how can we be trusted to put the news on the air? Who's going to believe what we say? In the eyes of the public, we're all criminals. Othello and I have talked this out together, and I agree with him."

"When have you ever *not* agreed with him?" Ike said softly. "I don't mean that in an insubordinate way, Joe, so please don't blow a valve. Othello owns the whole hog here, including the cloven hooves.'' She stole a glance at Noel, who was looking saintly and refraining from barnyard comments. ''I didn't mean anything by that, Noel.'' She rubbed her eyes and resumed with Little Joe. ''But I think we must have misunderstood Othello's memo to us today. I think he wants us to earn our salaries by coming up with some answers.''

''The answer is staring us in the face,'' Noel said benevolently, turning to stare at Hannah's abbreviated sequined blouse.

''Back off, old man,'' Hannah snapped. ''I'll chew you up and spit you out before you can even recognize my perfume.''

''*Eau de* Virginia Slims?'' Noel drawled, smirking at her.

Little Joe held up a hand. ''Now, now, children. Please. Let's try to get some perspective on this. You did not misunderstand the memo. Othello does not want a glut of Connie Candela stories. He wants the glut stopped.'' Joe glanced at the *Times*. ''The way I see it, Othello has asked us to use the resources of NTB News to see if we can't come up with some responsible measures that make it clear we're still the same reliable information provider we've always been, while forestalling the unfortunate publicity.'' He treated us to a woebegone smile. ''After all, we, of all people, ought to be able to do something rational about how Connie's death is treated in the media. We're supposed to be experts.''

''If giving Hannah a vote of confidence by putting her back in the anchor chair is your idea of rational,'' Noel said, with more spite—or more booze—than I'd ever imagined he had in him, ''then you might as well give my job to Mickey Mouse.''

''I've got news for you, Noel,'' Hannah shot back. ''Mickey Mouse already has your job.''

''That may be, Hannah, that may be,'' Noel said, measuring his words, ''but Connie Candela has yours, wherever she is. Very thorough young woman.''

There was an awful pause, pregnant with dismay.

Little Joe, demonstrating why he's the executive producer, slipped a slim leather notepad from his pocket without looking at Noel, opened it on the table, took a gold Cross pen from his shirt pocket, and made a check mark next to some scribbled notes.

"What? Are you taking minutes?" Hannah asked.

He glanced up, gave her a dark look, and said, "No, I'm about to delegate some responsibility."

She leaned forward to watch him read. "Oh, good," she said, looking up across the table at Ike. "Your new job is to get the writers to come up with a piece on NTB's own high-level, responsible in-house investigation. That ought to be worth about fifteen seconds."

Little Joe gave her a dirty look. "I'll handle this, Hannah." He transferred his gaze to Ike. "But that's correct. We have to put something on the air about NTB's concerns. You know the sort of thing. Committing our resources, and all that. Somewhere between an editorial and an expression of outrage. Not too stuffy, and don't make it sound like we're guilty of anything."

"Well, that's as clear as mud," Ike said. "I want to understand this. Do you mean that I should put something on the air about looking into Connie's death but refrain from actually conducting an investigation? You mean *lie*, don't you?"

"Like the Nixon White House," I offered. "If it hadn't been for Watergate, we'd be very grateful right now for the Twenty-second Amendment."

Joe frowned at me, like he was trying to get me in focus. "There's absolutely no similarity. We're a news organization, not the Committee to..." He closed his eyes and shook his head. "What the hell was that supposed to mean, Abby?"

"It's supposed to mean that if you're thinking of a cover-up, count me out."

"Nobody said anything about a cover-up." He thumped his pen on the table and then leveled the tip at Ike. "Look into the matter discreetly."

I snorted. Discreetly.

"Discreetly? What about Othello's memo?" Ike asked, ignoring me. "That 'get it accurate; keep it short' hoohah?"

"That's actual coverage. This is backgrounding. You of all people should know that seventy-five percent of what we investigate never gets on the air."

"Oh," she said sarcastically. "I'm ever so glad I asked."

Joe passed that. "Play it safe, Ike. Just do some nice memorial piece that exculpates the network, and look into what you can. You ought to know the rules better than anyone. If you get lucky, you're a hero. If you hit a raw nerve, you may get fired, depending on whose nerve you hit." He switched abruptly to Noel. "As for you. Uh, Othello wants you to button your lip except when you're reading copy expressly written for broadcast. And for God's sake, don't grant any interviews."

Noel waved his right hand around in the air, with apparent philosophical acceptance. "Discretion's the better part of valor."

Joe gave him a shrewd look. "Yeah. And brevity's the soul of wit."

Since we were trading proverbs, I wanted to say to Hannah, "Absence makes the heart grow fonder," but the atmosphere was already heated, so I controlled the urge, tapping reserves of nobility I hadn't used since earlier in the evening, when I sat without comment on the flabby cat's portion of the $2,700 couch.

Joe lowered his eyes to the page in front of him. "Abby, Othello wants the Plexiglas walls in Studio 57 struck. And I mean struck. They have to be down by this morning's broadcast. Othello doesn't want any more cheap laughs about people drowning in our 'aquarium.' Move in the flats from *Sunday Watch,* or whatever you think is best, until we decide what we want to do in there."

I raised my eyebrows. The aquarium was as much a fixture of the show as, well, Hannah. I realized then that nothing was a fixture anymore. The *Times* reference to the aquarium had apparently been one of those things that struck a raw nerve. I was glad I wasn't going to be involved in dismantling anything tougher than an inanimate object.

Hannah stuck her finger on Joe's legal pad. "I don't see anything on there for me."

"Hold your horses. If you need it spelled out, you'll have to wait until nine o'clock, when my secretary gets in. If you want your attorney or agent present, that's okay, too. In the meantime, Othello wants you to be on hand for any live, unscripted commentary or reportage from the anchor desk. You will be used on an as-needed basis, subject to Ike's judgment. That's the limit of your role on the broadcast."

"What?"

"That's it, Hannah. Emergencies only. The contents of that note found on Connie's finger made it into the *Times* story. And other media outlets too numerous to mention. These limitations are for your own benefit. The less you are seen to profit by Connie's removal from the job you publicly went to the mat over, the better for you, the better for all of us, the better for the show."

"I won't do it."

"Then I have been instructed to offer the job to Gabriella Munez at Channel Two. She's standing by for my call."

A calculating look entered Hannah's blue eyes. Noel used his eyes to stare cherubically at the ceiling, no doubt savoring this ball and chain being locked around Hannah's ankle. Ike was rubbing her eyes again, checking her watch, probably worrying about the Tokyo Bureau.

Goaded by some demon of tiredness, I found myself saying, "I wonder if we're missing the most pointed part of Othello's comments to us, which concerned our inflated salaries. Some people might think we make an awful lot of money to be sitting around merely devising ways to cover our asses. Our actual job descriptions remind me of the story of the three umpires."

Ike groaned.

Noel bleated, "Is that the one with the naked tattooed lady, the Irish perfume vendor, and the furry alligator?"

I raised my eyebrows at Noel.

"Never mind the story," Joe said. "What's your point, Abagnarro?"

"My point is that maybe we should prorate that $7,455,000, to see who has to work the hardest at saving our collective patoot. I'm just thinking out loud."

Ike made less money than anyone in the room, so it figured she'd be the one to squawk up and support my outburst. She was and did. "If the whole point of this murder was to destroy the show, it looks like it worked. We're acting like a mealy-mouthed public relations emporium, instead of a news organization. Abby's just cut through a lot of crap here." She flung her arm up in disgust. "We're getting nowhere with this bureaucratic backpedaling. What I think is that we should be talking about first things first, aggressively. Like how could Connie drown here—what sense does that make? Like if she wasn't drowned here, where did it happen? Like what devil styled her hair and put her in the studio after drowning her? But most of all, *why?* That's what's been bothering me from the beginning. Why not just kill her? Why the hell set her up in the anchor chair like a travesty of the show?" She stopped to get her breath. "I don't think we've done any fraction of seven and a half million dollars' worth of anything tonight." She pushed back her chair and stood. "I hope you will all excuse me. I have a TV show to produce. And I'm not lying for anybody."

I stood. "And I have a nap to take. I'll be lying on my couch."

We left together and walked down the hall, toward Ike's office.

She was still steaming, which was a relief from the frosty incarnation of the Wronged Woman I had left in her apartment.

"It doesn't matter what Othello meant," she said. "I hate this situation. We have to do something, something better than staff meetings." She stopped to consider the portrait of Connie Candela. "Why? Why her?" She put her head to one side and frowned. "Why drowning? Why yesterday?"

I gazed at the painting. The painting. The painting, the painting, the painting. I kept coming back, literally and in my mind, to the painting.

"Because," I said, trying to see the scenario in a fresh light, "because it wasn't yesterday, Ike. Maybe that's the wrong way to look at it. Let's not call it yesterday. Call it instead the first night of our AIDS theme week, the night after we had all those priceless paintings in the studio. And Connie tried to send you, or leave you, a message about those paintings—the package of prints. We don't know if Connie was just dreaming about a news story that would make her reputation, but since she was killed shortly after discovering whatever she thought she discovered, maybe she was really on to something." Ike was facing me, studying my face the way she'd been studying the portrait. "Ike, is there something else in that envelope? Is there some message we missed? Think. What are we supposed to see? Maybe there's something so small we haven't noticed it yet."

"Let's go to my office and look at the prints again. I'll get my magnifying glass."

"Let's check the envelope, too."

We hurried to 2744. She unlocked her door and pushed it open. Her office, unlike Noel's, was crowded with news-junk, and we had to step over and around several of Ike's toys—a Super Bowl game ball, one of Nick Faldo's golf clubs from his third British Open victory, a brass mandala puzzle from Tibet, an umbrella-shaped 60,000-volt stun gun she had bought on the Gainesville campus of the University of Florida, and the baby carriage used in *The Untouchables*. On a dart board above her desk she had tacked up a wine list from Au Bar in Palm Beach. The green envelope was on her desk, under a thick graffiti-marked chunk of the Berlin Wall. She shoved her keyboard aside, dumped the prints out onto the desk, and yanked a drawer open, rummaging around until she found her magnifying glass.

She picked the prints up one by one and examined them. She gave the envelope the same treatment. She shook her head and looked at me.

"Ike," I said, "I'll be right back."

"Where are you going?"

"I'm getting the tape of Monday's show."

I trotted down the hall to my office, unlocked the door, almost tripped over my skates, sorted through the tapes I had not yet filed, found the one I was looking for, and returned to Ike's playpen.

She was on the phone when I got there, talking with our Boston affiliate about the satellite uplink for the Heinous Face press conference that was coming up any minute. I stuck the tape into the VCR on a stand beside Ike's desk and started searching for the long segment on the paintings from the Museum of the Surreal. When she hung up, I was ready.

I pressed the play button. "Here we go. I wish I knew what we were looking for."

Concepción Candela, in a red dress, strolled in the living room set with Abel Chu, the curator from the new museum. They chatted about the paintings, set up on easels across the set. Chu said, "There is something very appropriate about this museum concerning itself with the fight against AIDS. Our subject matter is often the stuff of nightmares, the intrusion of the surreal into the mundane, the happy." There was more, and I tried to concentrate on what he was saying and on the paintings, but it was very disturbing to watch Connie, so full of life and promise. She was a natural on camera, poised and easy to take, vibrant.

Ike took the remote control from my hand and ran the tape back and forth, studying each of the works in turn, leaning forward and narrowing her eyes.

"Abby," Ike said slowly, wrinkling her forehead. "I think I know what Connie was trying to tell me. But it's not a written message." She pushed the pause button and hastily sorted through the prints on her desk. "There's nothing on these prints that shouldn't be there, as far as I can tell. But there is a message I can read. I can read it, but I don't understand it."

I waited.

"Abby, one of the prints is missing. The original promotion kit contained one more when I had it. One print for each painting they brought to the Emerald City. There were eight paintings in the studio." She gestured at the screen, touching it with her index finger. "See? These three on the left, the one they're standing in front of and talking about, and you can see the other four lined up just there, behind Connie's elbow."

"Okay. Which painting? What's missing?"

She moved her finger across the screen and pointed at the second painting from the left. Even I knew that painting. It was the only thing that had been familiar to me among the weird canvases the museum had brought to the studio on Monday under heavy guard. Three limp watches were draped around on a brown-and-blue landscape; a solid red one was under attack from shiny black ants. "The print of Salvador Dalí's *The Persistence of Memory*," Ike said quietly.

"What a weird mind he had," I said. "Limp watches."

"Limp watches. Floppy watches. Loose watches. Dalí himself called them the soft watches."

"I wonder what Connie called them." I shrugged my shoulders, not getting it. "She put the prints in an inter-office envelope. Prints of masterpieces we'd just had in the studio. But not all of the prints. She left one out. What the hell does that mean? Why would she leave that particular print out?"

"Maybe she didn't have it. Maybe she never got it. Or maybe she took it out." Ike's eyes were luminous and very large. "When I had the packet, it was complete. Either Connie took the missing print or somebody else did."

"Where did you keep the packet before you gave it to Connie?"

"In my office. But I left the door open, because I was letting the museum use my office. Everybody was in and out on Monday morning. And now there's a print missing and Connie thought she had a news story, something that would make her reputation as a journalist—so she must have meant a hard news story. Features don't make reputations. People with huge reputations can make a feature into a sen-sation, like Ed Murrow's *Harvest of Shame*, but it doesn't work the other way around. So Connie must have meant hard news. What's news about paintings? The only way they ever make hard news is if they're stolen or forged, and then only when they're really famous. Connie was trying to tell me something about *The Persistence of Memory*. Something that would be news. The print's missing. Maybe the painting is, too.''

FIFTEEN

"COME ON, Ike; that's such a famous painting," I objected. "If it had been stolen, we'd be the first to know. That would be news. And if it had been forged or something, how would Connie know that? She said she didn't know anything about art."

Ike looked reluctant and then disappointed, focusing on me like I was the mailman bringing her a certified letter. Those are almost always bad tidings. "But you gotta admit, Abby, that would be a painting worth killing for." She sighed and returned her gaze to the television screen where Connie Candela was frozen in her red dress against a background of surreal paintings.

"How much is worth killing for? What kind of money are we talking here?"

"Priceless. Incalculable. Millions." A faraway, whimsical glimmer leapt in her eyes. "More than the combined annual salaries of the two anchors, the executive producer, the director, and the broadcast producer of *Morning Watch.*" She smiled.

"Connie had a set of prints, not the painting. *The Persistence of Memory* is back in the museum. It doesn't make sense to murder anyone over a painting that's not missing."

"She was killed because she found out it *is* missing," Ike suggested, more than a hint of stubbornness in her voice. She turned her palms up. "I don't know. Abby, *something* has to be weird about that Dalí. What can you do with a famous painting except exhibit it, which is not news? Or steal it, which is news? Or forge it, which is also news, but only if it's found out? Can you think of anything else that makes sense about these stupid prints?" She stirred the seven prints around on her desk.

"It makes sense that Connie was trying to tell you something about that Dalí painting. But it can't have been stolen, Ike."

"What a drag. I thought I was V. I. Warshawski there for a minute." She tapped her fingernails across the seven prints. "It must be something simple. Connie obviously thought I'd get it right away or her note would not have been so obscure. Maybe I'm just supposed to figure out where the missing print is."

"In a small, uncomplicated place like Manhattan, that should be easy." I consulted the little cuckoo clock on Ike's desk. She'd have to head for the control room soon. "You know, Ms. Tygart," I said, "there's another approach to this."

"What?"

"Maybe it's not the painting or the print."

"What are you talking about?"

"The title. *The Persistence of Memory.* Could it be that Connie was trying to suggest something from the theme of the painting? There's a lot of weird stuff on that canvas."

"Limp watches." One of her eyebrows lifted. "How do you make a memory *persist?*"

Abby the techno freak. I know the answer to this one. "Videotape it. The cure for Newsheimer's. Or photograph it."

"You're giving Connie too much credit. She'd never see anything that abstruse. Whatever it was, she said she knew right away. It has to be something totally obvious."

"You're back to thinking the Dalí was stolen. Know what I think, Ike? We're too tired to be clear about this. I'd like to think we were earning some of that $7,455,000. Nobody else at that meeting will be doing anything more productive than buying diapers."

"Diapers?"

"To cover their childish asses."

"Yeah." She frowned. "Boy. Seven million bucks and change. The numbers are not that difficult to work out, Abby. Hannah makes less than Noel, for exactly the same job. That stinks."

"He probably gets a bonus for being tolerable to work with."

"It's because she's a woman."

"She's a bitch."

"She isn't paid less because she's a bitch. She's paid less because she's got incorrect hormones." Ike put her fingers on her chin. "Or do I mean genitals?"

"I hate to think about either one in the context of Hannah Van Stone, even though I'm the one who mentioned diapers."

She giggled and started stacking the prints. "I know. It's too fiendish for words, isn't it? Wasn't Noel a prince on the subject of her breasts?"

I laughed. "The persistence of mammaries. Noel certainly takes a lot of chances with his mouth."

Ike's phone rang and I grabbed it.

"Abagnarro."

"This is Jean. We've got the uplink from Boston. Ike said to let her know when Heinous Face was on the bird."

"She'll be right there. You got an editor standing around playing with his hands?"

"Yeah. If you want, I'll send *her* to an editing room, you sexist pig, and Ike can watch us take in the satellite feed from there."

"I'm glad you're on the Chauvinist Patrol, Jean. I'm so ashamed I could kill myself. Make it Edit Room 3."

Ike grabbed the phone from me.

"Jean?... Ike. I don't have a lot of time here. I'm behind on everything. You cut the tape with the editor. Good sound bites on the AIDS angle of the concert. A cut or two of a song. Crowds going gaga." Ike listened for a moment. "Knit together one chop of maybe thirty seconds. You and Noel can package another piece with narration. Make the longer piece about two minutes. Okay?... Thanks." More listening. "He's probably in his office. Sobering up, I hope."

That was the end of our colloquy on what makes a painting newsworthy. And for all I knew then, that was the extent of NTB's high-level in-house investigation into the death of Concepción Candela.

Ike sat down, brushed the prints into a drawer, booted her computer after she dragged her keyboard back into place, and forgot my existence. She's fast, and as screens popped up and disappeared on her monitor, at the aggressive insistence of her rapid fingers, show production was under way.

I had my own satellite problems to work on, since in addition to the Red Army's Tokyo road show, we were also going to carry the live debut of the London Symphony Orchestra's afternoon concert series in support of research on the HIV virus and a vaccine. And the wizards in the NTB Graphics Department had come up with some full-screen graphics for use with our orchestra story, so I headed for the other side of the twenty-seventh floor to watch them construct art on their screens and load pretty key graphics into their electronic queues. I like to tell them in person, when I can, to put their work into my preview queue so I can check the colors. I often think that the world of the graphics artists can be a little inhuman, partly because their bailiwick is animation. You can't supply too much of the human touch when you're putting in an order for animation, which was one of the things I was about to do, to open and close the two Heinous Face segments I now knew about.

It occurred to me to phone security for an escort through the tube, because I did not want to be caught again without an alibi. If someone was carrying a gun around, it wasn't too paranoid, I thought, to wonder who the next victim would be. It was a night for proverbs, and I was thinking of the old Sicilian adage: "Two witnesses may keep a murder quiet, if one of them does not see it," and I was wishing in my heart that I had witnessed something the night before to point at Connie's killer, and that someone had witnessed me witnessing it. Her murder had been quiet enough to be included in the Sicilian how-to murder manual.

And once again the tube was quiet. I checked my watch. It was almost 1:30. The door to Hannah's suite of offices was open, with the usual cloud of odoriferous gray smoke

issuing from the inner sanctum of the Mother Lung, one of
the fond nicknames we bestowed on Hannah over the years.
She was not allowed to smoke anywhere else on the twenty-
seventh floor, so she gassed up her office pretty thoroughly. The Mother Lung once told me that she smoked so
much before the show because she thought of it as "pre-
ventive nicotine," a huge infusion of drugs to prevent her
from withdrawing on the air.

I stopped at her door because there were chirpy squeals
coming out into the hall with the smoke. I waved my hand
around and saw Lourdes Ramirez, all four feet and seven
inches of her, attempting to drag a barber's chair around an
upright vacuum cleaner and across the plum-colored carpet.

"*Que pasa, Lourdes?*" I said. "*Dónde es Hannah?*"

Lourdes left off the squealing and puffing and tugging
and gestured toward the inner office. Then she gestured at
me. "*Puede usted ayudarme?*"

Even to help little Lourdes move a chair, I didn't want to
expose my breathing apparatus any more intimately to
Hannah's lair, but chivalry won out, and I went inside to
give Lourdes a hand. I wondered what Connie's personal
assistant was doing in Hannah's slave labor camp. Vacuuming had not been part of Lourdes's job description when
Connie was her sponsor.

Lourdes pointed with overbearing impatience to the spot
where the chair had already crushed a pattern in the carpet.
"*Ahi,*" she said. "*Dese prisa!*" Since I was already inconveniencing myself by continuing to breathe in there, Lourdes
snapping at me to hurry was a little rude. She looked like she
would smack me if I did not step lively to her bidding. But
in for a penny, in for a pound, I thought, wishing the proverb translated adequately into Spanish, and together we
shoved the chair back into place.

At the very moment that all the hard work was completed, Hannah appeared in the doorway to the outer office, having surfaced from the depths of murk within.

"Before you get any exotic ideas about this, Abby," she said, "let me inform you that I have assumed responsibility for the employment of this woman."

"Since when?"

"Since she was left without a job." Hannah narrowed her eyes at me. "Sometime around five in the morning yesterday."

"Well," I said, "being around all the Spanish should help you at the UN." I meant that sincerely, just using up some words until I could get out of there, but as soon as they were out of my mouth, I could see that Hannah thought I was prodding her.

"We'll see about the UN. She who laughs last, laughs best."

Another proverb. I was wishing I knew one about hiring someone in danger of losing her green card, someone who was on intimate terms with a woman who'd just been murdered. I had not seen any evidence recently that the poison of total self-promotion had been replaced in Hannah's veins with the milk of human kindness, so I assumed she had an ulterior motive in scooping up Lourdes Ramirez and saving her from an unceremonious trip back to Valladolid, Mexico.

I coughed and waved my arm around as Hannah lifted her nostrils at me and exhaled through them. And as I watched her through the smoke, she did not look at all like the woman who had kept America company for thirty years while it drank its coffee and got the kids off to school. With her deep nostrils flared and emitting trails of bluish-white smoke, she struck me as sharing the attitude, orientation, and heady allure of the exhaust system of an eighteen-wheeler churning down the New Jersey Turnpike.

But with her I couldn't just pull out and pass. I had often found that collisions worked best with Hannah, if anything was going to work at all. So, I said, "Lourdes hasn't by any chance had a sudden recollection of seeing you during those eleven minutes, has she?"

"If she has," Hannah breathed, "it would be a double alibi, wouldn't it? For me and for her."

"Well, has she?"

Hannah took a deep drag on her glowing stub of a cigarette. When she answered me, the words were punctuated by languid, drifting ribbons of acrid gray smoke.

"I haven't decided yet."

SIXTEEN

AFTER EXPERIENCING Hannah Van Stone's version of the surreal, I was beginning to think Dalí's limp watches were kid stuff. I didn't know much about art, but I knew what I liked, and I didn't like Hannah's creative attitude toward Lourdes Ramirez's memory.

I had resumed my interrupted course toward the Graphics Department, a small suite of partitioned cubbies on the opposite side of the twenty-seventh floor from my office, when Capt. Dennis Fillingeri stepped out from Studio 57, pulling the door closed behind him silently. He was wearing jeans and a dark blue sweater. Now that he was practically family, he was dressing casually.

"Did you bring a cot?" I asked, not politely.

"Can it, Abagnarro. I don't like this any better than you do."

"Well, at least you get paid for seeing me. I don't get a nickel for hobnobbing with you."

"You want to hear something funny, funny man?" Fillingeri smiled, like he really had something to smile about, flashing his perfect white teeth. "I get some small satisfaction from the knowledge that it's you who's paying my salary. *You're* paying me to see you."

"That's a hell of a note."

"Depends on your point of view. From now on, whenever I run into you, I'm gonna think about how I've got your taxes in my wallet. The way I see it, you're getting the pleasure of my company from both directions."

"I'm getting *something* from both directions."

He nodded his head, as if I were a good pupil in the Fillingeri School of Dunces. "That's the idea."

"I guess you used the taxes in your wallet to take my wife out to lunch."

"I was going to, but Mary is an independent woman." He seemed to think he was giving me the lowdown on someone I hardly knew. "I like that in a woman. She paid."

"That's good. Then she doesn't owe you anything."

He backed up against the plum-colored wall and crossed his arms. "What is it with you, Abagnarro? According to her, you're divorced."

"You ever been divorced, Captain Fillingeri?"

He shook his head. "No way. I'd have to get married first."

"Take it from me, then, Captain Homicide. Divorce is murder."

I left him standing there so I wouldn't have to look at him when he used his muscles to push off the wall.

There were a couple of artists in their cubbies, but not Fred Loring, the guy I was looking for. NTB graphics people are not like other people, or maybe they are and I just can't tell because they speak another language among themselves, which is who they're among most of the time. If you don't really pay close attention, what they say sounds like English, but it's not: "Wow, would you look at the ballooning low-rezz squib. It's deteriorating at the drag end, leaning way into the bag. You could hokk it out, but that would make South Africa give birth to high-tension twins. It's fishtailing in the seasick mode." Odd but true fact about our graphic artists—their union is the Writers' Guild. Imagine that.

I was looking for Fred Loring because he was bilingual and could occasionally make the transition from Graphic-speak to English. His cubby was empty, but I could see something that looked like the double red sun of the Red Army on his screen, so I figured he was already working on the Tokyo graphics and I'd wait for him in his chair while I caught forty winks.

Once I was seated, however, my fingers started doing the walking on their own, playing around on his keyboard because, well, *graphics is so much fun.* I tried to draw—build—a snowman, but between you and me, it was not of air quality. It soon occurred to me that, by golly, Fred was on Fillingeri's list, like me, and maybe Fred had some doodles left over from the night before that would help me pass the time while I suspected him of murder. It wouldn't hurt to see what had been on Fred's mind while somebody had been applying makeup to Connie. Besides, *graphics is so much fun.* I cracked my knuckles and gave myself a quick study of the keyboard.

I switched screens, checking the directory of Fred's hard drive for files that were keyed to AIDS or Heinous Face or surreal art, and stopped when I recognized a slug we had used on the show Monday—Dalítime. I called it out of memory: a computer-painted facsimile of the December 14, 1936, issue of *Time,* with Salvador Dalí's face on the cover, before he had curled his famous wire-thin mustache into stiff, oily spirals.

And in the same file, paged after the mustachioed face, there was the face of Concepción Candela, swimming before me out of a sea of blue. It was almost as good as the Samantha Harris portrait. I wondered vaguely what use Fred had ever seen for this piece of art, concluded he had just felt like building Connie's nice face, and went on to the next page. Another view of Connie's face, this time bathed in dappled sunlight. I was beginning to think Fred was a fan.

A series of carefully constructed pictures of her face—in profile, full on, from various imaginative angles—followed the first two I had found in this storage queue. He had built Connie's face electronically from all directions, and with great accuracy and even considerable talent. I was beginning to think Fred was more than a fan.

And then I found the nudes. If these were built from experience of the actual flesh, Connie had been as presentable in her birthday suit as she had been in street clothes. And if the pictures had been kindled, instead, from the fires of imagination, Connie had been especially presentable in dreams. I *knew* Fred was more than a fan.

"Get away from my tube, Abby," he squeaked, maybe an inch from my ear. I hadn't heard him approach. "You know about union rules."

I swiveled around in his chair. "Really, Fred. What union were you representing when you did the nudes? The Perverts' Guild?" Fred's not very tall, maybe five-eight, but he extended himself, especially from the shoulders up, and stuck his round chin forward in an effort to tower over me in the chair. But the main effect of the exercise was to make his thin brown hair, gathered by a rubber band into a long, stringy ponytail, seem to snake down behind his bony shoulder.

"Lower your voice," he squeaked, but in a deeper register, probably because he had stretched his diaphragm. "There's nothing wrong with those, not unless you happen to have a dirty mind." His small mouth looked prim and protective, and he pursed his lips furiously as he reached across me to punch a few keys to dump the file and lock his keyboard. Connie disappeared into the electronic void that her naked image had sprung from.

"I do have a dirty mind, Fred, and I don't think there's anything wrong with those pictures. But I also have a curious mind, and I wonder if there's anything wrong with you." I pointed at the now-empty blue screen. "That's a lot of work. How long did it take you?"

"Why don't you mind your own business? I've had a frank discussion with Captain Fillingeri about my, uh, portraits. I volunteered them as soon as I was told I was considered a suspect. If you've got a problem with that, go see him. I happen to know he's in the control room. I just saw him in there talking to Ike."

I may just have imagined that a nasty smirk had fastened itself to Fred's prim mouth.

"You're changing the subject, Freddie. Perhaps I should be blunt. Connie didn't pose for you, did she? You don't seem like her type."

"I'm very well aware of who her type was. But I have nothing to hide. My private artwork is my own business."

"You seem pretty well informed." And I almost added, "For a graphic arts geek." I ducked my head for a minute, thinking how best to pry the name of Connie's "type" out of the little worm. When I looked up, he was staring at me and I noticed how bloodshot his wide brown eyes were. He looked as tired as Joe Ayles had, and that I felt. And that made me think of the staff meeting. *When you want something, start at the top,* I counseled myself.

I took a shot. "Who'd have thought Othello Armitage would date the woman of *your* dreams?"

"I resent that. Connie regarded my trust and my dreams as a holy commission, like a karmic bond. A man's dreams, like a man's art, are sacred. Get out of my cubby."

I hid a smile behind my hand. I stood, not purposely choosing to make him feel like a dwarf, but I wasn't willing to crawl out of Graphics on my hands and knees just so Fred could pretend he was tall.

I smiled down at him. "You're imagining things. Connie never confided in you."

"She did, too," he yipped, goaded out of his New Age babble. "Not right away. She ignored me like all women ignore me. But I cast her astrological chart for her on my computer, and that changed things, made her feel close to me. Spiritually. Connie was a Sagittarius." Back to the babble. "She said I had an old soul and that Othello is an old man with a callow soul—Capricorn, you know—and that I was the only one who'd understand the sacrifices one makes for art. And I did understand."

"I'm sure you did." I patted his bony shoulder. "Were you busy doing some understanding between 5:10 and 5:21 yesterday?"

"I was working."

I gestured at his empty computer screen. "More sacred art?"

"Don't make fun of me. You're just a shallow philistine who'll never understand what I went through."

"Yeah, Fred, I've never suffered." I don't think I made a threatening move, because I don't assault wet fish, but Fred took a step back.

"I'm sorry, Abby." He sniffed. "Everybody knows how you feel about Ike."

"I doubt it." I did not want to discuss Ike with the man who had played electronic peekaboo with Connie Candela. "How did you feel about Connie?"

"Abby, I can't believe she's gone. The only consolation I have is that her current transmigration must be very peaceful for her, because she was so close to perfect in *this* life."

His face looked so pulled by emotion that I was afraid he'd start crying, but I didn't want to pat him again. I decided to give him some work instead, to take his mind off his karma. "I'll send you a memo in the next ten minutes regarding my requirements for the Wednesday *Morning Watch.* You'll be happy to know that as a member in good standing of the Directors' Guild, I'm allowed to touch my keyboard. And you'll find that my simple instructions won't require undue sacrifice on your part." I bent my neck to get a look at his bloodshot eyes, to see if he was coming around. "Just don't get my list mixed up with your sacred art, Fred."

His droopy look acquired a hint of combat. "I wouldn't. I'm a professional." He backed up another step. "You're so insensitive, so hard. What's you sign?"

"I don't know. I think it's opal. Or the dragon. One of those."

I left, wondering if Connie had been playing him or if she had taken that stuff seriously. I couldn't think of any reason for Connie to dangle a New Age small-screen artist on her string. Not when she could, apparently, dangle an old-fashioned big bucks artist.

Othello Armitage, I thought, as I strolled along the tube, whistling a little tune. *Othello Armitage, Capricorn.* If I could believe Fred—and I did, because his karma had been bleeding all over the place—the man who paid the anchorwoman's salary had bought himself the woman of Fred Loring's dreams.

I wasn't whistling when I entered Control Room #1.

The woman of my dreams, and my nightmares, was smiling slightly at something Fillingeri was saying. Maybe they were reminiscing about lunch. Or planning the next meal.

I sat down at my terminal screen, not bothering to spread greetings around, and booted my computer—if I needed someone to take my frustrations out on, Fred Loring was clearly available and uniquely deserving, as well as waiting for my orders. Before I started to put together that list of graphics for him, I considered sending Ike an electronic update on the love life of Othello Armitage, but at the moment she looked like she was thinking about somebody else's love life.

I dialed into Use-News and checked the directory of my electronic mail. At the top of the list were Ike's initials: *MET,* for Mary Emily Tygart. *Probably the early lineup,* I thought. I moved the cursor, pressed the enter key, and her memo appeared on my screen. I read:

Bulletin, bulletin, bulletin: Capt. Fillingeri has a warrant for Hannah. The note on C's finger has H's fingerprints all over it. Be cool. He's not going to serve it on her until after the show. Lots of cops in building keeping an eye on her sub rosa. You heard it here first.

I shot a sideways glance at Ike and Fillingeri, up a level from my station. Then I fired back a note of my own:

Oh, goody, goody, goody. I knew it. How'd she work the drowning trick?

I stole another glance at Ike. Her face was carefully innocent, just as though she and I were not carrying on an electronic conversation under the captain's nose. Or sub rosa. I could hear the electronic "ping" when my note reached her queue. She glanced at her "get" key alert and retrieved my note. She continued to kid with Fillingeri over the top of her screen as she read my note, then she typed and sent me another note:

Not known. But he's got fingerprints, and huge motive, and lack of alibi. AND she's a bitch. What more

could an officer of the law require? Too bad he's
wrong.

Fillingeri was wrong? I fired another note over to Ike:

One—does Captain F. know about the persistence of
you know what? Two—what do you mean he's wrong?

The answer came back while she bestowed a bewitching
smile on the captain:

One—not unless you told him, and two—just what I
said. Can't you read English?

I sneaked what I intended as a quelling frown at her
across the surface of the console, which was at my eye level.
Not a good angle for real hauteur.

Just then, the phone rang. Ike picked it up and listened.
She replaced the receiver with a bang. "Holy shit," she announced to the control room at large. "The Heinous Face
press conference. The *Boston Globe* just asked Satan Brown
about his secret six-month marriage to Concepción Candela."

Sure enough, the "bulletin alert" pings on every computer in the control room started going crazy simultaneously as the Associated Press put the story out on the wires.

Ike got busy at her computer. It's a good thing all of us in
the control room get the same wire service advisories Ike
gets, because nobody in this business likes to be even one
second behind the other prying, nosy snoops. It's not that
newspeople don't like to share. We do. Sharing is our life.
We just like to have it first before we share.

We all followed the story as it crossed the wires, accompanied by the pings every time a new angle or fact came out
that the AP thought warranted an advisory. All news copy
is written in the past tense, but we were reading the wires as
their reporters were taking in what Brown was saying: that
they had kept the marriage a secret because she had wanted

it that way, being on the rise at NTB News and not wanting the baggage of a personal life to carry up the network talent ladder; that the marriage had been an impulse, a few weeks after they had met when Heinous Face gave a concert in Houston; that they had both realized they had made a mistake and were ready to divorce; that he, Satan Brown, was not ashamed of that relationship, but since it had been a secret all along, there was no reason to suppose it had any bearing on the young anchorwoman's death; that he wondered how the *Globe* had found out.

Ike pounded her console. "Strike me pink! No wonder she thought she could get Heinous Face on *Morning Watch*. She could have gotten that band to appear on *Sunrise Semester*. Or C-SPAN."

I wanted to pound her console, too. I looked up at Fillingeri's face, which was a little too tightly controlled for a poker player to come along and ask to borrow it.

"This isn't news to you, is it, Fillingeri?" I asked.

"Brown's smarter than he looks," the captain growled. "He may have thought he could keep it from you guys, but he spilled it to the NYPD. We're not caught off-guard on this."

"Well," Ike said, "all I have to say is that the *Boston Globe* just made NTB News look like saps. I bet all they did was go look at public records in Harris County, Texas. They wouldn't even have to say 'please.'"

"Don't feel so bad, Ike," I said. "You would have been on it if it hadn't been for the *persistence* of other memories."

"No, I wouldn't. I'd have been in bed sleeping. I'm a complete boneheaded bozo. I should have assigned someone to public records. That's baby reporting. I'm supposed to be a journalist."

I clicked my tongue. "If your conscience really smarts in the cold, hard light of day, we can have another staff meeting, pass the hat, and mail whatever fraction of the seven million and change you think is appropriate to the *Globe*."

I turned back to my computer screen. Ike would have to deal with this nugget of news as a journalist-caught-napping. Pretty soon, "newsanoia" would kick in, that condition where a journalist imagines that every two-bit reporter in the country is laughing at her. If she needed me, she could just aim a swift kick under the console to get my attention.

In the meantime, I had the aquarium set to strike and artwork to requisition from the Graphics and Metaphysics Department. I couldn't resist the thought that Fred Loring was in exalted company. Othello Armitage had also bought himself the woman of Satan Brown's dreams.

SEVENTEEN

ALTHOUGH IT SHOWED something about Fillingeri that he was willing to wait to collar Hannah until we finished the show, he might as well have taken her at three in the morning. She never got on the air that Wednesday morning. The show was smooth as silk, and, under the stipulations of her new role, Hannah would only have made an appearance if we had needed her for breaking news or an especially tricky interview—or if the TelePrompTer had broken down, severing Noel from his lifeline to sense.

We led the first news block with the Red Army. That was Ike's call to make, and while nobody expected her to explain her reasoning, it was clear that she viewed a bombing in Tokyo as having far greater long-range impact than the love life of the show's late anchorwoman, even when that love life was Satan Brown of Heinous Face.

It's always uncomfortable for me, on principle, when journalists themselves become news, as they do all too often—for example, when they interview each other for sound bites on "think" stories like elections or spending the peace dividend—and Connie Candela had not only been a journalist (or, at least, an anchorwoman); her corpse had been found inside the New York headquarters of NTB News. Somehow, when we're reporting on ourselves, the news business seems to be feeding the monster it created itself, producing a Frankensteinish inversion of troubled ego, without the stern moral lesson of Mary Shelley's story.

So, in spite of an initial knee-jerk reaction to the *Globe*'s scoop from Houston (newsanoia), I did not feel that Ike had let her instincts betray her when she had concentrated her energies on Connie's recent New York activities. If Connie's murder was linked somehow to another, underlying news story, as her note to Ike seemed to indicate, and if NTB

News was going to nail the Connie Candela story, I thought
we'd nail it in New York. We weren't going to get it by
combing through public records in Houston.

Ike must have felt pretty burned by the *Globe*, though,
and she hauled in Arthur Landau again to do a couple of
two-minute pieces on the Heinous Face concert and press
conference, and he did a good job providing a succinct
roundup of Satan Brown's connection to Connie, both in
Houston and in the Emerald City the morning of the murder. It's not easy to get information overnight from Houston, but Landau woke up the Dallas Bureau and got them
involved, and at least NTB News was the first to break some
of the details of the marriage, including the date, the fact
that Connie had taken Brown's name, and that it had been
a civil ceremony—factoids not specified by Brown in his
news conference. Landau also dug up the hot item that it
was the first marriage for both of them. That may not sound
like major reporting, but at least we weren't simply moving
the wire stories through our printers and reading them aloud
on the air. And Ike had talked our Boston affiliate into
staking out Brown's hotel until we could fly Landau and a
crew in to take over. She also assigned Daisy Smith, a veteran producer, to start looking into a list of story ideas
Connie had submitted to Ike during a meeting the previous
week. Maybe whatever Connie had spotted about those
museum prints was a refinement of something she had been
working on earlier.

But Ike's coup—a thumb in the dike against what would
be the flood of media competition now that Satan Brown
had made her marriage public—had a New York peg. She
convinced Fillingeri to arrest Hannah at 8:55, instead of
waiting so politely until we went off the air at 9:00. *Morning Watch* was thus the first to break the story that our own
former anchorwoman, now on special assignment to the
show, had been arrested on suspicion of committing the
sensational murder of the colleague who had replaced her
at the anchor desk and who had also had the brief good
fortune to have been married to the nation's current heart-
throb.

During a commercial break about fifteen minutes before the end of the broadcast, Ike told Noel that he would soon have copy to read concerning Connie's murder, and she wrote the two sentences herself and sent them to the Tele-PrompTer operator, with instructions not to blab.

I was a little uneasy about making the announcement because of what Ike had written to me about Fillingeri being wrong.

"Are you sure about doing this, Ike?" I asked, during the weather report. "You said the captain had grabbed this particular frog by the wrong leg."

"He did, and I tried to tell him, but he just said finger-prints don't lie, or some cop talk like that. He also said"— she lowered her tone to a voice of doom—"that motive is the number-one criterion in his book. Nobody can deny that Hannah had a giant reason to hate Connie. I also get the feeling that there's huge pressure on Dennis to make a quick arrest—this is such a high-profile murder." She leaned forward over the console when the technical director stepped up to her level to get some coffee from the stand behind her chair. She whispered, "Besides, we'll only be reporting the truth. He *is* arresting her. And we're not going with it until she'd been read her rights. Fillingeri dangled the arrest right under our noses—we have to scoop the competition."

The control room phone rang at 8:58 on Ike's extension, and she snatched it up. She listened for maybe four seconds. She nodded to me, spoke into Noel's telex, and I cued the TelePrompTer. Noel read Ike's two sentences:

"Finally, my longtime colleague Hannah Van Stone has just been taken into custody by the New York City Police Department. She was arrested minutes ago in connection with yesterday's murder of her successor in the anchor chair, Concepción Candela."

Then Noel added the formula, and he did it right:

"There will be full details tonight on *Evening Watch*, on this NTB station."

He signed us off the air. No frills, no personal notes, no embellishments.

There were nine people in Control Room #1, the same cast that had watched Noel sign us off the air the day before with his farewell to Connie. We all stayed seated. Nobody spoke. I don't think anybody looked at anyone else. My eyes were focused on Noel, still on monitor three, but I don't remember seeing him.

That was no reflection on Noel. I was projecting my own feelings. What I saw was a hollow man, talking through a hollow wire, inside a hollow cavern, making hollow noises out of hollow events. *The real two-dimensional man,* I thought. The cardboard anchor. We could just fold him up and put him in a drawer until we needed him tomorrow. Then unfold him, fill him with hollow words, and fold him up again when we were finished using him. Television. We didn't even need news to happen. We manufactured everything we needed right in the building. Magic. The Emerald City.

I swiveled around in my chair and crossed my arms, leaning back to look at Ike. She was staring at the monitor, as I had been.

I swiveled back, signed off my computer, pushed my chair away from the console, stood, waved my hand in front of her face, and said, "I need to see you in my office."

She blinked. Without a word, she shut down her computer and left the control room. The phones were ringing, but she may not have heard them.

We walked through the tube together, going against the grain of traffic. I could hear phones ringing inside the offices we passed, and we were accosted by several NTB personnel who demanded to be told the whole story on Hannah, but they seemed to understand when we kept walking. They did not attempt to follow up, as they would have on any other morning. It could have been that our encircling cloud of gloom was interfering with normal news waves in the building.

When we were inside my office, Ike slumped into my desk chair and I perched on the edge of the couch, my elbows on my knees, my hands resting on the edge of the coffee table.

Ike lifted a piece of lava from my desk and picked up a small index card that had one word on it, spelled wrong: *P-O-T-A-T-O-E*. "Oh, my God," she said. "Where did you get this?"

"Alvin Healey in Washington sent it to me."

"Is it *the* crib sheet?"

I nodded. "The very crib sheet Dan Quayle used to make sure he did not screw up when he attempted to teach spelling."

"I'll give you my piece of the Berlin Wall for it."

I hesitated. I was intending to have that card framed. Healey had forced me to trade him the bustier Madonna had given me, complete with her autograph, for that piece of paper. "You can have it," I said.

"I can't just take it." She held the card out and looked at it like it was the kidnapped child she had paid the $5 million ransom for five years ago and who was only now being returned—safe and sound. "Can I?" she asked, between disbelief and lustful expectation.

I nodded quickly. I hurried into speech, to keep the lump from forming in my throat as she placed the card lovingly in her pocket. "Ike, that sure felt weird, just sitting there passively while Noel told the world about Hannah." I cleared my throat.

She rubbed the heels of her hands against her eyes. "I don't know about feeling weird. I shocked myself by not feeling anything. Like I was emotionally deficient, or dead inside."

The hollow woman, I thought. It was sure going around. "What makes you so certain Hannah's innocent?"

She drew a sigh. "It was what you said about your own actions when you walked to the control room yesterday morning—you know, the captain's favorite time period."

"What did I say? It can't have been anything earth-shattering. I went all over it in the statement I gave the cops. I went over it backward and forward. And Fillingeri has all that."

"You said you passed Hannah's office and smelled fresh cigarette smoke."

I slumped back against the cushions, disappointed. "Ike, she could have just left a cigarette burning. She didn't have to be in there smoking it."

"True, but *when* did she leave the cigarette? Cigarettes have life spans. How long do they burn? Five minutes? Seven minutes? If Hannah lit one and left it as a—please pardon the term—smokescreen, when did she do it? Before she drowned Connie? How long does it take to drown someone? Long enough for a cigarette to burn itself out. Or did Hannah race back to her office and light the cigarette *after* drowning Connie to provide herself with an alibi? Then did she race back for the body? Shouldn't she have been on her way to the studio with the body by that time? You said the cigarette smoke was fresh when you walked by, which was in the same time period when the killer transferred the body to the studio. How did Hannah do all of that? How could anybody?" Ike turned over her hand and patted the air. "If Hannah had simply lit a cigarette and left it burning in her office, it could not have stayed lit the entire time she needed to drown Connie, put on the makeup, and do her hair. If she lit it after doing all that, where did Hannah leave the body while she was in her office smoking?"

"Why couldn't she just take the body with her—before she moved Connie into the studio—when she took a mid-murder smoke break in her office?" Ike wrinkled her nose impatiently. "Wait a minute." I held up a hand. "That's it. Hannah could have done everything in her office. And smoked a cigarette while she was doing it."

"Don't be stupid, Abby. She didn't drown Connie in her office. Besides, Connie's body would have smelled like smoke when we found her. As nonsmokers, you and I would have noticed that. Hannah's office is a pit. She's been smoking in there for years."

"Connie did not smell like smoke," I conceded. "I wouldn't have missed that, as close as I got."

"Me, either. Connie's body was nowhere near Hannah's office, not after it was dressed and made up."

"Only those people who were on Fillingeri's list, which includes Hannah, could have been in Hannah's office during those eleven minutes. And nobody else on the list smokes but Hannah."

"They could have smoked that one time. It's conceivable."

"Okay, it's conceivable. But why pick that one time on that one morning to smoke? That doesn't make sense."

"What about Satan Brown? Does he smoke?"

"Nonsmoker. I read the research bio."

I thought for a minute. "What about the fingerprints on that note attached to Connie's finger?"

Ike shrugged. "Maybe it was Hannah's stationery. It was just ordinary notepaper, the kind we have all over the building. The killer clearly meant to make it look like Hannah killed Connie; that's been obvious from the moment I found that note. Why stop at writing her sign-off? Why not use Hannah's own supply of paper? Or the killer could simply have had a piece of Hannah's notepaper in his pocket. Just using what was convenient."

I could feel my facial muscles tensing into a frown, and I tried to relax them to tender Ike a smile. "Is this the reason you said I wouldn't understand? The cigarette smoke?"

She nodded. "Dennis didn't understand. Or he didn't think it was important. Men just don't listen."

"I've always listened to you, Ike." Before she could offer her usual resistance, I made a move for her hand and held it tight in mine. It had been clear to me when I was in Ike's apartment that I could not be what I wanted to be for Ike, but maybe I could be what *she* wanted me to be. "I listen even when you're saying what I don't want to hear." I saw a wary shadow in her fatigued eyes. "I'm listening to you now. Just tell me what you want me to do, or not do, or tell me to leave you alone. I'll listen."

She returned the pressure of my fingers. "I want to go to the Museum of the Surreal, to see those paintings again. I have to see what Connie saw that made her think she was on to a great story. And maybe what got her killed, but *not* by

Hannah. I want this to be over. But I also want the story. The whole story. Before anyone else gets it.''

"What do you want me to do?''

"I want you to go with me, to lend me your eyes.'' She grinned sheepishly. ''I'm afraid mine won't stay open.''

"I don't know anything about art. I'm happy to go, but I'll just be so much lumber.''

"Connie knew nothing about art, but she saw something that excited her.'' Ike's eyes brightened. ''In fact, Abby, maybe we should be looking for something that isn't about art at all.''

She tugged her hand away and reached for my phone.

"Ike. Before you do that. I've been thinking. Our gun person.''

She took her hand away from the phone. ''Yeah?''

"Why did he—or she—come up to the twenty-eighth floor? Nobody could have known we were up there. If someone was after us and knew we were in the building, they would have looked for us on the twenty-seventh floor.''

"And?''

"So they were after something or someone else.''

"Maybe Connie's packet of prints?''

"Maybe. Maybe something else.''

"He was probably surprised when the lights were on.''

"I mention it because, well, I was worried that maybe you and I are the next targets, after being up there then.''

"Why would we be?'' She picked up the phone and dialed.

I stood and stretched, glancing around for my skates. I saw them beside the end of the couch, grabbed them, and sat down again, placing them on the floor at my feet. I took off my sneakers.

I listened to Ike's end of her conversation with Abel Chu, the museum's curator, watching her as I tugged on my left skate and pulled the laces through the speed loops. I wrapped the lace once around my ankle and tied it. I reached for my other skate.

Ike covered the receiver with her hand. ''What's wrong with your skate?''

I lowered my gaze to the skate I had in my hands. "Nothing. These are my new ones."

She pointed toward the back of the skate. "What's that thing? It looks like you picked something up, there, between the brake and the last wheel."

I turned the skate over, and my heart skipped a beat. Lodged—deliberately pushed—into the small space was a dull aluminum canister, slim and ugly, about three inches long, maybe three-quarters of an inch in diameter, tapered at both ends. A small, heavily scratched canister with partially eroded Arabic characters and, below them, "CXTI-87"—the code numbers that indicate the country of origin, year of manufacture, and toxin, better known as the agent.

I couldn't read the other stuff written in Arabic, but I didn't have to. I had been in the press pool that traveled into Iraq with the first Coalition ground troops northwest of Basra. In addition to what I had learned from the medical and chemical briefings all the press had attended, the canister was familiar to me from supplies I had seen with my own eyes, small stores the Iraqi army had left behind in their sand bunkers on the "Highway of Death," where hastily retreating Iraqi troops were massacred from the air by the Coalition in what was probably the most fatal traffic tie-up in history.

It was a nerve gas canister. The mother of all terror.

For a substance that can kill thousands of people in something just over sixty seconds, nerve gas comes in surprisingly nonexotic and shoddy containers, ranging from big industrial drums (like the Ninja Turtles mess around with in the sewers) to the kind of pellet I was staring at. The toxin is packaged as a liquid that vaporizes like hair spray when its container is punctured or the pressure is released in some other way. Some canisters actually have spray nozzles. This one didn't, which meant that its metal housing was thin and probably vulnerable in the extreme.

I had no idea what mechanism was designed into this pellet, if any. The one idea I did have was that if anything happened to change the pressure in that tiny can of death while it was in my tiny office, Ike and I had zero—I repeat, zero—seconds to get out of the way. My hands tightened on the shoe of the skate. I did that because I could feel the shakes starting from my elbows, and I was afraid that the back wheel would respond to my terror and rub the canister.

I whispered, "It's nerve gas. Go. Quietly."

A picture flashed through my mind, a devastatingly scary videotape of what was believed to be the first use of nerve gas on people, a tape that had arrived anonymously at our Tel Aviv Bureau. It was a home video shot outside the Iraqi town of Halabje in March 1988, when Saddam dropped nerve gas from a plane onto a town of dissidents, reportedly killing five thousand people. The tape showed a whiteish cloud and a grayish cloud over the town, and then lots of dead people in horrible positions, as though they had died in excruciating pain, the kind of total-body agony that happens when a nervous system is instantaneously destroyed, shutting down all the other systems almost as an immediate afterthought. That's where the pain came from—the afterthought.

Ike put the phone down on the desk slowly, without hanging up. She stood. Slowly. She edged across my office, watching where she put her feet.

"Abby, put it down."

"I can't."

"You have to."

"No. Get out of here." I could barely hear myself, from the roar of my blood in my ears, and I was hoping the words were reaching her. I could hear little high-pitched squeaks coming from the phone.

"Put it down, Abby."

"I can't. My hands are paralyzed."

She took a step toward me.

"Get back, Ike."

"You have to put it down." She stepped slowly and with maddening, time-bending deliberation to the couch. She took one of the cushions from the back and slid it over the carpet until it rested against my leg. "Put it on the cushion, Abby," she whispered. "Just slow and easy."

I stared at the canister, and at my hands clenched on the skate. My elbows felt like they were floating at my side. I couldn't control the tremor in them.

"Pretend it's a tango, Abby. A smooth turn, a quick, light release. Nobody has hands like you."

My vision blurred for a second. "Get out. If you're in the hall, I can do it. I can't do it if you're here."

From my peripheral vision I saw the yellow blur of her dress moving toward the door, backing away from me. When she was out, surrounded by the white luminescence of the hall's light, I moved my arms, trembling, toward the cushion. A quick, light release, and the skate was on its side on the cushion, the canister an ugly, gleaming bulge. I ripped at the laces of the skate I was wearing and yanked it off. I stood and banged my shin on the coffee table. I crossed the room shakily and closed the door behind me.

Ike took my hand and we hurried to the fire alarm. I pulled the red lever.

In the bedlam of noise and confusion that followed, we did not head for the elevator, which you sometimes have to wait as much as twenty seconds for. We ran for the stairs.

EIGHTEEN

So we temporarily added another captain to our collection of NYPD brass, this one from the Bomb Disposal Unit.

Capt. Marvin Saddler, a tall African-American who looked to be about the right build but considerably too old for the Olympic shot put, arrived a few minutes after his underlings had removed the canister from the Emerald City. I was wondering what the NYPD feeds its sturdy captains when I saw Saddler arrive at the front entrance to the building, on Columbus Circle. He could have donated a few sculpted pounds to Fillingeri and still have no need to apologize for his shoulders as he bulled his way through the throng of tourists who had come to photograph the famous doors and had stayed to hobnob with the disgruntled/alarmed human contents of the building, some of whom might turn out to be famous, so why not try to get *all* their autographs and sort it out later?

The entire staff of *Morning Watch* was there to witness Saddler's arrival because everyone in the building had been evacuated to the street. Saddler was dressed in civilian clothes, unlike the masked men or women (hard to tell with the chem-armor protective suits) who had done the scary part and carried a black box and their atropine injections into the building and up to my office. The suits were in case the canister turned out to contain mustard gas, which attacks not only through the lungs, but also through the skin. The black box was an insulated environment that could be sealed hermetically against the escape or entry of any substance whose molecules move fast enough to keep them from bonding into a liquid—gas. And the atropine, that was in case the canister turned out to contain, as I already knew it did, nerve gas.

Atropine is the antidote to nerve gas. The scary part about atropine is not the needle. Atropine comes in autoinjectors you just press against an arm or a leg. You don't see the needle. What's really scary is that you have about nine seconds to figure out whether your symptoms (convulsions, choking, rapid and painful gasping) are caused by nerve gas or some other chemical, and, if it is nerve gas, to inject yourself with the atropine. If you wait more than nine seconds, you die from the nerve gas, which shuts down your nervous system. Unfortunately, if you figure wrong and it is *not* nerve gas, but you inject yourself with the atropine anyway, you have a fifty-fifty chance of dying from the antidote.

If I had punctured the container, I would have been spared the agony of that decision. I don't carry an atropine autoinjector on me. And although you never know what Manhattanites are carrying as the latest defense gadget, it would be a safe bet that if I'd made it out of my office and punctured the canister in a crowd somewhere, people around me would not have been groping for their atropine, or looking around to see who they could borrow from. The one line you will never hear in the one city where you will hear everything else is: "Pardon me, sir, but since you seem to have left your atropine autoinjector at home today, would you care to share mine?"

I had plenty of time to mull over the various other ways to compare life in Manhattan, between the East and Hudson Rivers, to life in that other cradle of civilization, between the Tigris and Euphrates, where people have been known to carry atropine as part of their daily gear, although I doubt they'd be any more likely to share it in a crisis. When the nerve gas canister had been removed, we were all marched in through the revolving door and herded into the elevators for another morning of questioning by New York's finest. Ike had to postpone our appointment with Abel Chu to go look at Salvador Dalí's most famous painting, after apologizing for leaving the curator on the line so mysteriously.

In addition, the twenty-seventh floor was searched for a supply, however small, of atropine, the idea being that anyone who wanted to kill me with nerve gas probably had not wanted to kill himself carelessly if the gas had been released prematurely. Almost certainly that someone had known enough to provide himself with the antidote. Othello had issued a general order to cooperate with the search, but he had drawn the line at allowing the bomb experts to dismantle his equipment, and the twenty-seventh floor is so full of electronic marvels and TV junk that no search short of one with a fine-tooth comb could possibly be anything other than a gesture. But even given the obvious loopholes in the search, it seemed to me that the cops received absolutely supine cooperation from the staff of NTB. After all, what if there was another canister of that stuff around? Would you want to be the one whose smart mouth distracted the cop from finding it?

We often have to cover dangerous, even deadly, situations to earn our grotesque salaries, but no one in that building was a daredevil for the hell of it. In fact, most of us are rank cowards who only got into the business because we couldn't tap-dance, sing arias, or tell jokes well enough to get more than a polite laugh—a bunch of mostly underweight show business wannabes, not a bunch of terrorists in training.

While the search was under way, the cops questioned everyone who had been on the floor for the overnight shift, which was when I had left my office unlocked and my skate had been tampered with. Nobody thought I had booby-trapped my own skate, so I was only kept around so they could ask me why I skated to work, where I kept my skates, if the canister had been there when I skated to work, who knew about my habit of skating, and if I had any enemies. When my answers kept coming out the same—"it's friendlier than the subway," "in my office," "no," "everyone," and "no"—they reversed the order of the questions to keep me on my toes.

Everyone else was asked five questions, different from the five I was answering. One: "Do you have any atropine?"

Two: "Have you been to the Middle East, and if so, when and which countries?" Three: "Have you had any training in chemical weapons?" Four: "Have you used Stapleton Airport in Denver in the last three years?" (The big American nerve gas depot is right at the end of the runway, not a comforting thought during a shaky landing in the midst of a snowstorm.) And, five: "What have you got against Abagnarro?"

Their answers, with one exception as far as I could determine through snooping and luck, were that nobody had anything against me, unless it was Ike. And that nobody had a supply of atropine. And that anyone who had been to the Middle East during the Gulf War had enjoyed all the benefits of training films and briefings on what Saddam might launch at them in terms of mass destruction and that nobody had slept through those training sessions, because, well, would you? And that roughly 50 percent of the staff of *Morning Watch* had, indeed, traveled to the Middle East recently, some to cover the war, some to visit their families, some for religious reasons. That if they had been in Denver, they had not toured the facility where all the really bad shit is stored. Of those on Fillingeri's list, only Lourdes Ramirez answered no to all four of the atropine, Middle East, chemwar training, and Denver questions. She also scored a no on the Abagnarro's enemies question. Apparently nobody answered that one with negative particulars, especially not with an explanation of what they had against me. It's nice to be popular.

Ike received the most intense fraction of Saddler's scrutiny because of the story she had done on the Sayeret Matkal, the Israeli assassination squad that just happened to feature nerve gas in its bag of dirty tricks. Ike had been more intimate with nerve gas than any of the rest of us. Her piece had been a classic of individual enterprise and there was nothing secret about her findings, but Saddler seemed fascinated by the detail that she had personally gone after the story. Didn't that mean that Ike was necessarily familiar with the antidote to nerve gas? Would she have been that courageous without making sure she had the right defense against the weapon she was investigating? Under questioning from Saddler himself about her knowledge of nerve gas, Ike offered the guess that my little canister contained "Taboon," a popular nerve gas among the chemwar crowd, and we later learned that she was right. And she confessed that she and her camerawoman had both carried atropine, but Ike denied bringing any back to the United States.

Ike was also the exception when it came to the question about who had anything against me. I gathered from Saddler that she had told him about our visit to the twenty-eighth floor, complete with gun-toting shadow, and that she had also told him that I had been walking in the twenty-seventh floor tube during the eleven minutes Connie Candela's killer had been transporting the body to the studio. I did not think she had spilled the beans about Connie's art prints and accompanying note, but I wasn't sure then, so I kept my mouth shut on those details. The soul of ignorant discretion.

Maybe Connie's killer, Saddler suggested, was the same person as the one who had brought a gun to the soap opera venue, and maybe, he suggested, that person was after me with nerve gas because I had seen something, either on the soap opera floor or during that walk through the tube.

So Saddler, who was ensconced in my office now that it was nerve-gas-free, asked me what I had seen the morning of Connie's death, and I went over the whole thing again. Fillingeri had returned to the Emerald City, having responded to the alert passed along by the Bomb Disposal Unit, and he made me go over it all again, too. He, like Saddler, seemed to think that my office would do nicely for command headquarters while the NYPD was in the building investigating NTB's latest excursion into exotic death-dealing. And, he was sitting in my desk chair.

After I had retold my story a couple of times, Fillingeri started on a side issue. "So what was your big idea about snooping around the twenty-eighth floor, Abagnarro?" he asked, his voice smooth, but his eyes fairly fierce under lowered brows. "Is this some more of your inside information? Did you go up there to get something you forgot when you picked up some cosmetics for Candela?''

I was at a topographical disadvantage, slumped against the back of the couch, but feeling it would be impolite to stand and look down at him, I merely raised my eyebrows, to offset his lowered pair. "I thought you arrested Hannah for that murder.''

"Answer the question. What were you after when you went up there?''

"Captain, did you look at the Costume Box?''

"Abagnarro, you've got a twisted idea of what's going on here. You have from the start. Let me see if I can spell it out for you: You are not a cop. I ask the question; you give the answer. Can you try that?''

"What was the question?''

"What the hell was your reason for going up to the twenty-eighth floor last night?''

"I wanted a beer.''

"That's not what Ms. Tygart said.''

"What did she say?''

"You're doing it again.''

"Doing what?''

"I ought to book you for back talk. You're so goddamn smug; you think I'm here for your amusement, don't you?''

"Is that what I think?''

He flung himself out of the chair and left my office in a police huff. I rose from the couch and reclaimed my chair, unpleasantly warm from Fillingeri's rump. *Just like the cat,* I thought. The creatures Ike collects.

Saddler shook his head slowly from side to side. "You're not making any friends, Mr. Abagnarro.''

"I don't want to be Fillingeri's friend.''

"Be my friend, then. Tell me who put that nerve gas on your skate. Tell me what you're thinking, or guessing. Whatever comes to mind.''

After Fillingeri, Saddler seemed almost human, so I offered him the one coherent guess I had. "Well, you cops keep asking about who was in the Middle East, or Denver. If somebody from NTB brought that little canister back as a souvenir—which is pretty hard to imagine—then anyone who has access to this facility probably had access to the canister. Odd thought, but you can get nerve gas at your local network headquarters.''

Saddler nodded again. "That's what I think. But it would take someone fairly knowledgeable to use it." He spread his large hands open in the air and closed them together slowly to make a tent. "Tell me something. How does a thing like that get through customs?"

"I don't know. But if I wanted to bring something that nasty into the country, I'd stow it with the gear."

"Like cameras?"

"What I'd do is open a videocassette, remove the tape, plop the canister in, reseal the plastic—who's to know? All you'd need would be a screwdriver or a good fingernail."

"You ever done anything like that?"

I raised my hands, the picture of innocence. "Me? I just thought that up on the spur of the moment."

"Yeah. What about getting something into your office? You keep your door unlocked?"

"It was unlocked overnight. I'll be more careful from now on."

Saddler lowered his chin to the top of his finger tent. "Yeah." He studied me over his fingers. "How good a skater are you?"

"Good enough."

"You use that brake much?"

So, Saddler knew something about Rollerblading.

"Not much," I said. "I mostly do speed-stops." Speed skaters, as Saddler apparently knew, don't use their brakes, opting instead for the small spin that turns the feet into a wedge and absorbs the speed when it's time to stop. More graceful, less wear and tear on the hardware. For most speed skaters, using the brake is like dragging an anchor.

He nodded slowly again, like his head was so heavy that if he got it going really fast it might fall off. "Still, you wouldn't have to use that brake to release the gas. It's plenty easy to puncture a nerve gas can. I expect a rock or a piece of glass would do it."

"Well, if that canister wasn't primed with a device to go off on its own, any sudden stop I didn't plan myself might do it, anything that backed me up against my brake."

"Like what?"

"Like in traffic, like rolling into the path of a cab or something."

"Don't get me wrong, Mr. Abagnarro. That little chemical toy was meant to kill you, and it would have killed you today, not tomorrow. I just like to narrow the possibilities, try to get into the mind of the person who rigged this apparatus. You got any ideas?"

"Nope." I held up my hand and extended my index finger. "I mean yes. I have one idea. Whoever did it is crazy. There was no way to guarantee that I'd be the only one to die."

"True." More slow, slow head shaking. "But at least it would be guaranteed that *you'd* die. Very quickly. Within maybe sixty seconds, tops, and you'd be in no shape to know anything after, say, the first ten seconds." The head shaking stopped and Saddler's eyes came at me straight on. "Somebody wanted you dead—dead in a hurry. Real dead. Real quick."

We sat in silence for a while, not a companionable silence, but there was nothing adversarial between us the way there was with Fillingeri.

"Captain," I said, "what's Fillingeri got against the media?"

"Nothing special that I know of. Just the usual."

"What's usual?"

"You guys never give us the benefit of the doubt, except when it suits you to ride along with your cameras on a drug bust. That's the usual."

"You make us sound like ingrates."

"Yeah." That slow, slow nod again. "I'm not complaining. But you asked."

When Saddler finally left my office, about 12:30, I tried to sneak over to Ike's office, but *Evening Watch* was in possession of the tube, waiting to pounce on me unless and until they got another memo from Othello Armitage, who was probably chewing the green marble floor in his office because a couple of enterprising photographers had flowed into the Emerald City with the postevacuation crowd and had captured our chaos with the magic of celluloid. This was definitely more of the kind of bad publicity that's not good.

After navigating the trashy jokes and bald curiosity of the *Evening* rubberneckers (one of them tossed me a can of Coke and yelled, "Hey, Abagnarro, heads up and reach for your atropine!"), I dodged into Ike's office and shut the door behind me.

"I'm hungry," I said. "I'll treat you to lunch at Gypsy's."

"You mean your mother will treat me." The only reason cynicism didn't drip from her tone was that she was too engrossed with her computer screen to give me the full Tygart repertoire of overflowing anti-Abby sentiment.

"Okay," I said, with generosity based on a wallet full of credit cards. "I'll take you somewhere else." But I wanted to show Ike that my generosity was also tempered by financial responsibility and common sense. "Within reason."

"I have to go over to the Circle Rep to see if I made the cast of *Hamlet*. I'm already late, and I don't have time to eat." She turned to give me a dirty look, one that did not quite say I had inconvenienced her by allowing someone to rig my skate with a canister of Iraqi nerve gas, but one that nevertheless let me know that offering to pay for her lunch in my company was an insensitive gesture, perhaps well meant but definitely not appreciated. "Without your skates, you'll just slow me down."

"Well, pardon me for being a victim." Apparently the new goodwill and understanding between us had evaporated with her temper, which was obviously fraying under the ministrations of the Bomb Disposal Unit. Plus, it probably had not made her feel too jolly to watch me hold a canister of nerve gas. At least not while she was in the same room. But I wondered if something fresh was eating her.

Her phone rang and she jumped. She lifted the receiver.

"Tygart here."

She listened, reached for a pencil, and started making notes. I decided she didn't need me as an audience and was turning to go when she held up the hand with the pencil. She tucked the receiver under her chin and muffled it against her shoulder.

"Abel Chu has to give a class this afternoon at MOMA. Then he has a cocktail party. He'll meet us at the museum at 8:30 tonight and open it up just for us." She lifted the pencil hand. "If you still want to go?"

"I said I'd go."

She leaned into the phone. "We'll be there. Listen; we really appreciate this. NTB appreciates it."

Ike made a few more nice noises and hung up. She looked limp sitting there, tired and defeated. Her pretty yellow dress was wrinkled, and the shadows under her eyes were gray.

She knuckled her eyes with her fists, like a child. Still rubbing, she said, "The Dallas Bureau is pulling out the stops looking into Concepción Candela's pre-Houston, pre-career-clawing past. We've got a freelancer in Mexico seeing if they can find any dirt on Lourdes Ramirez, other than her nasty temper. Arthur is going to travel with the Heinous Face tour to Buffalo today."

"But Satan Brown could not have rigged my skate, Ike. He was in Boston, with our own news crew staking him out."

"I know, but he was part of Connie's life. Also, it does not automatically follow that the nerve gas fiend is also Connie's killer. Maybe the two events are unrelated."

"Maybe. But they're stacked awfully close to each other in time."

She nodded. "I don't believe for one minute that we're dealing with more than one fiend. But I'm not letting the *Globe* sneak up on me again. This nerve gas flourish is going to make everyone jump on the story, even those who didn't twitch when Connie died."

"What else?"

"Strictly on the q.t., I've borrowed a couple of people from the Investigative Unit to eyeball Fred Loring's dreary past." She lowered her fists and wrinkled her nose. "What

a creepy thing he is. What creepy things we are." She
yawned. "The creeps from the Investigative Unit are also
doing Noel."

I gawked. "Noel?"

"Noel. He's on that eleven-minute list, he was available
to fix your skate, and he knows this building like the back
of his hand. Costume Box, makeup, everything on the
twenty-eighth floor—he probably knows the ins and outs of
every floor, including the penthouse; certainly he knows this
floor. If someone had nerve gas, he might be the one to
know. He's made NTB his life over the past thirty years.
Besides, we all know he has an eerie mind."

"Not that eerie. He's a nice guy."

She lifted her shoulders as though the exercise took all her
concentration. "Abby, what do we actually know about
Noel Heavener? Beyond his life here? He's a recluse."

"What in the world are you looking for with Noel?"

"Easy stuff. I want to know about his memberships in art
museums, on the chance that Connie was actually on to
something. The one and only interview he ever granted, the
piece in *Rolling Stone* in 1979, profiled Noel's watercol-
ors—his hobby is painting pictures of children and horses."
She wrinkled her nose fastidiously. "Also an occasional
portrait. And we're checking with auction houses and galleries to see if he's a buyer. That's easy, just telephone legwork. I've also asked the Tel Aviv Bureau to send me an
itinerary of his tour of duty in Israel during the war. I was
busy with the Sayeret Matkal, and I did not keep an eye on
him. This may be one area where we have an advantage over
Fillingeri and over other news organizations—our own
Mickey Mouse in the Holy Land."

"We had two sets of Mickey. I was in Saudi Arabia when
you and Noel were in Israel. So was Fred Loring, only then
I didn't know Fred had something in common with Noel.
Fred calls it 'sacred art,' and he doesn't paint children."

"What's sacred art?"

I told her about Fred's nudes.

Ike stared at me. "Fred? He's painting nudes over in
Graphics? He's painting nudes? Of women?" Suddenly she

laughed. "I guess I should be relieved that Fred-the-Dread is painting *humans*."

"Don't make fun of Fred. He doesn't like it." I told her about Fred's fact or dream about where Othello Armitage fit into the Connie Candela story.

"How would Fred know? I mean, everybody speculated, but does Fred think he caught them in the act or something?"

"It was some hogwash about past lives and karma. Fred and Connie were, according to Fred, soul mates, which is probably better than no kind of mate at all. He did her horoscope, instead of the part of Connie he really wanted to do. Pure sublimation. Harmless Shirley MacLaine stuff like wandering souls and horoscopes."

"God, why didn't Connie just read the newspaper like everyone else?" Ike's computer emitted a ping, and she turned to her keyboard to retrieve what the wires were moving. "Oh, this is nice. There's a severe thunderstorm watch for Medicine Lodge, Kansas. Bless my soul." She punched keys and shut down her terminal. "Jeez, you'd have to be a real newsaholic to get excited about that."

"Or live in Medicine Lodge."

"If I lived in Medicine Lodge, I'd become a newsaholic. What else would there be to do?"

"Ike, you're so chauvinistic. I'll bet there's lots of nice people in Medicine Lodge."

"Yeah, but what do they *do?*"

"Maybe they do the same things everyone does. Or wants to do." I grinned at her. "Like make love and sleep and eat Italian food."

"Yeah. And maybe they draw dirty electronic pictures and carry around nerve gas canisters." Her voice was thick with sarcasm. She put her palms flat on her hips, the way she does when she's being an authority on something. "You really have to get over this idea that people are the same all over. Just think of Fred Loring."

"I don't want to think about him."

"Who does? But do you suppose Fred concentrated on Connie? Or did he have a thing for NTB women in gen-

eral? I hope it doesn't turn out that Noel has a tawdry little
sleaze-life, too. I almost hate snooping into the lives of
people I actually know. It seems that everyone at NTB has
a dirty little secret.''

"Well, I doubt Noel's a pervert." I couldn't imagine Noel
Heavener having a dirty little secret. "Ike, Noel asked me
about my skates. Just yesterday.''

"What's he say?''

I scratched my head, trying for the exact memory.
"Something about whether I went everywhere on my
skates.''

"Maybe he's a diabolical terrorist." She shook her head
tiredly. "On the other hand, who knows what Noel really
thinks he means when he says anything? God. Maybe he just
wanted to know if you could get him hockey tickets.''

I smiled. "What about Hannah? Are you skipping her?''

"No way. The more I know, the better. But Hannah's my
hole card. I have two advantages and she's one of them. I
know she didn't kill Connie.''

"You don't know that. You think that.''

"Well, it's still an advantage. I'm the only one in the media who thinks it. Everyone else will be concentrating on her
life story and wasting their time. And I think they'll get a
big, fat nothing. Hannah's life is more of an open book than
any of the others'. She's always courted publicity. If she has
any secrets, it can only be stuff that slipped her mind when
she was giving everyone an ear job over at *Time* magazine.
But I can afford to specialize; I don't need Hannah's life
story, because of my other advantage—those art prints.
Even though I don't see how she could have killed Connie,
I've got people looking into Hannah's contacts in the art
world, same as for Noel. No one else will be covering that
angle. It's still mine exclusively.''

"What about the nerve gas?''

"Hannah was in Saudi Arabia with you guys. You tell
me.''

"She was with the first press pool into Iraq. She saw the
same nerve gas stores I did. But I didn't see her tuck any
sinister canisters into her bra.''

Ike took a deep breath and gave me a stern dose of her eyes. "Abby, just so you know, the Moscow Bureau is making contact with your BBC bimbo. Your little *prastitutka*." She leaned on the last word, giving it an unnecessary emphasis. But there was nothing wrong with her pronunciation. Russian doesn't have all that many words that are cognate with English, but that one is, and it would have been easily translated down on 42nd Street where they rely on a brand of pidgin English known as Trash Talk. "Don't gawk at me like that, Abby. We are looking without prejudice into everyone, especially if they have a kink in their past. We have to cover everyone on Fillingeri's list."

"Including me?"

"You heard me."

NINETEEN

My BBC *prastitutka* was the *mistake,* of course.

The fall of communism in the Soviet Union and the end of the Cold War had marked the beginning of the very heated war between Ike and me, as well as the fall of our marriage. I'll always associate Gorbachev's ouster with my own, although what happened was hardly his fault.

During the final days of the Soviet Union, I was assigned to the Moscow Bureau to direct the series of shows we anchored from the Russian capital. Moscow is one of the few hardship bureaus NTB still operates around the world. A hardship bureau is defined as a place where the conditions are so bad that no one has to work there more than three years. NTB is all heart.

I was only assigned to Moscow for five weeks, but that was long enough to convince me that three years would be a hardship. It was bitterly cold. I was living in the Rossiya Hotel—which we called the "Roachsiya," for obvious reasons. The bathtubs don't have plugs and they don't have showers, so you make do by splashing cold water from the faucet with one hand while you brush the roaches away with the other hand, and Muscovite roaches are eager for intimacy.

The Rossiya is the largest hotel in the world outside of Las Vegas, it's right across from Red Square and provides a magnificent studio backdrop, with Saint Basil's and the Kremlin—but it's also the most depressing, dirty, dimly lit, paranoid, bug-infested institutional setting I've ever experienced. Just for the privilege of entering your room to bathe with the roaches, you have to turn over your passport and other ID to the "Key Lady," who waits in a dark hall at her desk to hand over your room key if she likes your ID.

But it wasn't just the Rossiya and the filth and the cold and the paranoia. It was the food shortages, the swarming rats, the haunted faces of unhealthy old women standing in long food lines for stale bread—or, worse, no bread at all—and the closeness among the press corps in the face of adversity. These had been my excuses.

The woman Ike called *prastitutka* didn't need any excuses as far as I knew. She was a veteran correspondent for the BBC and had a reputation in the press corps for getting around among men as expertly as she got around wars and other hardship zones—Iran/Iraq, Afghanistan, South Africa, and, of course, the usual bloodletting in the Mideast that keeps tourists from mistaking it for, say, Utah, which it resembles in places. She had made her reputation in Beirut, which makes Moscow look like Disney World.

Ten years older than me, inured to backward living conditions (she thought the Rossiya was "magical"), and many years more experienced with the special sexual rules of hardship zones, Sarah (I don't call a woman with her credentials a *prastitutka*) had asked, and I had said yes. I'm not saying it was Sarah's fault. It wasn't. I didn't say no, and when I said yes, it wasn't lukewarm.

And when Ike found out, she wasn't lukewarm. One of the first things Ike and I had done, years back when we decided we were serious about each other, was attempt to draw up a constitution. We were sharing tapas at El Internationale, all the way down near the foot of Broadway in the Financial District, when the idea came up. Ike, who is always prepared, took a fresh notebook from her purse, opened it to the first page, and put it on the table between us. We looked at each other and, practically in the same moment, said the same word. And we never got beyond the first word—*loyalty*—because that said it all for both of us.

So, my saying yes to Sarah in Moscow had said something else, too. My answer was not only unfaithful. It was unconstitutional.

Now, on the twenty-seventh floor of the Emerald City, with Ike telling me that my past and Sarah's were being probed as part of Ike Tygart's investigation into Connie's death, that moment made it clearer even than the divorce had been on the subject of our constitution. It wasn't temporarily revoked; it was destroyed forever.

"Thanks," I said. It came out icily, but I felt hot all over. "That's really nice. How many people have you told? This is great. I get my skate and my reputation screwed in one day."

"You'd better not get me started on the subject of screwing."

"You started it yourself. Dammit, Ike, how long are you going to keep this up? I don't even remember what Sarah looks like."

"I'll just bet." Ike rose from her chair and slammed it against her desk. "The only thing I care about concerning your memory is what happened during those eleven minutes. This is only a news story to me, nothing more. The only reason that *blyad*—that BBC journalist—came up is that I want to know who's playing with nerve gas."

I was surprised Ike knew the word *blyad*, which is much dirtier than *prastitutka*. "What does Sarah have to do—in your demented mind—with that nerve gas canister?"

"She staked the BBC to that exclusive report on the Soviet nerve gas factory at Voronezh. And she was in Baghdad before Moscow. She's an expert on nerve gas. Besides, I wouldn't be the first to suspect that a canister of Iraqi nerve gas, complete with Arabic lettering, really made its way to the desert via a Soviet freighter in the Persian Gulf."

"You're reaching, Ike."

"I have to reach. I want this story."

"You sound hysterical."

"I'm not hysterical." She ran her hands through her hair, forgetting she had braided it, and the result was a mess. "I'm scared, Abby. I knew about nerve gas. It's not a terrible novelty to me. I'm an expert, too. It's a weapon that insane people use. Somebody insane is after you. And they have access to this building."

"I wish I thought this hysteria was coming from concern for me, some core of feelings you didn't know you still had."

"It isn't!" Her voice went up a couple of notches. "I wouldn't waste my time being concerned about someone who's thinking about his *prastitutka*."

"You're so stupid, Ike. How could I find the time to think about her when I spend every waking minute thinking of you? God, I even spend my sleeping moments thinking of you." I grabbed her arm above the elbow and held on. "I'm crazy, I think about you so much." She shook her head quickly, like she didn't want to hear what I was saying. "Ike, you started this—let's talk about screwing." She winced and tried to pull away. "I screwed everything up with a half-hour liaison in Moscow. I hate what I did. But you're screwing everything up, too. I'm the same person I always was. I was human when you met me, and I was human in Moscow. I screwed up."

But Ike only heard part of what I said.

"Half an hour? You gave that creature half an hour? That's worse than I ever thought. I thought it was just some little ten-minute fling. But *now* I find out you practically gave her the full Abagnarro treatment." She jerked her arm. "Let go of me. I hate you."

"I'm not letting go. I should have held on tighter all along. You had no right to divorce me. You belong to me."

She gasped. "What a double standard! I suppose you didn't belong to me?" With her free hand, she reared back to take a swing. "I don't belong to you now; that's for sure." I grabbed her other wrist before she could get the swing going. Somehow I lost my balance, and together we tumbled over onto her couch. I heard something rip and we both froze.

She was pinned against the back of the couch, and I sat up to take my weight off her. She reached and pulled at the torn pocket of her dress. She extracted the index card bearing the vice president's P-O-T-A-T-O-E autograph. Actually, the two pieces. She held them up and peered at me over her fingers.

"I hope you're satisfied, Abby." She hiccupped.

"I'm not. There's only one thing that will satisfy me."

"If you touch me, I'll scream." She said it low and hiccupped again, impaling me with her eyes, but there was a soft, crazy edge to the shaft of her eyes. I may have imagined a light in her eyes that was strangely inviting.

Very gently, I moved closer to her, shifting my weight so I wouldn't tear her dress again. "I can't tell if you're teasing me, if you're serious, or if you're hysterical."

"I'm hysterical."

"Then I won't touch you. I may be a screwup, but I'm not a rapist."

She leaned her head back against the arm of the couch, closed her eyes, and tried to hold her breath, but the hiccups kept interrupting her. She opened her eyes, keeping her lips and cheeks pushed out while she held her breath.

"You look like Donald Duck," I said.

Finally she expelled her breath and hiccupped again.

I moved away. "Why don't you give me a call when you're ready to go to the museum tonight?" I said. "Give me a few minutes to get ready." I stood and stretched. "Have a nice day. I hope you get good news at the theater."

"Where are you going?"

"What difference does it make? I don't belong to you."

I left her office.

I may have salvaged some shreds of my pride, but my transportation was completely gone. Captain Saddler had confiscated my wheels. I'd have to walk to Gypsy's.

When you're used to cruising the sidewalks of Manhattan at thirty-five to forty miles an hour, becoming a pedestrian again is a difficult adjustment. People seem to move in slow motion. Storefronts seem frozen in time. But cars seem to fly by at warp speed.

I arrived at Gypsy's at the height of the lunch rush. My mother's soap opera buddies were gathered at the bar, eating *spinach tortellini Carole,* drinking the house Chianti from the crystal flutes that normal customers are never allowed to touch, and not talking because *Meg's Children* was in full spate. I took a seat at the bar, and my mother poured me a glass of wine without taking her eyes off the tube. The soap opera must have been especially absorbing that day, because I got my wine in crystal.

"You know, Ma, it's your fault if I get soused on an empty stomach."

"Hush. Arnie's just been arrested."

I watched two cops escort Arnie from one of the living rooms and out through a door in the little world imprisoned inside the television set over the wine rack. It's funny, but even after you've seen what the sets are made out of, they still look real on television. And we've mastered sound technology to the point where I couldn't hear their shoes squeak on the concrete floor when they departed the living room carpet.

Arnie's departure was followed by a commercial for—believe it or not—soap, and my mother dragged her eyes away from the set.

"You look rotten again, Abby."

"No, Ma. I *still* look rotten."

"You should go home and go to bed, instead of hanging out in bars."

"I will. Soon. Can I have some of that tortellini?"

She signaled to a waitress.

"Abby, I don't like what's happening on your *Morning Watch*. The idea of telling everyone Hannah killed that girl."

"We didn't say that."

"You did, too. I heard it with my own ears."

There are some things you just can't tell Carole Abagnarro. "Sorry, Ma." I yawned.

"And now look where it gets you. You look like idiots."

I sipped the Chianti. "Why? We broke the story."

"Maybe so. But CNN broke the story that the cops let her go. We were channel switching just before you got here, and that's what they said."

"What? Hannah's out?"

"CNN doesn't lie."

"Oh, and we do?"

"I didn't say that."

"Ma, did they say why the cops let Hannah go?"

"It was something about she's got an alibi. That Mexican girl. She would have spoken sooner, but her English is not good, and she did not understand what the police were asking."

I was willing to bet that Lourdes Ramirez had been interviewed by a bilingual cop. The only thing she had not understood was how much she could sell her story for. I wondered if Ike had heard the news yet, if she was near a TV.

I gulped my wine, wondering how much a television anchorwoman pays a personal assistant to lie. A nice little bonus, and Lourdes got to keep her green card, too.

The commercials were over and Meg's kids were back at it. I faded out of existence for my mother as she returned to the magic from Soundstage 28-A. The waitress brought a plate of tortellini, and I ate, keeping half an eye on the television. Arnie was sitting across a table from a guy in a suit, obviously his attorney, and Arnie was pretty steamed about how unfair life is and about what liars people are. I thought, *Yep, if you pay them enough.*

My wine glass was empty, and my mother took it away, replacing it with a Heineken. "You won't sleep well with a Chianti headache," she whispered.

"Ma," I whispered back, "did CNN say anything about the nerve gas at the Emerald City?"

"Yes, but they didn't have any pictures of you, so I didn't really pay attention."

Motherly devotion. I could have died, but CNN didn't have pictures, so why break into a sweat?

I finished the tortellini and the beer. I stood up to go, and my mother must have seen me out of the corner of her eye.

"Wait, Abby. I've got something for you. Wait 'til the commercial."

I resumed my seat on the bar stool. I was getting a crick in my neck from watching Arnie's struggles with the law. I put my elbows on the bar and closed my eyes.

The next thing I knew, my mother was poking me gently with a long, thin Tupperware container that sounded like a maraca. I forced myself to wake up completely and saw that the Tupperware contained uncooked homemade spaghetti. Dry pasta is surreal if anything is, worse than a fur-lined teacup; pasta is supposed to be floppy.

"Thanks, Ma."

"It's not for you. You'd only ruin it. It's for Ike."

"Thanks." I can cook pasta, but that's one of the things you can't tell Carole Abagnarro.

"Shh. The show's back on. Go home and sleep."

I rubbed my eyes. "I'll probably dream about loud spaghetti and floppy watches. Or floppy spaghetti and loud watches."

I clutched the Tupperware cylinder in my right hand and started to rise.

"That's a good boy," she said, reaching to pat my hand absently. "You do that."

When I was standing, turning to leave the bar, she touched my sleeve and whispered, "What do you mean, floppy watches? If this is more inside stuff about *Meg's Children,* like what you said about Roman Nights, you gotta tell me."

I blinked. "I wasn't talking about your soap, Ma."

"Yes, you were. The floppy watches."

"Ma, you just don't listen. Sometimes I wish I were on television so you'd actually hear what I say."

My mother glanced back up at the television. Arnie was shouting at some redheaded woman with a sickening smile and a mole on her chin. Then the scene switched to a tavern, and I recognized parts of the saloon I had seen being unloaded the day before and taken into the Emerald City through the loading dock.

"This is so good," my mother said, pointing at the television. "I told everyone there'd be a new tavern. I love to know ahead of time. What's this about the floppy watches?"

I sighed. I didn't want to sit back down because I was afraid I'd fall asleep and never make it to my apartment.

"It's just a painting, Ma. Really crazy. It's kind of a land-scape, but it's got these watches, loose like pieces of balo-ney, and they're hanging on a tree or something. Go back to your show."

"I know that painting, Abby."

"Everybody knows that painting. It's famous."

She raised an eyebrow. "How'd it get famous?"

"It got famous because it's supposed to be really great. I don't know. How do paintings get famous? I don't know what makes the Mona Lisa so famous. I think she looks like Lee Iacocca in drag. Why are we talking about this?"

"You brought it up. I thought maybe you knew some-thing about *Meg's Children* that I can tell everyone."

"What does a painting with floppy watches have to do with that show?"

"That painting was in Roman Nights on Monday, when Jessica and Arnie had their big fight. She was drunk and threw a drink at him."

I was awake then. I grabbed my mother's arm, the sec-ond time that day I had manhandled a woman I love. "Come to the kitchen."

"In the middle of the show?"

"Ma."

I guess she could tell from the look on my face that if she didn't do what I said I'd be creating a better show than anything she was likely to find on her nineteen-inch TV set.

She came around from behind the bar, and we walked to the kitchen. I reached past her to push the swinging door and followed her into the gleaming chrome and copper re-gion where Gypsy's celebrated pasta was made fresh daily, just like the menu said. Various red-jacketed underlings and two busy female chefs in full-length white aprons glanced at us, a welcome in their eyes for my mother, suspicion and reproach for me. I didn't know if they had been watching murder news on CNN or if they just didn't like having their kitchen invaded by an outsider. I may be Carole Abagnar-ro's baby boy, but I am never received with open arms in the kitchen at Gypsy's.

The chefs went back to chopping vegetables and stirring things at the island range. Garlic, fresh tomatoes, onions, and basil perfumed the air. Italian food is really the only cuisine that smells just as good when you're full as it does when you're hungry.

"What did you say? I demanded, leaning against the stainless-steel side of a mammoth double refrigerator. "Did you say the floppy watch painting was in Roman Nights on Monday, on your soap opera?"

"Yes. Are you going deaf? I worry about you, Abby. You should see your face. You look like you haven't slept for two weeks."

"Tell me about the painting."

"Why? There's nothing to tell. It was just on the wall."

"And what about Tuesday? Was it still there?"

"No, I don't think so. But I don't think they showed that part of Roman Nights."

"Was the picture framed?"

"Of course it was framed. You think they just have cheap junk in Roman Nights? That's a very respectable place, I'll have you know. You have to wear a jacket and tie to go there. Arnie made a lot of money when he had the investment firm with Carl, and he didn't spare a penny when he decorated Roman Nights after his first marriage to Jessica hit the skids. And—"

I held up my hand. "Ma. Please. I only wanted to know about the picture."

She snatched a green onion from the smooth butcher-block surface of the center island, in an extraordinary feat of timing and dexterity that I wouldn't want to try—one of the chefs was chopping the onions with a cleaver about the size of a lacrosse stick. "What's so important about that awful picture, with those awful wriggly watches, that you took me away from my show?"

I shrugged. "I wish I knew."

TWENTY

I WONDERED IF you took a poll, how many of *Meg's* legions of loyal viewers would remember that painting on the wall of Roman Nights? When they were watching all the agony, did they also watch the walls?

You know, it's like I said in the beginning, with the three umpires. So much depends on how you look at things, and it wasn't just that painting.

Take the canister of nerve gas.

One way to look at it was to think it was meant to kill me. That point of view almost stared back at me when I considered it, with the unquestioning assurance of my own reflection in a mirror. *But,* I thought, as I walked north on 9th Avenue, *mirrors are full of tricks*. And nerve gas is designed for at least two purposes—killing and *terror*.

So, one other way to look at that canister of nerve gas was to think maybe it was a trick, a deadly trick whose object was to produce terror—perhaps to evacuate the building, every floor, starting with the twenty-seventh, where the nerve gas was planted, and including the twenty-eighth, which happened to contain the missing print from Connie Candela's museum packet, or something that looked a lot like the missing print, if Carole Abagnarro's eyes are any good.

What did the twenty-seventh floor have in common with the twenty-eighth, other than the fact that television programs were produced on both floors? Only one answer occurred to me: both floors had played host at one time to a print of Salvador Dalí's *The Persistence of Memory*. So what was the object of the evacuation? *To get that picture of limp watches,* I thought, answering my own question. Certainly the beer in Soundstage 28-A wasn't worth all the trouble.

Still, a full-scale evacuation seemed like a lot of trouble for a mere print.

I stopped at the Emerald City's loading dock. A couple of NTB trucks were parked at the concrete, their gates down. I climbed the small flight of green stairs, strolled across the concrete, and took a peek inside the trucks. One was empty, the other full, full of furniture and fake greenery and the yellow taxi we had seen outside Soundstage 28-A the evening before. I wondered why they didn't just drive the taxi away, and then I realized it probably didn't have an engine. A prop, not a vehicle. Television reality.

I showed my ID to the same squat, dark-haired forewoman who had been superintending traffic in and out of the cargo bay on my visit the day before.

She took my card from my hand and studied the photo.

"That guy looks just like me," I said, more brightly than I felt.

She gave me a bland look. "Yeah, I can see the resemblance." She nodded at my Tupperware cylinder. "What's that?"

"Spaghetti."

She took the Tupperware from me and shook it before she handed it back. She looked at my ID again. "News, huh? What are you using this entrance for?"

I lifted my shoulders. "Newsheimer's. I sometimes forget how to get in from the front."

She held out her clipboard and made me sign. Then she compared my signature to the one on the ID and returned the plastic card to me. "First door on your right." She gestured in through the big cargo door.

"What are you talking about?"

"The clinic," she said, tucking the clipboard against the hip of her jade green coveralls.

"What clinic?"

"All the news diseases are treated in there."

"Are you making fun of me?"

"No way. But there's a guy in there with newsanoia, and he thinks everyone's making fun of *him*. You two might get along."

She was a surprise to me. She never once cracked a smile.

"What do you do in your real job?" I asked. "I mean when you're not playing receptionist out here for the journalism clinic?"

"This is my real job. Security is my life."

"Where'd you get your training?"

"Princeton."

I could feel my eyes getting bigger. My SAT scores had practically guaranteed that I couldn't even *spell* Princeton without counting on my fingers. "Princeton? And this is what you want to do with you life?" I waved my hand around the dock.

"I make eighty thousand a year and benefits," she said, with no special smugness, just reporting facts like I was the IRS. "No paperwork to drag home, no stress, no extra hours. All the free time I can use. Princeton doesn't graduate any dopes."

"I guess not." I was still musing on the quality of the NTB Operations Division's personnel as I walked into the bright and nearly empty arena of the Emerald City's first floor. It had the feel of Yankee Stadium before a game—clean, vast, full of yesterday's echoes.

Apparently security thought that keeping its waiting room empty made for ease of traffic control. There wasn't even a stray box to hide behind, if I were so minded. But the elevator was situated just inside the small green door off the loading dock's cargo entrance, next to the green stairs. If the killer had sneaked in that way, he wouldn't have had far to go.

I took the service elevator to the twenty-eighth floor.

When the doors opened, the scene was very different from the night before. Daylight was spilling in from the tall windows, casting a dirty yellow haze over the clutter and through the dry dust particles floating in the air like Peter Pan's magic flying powder, and the place was crowded with people—people reading scripts, people moving green canvas hampers on wheels, people carrying cartons of food, people with towels around their necks to keep their makeup off their costumes, people walking around and talking on cellular phones. With people around to show the scale, the two soundstages looked smaller in the daylight, less alien.

Nobody paid any attention to me as I headed for Soundstage 28-A. I was probably a delivery boy or an electrician. Why put on a smile or offer a greeting? They probably reserved those for the media. I made a mental note to send Noel Heavener up to let them know how important I was.

When I entered *Meg's* soundstage, I blinked. The lights were hot and bright. Hotter and brighter than in Studio 57. They were taping a scene in a hospital room. I didn't recognize any of those characters, but I would be able to tell my mother that the guy who played Arnie was smoking a cigarette near the soundstage's other open door while he flipped through the pages of a thin script. I made a private vow to bring my mother up for a tour of the soundstages if the hours of our free time should ever overlap.

I took in the panorama of sets ranged around the walls. Roman Nights was gone. In its place was the new hangout for Meg's family, with the jukebox and bar I had already seen. They must have built the set that morning. I did not think my mother would like it as much as she had liked Roman Nights. The new set struck me as cold and phony, but maybe that was because it had not yet had time to absorb enough agony to give it character.

I stepped back outside the soundstage and made for the other door. Arnie was putting out his cigarette on the floor, grinding his loafer against the concrete—littering and defacing NTB property. Even in real life he was a loser.

"Where's Roman Nights?" I asked.

"Gone the way of the dinosaur, I'm afraid," he drawled, turning his hand languidly in the air. "The transitoriness of all things finite. Here today, so much dross tomorrow."

"Sic transit gloria mundi," I said, making another mental note, this time to try the phrase on the Princeton graduate. My SATs were laughable, but languages stick to me like lint. "But Roman Nights didn't just vanish, did it?"

"Was that German?"

"Swahili. Where's the set?"

"I wish I could speak another language." His hand swept out, describing another languid circle in the air. "Ah, but the intrusion of the prosaic—who has time for intellectual pleasures?" His hand came to rest on his script. "Roman Nights was the first thing out this morning. I expect it's halfway to Brooklyn by now. *Meg* is donating some junk to the Drama School at LIU."

"Was Roman Nights taken out before the bomb scare?"

"All I know is that it was removed before anyone thought to make coffee. It's very difficult to *think,* much less *see,* before coffee. How full of briers is the workaday world. You know?"

"Yeah. I practically invented briers."

I turned and hurried toward the elevator, catching a glimpse of the Costume Box as I went by. The door was open, and the television was on. The pile of empty green interoffice envelopes was still there, gathering dust. Or Pan-Cake makeup. Or Peter Pan dust.

When I reached the ground floor, the trucks were still there, gathering dust and whatever else constitutes Manhattan's piece of the planetary atmosphere. Maybe even some Peter Pan dust. The empty truck was just as I had last seen it, but the other truck's door was closed and a couple of men were snapping the locks shut.

"Hey!" I shouted.

The Princeton graduate was at my side quickly, offering me her clipboard.

"I gotta get in that truck," I said.

"Did you forget your taxi fare, little boy?"

I drew a deep breath, hoping she was as smart as she ought to be, or at least brainy enough to veto the rule book when somebody gave her a good reason. "Look. Something that belongs to me is on that truck. It was taken out early this morning from the twenty-eighth floor."

"News is the twenty-seventh floor."

"I migrate. The beer's better up there."

"What is this thing that you think belongs to you?"

"A picture in a frame. It has sentimental value. Otherwise it's just so much Peter Pan dust."

"How much?"

That threw me off stride. "How much what?"

She made a noise. "How much money. The bribe."

"You want a bribe?"

"Of course I want a bribe." Again there was no sign of a smile. "I majored in economics. Four-point-oh GPA in coursework for my major."

"I bet you did all right in drama, too," I said, letting my disappointment show on my face. "You had me convinced for a while that you were a nice person."

"I'm not." She stuck her hand at me, palm out, waiting.

I looked at her hard brown eyes.

Asking me to pay a bribe is like asking Bangladesh for a farm subsidy. I tucked the Tupperware under my arm, felt in my pockets, and came up empty. "Do you take American Express?" I asked.

She pushed her hand at me. "I'll hold it hostage until you have cash."

I dug out my wallet and extracted my card, but I kept my eye on her while I did it. For all I knew, she might have designs on my watch. Or my mother's spaghetti.

I handed over the Amex card, which she pocketed after looking at the signature on the back, and, by golly, she handed me the clipboard and made me sign.

"What about those guys?" I asked, pointing at the men who had loaded the truck. "Will they jump me if I break into the truck?"

"I doubt it. You don't look dangerous. Besides, they're paid by the hour and it's not their truck. They can take NTB money for standing around while you sweat." She elevated an eyebrow by about a quarter of a centimeter. "They're not stupid either."

"Harvard graduates?"

It was something like swiping computer disks, I thought. We were all stealing from Othello Armitage, one way or another. I decided to clock myself as I searched for the print. Not that I had any intention of reimbursing Othello for their time, but I was curious to see if their ethics were as bad as mine.

It took me half an hour to find the print. I had to move furniture aside, fight off the plastic greenery, squeeze between boxes, crawl over the taxi, and sort through all the framed things in the back of the truck, including the phony mirrors that I could not see myself in, which, in a way, was kind of a relief. At least the cardboard man, that ubiquitous reflection, had not followed me into the truck.

When I located the print at last, sandwiched among the mirrors, I had four splinters and BO. It was hot in the truck.

I carried my prize out into the sunshine and wiped my forehead on my sleeve.

"That's a fantastic print," the pride of Princeton said. "It looks exactly like the real thing. I mean *exactly*. I'll give you your Amex card for it."

"You've got good taste to go with your crummy ethics," I said. I took a second to figure out my own crummy ethics. I had lied about the print belonging to me, but she didn't know that. To her, I was just a poor schmo who had lost a picture and wanted it back. I decided she was worse than me, so I wanted to give her something to think about that would hit her where it hurt—her bank account. I held the frame just out of her reach. "The reason it looks exactly like the real thing is that it is the real thing. I was going to give it to you, but you disappointed me with your low morals."

"My morals are very fluid. I'm extremely high-minded when it comes to art. If that's the real thing, what was it doing in that truck?"

"It was part of an intelligence test designed by the Operations Division, for which I am a spy. You passed the art recognition part, but I'm going to report your lax attitude toward security out here. You're extremely easy to bribe."

She puffed air out through her lips, the minimum physical expenditure of condescension. "You didn't bribe me to get in or out of the building." Then she actually sneered at me. "Don't be such a baby. I rolled you fair and square, and you know it. I allowed you to pay me to look through the garbage. If anybody failed an intelligence test, it wasn't me."

That was certainly one way of looking at it. She reminded me of someone. I thought a minute. Dennis Fillingeri. I was paying him to harass me; I was paying this Princeton financier so I could root around in the castoffs of *Meg's Children.* I was paying for some odd privileges.

The sun was hot, my shirt was wet, the frame was unwieldy, since I was also carrying spaghetti, I could hardly keep my eyes open, and she had my American Express card. *Really,* I thought, *I have to do something about this.* I couldn't stop paying my taxes to line Fillingeri's pockets, but this woman probably had her own Amex card, probably a nicer, gold one. She didn't need mine.

I held the print up to get a different angle in the sunlight. "You really think this is a good print?" I asked.

"It's awesome."

"Your offer still good?"

She nodded and slipped my pitiful green credit card from her pocket. She held it toward me by the corner.

So I took it from her, stepped to the edge of the dock, dropped the five and a half feet to the sidewalk, and looked up at her. She squawked but seemed stymied by the drop.

"I guess your grades in phys ed weren't so hot, huh?" I suggested. "Probably kept you out of Phi Beta Kappa."

"You owe me," she said, glancing at my signature on her clipboard. "Abagnarro."

"Don't be such a baby. I don't owe you anything. You're holding the autograph of the best tango artist in Manhattan. The Mikhail Baryshnikov of the ballroom. See you around. *Sic transit gloria mundi.*"

I missed my Rollerblades on the way to my apartment because I had to watch where I was going.

When I dragged myself into my lair, I tossed the framed print onto my desk—where it skidded across the chrome surface, producing a hideous screech. It sent pens and pencils scattering into what my building management calls the "kitchenelle" and followed them onto the floor, the black and white tiles that the management calls the "modern appointments." I carefully deposited the spaghetti on a chair (I owe Carole Abagnarro a lot more consideration than I owe Salvador Dalí imitators), flopped onto.the couch, dialed Ike's number, and got her machine.

"It's me," I mumbled. "I've got the print. And some spaghetti." I fell asleep without pulling down the blackout shade.

TWENTY-ONE

WHEN YOUR HOURS are chronically screwed up, which is the case with most newspeople because that's also the case with most news, you learn to make the most of what sleep you get. Jack Swanberg, for example, who is the foreign editor at NTB News, can fall exhausted into a nap in his office after a crisis in the Philippines and wake up twenty minutes later with enough energy for what's going on in Thailand or Tokyo, and so on as the Earth rotates through his twenty-four-hour shift. Granted, Jack has the worst hours of anyone at the network, but I think that even those of us with lesser problems—or better hours—can take the plunge into deep, brief sleep with almost no effort and with almost no negative side effects. I know I dream a lot, so I'm not even missing the important REM part of the cycle.

And, of course, I always have Jack to compare myself to, which helps, because a large part of sleep psychology is reckoning how much better off you are than you could be. When Ike called at 6:30, I'd had almost three and a half hours of sleep, a block of time Jack could have used to deal with two coups and a stock market plunge, so I felt pretty good.

"Abby, I got your message. You must have spent the afternoon in a bar."

Now Ike's a slightly different case when it comes to sleeping. She tends to hold off the inevitable until she crashes, and then she sleeps for a couple of days straight. She could never be foreign editor, because the Earth never goes two days straight without a crisis flaring up somewhere on its thin, troubled surface.

"I spent my afternoon working—not drinking." I yawned, but that was merely a ritualistic response to being awakened suddenly. I was fully alert. "I'll bet you didn't sleep."

"I'll tell you about my afternoon in fifteen minutes. Meet me at the All-Souls Cafe. We'll grab a bite to eat before we head downtown to the museum." There was a pause. "Don't worry. I'll pay."

"I'm not worried. They're letting me run a tab again."

I threw on a pair of denim shorts and a white shirt that happened to be draped over a doorknob. I slipped my feet into sneakers. This time I skipped the Cool Water. Why waste gas on a car that's not going anywhere?

The All-Souls Cafe is next door to Playtime-in-Brazil on 72nd Street, which is how Ike and I came to be so familiar with it. All-Souls is very good about running tabs for regulars, but I'm sort of a special case. I suppose I was a little careless for a while, and after a streak of more than eight months, I found myself with a bar tab (that includes food) of $3,100.21. When I finally paid it off, John-the-Romanian (who tends bar and, rumor has it, owns the place) had a small brass plaque nailed onto the end of the bar where I usually sit. The plaque has my name and the date I paid off that tab.

I walked past Playtime-in-Brazil and noticed that the top hat was catching the slanting orange rays of the evening sun and sparks of orange light flashed from the silver shoe like someone was dancing on fireworks.

The tiny red-and-white canopy over the entrance to All-Souls looked dingy in that light. I started down the small flight of stairs, which abuts the flight of stairs going up into Playtime. I could see Ike sitting at the bar when I glanced through the window on my way down into the cafe.

All-Souls is dark, and the jukebox is always loud. It's the best jukebox in New York. The selection of songs ranges from "Springtime for Hitler" to "Ninety-nine Red Balloons." Try finding both of those songs on any other jukebox in the five boroughs.

With the framed print and the Tupperware tube of spaghetti at my side and my backpack in my hand, I went in and sat next to Ike near the end of the bar. She was reading *Time* and sipping a ginger ale and wearing cutoff denim shorts and a white bodysuit with long sleeves that hugged her shapely arms and ended in scallops at her slim wrists. She was sitting on the bar stool with her legs crossed Indian-style, concentrating on the letters to the editor. She always reads the letters, sometimes when she doesn't even have time to read the news pages or the movie reviews. She says she likes to figure out how much editing has been done to the letters to make them sound so much more rational than the people who phone us when they think we've screwed up. That's the way it works in the news business—you take time to sit down and write to magazines and newspapers when you're steamed about something, but you pick up the telephone immediately and call television networks without even preparing your case. Hit-and-run criticism.

John-the-Romanian waved to me from the other end of the bar and reached for a Heineken. I shook my head, and he brought me a bottle of ginger ale.

"Not drinking tonight, Abby?"

"Got a hot date, John. Tonight's the night Ike lets me take her home."

Ike lowered the magazine slowly to the bar and gave me a look, a look that said, "That will happen right after I let a boa constrictor help me into my jacket."

"What's the deal on NTB, you guys?" John-the-Romanian asked. "First your anchor gets herself killed; then you have the gas scare. It sounds like things are pretty hairy in the Emerald City."

"They are," I said. I lifted my goods onto the bar, sliding the Tupperware in front of Ike. "First things first. Homemade and fresh from Carole Abagnarro."

Ike stood the cylinder on end and peered at the yellow sticks of pasta. "God, nothing's as good as Carole's pasta. Italian ambrosia."

"Second things second," I said, turning the print faceup and sliding it over next to the spaghetti.

Ike blinked. She got her legs uncrossed, lowered her feet to the brass rail, and leaned closer to the bar, her face almost touching the surface of the print. "You weren't just babbling when you left that message. Where'd you get this?"

"Soundstage 28-A. Well, actually, from a truck that was taking it away from the building. It *was* in the sound-stage."

"Where?"

"The set of Roman Nights, that tavern from *Meg's Children*. The derelict bar where we got the warm beer."

"What made you go back?"

I raised my shoulders. "I'm smart."

She held the print at arm's length and nodded. "You certainly are. So this is Connie's missing print. I wonder how it got framed. How it got to Soundstage 28-A. Who put it there. Why they put it there. Why anybody went to all the trouble." She turned the frame around so it faced John-the-Romanian. "John, what's so special about this picture?"

He cocked his head to one side and gave the print as much of a study as the dim light allowed. "That's such a fucked-up painting. It's great. I've always thought Dalí must've been nicely baked, stoned around the edges, sizzling."

Ike lowered the print to the bar.

A waitress I didn't know carried a tray out from the kitchen, jostled her way through the crowd standing around the jukebox with their drinks, and stood next to Ike, un-loading Mahicado salads—a fish and avocado concoction in olive oil and dill, the house specialty at All-Souls. I grabbed the print, leaned it against the wall, and realized I was hungry.

Ike and I ate in silence while John-the-Romanian tended to a huge drink order from the cafe in the back. When he returned, he parked his elbows on the bar.

"So, when are things going to settle down at NTB?" he asked, in his gentle, nonprying way. John could ask a woman about her sex life and make it sound like he was merely making conversation about the weather.

"John," Ike said, dipping a piece of mahimahi into the olive oil and dill mixture and waving her fork in my direc-tion, "a lot depends, I think, on that little print leaning against the wall next to the horny television director with the big mouth." She raised her eyes to John's gentle, noncommittal blue eyes. "I think Concepción Candela was killed because of this picture. She knew something about it that made her dangerous." Ike waved her fork in the air. "Whatever Connie knew, it was something she found out after Monday's show, and she was dead before Tuesday's show." Ike transferred the direction of her fork to the print. "That print was upstairs on the twenty-eighth floor where they make the soaps. Connie was up there at some point, probably Tuesday during the overnight. She left me a note that said she was on to some big news story. Somehow, after she wrote that note, somebody drowned her, got her downstairs, and stuck her in the studio in the anchor chair. Oh, and after the drowning but before the trip to the studio that same somebody did her makeup and her hair."

"Wait a minute," I said, remembering the muddy picture on my monitor, as I had first seen Connie that morning. "And put her in that forest green jacket." I turned to Ike. "Remember that green jacket?"

She nodded and brought the piece of mahimahi to her mouth.

"Ike, Connie was on the air in Houston, where they're not so backward they don't have weather graphics. She'd know better than to wear green to anchor our show. So somebody also put a bad jacket on her."

"Yeah." Ike pursed her lips. "I already thought about the jacket. Connie knew better than that. She wouldn't wear green." She cocked her head. "Actually, it was more of an apple green, a dark apple green. Don't feel bad, Abby. Women are just better at identifying colors than men. I wasn't criticizing."

John-the-Romanian looked puzzled. "You can't wear green on TV? I know I've seen people on the tube in green."

"You mean like on sitcoms," Ike said. "They can wear anything. Green's only a problem for a news anchor or someone who's going to be interacting with a chromakey screen, which is usually also green. It'd be a problem for someone doing the weather, too. It's like if you're wearing green, your torso becomes the place where the graphics show up. John, say I wear green and walk onto a weather set, which is just a big, empty green board. All the maps and stuff don't really exist; they're all superimposed on the picture electronically. The weather set already has a green background keyed to the graphics, and I then *become* the background, at least that part of me that's wearing green. All those maps show up on my chest and arms. You watch the Weather Channel and see if those meteorologists ever wear green—they don't.''

He seemed to mull that one over. ''Ike, you mean that when the weatherman points to places on the map behind him, he's really looking at a blank green board? He doesn't see any maps? How the hell does he know where to point?''

''Check how often he looks to the side. He's looking at a monitor off-camera.''

John-the-Romanian looked like he thought Ike was pulling his leg.

''Just think about it, John,'' Ike said. ''Anyway, Connie was put in the studio between 5:10 and 5:21. Whoever killed her had to use those eleven minutes to get her moved. And Abby was using those same eleven minutes to get to the control room—he was out in the hall at the same time.'' She reached across the bar to grab a couple of napkins, but John-the-Romanian met her halfway and stuffed a stack in her hand. ''Then, today, we have the nerve gas. The canister was attached to Abby's skate last night. And I think it was meant to take him out because of something he saw during those eleven minutes.''

''But,'' I interrupted, ''two things are wrong with that. One, I didn't see anything.''

Ike gave me a look that said I was just too lazy to figure out what I saw.

''Two,'' I went on, ignoring the look, ''maybe the nerve gas was meant to do what it actually did—evacuate the building.''

''Why do you say that?'' Ike asked, putting down her fork.

''Because maybe the killer wanted to retrieve the print and that's the only way he could get it before it was taken away

on the truck. The set of Roman Nights was already dismantled when we were up there together and our gunperson had
to have seen that—it was ready to be trucked out to the hin-
terlands. The killer had to act during the day, today, which
would be bad timing from his point of view, because that's
when the soap opera venue is full of people. Ergo, he gets rid
of the people.''

Ike made a face. ''Why didn't he just take the picture
when he was up there last night, when we saw the gun
shadow from the Costume Box?''

''Because,'' I said, on a note of triumph, ''because he, or
she, couldn't take it out of the building then; and he, or she,
also didn't want to be caught carrying it around with him.
Or her. English needs some new pronouns.''

''You can always call the killer 'X,''' John-the-Romanian
suggested.

''No thanks,'' I said. ''I was never any good at algebra.
Anyway, maybe he, or she, *had to attend a staff meeting*
that same night on the twenty-seventh floor and didn't want
to show up carrying this print.''

John-the-Romanian, who must have entered thousands
of conversations-in-progress, seemed to be holding his own,
picking up the salient points. ''Who was at the staff meeting?'' he asked.

Ike looked off into the dim middle distance. ''Me, Abby,
Othello Armitage, Joe Ayles, Hannah Van Stone, and Noel
Heavener.'' She stared some more at something that wasn't
in the cafe. ''And we also know that Lourdes Ramirez was
in the building all night.''

''Yeah,'' I said. ''Being paid to lie for Hannah.''

''What?'' Ike said, returning her gaze to All-Souls.

''Hannah practically told me that she was going to pay
Lourdes to come up with an alibi.''

''My goodness,'' Ike murmured. ''What a nasty trick to
teach someone new to this country. Hannah will make
Lourdes an American in no time.''

''Yeah, she can pass her citizenship test as soon as she
cashes Hannah's check and bribes the INS proctor.''

"Well, with Lourdes in the building last night, that's Fillingeri's list. No, wait. Satan Brown, but he wasn't even in the city. However, Fred Loring was there overnight as always. You saw him, right?"

"Right." I swallowed Mahicado the wrong way and coughed. I took a drink of ginger ale. "Pardon me for mentioning this, but there was another interesting person in the building overnight. Captain Dennis Fillingeri." I took another drink. "Just thought I'd mention it."

Ike rolled her eyes. "Yeah, and he also rigged your skate with nerve gas to evacuate the building. Nerve gas to evacuate the building! You shouldn't be allowed to think, Abby."

John-the-Romanian poured himself a glass of orange juice and snagged a cherry from the lazy Susan beside the napkins. "I gotta say, Abby, I agree with Ike. Somebody puts nerve gas on your skate, who's to say it won't kill you? If I had to bet, I'd say it would."

Ike nodded vigorously. "Abby, if I hadn't been in your office, you would never have noticed the canister. You would have skated blithely away to your painful death. Therefore, your evacuation theory is baloney."

Before she could see it coming, I planted a big, smacking kiss on her cheek. "You saved my life, Ike." I winked at John-the-Romanian. "Correct me if I'm wrong, John, but if we were in China, wouldn't that obligate Ike to go to bed with me? Isn't that how it works? Isn't there an old Chinese proverb?"

He grinned enthusiastically. "Something like that. I'll tell you what, Abby. You get Ike into bed any time during the next twelve months and I'll nail another plaque to the bar."

Ike snorted inelegantly. "This isn't China."

John-the-Romanian smiled and walked away to take a drink order from a man at the other end of the bar who was waving his glass like it was a flag.

"Abby," Ike said, pushing her empty plate forward to make room on the bar for her elbows, "go over it again. What did you see during those eleven minutes?"

"A big, fat nothing. I'm tired of saying it over and over again. I'm sorry, but I saw nothing. I wish somebody would believe me."

Ike put her forehead down against her wrists. "What about motive?"

"What about it?"

"Don't be so dense. Who had one?"

"Hannah."

"She didn't do it."

"Have it your way." I felt like putting my head down on her wrists. "Noel."

"What's his motive?"

"He was afraid of Connie. Thought she'd get his job next."

"Noel was probably right. That's the way the wind is blowing. Younger, better-looking anchors. No reporting experience necessary. No qualifications that are more than skin-deep."

"Noel never had any qualifications," I said. "He's always been a reader."

"He came out of the radio school of broadcasting—unload the melodious tones and lull the audience. Having a great voice was a qualification then."

"Okay, well, there's Othello, speaking of people who came out of the good old days of radio. And he has a key to the back door of the Emerald City. I like that in a murder suspect."

Ike rubbed her forehead back and forth across her wrists. "Why would he kill Connie? He wanted her to lead the way into the shiny new age of information broadcasting. Plus he'd just spent a fortune on promoting her."

"Maybe she was leading the way into her shiny bed-chamber with men he didn't approve of, meaning other than himself. Jealousy's a powerful motive. I oughta know. I'd like to kill Dennis Fillingeri. I'd like to kill him a few times, in fact."

She raised her head from her wrists and gave me a smol-dering look. "Leave Dennis out of this, will you? In fact, leave jealousy out while you're at it." She returned her forehead to her wrists. "No, leave it in. I'm glad you're jealous. Serves you right, you lousy cad."

"I'm not a cad. I'm a lousy two-timer."

She drew a sigh that raised her shoulders and tightened the white bodysuit across her breasts. "You got that right, Abagnarro, you lousy two-timer. Let's not talk about you. What about Lourdes? What kind of motive could she possibly have?"

"No clue. Unless Connie was threatening to send her home. Maybe Lourdes knew who was going in and out of Connie's bedroom door and was threatening to tell the big guy, the guy who writes the paychecks. So Connie was going to pack her off home to Mexico, and that pissed Lourdes off."

"Don't be a sap. Killing Connie wouldn't keep Lourdes in the U.S. The only way I can see that Lourdes would have killed Connie is if she simply lost her temper. I've never met anyone as out of control as Lourdes. What about Joe Ayles?"

"Joe's not even on Fillingeri's list."

"He's on mine. We still don't know why he couldn't be found that night, and he's probably got a key to the loading dock door, too."

"Joe? He said he was asleep. On motive, you've got me. If I'm just taking a wild-ass guess, it could be he wanted to get through the bedroom door and there was already somebody standing there. I don't know."

"Somebody like Fred?"

"I doubt it. If Fred knows anything about bedroom doors, he must have taken a carpentry course."

Ike sighed again and sat up. She looked at her watch. "We'd better roll. Got your skates?"

"In my backpack. My old skates."

"We can't skate all the way. "We'd never make it in time. Why don't we get a taxi to, say, City Hall, and skate the rest of the way? I've had zero aerobic exercise today. That could be what's wrong with my energy level."

I signaled John-the-Romanian for the check, signed it to my tab, and slid the framed Dalí print under my arm.

"I gotta tell you, Abby," John-the-Romanian said, "your tab's up to four hundred eighty-nine dollars. You're getting in deep water again."

I tapped the brass plaque. "I'm working on it."

"Well, if somebody's after you with nerve gas, you may not be able to pay it off. Take care of yourself, huh?"

Ike laughed. "You're all heart, John."

"I know."

I handed Ike the spaghetti and we left. We walked to West End Avenue and grabbed a cab headed downtown.

We used to do a lot of fooling around in the backseats of cabs. It was kind of a game, to see how far we could go without the driver getting wise. So, my first impulse was to reach for Ike's thigh after I gave the cabbie our destination, but I reined in my temptation by keeping a grip on the frame.

"Abby?"

I glanced over and saw that Ike was stroking the Tupperware absently. "What are you doing to that thing?" I asked.

She lowered her eyes and seemed surprised that her hands were so busy. "Nothing." Her hands were still. "Abby, I may not have found anything as titillating as that print, but I did go over to Connie's apartment this afternoon. And I talked to her maid. Connie was at the Tonys Monday night, but her maid didn't know who with. So I went down to the St. James and bribed them to show me their guest list. Connie's name wasn't on it. She must've used one of the few complimentary passes, but it was no dice trying to find out if she was escorted or if she went alone or who she got the pass from." Ike wriggled around on the seat to face me. "But nobody goes alone to the Tonys, do they?"

"I don't think so." The cab was clipping through the deepening shadows on West End, and I stared out at the Hudson. The apartment towers over on the Jersey shore looked like dominoes: small, black, and neatly stacked. Ike was right about how few complimentary passes the American Theater Wing gives out. Therefore, I *knew* who Connie's date had been, and I *knew* whose complimentary passes they had used, as surely as if I'd seen them going into the St. James with my own eyes. I didn't know if Joe Ayles had offered or if Connie had connived, but they had gone together or I was not the most accomplished tango artist in Manhattan. I also did not know if, in addition to courting Othello Armitage, Connie had been helping Joe Ayles warm his sheets at night, but I did know that Ike was not going to like my conclusion, mainly because she was not going to like my inside information on the tickets. "Ike, my dear, about those passes to the Tonys."

"Yeah?"

"They were mine."

"What?"

"But I gave them away."

"You gave away tickets to the Tonys?"

"I gave them away so I could dance with you Monday night."

Her breathing was coming in irregular spurts. "You . . . you . . . you had tickets to the Tonys and you callously gave them away . . . so we could compete in a tango contest? Are you nuts? Have you gone totally around the bend?"

I decided to affect ignorance. "Oh. Would you have liked to go? I didn't think you'd want to spend that much time in my company sitting down."

"I'd spend time with Godzilla to go to the Tonys, you slimeball. You gave your tickets to that unconscionable bimbo?"

"I did not give my tickets to Connie." I shifted the print on my knees and tried to look indifferent. "I gave them to Little Joe."

"Oh, that's just great!"

"Calm down, Ike. It's just an awards show. We always used to make fun of them when we watched on TV."

"Watching the Tonys on a tiny tube in your living room is not the same as watching them from the audience, an audience composed entirely of the New York theater's movers and shakers." She folded her arms across her chest and looked pained.

Both of us faced forward as the cab made the left onto 14th Street and headed toward Broadway. Silence reigned, but not the fun kind of silence that used to characterize our taxi rides through Manhattan. It was a long ride down Broadway.

Ike finally broke the silence as the cab pulled over to the curb outside City Hall. "Do you have any money?" she asked coldly.

I grimaced, she pulled some bills out of her pocket and shoved them into the dish, and we got out of the cab. It was getting dark, and the streets were empty. Our cab was the only car in sight.

"You want I to wait?" the driver asked, in a thick Ukrainian accent. "Thirty dollars, ten minutes, I wait, you come back, thirty dollars."

"Vodka," Ike said, culling from her thin Russian vocabulary. "*Das Vadanya. Olga Korbut. Catherine the Great. Blyad.*"

On the last word, he pulled away from the curb with a quick, angry jerk of the steering wheel and authoritative pressure on the gas pedal.

"That wasn't very nice," I said. "Of either of you. You were both looking for a victim."

Ike sat down on the low iron railing that borders the grass of City Hall Park. She tugged her skates from her backpack, thrust the Tupperware tube in their place, and pushed her sneakers off by rubbing the backs against the sidewalk. I sat down beside her, looked around for a place to put the frame, found nothing promising, and dumped it on the sidewalk while I got ready to skate.

When she had her skates on, she stood and waited. "I'm sorry, Abby." Her voice was soft. "They were your tickets. You had every right to do what you wanted with them. It isn't like I've been so superfriendly lately that you'd just automatically think I'd want to go with you."

"That's for sure," I grunted, bending to tie my laces.

"How'd you get tickets in the first place?"

"Carol Channing gave them to my mother."

"Oh."

Something nagged at a corner of my brain. When I realized what it was, I could have kicked myself. After all, this was a theater conversation of sorts. "Ike," I said, "did you get the part in *Hamlet?*"

"Yes. We start rehearsal in two weeks."

"I'm sorry I didn't ask right away."

"That's okay. We were thinking about other things."

"Congratulations, Ike. You've waited a long time for this break."

"Thanks."

I stood, gave her a brotherly hug, bent to retrieve the print from the sidewalk, and we rolled down Broadway. The streets were practically empty, except for an occasional private car—no taxis, only a couple of buses at that time of the evening. After about seven o'clock, the city south of Canal Street is as close to a ghost town as New York ever gets: even the most maniacal financiers and politicians have given up for the day and gone home, except for the few who have stayed behind to kill themselves—and they're not out on the streets.

We skated the eight blocks to Wall Street, using the middle of Broadway for the most part, because streets are cleaner and more reliable than sidewalks in Manhattan, and it was a rare treat to be able to use them freely. I leaned forward on my skates, loose at the knees, slipped the hand that was holding the print high onto my hip, and kept my other arm tucked to my side. We skated fast, a great workout, and it was exhilarating to skate for pure speed without an eye to traffic and other moving obstacles. We swung left onto Wall Street at Trinity Church, no longer the filthy "Black Widow of Broadway" now that it's had a facial, and we were in the Canyons—the dark, narrow, and usually windy chasms whose steep cliff walls are the office hives of the Financial District.

Rollerblades are much quieter than roller skates, but even so, our wheels at that speed created a whirring, liquid sound that echoed through the Canyons as we whooshed past the stocky (no pun intended) gray edifice of the New York Stock Exchange and the ponderous stone steps of Federal Hall.

We flew around the corner into William Street and slowed in front of the brick and brass facade of the Museum of the

Surreal, which is housed in what used to be Fisherman's
Bank, four stories high and black with the centuries-long
caress of dirty air. Lights were on inside the museum, shining in dull gold tones through the tall, narrow, heavily
barred windows.

There was a brass rail bisecting the fifteen steps up to the
double doors that were themselves intricately laced with
brass fittings. We climbed the stairs on opposite sides of the
rail, doing an awkward skate-walk called the "herringbone." Ike found a doorbell and gave it a long push. We sat,
took off our skates, put on civilian footwear, and were re-
warded for our fast timing when Abel Chu opened the door
just as we both stood.

"You're right on time," he said. "Welcome to our house
of dreams, fantasies, and the inconceivable."

TWENTY-TWO

WE STEPPED ACROSS the highly polished and refractive oak floor of the cozy entrance foyer and, passing through a low oak-beamed doorway, stopped under the small blue dome of the renowned "Flower Rotunda," whose ceiling sparkled with thousands of gilded cornflowers painted on a pale azure vault of plaster that was ribbed by oak supports. Even the oaken radii of the dome glinted with the tiny flowers outlined in gold. The dome was lit from below with muted yellow electric bulbs that were incorporated into the design of the candle sconces that had served to illuminate the dome when the building was erected by Dutch craftsmen in 1701. I'd read the museum's brochure before Monday's show, and it was nice to have the facts at my fingertips.

"I never grow tired of this charming antique," the curator said, taking his right hand out of the pocket of his black sport coat to make a circular gesture that encompassed the walls and dome of the rotunda. "I do not think the Surrealists would be disturbed to find their works juxtaposed against the background of this eighteenth-century flight of fancy. The principal philosophical mistake the Surrealists made, after all, was supposing that their generation was the first to hunger after the liberation of imagination. The emotional and intellectual force that created this spread of fantastic cornflowers was at least as ambitious as those that created the works on display beyond this pleasure dome."

"It's beautiful," Ike breathed, pirouetting to take in the endless and random parade of flowers that circled the dome without beginning, without end, seemingly without even a thought to order. "I've never seen anything like it."

His black hair falling across his smooth forehead as he executed a quick bow, Abel Chu smiled to himself, self-consciously. "That's what I meant to say: it's beautiful."

Behind his wire-rimmed glasses, his dark eyes glimmered, reflecting his obvious delight in Ike's response.

"Abby, look! It's like standing under a sky of flowers. It's impossible and perfect."

"We should have brought a camera down here for Monday's show and done a remote from under this dome," I said with real warmth. "This room is worth the price of admission, much better than standing around looking at a bunch of spooky..." I caught myself and stopped guiltily.

Chu laughed out loud. "Mr. Abagnarro, you, perhaps, do not admire Surrealist art?"

"Well," I said, and, having already embarrassed myself, I added, "you have to admit those paintings you brought to the studio the other day have nothing to do with life as we know it on this planet."

"Abby's a philistine," Ike said, laughing.

"But he's an honest philistine," Chu said, combing his fingers through his straight black hair. He turned to me. "Mr. Abagnarro, would you say that this rotunda is an accurate reflection of life as we know it?"

I gazed at the rounded perfection of the flowered dome. "I know what you're trying to say. But this flowered dome makes more sense than"—I offered him the framed print—"this."

Chu took the print and scanned the surface of the picture of four watches on a landscape that was at once bleak and luminous. Three of the watches were limp, their blue faces draped over what seemed to be incidental aspects of the foreground; the fourth timepiece was red and firm, but it was being eaten by fat and shiny black ants.

"Dalí claimed that a piece of soft cheese inspired this painting one night when he had a headache," Chu said. "Camembert," he added, with a touch of gentle humor and a shy smile.

"I can believe that," I said. "Only I would have thought he had worse than a headache."

"Shall we look at the real thing?" Chu asked. Carrying the framed print at his side, he led the way through another oak-beamed door on the opposite side of the rotunda. We

followed him into a long, narrow room whose walls were
lined with paintings. "These on the right are by René Magritte, who some say was more rational than Dalí." Chu
paused before a painting that presented a streetscape at
night, with lighted windows, a glowing street lamp, and
midnight shadows, but the sky was as bright as day, pale
blue and fretted with puffy white clouds. "This is typical of
Magritte's work. It's argumentative, presenting two realities side by side, almost as though they offer a choice, like a
good mystery, an intriguing puzzle waiting to be solved.
Dalí's paintings are not so forthright, so clear in their options."

"He would have gotten a kick out of the three umpires."

"Excuse me?"

"Never mind."

Ike trailed behind us as we crossed the room. She seemed
to be ensnared by the Magritte paintings, and Chu waited
patiently in the far doorway until she caught up with us.

The next room was huge, and it was given over completely to Dalí, but my eye quickly fastened on his most famous painting, placed in the center of the left wall, under a
burst of track lighting. It looked exactly the same to me as
the print Chu clasped at his side.

Surrounded by larger canvases in this room, *The Persistence of Memory* seemed smaller than it had in the studio on
Monday morning when it had been propped up on an easel. Chu and I crossed immediately to stand before the
painting, but once again Ike was caught by other works, and
we waited for her.

"I've always wondered why museums don't put protective glass over a painting this valuable," I said, bringing my
fingers within a couple of centimeters of the canvas. "Aren't
you afraid that people will touch it all the time and ruin it?"

"People who come to art museums have very good manners," Chu said. "And they come to see paintings, not
glass." He grinned, a conspiratorial grin. "And when we are
open, there are always two guards on duty in this room.
Very big guards with bad manners."

Ike moved between us and gazed at the painting. "How can you be sure that this one is the real thing?"

"I can authenticate it by several esoteric means, all of which I have used this evening before your arrival, but there really is no question. Not only do we have the archival evidence that traces the travels of this painting, but also the brush strokes are unmistakable."

"I don't see any brush strokes," Ike said, peering at the surface of the painting. "It's as smooth as glass."

"That's part of the Surrealist paradox, to make the painting seem so *real,* almost like a photograph, that its unreal subject matter takes on an authority over the actual— becomes surreal, superreal. But, believe me, there are brush strokes. There is no question."

Ike gestured at the framed print. "Mr. Chu, is there anything unusual about this copy?"

Chu lifted the print and held it beside the original. "An uncommonly good photograph. That's all it is."

In their frames they still looked identical to me, and I said so.

Too polite to call me an art ass in so many words, Chu extracted an extremely fine magnifying glass from his coat pocket and offered it to me. The glass was set in a golden rectangle, and the handle felt like onyx, heavy and cool and smooth.

"Hold the glass half an inch or so from the canvas," he said. "You will see thick canyons and jagged escarpments and sharp valleys and angular plateaus. It should resemble a desert disturbed by earthquakes: dry, cracked, deeply gouged by the elements, buckled by cataclysmic forces."

I help up the glass and peered through it, shutting one eye, and sure enough, there was the desert.

"Now, look at this print," Chu said, holding the framed imposter under the light.

I looked. What I saw was a shallow and uniformly dimpled plane, its smooth regularity in stark contrast to the messily chaotic microcosmic world of the Dalí painting. I handed the glass to Ike, and she performed the study I had completed.

"Pretty convincing," I said.

"There never was any doubt," Chu said mildly, dismissing the print. I don't know how he did it, but Chu made his firm pronouncements sound almost like sweet apologies. "The very authentic painting you see on the wall is on loan from the Museum of Modern Art. Their security arrangements, and ours, are very good. It's utterly impossible that we would have a bogus Dalí here and not know it."

"Are you saying that the museums are theft-proof?" Ike asked.

"No, not at all. I'm sure there are very clever thieves who could rob us blind. What is not possible is that we could remain in ignorance of such a theft."

Ike jammed her fists into the pockets of her shorts. She took a turn around the room, absently admiring the paintings. When she returned to our position before *The Persistence of Memory,* she said to Chu, "Can you think of any reason that Concepción Candela would regard this painting as a potential news story? A big news story?"

"That it is on loan from MOMA to this museum is news in the art community, but, of course, the larger community would not care about that."

"Well, what would make it news?"

Chu smiled. I was beginning to wonder if he was always happy. He certainly owned an eclectic collection of smiles. "The destruction of the painting—by fire, or vandalism." Self-deprecating smile. "A clever forgery that garnered millions of dollars." Wavering grin that wrapped around his lips like mist on ivy. "If, as you suggest, someone had stolen the painting." Mournful half-curve that gave him the dolorous and sweet otherworldly distance of a Madonna. "If we discovered something odd about the painting itself. Those would be newsworthy things." Flat smile that signaled he was finished, like "the end" written across the lower third of his face.

"What do you mean, something odd about the painting?" Ike asked.

"Let me see." Chu's flat smile broadened and took on dimension. "If the painting concealed another painting, or the *Communist Manifesto*, something like that—which is definitely not the case. Or if we discovered the Dalí had not, indeed, painted it—if, for example, his wife, Gala, had painted it. Or if we discovered that the paint is not paint but Camembert cheese. Those would be oddities worth reporting."

Ike pursed her lips, but she didn't smile. "What would make that print newsworthy?"

Chu smiled ruefully, yet another fresh example from his assortment. "I can think of nothing. Unless, and here I am letting my imagination liberate itself, as it were, there is a code to a secret military complex embedded in the structure of the photograph's grains." He giggled. "You see, it's really quite fantastic to imagine anything worthy, much less newsworthy, about that print. It's just a print. Worth, I would say, twenty-five dollars."

"Darn," Ike muttered. "I guess Connie dreamed it."

In addition to his smiles, Chu's utter lack of curiosity about the purpose of our visit struck me as, well, surreal. Apparently if it didn't look like a desert rearranged by an earthquake or if it wasn't inspired by Camembert, he wasn't interested. But he was sure nice.

"Mr. Chu," Ike said, "have you checked the other seven works you brought to our show on Monday morning?"

"Oh, yes. Safe and sound, each one. There really can be no doubt about them at all."

We thanked Chu and he showed us to the door; he smiled at us tenderly and with fatherly approval when we stopped to drink in the Flower Rotunda once more.

When we were on the outside, we could hear him sliding the bolts on the double doors, and the click of the alarm system being engaged must have been audible from the sidewalk. That suggested to me that Chu slept on the premises. Nobody would be using that door again tonight.

We sat on the steps to get equipped for skating and to accustom our eyes to the darkness after the museum's bright interior.

"Let's head over to the World Trade Center," I said, looking at the lighted dial of my watch. It was ten minutes past nine. "We can probably find a cab there for the Windows on the World traffic." Ike and I had often wanted to dine there, in the highest eatery in Manhattan, on the 107th floor of the World Trade Center, but we always lost the impulse because after the impulse comes the three-month waiting period for reservations. We're both instant-gratification eaters.

I gave Ike my hand and helped her to her feet, and out of the corner of my eye, down the street to my right, I caught a piece of the darkness sliding out of the rest of the darkness. A small car detached itself from the gloom at the corner of William and Wall Street; it rolled toward us without its lights. *Not a promising sign,* I thought. Good and honest cars show their lights at night.

As the car neared, I quickly pulled Ike into the tiny recess provided by the museum's door.

Three things happened simultaneously, in the space of maybe two seconds. The car pulled even with the museum, a sudden burst of reddish-orange light erupted from the car and was gone instantly, and a deep thump echoed in the panels of the door. I jerked my head to the side and was just able to make out a ragged, splintered hole in the door. The driver was using a gun with a silencer.

Another burst of red light flared from the car. I could feel Ike react to the splintering "thwack" on the surface of the door between our heads. She ducked at the same time I ducked, and I squeezed her hand.

Our options were limited. We couldn't just stand there and ring the bell again, waiting to be admitted while we dodged bullets. I held the framed print out and in front of us, gave Ike's hand another squeeze, hoping she would follow my lead, and pushed off down the stairs, toward the car. It was a huge risk, but we were low on choices.

I don't think there was another shot as we went bouncing down the stairs on our blades, gathering speed as we flew through the air. I heard the car's engine and then the tires squealed, speeding away into the darkness.

We sailed onto the sidewalk and circled together to a halt.

"What the hell?" Ike shouted. "Why didn't they kill us?"

"Maybe they didn't want to damage this," I replied, lowering the print to waist-level. "Let's get out of here."

I hung onto her hand and we leaned onto our edges, building speed quickly and taking the turn onto Wall Street at about forty miles per hour, whizzing past the corner so fast we created a draft I could hear echoing off the buildings.

At the end of the canyon, the dark and narrow spire of Trinity Church loomed, a blackness upon the blackness of night. And also at the end of the canyon, the car reappeared beside the graveyard on the right and turned silently into Wall Street. The car crept down the block toward us, passing the stock exchange without its headlights. There was nowhere to go but back.

With another desperate hope, I signaled Ike with the pressure of my hand. She never missed a beat as we turned suddenly, spinning together so fast the darkness blurred, a wild and frightening high-speed trick we'd never tried before, and we skated like demons back to William Street. A chunk of stone shot into the street over our heads as we rounded the corner.

"He's shooting the goddamn buildings!" Ike screamed. "God, I hope that's what he's aiming for."

"I don't think so!" I yelled.

Together we hurtled down the center of William Street. A burst of nearly silent gunfire churned up the pavement as we took the turn into Beaver Street, and Ike stumbled on a fragment, a fractional loss of momentum that almost took us down. We were hanging onto our balance on our edges, almost out of control.

Regaining some measure of balance from sheer forward motion, we raced west on Beaver. I did not look back as I heard the car's tires scream around the corner behind us, not even a second later when I heard the shrill, ragged blast of sound that must have been the car spinning out of control and clipping a building. The sound of our skates and the

wind roaring in my ears combined to distort the noises made
by the car. But I could tell it was still in pursuit.

As we flew across Broadway toward the trees of Bowling
Green, I was hit. A sharp, tearing heat flashed across my left
shoulder, and I nearly dropped the print. I don't remember
crying out, but I must have, because, an instant later, Ike
signaled with her hand that she would lead. She took us
around the little park, on a quick jog to the north, and then
down the other side so we could get a look through the trees.
It was too dark to see the car, but I saw another burst of red
light, and leaves were sheared off some lower branches of
the trees and showered down over the park.

My upper left arm felt like it was on fire, but I held on and
Ike steered us south to State Street, past the U.S. Custom
House, a hulking mansion in dark gray granite. The four
white limestone monuments in the front seemed to spring
out of the night at us as we flashed by the building.

The lights of the South Ferry Terminal Building shot up
before us at the foot of State Street, and Ike signaled to pick
up speed. I must have been slowing down without knowing
it.

We skidded over gravel and under the belly of the terminal, through the parking lot. The Staten Island Ferry was
just pulling away from the slip. The chain was already up
across the deck on the lower level, the car level. The boat
was too far out for us to make it. We were almost out of
skating surface, trapped at the end of Manhattan.

TWENTY-THREE

ANOTHER VOLLEY of bullets tore into a concrete pillar on my left, sending showers of dust and tiny scraps of debris flying into my face.

"Hang on, Abby," Ike warbled, and I could hear her terror. She squeezed my right hand, gave it a tug, and we put on a final burst of speed, sailing up into the air off the pavement, up and over dark water, over eight feet of open space, and landed on the back of the boat, our skates screaming on the steel deck.

"Duck!" she yelled, and we slid under the chain and into the bowels of the ferry.

We were going so fast that, even in a crouch, we didn't stop until we reached the forward end of the vast and dark and nearly empty auto deck. We stood and breathed.

"Thank God," Ike managed to say, bending over her knees and flexing the tension out of her arms and knees.

"Somebody's sure pissed at us." I was breathing hard, taking in the old exhaust fumes coating the walls of the deck.

"Let's get upstairs into some fresh air, Abby."

The Staten Island Ferry is the best place to be if you really want to see Manhattan at night, especially if a car is chasing you and it just missed the boat. As you sail farther away from the island, more and more buildings pop up out of the ground, and the city seems to build itself little by little from the Wall Street area northward, just the way it did over the course of history. You can't even see the Empire State Building until you're about ten minutes into New York Harbor, so that's about one minute for every thirty-year span of historical time. The city unfolds its spectacular skyline like a pop-up toy, and it's such a compelling show that it's easy to forget that there are other famous sights in the

harbor, possible to miss even the shining beacon of the
Statue of Liberty until the ferry is almost on top of her.

The ferry was not crowded, not that sharing the boat
would have made any difference to us, because not even a
tourist would want to get involved with a couple skating on
deck if one of them was bleeding from a fresh gunshot
wound, which I was.

We skated around the measly two cars on the vast lower
deck and once again used the herringbone walk to climb
steps. Ike went first and held my hand. When we were top-
side, we skated in through the doors to the upper deck, past
the long wooden, high-backed benches that extend the
length of the ferry like pews in a particularly large church.
We skated the length of the boat and, at the rear, we collapsed onto a bench and caught our breath as we watched
the skyline taking shape.

"It's like old times," I said. "Remember how we used to
ride this old tub at night when we first started dating?"

She didn't give me a snappy answer. From the look on her
face, even in that gloom, I could tell that her memories were
as nice as mine.

Ike arose after a few minutes, as the Chrysler Building
reared its silver shoulders on the skyline, and she went to the
ladies' room to acquire and soak some paper towels. When
she returned, she smelled semi-industrial. With her help, I
stripped off my backpack and shirt. I leaned my head
against the rock-hard back of the bench. I'll never understand how people can sleep on the ferry.

Ike sponged my wound efficiently and quickly, but then
she's been on battlefields and I wasn't the first casualty she'd
treated. There was a respectable amount of blood for what
turned out to be a small, jagged scratch. My left arm felt like
there were bells inside, jangling spastically to some erratic
tune being played along my bones.

"Did you ever get a look at him?" I asked, not raising my
head from its berth on the hard wood.

"No. I don't even know what kind of car it was."

"Me neither. Except that it was small, probably Euro-
pean."

She took nail scissors from the front pocket of her back-pack and started snipping at the sleeve of my bloody shirt.

"You don't have to cut the shirt," I whined. "I paid sixty bucks for that at Bloomingdale's."

"You mean you charged it. Shut up; I'm making a bandage."

I cooperated while she did things to my shoulder. I knew the wound was too slight to warrant such a fuss, but it was very pleasant to have her hands on me. I closed my eyes while she tied a strip of the sleeve around my shoulder. When she was finished, I opened my eyes and looked down along my chest. There was a drop of bright red blood in my navel, and at first I thought I'd been hit there, too, but I quickly realized the drop was merely the pitiful runoff of the shoulder wound, hardly serious enough to use as pressure on Ike's sympathy gland.

"Will I live?"

"To a ripe old age," she said, gathering up the remains of my shirt and restoring the scissors to her pack. There was a thin streak of blood on her pretty white sleeve.

I put my right arm around her and drew her against my chest. We sat like that as the boat drew even with the Statue of Liberty, her torch lit up brighter than a hundred TV stage lights and her drapes gleaming white against the night sky.

"Ike," I said, rubbing my palm rhythmically and slowly against the soft fabric covering her arm, "I never told you this, but I used to fantasize about growing old with you, to a ripe old age." I rested my cheek against her soft hair. "I always pictured you as a kind of grumpy but very pretty old lady, chewing me out when I forgot to do something—like pay my bar tab." I leaned back a little so I could look at her face. "I'm really sorry about the way things turned out."

"Me, too." She sighed and nestled her shoulder against my armpit. "I used to do the same, only I pictured you as a lazy old geezer who took a lot of naps. But you always looked as graceful as Fred Astaire when you were asleep, and even when you were ninety, you were an awesome lover."

"That's nice."

"Yeah. It was nice."

You're not supposed to stay on the boat when it pulls into the slip at Staten Island; you're supposed to get off and, if you want to return to Manhattan, reboard the boat through the Staten Island entrance. The rule is designed partly to prevent homeless people from thinking they've found fairly decent lodgings for only fifty cents per night, and to get them up on their feet so they don't turn the boat into a floating hostel.

It still amazes me that the best ride in New York is so cheap. And that we don't just let the homeless sleep, instead of waking them up so they can get back on the boat to resume their naps. Fifty panhandled cents per person for a partial solution to the homeless problem seems like a big civic bargain to me. With suspicious types like Ike and me, the transit authorities should be glad for the relative safety of homeless passengers.

Since Ike and I had not paid any toll and were ferry outlaws anyway, we exempted ourselves from the rule and took our chances. Nobody paid any attention to us, maybe because we were not sound asleep. While the ferry was parked, Ike went to buy us a Coke from the ferry's snack bar. They were out of Coke, so we shared a carton of orange juice.

When we were under way again, heading back to Manhattan, I picked up the print from where it lay beside me on the bench. Some blood had dripped across the blue-and-brown landscape, and had dotted the limp watch hanging from the branch of the dead olive tree.

"Whatever this was worth, if anything, I don't think I've improved it," I said. "It looked better without the blood."

Ike sat up. "Give me that."

I handed her the print. If we hadn't been so busy running from bullets, we probably would have taken the thing apart sooner. Ike took out her nail scissors again and went to work on the four screws that held the frame together. In the process, she blunted the tips of the scissors and broke a nail, and she had to wrench the pieces of wood apart, but she finally got the print out of the frame. She held it stretched between her hands and waved it; the print was surprisingly thick and supple.

"Hello," she said. "This is a strange photograph." She bent forward, and the place she had warmed on my side by sitting so close was exposed to the night air. A chill danced over my skin, and I shivered.

She picked gently at the upper right corner of the print, lifting up a large-enough section to begin to peel it back. I could see that there was plastic under the print, some thin sheet that looked like ordinary Saran Wrap. And under the plastic was another picture.

Ike glanced at me over her shoulder, her eyebrows raised and her blue and green eyes enormous. She bent over the frame and peeled the Dalí print and the film of plastic back with infinite slowness, centimeter by centimeter. I sat up to watch the slow operation.

There wasn't anything complicated about the arrangement Ike found: rolled scraps of Scotch tape held the neat layering of plastic to the back of the print, and the whole thing was carefully pressed over a piece of canvas. By the time the Statue of Liberty was again visible through the port windows, we knew what was on the canvas, although Ike did not have to peel the entire print back for us to recognize the work.

"My, my," Ike marveled. "My, my, my."

"I'll be damned," I said.

"We've been fools, Abby. Cretins, dopes, and dum-dums. We don't know how to read plain English. Connie said in her note that she didn't have any training in art. But she said she recognized 'it' as soon as she saw it. What else could possibly have hit her over her thick head like that? Of course a total narcissist like an anchor would recognize her own portrait."

It was obviously Samantha Harris's most recent portrait study, and I was betting it had to be the real thing, because somebody had gone to a lot of trouble to hide it and to attempt to kill us for getting our hands on it. But if Ike was holding the real thing, what was hanging on the curving wall of the twenty-seventh-floor tube in the Emerald City?

"Ike, is this thing worth money?"

"If it's the original, it's worth a fortune. Harris is mostly known for her Abstract Expressionist work—"

I interrupted. "You mean splashes and squiggles?"

"Yes, you philistine, but, I was going to say, the NTB portraits are her only extant realistic work, as far as I know. The story is that she destroyed her early representational stuff when she joined the Abstract Expressionists like Jackson Pollock and Willem de Kooning. I've told you a million times that those Harris portraits are worth a king's ransom."

"Yeah, but you never think about something you see every day. I mean, we work with fantastically valuable cameras and we don't spend the night kowtowing to them." I stretched my legs out into the aisle, beginning to feel cramped. The benches on the Staten Island Ferry were not designed for tall people, with or without homes. "So Connie was killed because she recognized her own portrait. Meaning, on Monday after the show she recognized that the one hanging on the wall of the tube is a fake, which she would know because she would know how her own face looked in a recent portrait."

"And the real Dalí painting had nothing to do with it," Ike said, suddenly standing. I pulled my legs back and she skated across the floor to the window, gazing out at the retreating figure of the statue in the harbor. Ike stood there a couple of minutes. When she turned away from the harbor, she wasn't smiling in triumph because we had finally begun to unravel the motive, or part of it, for Connie's murder. In fact, the look on Ike's face suggested that she'd just received some bad news.

Ike skated back to our pew and slid onto the bench next to me. "But we still don't know who killed Connie or how she was drowned. You've gotta have some major water to drown somebody, like New York Harbor, or at the very least a decent bathtub. I don't think any of those sinks and plumbing whatnots in the soundstages are real, are they?"

I shook my head. "They're not connected to water. The only water on the twenty-eighth floor is in the toilets and bathroom sinks and the water fountain. Just like the twenty-seventh floor."

"And we don't know why she was put in the anchor chair."

"Or who's after us. Or should I say, after this painting, this Samantha Harris original."

"Abby, are you sure you didn't see *anything* during those eleven minutes?"

She started unlacing her skates.

"Jesus, I wish you'd stop asking. What are you doing?"

"Changing. You shouldn't skate when we reach Manhattan—you may open that scratch on your shoulder. I'm not at all cheery about my nursing skills. I don't want you to sue me for malpractice. I'll help you with your skates in a minute." She slipped her feet out of her skates and grabbed her backpack. "Abby, just try one more time. Try to remember if you saw anything. You must have."

I closed my eyes, resigned to another recital. "I stopped and looked at the portrait. I guess I was looking at the fake. Shows what I know about art. I actually got a little choked up admiring it." I opened my eyes, realizing that sleep was not all that far away.

"Maybe the murderer saw you staring at the fake." Ike dropped her sneakers on the floor and stepped into them. She hiked her right foot up on the bench to tie the shoe.

"Maybe."

"But I don't think that would be enough to make him go after you, which he did with the nerve gas—that was before we had the print in our possession, so he was definitely after you." She started on her other sneaker. "No, it couldn't be because you were seen looking at the fake. Lots of people looked at that phony portrait of Connie and didn't notice anything. You were the only one targetted with nerve gas."

"But stopping to look at the fake painting was the only interesting thing I did. After that I walked past the talent offices, and..."

"Tell me what you saw. Everything."

Reluctantly I closed my eyes again. I was drowsy, but I tried to call up the memory of that eleven-minute stroll. "Noel's office door was open. It was just, you know, clean, like it always is. His computer, his Parsons table, his tie rack, nothing special."

"Then what?"

"Then Hannah's office. The smoke. That's what made you decide she couldn't be the murderer."

"Then what?"

"The Green Room. The guitarist strumming. Nobody else in there. The smell of fresh-brewed coffee. Connie's briefcase, that red eelskin thing. Her glasses." I rubbed my eyes and opened them. The Manhattan skyline was winking out from the north, building by building. Soon there would be only the dark wall of structures surrounding Battery Park, the remainder of the skyline having dropped out of sight behind the buildings close to the harbor. I yawned.

"Don't fall asleep now, Abby." Ike smiled encouragingly at me and took a peek at my makeshift bandage. "Go on. After the Green Room. Then what?"

"Then nothing. I went to the control room."

She shook her head and blew out her breath. "I can see why you're sick of telling it. There's nothing to tell."

"You think I don't know that?"

She put her chin on her knuckles. "Maybe it was something else you saw, not during those eleven minutes."

"Well, that only includes the rest of my life. We'd better get started if you're interested in co-writing my autobiography."

"Maybe it was something you saw on the monitor." She scooted off the bench and squatted beside me, untying the laces of my skates.

I forced myself to concentrate. "The only thing I saw was dead Connie. And her jacket was all wrong." I thought a minute. "And I sent a note to Lourdes, giving her a mild scold."

"Okay. What about what you saw in the studio?"

"I saw the same things you did."

"What about after?"

"God, I don't know. Nothing."

"It has to be something, Abby."

She had my skates off and was taking my sneakers from my backpack.

"Ike, I can't think. The cops came. No, wait. Noel got there first."

"And?"

"And nothing. He just got there and said something goofy."

"What'd he say?"

I swallowed. "He wanted to know if Connie and I were having what he called 'a love rehearsal.' You know how strange he is."

"Did Noel touch the body?"

"Never went near it."

"Then what?"

"The cops. And Hannah came in." I sat up suddenly. "Ike, Hannah had her makeup on. Why would she have her makeup on? She'd have no reason to think she was going on the air."

Ike's hands came to rest on my shoes, which she had been tying. "Gosh. I wonder if that's it?" She finished tying the shoes and stood. She grabbed the Tupperware container and studied it. She opened the top and spilled the spaghetti onto the bench.

"What are you doing that for?" I demanded. "That's homemade."

"I hope some homeless person recognizes it as food." She cocked her head to one side. "It looks like broom straws." She took the Harris painting carefully by a corner, rolled it, and slid it gingerly into the container, pushing it down before she sealed the Tupperware. "We can't just carry this around like it was a cheap print. It's a Samantha Harris original. At least I think it is."

"You're derailing my train of thought. What about Hannah's makeup?"

"Abby, I have to stick by what I said about the cigarette smoke. Hannah may have been in makeup because she was hoping against hope, dreaming that some emergency would put her on the air. Maybe it was force of habit that made her do her face, just a pathetic gesture. Or, and I like this one, maybe she was wearing makeup as part of her campaign to make us all uncomfortable—you know, to rub it in what louses we were to take her off the air."

"You're awfully stubborn about that cigarette smoke, Ike."

"I am not." Her chin jutted out slightly. "I'm right."

"It has to be Hannah's makeup. There isn't anything else, Ike. Everything was so straightforward. The cops, Hannah being a bitch, me wishing you were there to hear her, the cops wanting the lights turned on, Noel stuffing his ties in his pocket, the security guards looking useless, then you on the intercom, and the emergency plane landing, and the police captain with two names."

"What ties?" she said. "Noel had more than one tie?"

"Yeah."

"Why?"

"Maybe he couldn't make up his mind." Then I corrected myself. "What passes for his mind."

"Go back a minute. You said you saw his tie rack in his office. Were there ties on it?"

I shook my head. "Empty."

Ike gazed at the front of the boat as it neared Manhattan. When she spoke, it was a monotone, like she was thinking out loud and her thoughts were so fragile they'd break if she hurried or changed her tone any. "He wore a brown suit that morning; I remember vividly because of the emergency landing of the Tell-Air plane. It's, like, imprinted on my memory. I can see Noel as clearly now as I saw him then on the control room monitors." She turned to face me. "Abby, Noel was wearing a blue tie with pink splashes. It was all wrong. It was a bad tie for that suit."

I met her eyes. "The two ties he had when he came into Studio 57. They were both way too flashy—one was the blue one he ended up wearing, and the other had green and yellow stripes on a gray background. Noel can't have meant to wear either one of those ties. And he would not have wrinkled them by stuffing them in his pocket. He's a goddamn anchor—if they get any part of broadcasting right, it's the part where they have to look good. What the hell was he doing with those awful ties?"

"Maybe," Ike said, her eyes sparkling, "maybe something happened to the tie he wore to work. Maybe he got something on it." Her eyebrows moved up and down like Groucho Marx's. "Like makeup. Maybe Noel had to ditch his tie after he drowned Connie and played dress up with her corpse."

"But that's what it comes down to, Ike, and where it always breaks down. *Nobody* could have drowned her. This is too weird: first the drowning, then the gun, then the nerve gas. There's too many weapons."

Ike put her hands in her hair and closed her eyes. "Nerve gas. Nerve gas. Atropine. Taboon. Iraqi Taboon. Soviet Taboon." She sounded like she was in a trance. "Drowning. Lungs. Breathing water into lungs. Taboon. Nerve gas shuts down the sympathetic nervous system. The antidote." She opened her eyes suddenly. "Abby, anybody who plays with nerve gas always carries the antidote. That's just a fact. The antidote is atropine, a drug like belladonna. In the absence of nerve gas, the antidote itself can be deadly. Atropine speeds up sympathetic nervous reactions." A victorious gleam showed in her eyes. "Atropine speeds up breathing. You hyperventilate like a son of a bitch if you inject yourself with atropine. You breathe so hard you *can't* breathe. Your mouth dries up. If somebody shot Connie with atropine, she could have drowned while drinking a glass of water. Her breathing would be so screwed up she'd inhale the water. Bingo." Ike waved her arm with a flourish. "That's how she was drowned."

"Why didn't the autopsy show that?"

"I bet it did. Or would. When they found Connie's lungs full of water, they were satisfied she drowned. Why look for something more esoteric? Besides, the way your system spazzes up with atropine is the same way it spazzes up when you drown. She would have been the perfect picture of drowning, because she did drown, and nobody would think of atropine. There'd be no reason to."

"You think the killer gave her the water after injecting her?"

"Probably told her it would make her feel better."

"And then brought her body to the studio. Why?"

"To get her as far away as possible from that print she must have discovered on the soundstage." Ike squirmed, and I found myself catching some of her excitement. "To paint a different picture of the murder. It was a set piece to distract everyone from the Candela portrait."

"How'd Connie know the print was up there in the first place? Why did she go up to the twenty-eighth floor?"

"She probably didn't know. All she knew was that her portrait was gone. And she knew that one of the prints was missing. And just maybe she was one of millions who watched the soap. Connie would spot the print and realize it shouldn't be on the set of *Meg's Children* because she herself was supposed to have that print in her packet. Or maybe she was up on the twenty-eighth floor for some other reason and she spotted the print. She could have found out where the print was a number of different ways. Nothing Connie figured out took any brains—everything she figured out had something to do with her personally. Good old Connie herself—her portrait, her print." Ike clapped her hands together and squeezed them, apparently to keep herself under control. I've seen her do that before many times when she was ready to nail a story. "The killer must've taken the print to cover and hide the portrait he had just stolen, thinking nobody would miss the print—it was just junk from a press kit. The portrait of Connie had only been in the building a few days. The killer must have taken it sometime after Monday's show. That's when Connie noticed the switch. That's what her note said. She noticed it on Monday."

I grabbed Ike's hands because she was squeezing them so hard the knuckles were turning white. "So," I said, "when she went to the soap operas to look at the print, she was just curious. The thief may have gone up to check on the print, or maybe Connie told him she was going up there. Or maybe she followed him. Then she caught him in the act, making the switch or doing something with the print, and she confronted him.'' Ike unfolded her fingers under mine. ''All of this was on Tuesday during the overnight. And he killed her. And her makeup would have been ruined by all the water spraying around because she would have been convulsing. He had to redo her face completely because the makeup in the Costume Box would never match what she was wearing. But I'll bet he didn't have to restyle her hair—probably just comb it into place. And he probably ruined her jacket with the mess, and that's why she was wearing that apple green thing. And he ruined his tie in the process.'' I picked up the Tupperware and considered its smooth, innocent plastic surface. ''A human life for this little thing.''

''I wonder if he had the atropine on him when he went up there.''

''I doubt it. Perhaps when she confronted him, he told her to stay put, that he'd explain how it was all a misunderstanding. That he'd be right back with something that would explain everything. That's when he got the atropine, and that's when she wrote the note.''

The ferry was closing the distance to its Manhattan slip rapidly. We walked to the forward deck.

''Think we'll have a greeting committee waiting for us?'' Ike asked.

''What can we do if there is?''

''Well, we can't ride this boat all night, that's for sure. You need to have your wound looked at by a doctor. Maybe you're supposed to have a tetanus shot or something. We'll get off, use the first phone in the terminal, and call 911. He won't shoot at us in the terminal.''

As the boat churned across the inky water and drew closer to Manhattan, I started watching the docking area nervously. When we were maybe ten yards out, I spotted a dark figure emerging from the side of the tall pilings. I did not think it was a transit worker.

I nudged Ike and she saw the same figure. We stood together on the deck, the breeze whipping around us, watching to see what the figure would do. Surely no one would shoot at the Staten Island Ferry, with a full complement of captain and crew getting ready to dock her.

When we were about five yards from the slip, a tiny flash of metal showed in the air, arcing against the black jumble of sky and buildings, and something was lobbed onto the deck and dropped at our feet, striking the deck with a metallic clink. We leapt back, away from it. In the spill of light from the wheelhouse, I could see what it was—a canister of nerve gas.

But this time the metal container was hissing.

TWENTY-FOUR

THERE WAS NO TIME to think. Not even a second. Nerve gas gives absolutely no margin for thinking—and a margin for error only to the very, very lucky.

I grabbed Ike and we went crashing over the side of the boat into the black, heaving water of New York Harbor.

My fear of the nerve gas was only slightly greater than my fear that we'd be crushed against the dock by the ferry. As we hit the water, I pulled Ike's arm with all my strength and dived. Thank God she's a great dancer; she followed my lead like we were in a ballroom, and we went deep.

I stroked wide to what I hoped was the west, away from the ferry's slip. It was black, blacker than night, under the water, where I couldn't make out even a shadow of the giant hull; there was nothing for my senses except the cold embrace of the water and, even in my terror, even struggling to hold my breath, the acrid smell of diesel fumes and grease.

We burst through the oily surface about three feet to the west of the ferry's slip, both of us gasping and choking. The boat's wake pounded over us and threw us against the slick and weathered wooden pilings, which I scraped with my already-sore shoulder. The walls were too slimy to provide a handhold, or any purchase at all, and we struggled against the water's wild action. The waves tossed us against the pilings again and again.

"Now we're even," Ike sputtered, over a trough in the buffeting force of the wake.

"What?" I shook water out of my ears.

"We're even. You saved my life. We're even. Now I don't have to go to bed with you, not even in China."

I could barely make out the pale oval of her face or the white fabric covering her shoulders. I renewed my grip on her arm, afraid if I let go her slim form would be flung back into the ferry's path. "You okay?" The grinding noise of the ferry's engines seemed to take my words and shred them into the night.

"Fine. What about you?"

"My nervous system works, but my shoulder hurts like hell. That'll be my handicap; I'll race you to the Battery. That crazy shithead probably saw us dive—we gotta get out of here."

"I've got a handicap, too."

"What?"

The white shape of her arm shot out of the water. She raised the Tupperware cylinder above her head. "A fortune in art." She laughed.

My nervous system checked in by giving me a nasty stab of butterflies in my stomach. "Jesus, not so loud. Don't gloat yet—let's get that pretty picture to dry land."

"Not to mention our butts," she said, close to my ear.

I thought I heard voices on the ferry and a siren in the far distance as we struck out toward the open water—the distinctive deep and reverberating siren of the harbor patrol. We steered by the distant lights shining across the Hudson from the Jersey shore, away from the bleak and jagged indistinctness of the shadows where the water met the artificial shore of Manhattan, away from the rusted, crusted things that jutted out into the water, away from the action of the harbor against the hem of the island. We rounded the tip of Manhattan powered by clumsy breaststrokes. I wasn't sure where we were, because the Manhattan shore was so dark and it was difficult to sort the blackness into reference points from the water, but we finally clawed our way up the slick cement walls of the Battery.

We rested there for a minute, on our hands and knees, dripping and breathing. We got to our feet and staggered to the grass, where we collapsed.

I raised myself on my elbow, winced at the pain in my shoulder, and scanned the big, open park. Battery Park has few trees and nowhere to hide. We were alone.

Ike's eyes were closed. Mine weren't. Her wet bodysuit might as well have been made out of cellophane.

"When you save a person's life after they've saved yours," I said, taking a deep breath and leaning over Ike, dripping on her, smoothing a lock of wet hair out of her eyes with my hand, "you're obligated to go to bed with them. That's a little-known Chinese proverb. You've left me no choice."

I didn't care if she slapped me or wounded me with stinging words. I touched her.

She shivered. Her arms came up to encircle my neck. "Abby, I never told you. Being frightened turns me on. Isn't that bizarre? You should have seen me in the Negev. There I was, crawling across the wilderness in the dark, and I was thinking what it would be like to be a snake in heat."

"I wish I had seen you. Are you turned on now?"

"Yeah." Her eyes sparkled with crazy fire. "Let's do it."

"Here?"

She nodded. "Here."

"Now?"

She nodded. "Now."

"Since when have you become so totally abandoned? Somebody might see us."

"I hope everyone in New Jersey has high-powered telescopes trained on us right now." She rolled over against my chest, her clothes cold and clammy, but her flesh warm beneath them. "I'm a divorced woman. I can be as abandoned as I like."

It wasn't what I had pictured in my sad and lonely afternoons, spent in my cell of an apartment, since the divorce. No soft music or fragrant breezes, no palm trees, no whatever. Just a willing and intensely cooperative Ike, who was evidently as hungry as I was for solace and warmth and the security of closeness. At least, she was hungry for something—all those months, if I'd only known about the fright factor, I would have arranged for plenty of shit to scare the daylights out of her. How hard can that be in New York? Who needs the Holy Land?

In the black shadows of Battery Park, New York's dark
and empty Financial District hulking as the unromantic
backdrop to a soggy pair of badly frightened people, the
summer air touched with diesel fumes from the harbor at the
foot of Manhattan, the Statue of Liberty's torch twinkling
at the horizon of my line of sight, the scratch on my shoulder throbbing and sending sparks and needles of awareness
down my left arm in a shower of intimate reminders that we
might still be in danger, I made love to my ex-wife.

I hope the nosy people in New Jersey who were watching
us through their telescopes got an eyeful. Frankly, I like to
think that if they gave out trophies for such crude behavior
as fornicating in Battery Park, we'd have owned another
hunk of pewter to fight over. And if I ever talked to tourists, which I try not to do because I'm the sort of New
Yorker who only confuses them, I'd recommend sex in the
park at night after a terrifying leap into the filthy, stinking
harbor.

Breathless, warm, and happy, I was tenderly buttoning
Ike's shorts when she said, "I have to call Dennis."

I felt like somebody had slugged me behind the ear. I
blinked and shook my head.

"What?" I shook my head again. I stared at her. "Why?
Does Dennis require you to make full reports?" I gripped
her waistband and tugged, hard. "What the hell kind of
thing was that to say? How can you utter another man's
name when we've just coupled ferociously in a public
park?"

She fixed her lovely eyes on a tree limb above us and
seemed to be contemplating life, her face was so thoughtful. "You know, Abagnarro, I like this jealous side of you.
I'm going to cultivate it. Divorce may be the making of us."

"I hate being divorced." I tugged at her shorts again,
slipping my hand inside along her waist. "I liked it better
when I had rights."

"Well, that's just too bad, because I like it this way." Her
hand came around my wrist and pulled.

"Jesus." I lay back on the thin grass, staring up at the
black limbs and black branches of the scrawny tree over-

head, its black skeleton a grim shadow on the throat of night. "What's to like?"

"For one thing, you've stopped taking me for granted."

"I never took you for granted."

"Yes, you did. Plus I have more free time, without you underfoot. I can devote myself to my craft."

"Which craft is that?"

"Acting, you dope. The other things I do are not crafts. They're more like tire changing—skills. Useful skills, but merely skills nonetheless."

My shoulder was numb. My thoughts were numb. *Let her call Dennis,* I thought. I searched in my pockets, trying to oblige with some coins but coming up empty, as usual. "I hope you have a quarter," I said. "Next time you screw somebody, you'll have to bring change. I'm temporarily out of funds for calls to NYPD captains."

"Oh, I'll just call 911," she said breezily, "and have them patch me through to his home number." She sat up and reached for the Tupperware.

"You have his home number?"

"Certainly. If all I got out of buying him lunch was the pleasure of watching him drink anisette, I'd have been wasting Othello's money." She popped off the Tupperware lid and slid the painting out with tender care. "God, I wish I owned stock in Tupperware. This stuff is awesome." She spread the painting open, and even with the mask of the imitation Dalí partially in place, in the darkness the Samantha Harris painting looked . . . well, I'd better skip artistic hyperbole. I'll just say it looked dry.

"I thought you said *Dennis* made a pass at you. That sounds like you got something besides his phone number."

"Don't be so crude, Abby. Just because someone makes a pass doesn't mean you have to let them have their wicked way, like a *prastitutka.*" She waved the painting at me. "At least, that is," she seemed to correct herself, "I haven't let him have his wicked way *yet.*"

"Well, what are you calling the captain for then? Is it time to make an appointment for his wicked way?"

She was rolling the painting again as she had done on the ferry, this time into a tighter, neater coil, and she shot me a look. "No. I'm calling so he can execute the search warrant for Noel's apartment."

"I don't think it's all that easy to get a search warrant, Ike, especially at this time of night." I held my arm up against the outline of the skeletal tree and glanced at my watch. It was 11:23.

"Oh, Dennis already has a warrant. We had lunch this afternoon before I went to the St. James, and I told him to get one, just in case."

I decided not to react to their second lunch, not even to ask who had paid. "Come on, Ike. You didn't know then that Noel was the killer. You don't know it now."

She crammed the lid on the Tupperware and burped it. "I didn't *know*, but I thought it might be." She started grooming her wet hair with her fingers. "Think about it. It had to be someone from the captain's eleven-minute list."

"Or Othello—he has keys to the loading dock door. What you might call total access."

"Or Othello," she agreed. "Well, just look at the list. I crossed everyone off one by one." Ike was enjoying herself. Exercising her tire-changing skills. "Let's start with Hannah," she said, "because she's so easy. It wasn't her because of the smoke."

I grunted.

She proceeded to her next item. "And it wasn't Satan Brown."

"How'd you figure that? Oh. Because he was in Boston when someone accessorized my skate with chemical brakes."

She nodded, working her fingers through her hair, separating it into strands. "That made it obvious, but I was pretty sure even before he went to Boston. The killer had to be somebody that knew about makeup and our setup in the studio, because the lights over the aquarium were so carefully arranged, which had to be done quickly—you'd have to know where the lights are, and which switches do what, to accomplish that without taking time out to locate them.

And then, as you said, when Satan Brown was in Boston when your skate was rigged, that clinched it."

I hadn't thought about the lights like that. "Okay. It wasn't Brown. Thank goodness. He's the best drummer since Buddy Rich."

"Who's Buddy Rich?"

I sighed. The things we don't have in common. "Never mind. Go on."

"Let me see. Oh, yes. It couldn't have been Lourdes Ramirez."

"Why not?" I asked, thinking of the young Mexican's fiery temper. The little tyrant seemed capable of murder to me, and she knew Studio 57.

"Because of the nerve gas. I don't believe Lourdes Ramirez knows diddly about chemwar." Ike started braiding her wet hair. "And also, there was the note on Connie's finger. Lourdes is so excitable, she couldn't possibly have had it together enough after killing Connie to write perfect English. Even when she's lucid, her English is terrible. You must know that, Abby. You've been writing her notes in Spanish."

Yep, I thought, *I'm a dope. Yo soy un hombre estúpido.* I eyed Ike's wet bodysuit. *Desvístase, por favor.* Pain was returning to wake up my numbed shoulder. *Me duele.* "Okay."

"And it couldn't have been Othello."

"Wait a minute. Why not? He could have used his key to come in the back way. And he knows all about makeup and the light switches and all the other stuff."

"True, but Othello wouldn't screw with his own bottom line. Hannah pointed out the fact that NTB stock took a dive after the murder. Everyone knows what a tightwad Othello is. He's got barking killer dogs chained to his wallet. Just think about it: He only okayed the new promotional campaign after thirty years of producers whining at him about ratings. He hates to spend money, and he hates to lose money. He wouldn't kill the woman he'd invested that much money in. Othello would find a more cost-effective way to make sure she got what was coming to her, whatever he thought that was—like giving her squat jobs on the weekend news. That was my thinking this afternoon, but now that I know about the painting, I know it couldn't have been Othello. He wouldn't steal the painting.''

I nodded. ''Because he already owns it.''

''That's right. But even before I knew about the painting, that left you and Fred Loring and Noel.''

''So?''

''On Fred, I took a wild guess, but I based my guess on the fact that he's a graphics freak. You know how graphics-consumed those people are—they even have their own language. They eat, breathe, and sleep with graphics. So, the last thing Fred Loring would put on Connie Candela would be an apple green jacket. Graphic artists shudder at the very sight of green. They're allergic to that color. It's their precious weather graphics that get whacked in the presence of chromakey-unfriendly clothing.'' Ike's hair was sleek, neatly pulled into a wet braid. She twisted the end into a knot to hold it. ''So that left you and Noel.''

''And you ruled me out because I'm such a nice guy?''

''Don't be silly. I ruled you out because I knew what you'd been doing all night while the murderer was busy.''

''How'd you know? How could you possibly know?''

''Simple. You always sleep like a log after a dance contest. If you didn't spend the night on your couch, I'm the mayor of Medicine Lodge, Kansas. Besides, you were still yawning when you came into the control room. I heard you when you were dangling over my shoulder.''

''I didn't think you even knew I was there.''

''I knew.''

She stood and offered me her hand. She helped me stand, even going so far as to slide her arm around my waist. I put my arm across her shoulders.

''Think they saw anything worthwhile in their telescopes?'' I asked, waving my wounded arm stiffly at the Jersey shore.

She smiled up at me. ''If they didn't, it wasn't your fault. I must say, Mr. Abagnarro, you even tango extremely well dripping wet in Battery Park and with a wounded arm. We'll have to do this again sometime. It was fun.''

It was fun. Gee.

We walked to a phone booth at the edge of the park near the water.

I brooded, leaning against the booth while she called 911. She had said it was fun. I had poured heart and soul into making love to Ike, and she thought it was *fun?*

"Dennis?...Hi. This is Mary." I watched her through the Plexiglas windshield of the booth. "Can you meet me at Noel Heavener's apartment?" There was a pause. "Oh, you heard already. Well, I can't explain it all now. I'm sort of indisposed. But we jumped over the side of the boat when we saw the canister." She listened, holding the phone slightly away from her ear. I could hear Fillingeri's voice from where I stood next to the booth, but I couldn't make out the words. He spoke for a few minutes, and then Ike said, "Thank God for that, Dennis." She slung the phone against her shoulder and consulted her watch. "Half an hour? Okay." Another pause. "Oh, can you send a car to Battery Park?" She tapped her fingers on the Plexiglas. "Good. Okay, I'll see you soon, Umberto." She cradled the phone on its hook.

"Umberto?"

She smirked. "Just a little nickname."

"What business do you have giving that anti-media goon a nickname? Umberto?"

She patted my arm. "Mind your own business."

"What'd he tell you about the ferry?"

"The Bomb Disposal Unit just got there. Nobody's dead, although one crew member who was working the forward deck has been taken to the hospital; the canister rolled off the deck into the water, but the sick guy saw it and recognized what it was before it rolled, like we did. He apparently recognized it from the pictures he saw on CNN today of the NTB canister. He was farther from it than we were, apparently, and he said he saw a dark gray cloud rising from the canister before the wind whipped the gas into shreds. He shouted a warning, and the ferry reversed its engines. Dennis said that's an almost automatic procedure. The canister's still floating in the harbor—hissing. They're shining lights on it, to keep it in sight. The Coast Guard and the New York Harbor Patrol are setting up a perimeter in the water to keep traffic away. That's all Dennis knew. Saddler called him because he thought it might be related to the NTB murder. Dennis said you don't often get two canisters of nerve gas in one day in Manhattan.'' She patted my arm again. ''New York may be one screwed-up city, but not *that* screwed up.''

We only had to wait five minutes for the car, and it turned out to be a measly yellow cab. If the driver had not been dispatched by the NYPD, I was thinking, he wouldn't have stopped for us. We had to have looked like ugly customers, with my nicked shoulder and naked torso and our wet clothes and maybe the look on my face. Fun. Umberto.

Ike opened the door and motioned to me to enter the cab first.

''Couldn't Dennis send a cop car?'' I asked, still sulking.

''He probably doesn't want his attentions to my personal comfort to appear too marked.'' She gave me a stoic smile.

I ground my teeth and got in. I slid over to make room for Ike on the backseat. She followed me, told the driver to take us to Park Avenue and 51st, and slammed the door.

This driver was a cowboy, and he hit the gas with the frolicsome macho enthusiasm of a stallion let loose on the stud farm, taking us back past the Staten Island Ferry Terminal and up onto the elevated highway that sweeps the eastern side of Manhattan's broad tip. From there we could see the string of bobbing lights forming a semicircle in the harbor around the ferry terminal.

We headed north, and, as we tore up the FDR Drive, we did our part to send Manhattan's worn infrastructure crumbling back into the Dark Ages. The taxi complained all the way, howling out some grinding noise from its engine, but our driver never let up, and we passed the United Nations at such rattling speed that I didn't even have time to picture Hannah Van Stone pounding a beat outside the General Assembly Building.

By the time we screeched to a shuddering halt in front of the ornate, solid, and heavy bulk of Saint Bartholomew's, my shoulder felt like it should be screaming as loud as the cab's engine problem, and that was just from the *new* bruises. We climbed out of the cab and started toward the east.

"Hey!" the driver shouted. "You just had the ride of your lives. Who's gonna pay?"

Ike turned around, opened the front passenger door, and leaned into the cab. "The New York City Police are paying. Didn't anybody tell you?"

"Come on, lady. You can't tell me a story I haven't already heard a thousand times. Just pay like a good girl and I'll be on my way home. It's been a long day."

"I'm serious. The police dispatched this cab."

"No way. I don't even have a radio."

Ike glanced quickly at the dashboard. I leaned against the cab to see what she would do. There was no radio. It was a gypsy cab.

"I guess we got in the wrong car," she said, offering the cowboy a weak, twisted smile and backing out onto the sidewalk.

"I guess you still gotta pay," he said, not smiling. "What is this?"

Our backpacks, meaning all of Ike's money, were still on the ferry.

She turned to me. "You don't have any money, do you?"

"Not a cent."

"Jesus, Abby! Just once I wish you'd learn to plan for things."

My mouth fell open. "You wanted me to plan to take a cab to Saint Bartholomew's Church, just before midnight, having taken a dip in the harbor, wearing practically nothing but my skin, after a rousing royal screw in Battery Park—and still have money to pay the cab off? I suppose you think I should also have exact change!"

The driver opened his door and came around to confront us on the sidewalk. "I don't care who got screwed as long as it's not me." He stuck out a meaty hand. "Come on; it's late."

I sighed and, for the second time that day caught without cash in a real emergency, fished my wallet out of my shorts and flipped it open. It was soggy, and the folds were stuck together. I pinched the green plastic from the sticky center slot. "Do you take American Express?"

TWENTY-FIVE

THE COWBOY SNATCHED my Amex card, trotted back to his open door, jumped in, and put down some serious rubber on Park Avenue.

Ike started hopping up and down on the pavement as the cab roared away past the elegant banks of flowers and shrubs in the center divider of Park. "Are you *nuts?*" she screamed. "What'd you do that for?" She flung a fist in the air. "I swear, Abby, you'll never understand money!"

"Well, I got rid of him, didn't I?"

"Oh, just wait until you get your next bill; that's all I can say."

With some difficulty, I reached for one of her flailing elbows. "Ike, it's just a thing. A little green plastic thing. I'll report it stolen from the next phone I see. The most it will cost me is fifty dollars. This has still been a cheap date, all things considered."

She yanked her elbow out of my grasp and marched down 51st toward Lexington, talking to herself and flinging her hands around, one of them gripped tightly around the Tupperware cylinder.

I caught up with her at the corner. Across Lexington on the north corner was East Rock, Noel's building, a modern glass-and-marble tower of apartment homes: sixty stories of fairy-tale dwellings, the cheapest of which (a two-bedroom flat with a view of Brooklyn, only suitable for your butler) probably sold for 2 million bucks.

That is a very nice address, and not just because it's across Lexington from the corner where Ike and I were standing, the very corner that boasts the very subway vent that breathed the very gust of steamy air that lifted Marilyn Monroe's skirt in that very famous scene from *The Seven Year Itch*. I'd never been inside Noel's apartment, but I've been in a couple of other apartments in the building, mostly when I was visiting my butler friends. Nice address. Very nice. Very. Nice.

Noel never gave parties or had people over for dinner or, for all I knew, had a butler. Noel had been a recluse for years, and I hadn't even heard any rumors about the wonders of his sixtieth-floor penthouse. Usually we find out everything we can about the lifestyles of our rich and famous anchors, but Noel's life and abode had resisted our prying, mainly because when we were so frustrated, so driven against the ropes of our curiosity that we'd actually sink to asking him a direct question, he'd just look confused and say something completely irrelevant, something like, "Well, my place is very clean." That wasn't the kind of factoid to build a legend around. Cleanliness is a blank, especially when what you're after is dirt.

There were three cop cars and an NYPD van parked on the street, their bubble gum machines revolving and emitting arcs of light. The building's doorman, who was about nine feet tall and dressed in a gray morning coat and shako, looked dignified and uninterested in whatever trashy, low-life thing the cops thought they were doing in his neighborhood.

Fillingeri and Saddler were standing beside one of the cars, Fillingeri talking into a phone. Ike waved, and he responded with a tight wave of his own. He leaned into the car to replace the phone.

Ike started to cross the street, but I put out my arm.

"Wait," I said. "Your suit's still damp, your nipples are showing, and the light's against us. I wouldn't want you to get a ticket. Two tickets—flaunting and jaywalking."

She snorted and jogged across Lexington, dodging cars like a native New Yorker, which means carving out the path you happen to feel like and assuming the cars will get out of your way.

Having taken a stand, I waited primly for the light. I watched as Fillingeri came around his car to meet Ike, eyeing her bodysuit and touching her elbow in a familiar way and leaning close to her while he listened to something she was saying. When the light changed, I strolled across the street.

"You mind stepping on it, Abagnarro?" Fillingeri snapped. "We've got a crazy man on the loose with nerve gas. Maybe you hadn't heard."

I waved my arm negligently. "Please don't wait for me. I wouldn't be any use as backup anyway."

"I can tell that by looking at you," he sneered, running his eyes scornfully over my chest.

"Oh, well," I replied airily, "I'm sure I pay you too much money for you to require any assistance from an innocent civilian like me to do your job."

He cracked a laugh. "That's for sure." He eyed my chest again. "I don't know what got into me, Abagnarro, thinking you might have been a killer. Your kind hasn't got the nerve."

"You ought to be grateful for that, Captain."

He narrowed his eyes at me, clearly not sure what to make of what I'd said. "Maybe. But what I'd really be grateful for is if you'd give me a good reason to act on this warrant." He took a folded paper from his shirt pocket and slapped it against his palm. "What's the story?"

Ike rattled off her conclusion about Noel's necktie on the morning of Connie's death. Fillingeri watched her in what was impatient and obviously growing exasperation, Saddler with quiet thoughtfulness.

When she finished, Fillingeri said, "You want me to invade this guy's fancy home and search through his golden Cheerios and diamond pillowcases for nerve gas—let me get this straight—because he wore the wrong tie?"

Ike stamped her foot. "Did you listen to me? Noel's the only one who could have, would have, done it. If you don't search his place, you may never get the evidence. He's got nerve gas, Dennis!"

Saddler stepped forward. "You have good reason to believe there's nerve gas in that apartment?"

"Yes."

"Can I consider this a civilian distress call?"

Ike eyed Saddler in dawning admiration. "Yes. You bet. I'm distressing like mad."

"Somebody told you there was nerve gas in there?"

"Yes," Ike lied.

Saddler directed a keen, clear look at Ike's eyes. "The Bomb Disposal Unit doesn't need a warrant," he said. "Not when the public safety is at stake." He signaled to the police van by raising a big hand, and immediately four guys in T-shirts and jeans jumped out and joined us on the sidewalk. Since they already knew that any gas they found would be the nerve variety, they weren't wearing the kind of suits that the bomb disposers had worn to the Emerald City, when, for all they knew, they could have been up against mustard gas or some other chemical toxin. These guys knew what kind of agent Noel specialized in, and for nerve gas the only protection is atropine.

"Let's go," Saddler said curtly.

Ike tossed Fillingeri a look that said he was a cowardly and utterly unimaginative worm, and that the disappointed committee had unanimously voted to revoke his overly generous privileges at the worm farm, and that he shouldn't dare to dream of reapplying for membership even in that low brotherhood. She grabbed my hand, which I thought— when I saw the look on Fillingeri's face—was *fun*.

We followed Saddler into the building's black-and-white Art Deco lobby, where he dealt with the looming and censorious doorman according to the enviable methods of the NYPD. In some situations, an NYPD shield is worth much more than an American Express card.

When the doorman had returned to his post, Saddler took Ike and me aside in the lobby, slipping two atropine autoinjectors from a small leather bag slung over his shoulder.

"You both know how and when to use these, right?" he asked. "You've been trained, right?"

I nodded, taking one from his hand. Ike reached for the other one. Apparently, Fillingeri had already been given his, with instructions for use suitable to a captain.

"If you shoot this shit without being exposed to the counteragent, meaning nerve gas," Saddler warned us, "you may die. I hope you're not trigger-happy."

I hoped I wasn't, too.

Saddler commandeered two elevators. We rode up to the penthouse with him and Fillingeri, the bomb-disposing troops taking the other car.

The elevator doors opened onto a glass-domed hall that was bigger than but not as pretty as the Flower Rotunda. Very few stars are ever visible through Manhattan's haze and pollution, so the dome just looked black, in keeping with the building's color scheme. A set of black double doors opposite the elevator was flanked by long, low black tables on which were positioned forests of tropical plants.

Our two groups gathered in the elegant little domed foyer, eight people carrying what could be deadly substances that they themselves might administer to their own systems. The foyer would be a perfect environment for nerve gas to work at maximum efficiency. It was enclosed and the temperature was on the cool side—just the kind of conditions that the manufacturers of nerve gas dream about when they're designing their brochures.

The black double doors were opened suddenly and silently from within, and Noel stood there, in a sport shirt, slacks, and bare feet. He looked sad and myopic. In that startled moment, I noticed that one of his eyes was a lighter brown than the other, and I deduced that he had lost a contact lens—before I saw the little canister in his hand. This canister had a spray nozzle, and Noel's finger twitched and hovered over it.

Almost simultaneously I caught the nearly inaudible swishes and light rustling of clothing as eight people moved to draw their atropine autoinjectors into position, ready to shoot themselves if Noel moved the hand that held the nerve gas.

Noel took a step forward, toward us.

From the straining perspective of my peripheral vision, I saw Ike lower the autoinjector over her forearm.

"Don't!" I managed to gasp out, my heart turning over sickeningly in my chest. "The canister's empty."

I was seeing Noel's canister from the side, and I could tell that the nozzle was bent. It was a used container.

Noel shook his head, apparently surprised to hear my voice. "You won't be needing those things," he said mournfully, pointing at the autoinjectors in our hands with the hand that held the canister. "Abby's right. I haven't got any bad juice left."

Bad juice. So that's how he thought of it.

But nobody moved immediately to put their needles away. Saddler stepped out of the group and approached Noel slowly. A large, firm black hand covered the trembling white hand, and Saddler had the canister. With his autoinjector held ready in his left hand, he lifted the aluminum container with his right, holding it up to the recessed lights under the dome and studying it. He shook the canister. Since nerve gas, when it's still in the can, is liquid, shaking the thing probably gave Saddler all the information he needed. Of course, the problem is, when you need that kind of information, it takes real guts to shake a can of nerve gas.

"Abagnarro," Saddler said, "you've got good eyes."

Everyone breathed at once.

Fillingeri stepped forward, his laminated *Miranda* card in his hand, not taking any chances that this moment would be lost when Noel got around to hiring an expensive lawyer. In a weirdly unemotional, low-voiced monotone, Fillingeri read Noel his rights. When he was finished, Fillingeri barely paused before launching into a question to make Noel's admission official and admissible in court. "Heavener, are you saying you've already used nerve gas today?" It may have been my imagination, but I thought Fillingeri's voice shook a little when he left the *Miranda* script and had to invent his own lines.

Noel nodded. "I'm really sorry. It was all I could think of to do."

"Where'd you get it?"

"In the Holy Land." His lip quivered, and I thought he was going to cry. "Isn't that sad? The Holy Land?"

"It wasn't too sad for you to bring it back to the United States, was it?"

Noel gazed at Fillingeri in what appeared to be genuine horror. "Oh, I never meant to use it. I just found it so sad, and fascinating, that such stuff would come from the Holy Land." Noel blinked, on the edge of tears. "Where little Jesus was born. The Holy Land. It's the only time I ever brought home a news souvenir."

"Yeah, it's sad," Fillingeri said. He wasn't wasting any sympathy on Noel's social or religious insights. "Was it sad when you killed Concepción Candela?"

Noel kept his eyes on Fillingeri, avoiding looking at Ike and me, turning his shoulder slightly and seeming to shrink into his shirt. I wanted to avoid looking at Noel, because he was so pathetic, but I couldn't take my eyes off him.

"No, it wasn't sad exactly," he said, still in command of his wonderful, deep TV voice even when he had lost the rest of his physical presence, "but I don't want you to think I meant to kill her. Everything just happened so quickly that I couldn't *think*. She was threatening me, saying she'd have the show all to herself. She was going to tell Othello about her portrait." He held out his empty hands, turning the palms up, in a peculiar expression of fatalism. "And then Othello would have found out everything. What else could I do? I'm not going to lose my job because of a tramp like her. It wouldn't have been so bad if it had been Hannah threatening me, because at least she's a decent woman."

Noel's reasoning was too twisted for me, but I could tell that Ike had gotten his point.

"Noel," she said softly, "you actually care for Hannah, don't you?"

"Certainly. Why, we've been together most of our adult lives. We're the same, Hannah and me. I hated it when she was kicked off the show. But I didn't kill Connie for taking Hannah's job. I killed her because she was going to take *my* job." Noel tried then to focus on both Ike and me, and I moved closer to her side to make it easier for him. "I love my work," he said.

Fillingeri seemed at a loss. He flapped his hands at his sides for a couple of seconds in the dead silence that followed Noel's bald and simple confession. He took a step back and said, "Where's your phone, Heavener?"

Noel waved toward the interior of the penthouse. "Please. Help yourself. It's in the kitchen."

Fillingeri circled around Noel and disappeared inside, accompanied, at a gesture from Saddler, by the bomb disposers.

Noel looked at Ike and me again, and then he seemed to notice my shoulder. "It broke my heart to attack you sweet kids. But, you see, you would have made me give up my job, too. I belong on the air, and I had to try to stay there." He wiped a hand across his eyes, and then I did look away. "I can't do anything else, you know."

Ike bit her lip. She hesitated a second or two, but she ignored the pleading, defensive look on Noel's face and said, "Noel, I have to know. Did you figure it out yourself that Connie would drown if you gave her water? You did give her water, didn't you?"

"I thought she'd die, but easier, softer. She was gasping, and she couldn't breathe. She was all bent over a yellow cab upstairs. There was a water fountain. I thought it would help her get through the terrible ordeal of the atropine. Ike, it was worse than what we saw in the training films in Israel."

"I'm sure it was." Ike looked sick. Maybe Noel didn't realize that they didn't actually kill people to make those chemwar training films. Maybe he thought he had been watching actuality, a piece of footage.

Saddler clasped Noel's elbow, gently but with authority. "Let's go inside so you can put on some shoes."

Noel led the way into the last thing I would have expected of a penthouse in that building. The mammoth living room, with plate glass where most people have walls, commanded a magnificent view of the island—east, south, and west. But that view was the only orthodox thing about the room, if anything can be orthodox in an apartment that probably cost more than Noel made in a year. The only objects in the room were an empty easel, over by the west window, and a low-slung canvas stool and a tidy table with a jar of paintbrushes and a fresh, clean palette. The room was otherwise bare. No sectional sofa, no wet bar, no grand piano, no television, no nothing. The emptiness was stunning. I could have done cartwheels across the room without fear of breaking a thing except my own bones.

Saddler followed Noel as he trudged across the thick gray carpet on his bare feet. They left by another door in the north wall.

Ike and I wandered around and finally found Fillingeri, several acres of carpeting later, in Noel's kitchen using a white and ordinary wall phone. I'd have thought an anchorman would at least have a speakerphone.

What I could gather from Fillingeri's part of the conversation suggested that he was on a conference call with the police commissioner and Othello Armitage. That chain of command struck me as odd, but maybe the NYPD was angling for some strokes from the media, or maybe the media was angling for some strokes from the NYPD. I could almost hear the mutual hand washing coming from the line. Othello must have decided that he could not trust his staff to control the spin on his most senior anchor's arrest. It occurred to me that Fillingeri might have to revise his opinion of the media after getting a feel for Othello's hand on the helm, only I wouldn't have put a nickel on which direction Fillingeri's revision would go.

The kitchen was as devoid of personality as all the rooms. There were cupboards and built-in counters, but nothing that Noel could have added himself, not even a box of golden Cheerios. It was empty, impersonal, worse than his office. Ike and I passed Fillingeri as we went through into the next room.

Ike found a light switch, flipped it up, and the room was bathed in a warm and luxurious silken white radiance—and on the walls of the room, which was innocent of any other furnishings, was a line of portraits that were more than familiar to me.

I heard Ike gasp. "Abby. My God. They're all here. Noel took every blasted portrait over the years. Even the dog. It's a broadcasting museum."

"It sure is," I said. "And look whose portrait has its own wall."

She spun around. On the north wall, in lonely state, was the thirty-year-old portrait of Noel Heavener. He hadn't changed that much in thirty years, if the Samantha Harris portrait had captured the younger Noel with anything like accuracy. The same round face, the same brown eyes, the same unlined face, untroubled by self-doubt or uncertainty or, perhaps, much concern for others, for all the problems of the world he'd been reporting over the years. Thirty years, and nothing had gotten to him until he encountered nerve gas in the Holy Land, at least, not until his job was threatened. And here was his shrine to his job: just Noel, alone on one of the walls, the serene expression on his face showing that he was maybe thinking about what a great job he had. And, I thought, that was undoubtedly the first portrait he stole, the one that gave him the idea.

I sat down on the carpet, my right elbow on my knee, my left arm stretched so I could rest my hand on the thick pile of the carpet, where I could see the deep strokes left by a recent vacuuming. I pictured Noel vacuuming his private museum, and I thought about him swiping these pictures over the years, taking each one as it was entered in the NTB gallery, replacing it—with what? Who had painted the portraits I saw every day I went to work? Did Noel study the Samantha Harris portraits during the overnight and then come home to his empty nest and reproduce them from memory? Did he frame the fakes himself? Had he made the earlier switches simply and directly, during the overnight shift? And why had Noel taken the originals home to live with him? If it was for the monetary value of the paintings, it almost made sense. He had cornered the market on Samantha Harris's only realistic work.

But I thought Noel's project went deeper even than greed, deep down into the well of the most narcissistic ego I had ever encountered: These images on the wall were Noel's company, his two-dimensional compatriots, his friends, his lovers. Himself.

Ike was by my side.

"I'm sorry, Abby. You need to get to a doctor. That little dent might fester or do some medical crap like that."

"I don't need any doctor. What I need is to get out of here. This place is so pitiful it makes me feel sick."

"Let's go."

We left the Noel Heavener Museum, turning out the light as we went.

When we returned to the kitchen, Fillingeri was just hanging up the phone. His hand was still on the receiver as we passed by, and Ike practically snatched it from his fingers. He stepped away, and she dialed the number for Control Room #1.

"Hi, it's Ike. I need you to send a crew to Noel's apartment. Tell them to wait downstairs with the doorman and get pictures and sound when the cops bring Noel out." She glanced at her watch. "And tell the radio desk that Noel has been arrested for Connie's murder. He confessed." Ike listened for a moment. "No way. I heard him with my own ears. They can quote me." She replaced the phone on its hook.

Fillingeri opened his mouth, like he thought he was going to object to Ike's high-handed management of his turf.

"Don't try to mess with Ike's press freedom right now, Umberto," I said. "She's not in the mood. She hates to be contradicted right after sex."

"I do not," she said indignantly. Then she blushed. "That was really low, Abby."

Fillingeri's brow seemed to contract as his eyes widened, and it looked like he was going to say something as soon as he could decide what that something was, but Ike didn't give him time to let his cerebral machinery grind out whatever response he was working on.

"Listen, Dennis," she said, "my crew will be in place in a few minutes. They have nothing to do with you."

Fillingeri cleared his throat. "But, just now," he said, "Mr. Armitage said he didn't want any cameras...."

"Never mind Othello." Ike wasn't having any helpful hints from Captain Worm. "I'm not taking any orders relayed through a police flunky. If Othello Armitage has any orders for me, he can tell me himself. And if you rat on me, Dennis, I'll tell Othello you got the message wrong. It won't be my neck if you screw me on this."

"Or at all," I offered, wishing I had the kind of muscles that ripple menacingly. Still, I thought, taking Ike's hand and steering her from the kitchen, there's something to be said for tango muscles, as I had reason to believe the good citizens of coastal New Jersey had learned through their telescopes that night.

When we reached the living room, with its uncanny view, Noel and Saddler were standing over by the south window. Noel had put a pair of loafers on.

Saddler came to meet us halfway.

"He says he painted those pictures that are now hanging in the Emerald City. They're all fakes."

"I know," Ike said quietly. "We just saw the originals."

Saddler raised his brows and shook his head. "Heavener keeps extra frames in one of his bedroom closets. Identical to the frames on the anchor portraits hanging in that hallway at the Emerald City." He shook his head again. "Frames. In a closet. Like they were clothes or something."

"They *are* clothes," I said. "High fashion for the only friends Noel has."

"Some friends. You know those prints Heavener has on the wall in his office at the network?"

"Yeah?"

"They're his own work. Horses and children, stuff like that. Even aside from his copies of the anchor portraits, Heavener kept himself busy. He'd bring in his latest ponies or whatever to hang behind his desk, to 'freshen up the place,' he said. And then he'd take the older pictures down from his walls and walk them upstairs to the soap opera set as gifts to the art director, already framed and everything. Heavener's paintings have been on afternoon TV a lot. Anything new showed up there in the soundstage, they always knew it was from Heavener. He escorted a whole lot of paintings in through that revolving door at the network over the years—and out the door.''

Ike made an impatient gesture with her hand. "Didn't Fillingeri ask anybody about that?''

Saddler spread his huge hands at his sides, flexing his fingers. "No reason to. Fillingeri wasn't looking for a painter; he was looking for a killer.''

I glanced over at Noel, who was staring forlornly out at the city through his empty penthouse's wall of windows.

"What made Connie's portrait different?'' I asked. "Why didn't Noel just do it neatly the way he did all the others?''

Saddler sighed. "He said he couldn't get his own version of the Candela portrait framed in time, something about the brass nameplate not being ready. He couldn't afford to wait to substitute his copy for the authentic portrait because that other anchorwoman had already trashed the studio, and he was afraid the Samantha Harris portrait of Candela would be the next target.''

Ike blinked. "I guess Hannah just didn't think of it. That would have been awesome revenge.'' She frowned. "No. Not even Hannah would vandalize a Samantha Harris.''

"I wouldn't know about that,'' Saddler said. "What I do know is that Heavener was afraid of both anchorwomen. Afraid the older one would ruin a valuable painting, afraid the younger one would get his job. And after he killed Candela, he was afraid to take the authentic painting out of the building, afraid he'd get caught finally. But you know what scared him most? He was so afraid of something happening to the Candela portrait that he did what he called 'a risky trick.' You want to know what he considers a risky trick?''

I nodded. Ike nodded. Over by the window, Noel just kept staring out at the city.

"A risky trick,'' Saddler said, "is covering an expensive oil painting with Saran Wrap and a cardboard picture—he says you have to protect the painting. Can't let anything bad happen to the precious brush strokes. Can't expose the poor, vulnerable painting to any harm. Thank God for Saran

Wrap, he said. Art thieves have been using plastic wrap since it was invented, he said." Saddler looked over his shoulder at our lonely anchorman. "If Heavener calls that a risky trick, I wonder what he calls murder."

Ike nodded slightly toward Noel and drew a deep breath. "Has he talked about Connie?"

"Enough. Just to say he brought her body down from the soap opera floor in one of those green hampers, dragged her into the studio, left her in the chair. Said he thought he could fix it to look like Hannah Van Stone had killed her, but he was sure Hannah had an alibi because she always smoked her brains out in her office at that hour. He said she was so addicted that it was an unbreakable habit. Basically, he thought he'd committed the perfect crime, and that he and all his friends would escape what he calls 'negative attention.' Said he didn't want anyone to get in trouble over what he did." Saddler shook his large head slowly. "He also said he couldn't resist returning to the studio when he saw Abagnarro go running in there Tuesday morning. He says Abagnarro has the best eye in the business, and if what Heavener had done to Candela could fool Abagnarro, it would fool everyone."

I was not overcome by Noel's flattery, well intentioned or not. "It fooled me," I said. "I guess my eye's not so terrific."

"Pish, posh," Ike said, "you were the one who got everyone started in the right direction. If you hadn't noticed her makeup, maybe we wouldn't have figured out the whole thing."

Saddler gave her a quick, solemn smile. "We might all be dead or damaged now from atropine if it hadn't been for Abagnarro's eyes. I'll take that over solving a murder any day. Cases-solved statistics don't impress me. Survival numbers do."

We left without saying good-bye to Noel. Or Umberto Fillingeri.

At the street, the doorman wanted to hail us a cab, probably to get the sleaze factor out of the neighborhood quickly, but we had no money. The fastidious doorman would not be happy, I thought, if he knew the kind of sleaze that was on its way over in an NTB truck to take his picture.

One of the bomb disposers offered us a ride in the van, and he took me home first. I showered and put a couple of Band-Aids on my shoulder and changed, wondering why I felt so sorry for Noel instead of feeling angry that he'd tried to kill me at least three times.

The staff of *Morning Watch* was subdued that night, but we got the show on. I don't think it gave Hannah any satisfaction to have the tables turned when she reported that Noel Heavener had been arrested for killing Connie. She didn't stumble, because Hannah never stumbles, but she didn't look like her usual granite-hearted self. In fairness to Hannah's massive self-absorption, though, maybe she was so glum only because the arrest news she was reading wasn't a scoop. It was used news—the NTB Radio Network had broken the story.

After the show, I called American Express to report that my card was missing. I thought about calling the All-Souls Cafe to make a different kind of report to John-the-Romanian, but I vetoed the impulse when I realized the bar wouldn't be open that early in the day. Besides, I didn't really want another plaque on the bar with my name on it.

I wasn't jaunty when I left my office and locked it and walked down the tube past the phony portraits. I didn't even have the energy to kick myself for pretending I had admired them for years.

When I left the elevator at the lobby, I could see Ike through the great sea green doors. She was out on the sidewalk, watching as tourists photographed the etched faces in the glass, one of which was Noel's. I guess he would have stolen the doors, too, if he could have figured out a way to sneak them home to his broadcasting morgue with the nice address. Very nice address.

I signed the logbook and went out through the revolving door.

We walked together to the corner of Columbus and 60th. The crowds are lively at 9:30 on a Thursday morning, and we were jostled as we stood there. To avoid unnecessary contact with the herd, you really have to keep moving.

"Abby, do you think Noel's crazy? I mean, certifiable?"

I sidestepped as a man dragging a little kid and a brief-case broke from the crowd to make the light.

"I don't know. What's crazy anyway? Who's to make that decision? It all depends on how you define crazy."

Ike shook her head unhappily. "The existential night-mare. Twentieth-century angst. Anything goes; there are no rules; every man for himself. I'm surprised at you, Abby. There have to be *some* absolutes, even when it comes to sanity."

"Didn't Connie's murder teach you anything, Ike? The whole thing completely depended on the fact that we see things the way we expect to see them, the way we already have them organized inside our heads. It's a trap to think that we know anything at all for sure. You nearly killed yourself with atropine because you thought Noel's nerve gas canister was full. You're the same way with the divorce. Once again, I can't help thinking of the three umpires—"

"Okay, okay. What's the deal on this story? You've been trying to tell me for three weeks." She crossed her arms and planted her feet against the flow of pedestrian traffic. "Well? I'm waiting."

"Here?" I gestured at the people massing around us on the sidewalk as they waited for the light to change. "Jeez, Ike, this story is about the entire history of philosophy."

"I thought you said it was about umpires."

"It is. It's both. It's about how people look at things."

"So get on with it. Right here. You brought it up."

"Well, it never occurred to me that you'd actually let me tell the sucker."

"I'm waiting, Abby."

The sun was warm. I shrugged my arms out of my jacket, slung it over my arm, and took a step back, accidently treading on someone's ankle.

"Watch it, buddy!" he snarled. "Are you blind?"

"As a matter of fact, I am," I said, turning slightly and groping the air.

He lowered his eyes, hunched his shoulders, and mumbled an apology.

I turned back to Ike.

"Well, you see," I said, "there was this ball player who'd been having a bad season. His batting average had sunk to .198, and he was getting a little desperate. He's down to the last three games of the season to raise his average above the .200 mark before management starts typing new contracts. So in the first of those games, he steps up to the plate.... Wait a minute, Ike. This works better if I act it out."

I handed her my jacket, unbuttoned my shirt cuffs, and pushed my sleeves up to my elbows.

I got into a batter's crouch, holding an imaginary bat over my shoulder and looking into the distance toward the pitcher.

"Is this really necessary?" Ike asked impatiently, stuffing my jacket over her arm.

I shifted my gaze to her face. "You'll see." I resumed my confrontation with the pitcher as the light changed and the crowd started to move. I felt a twinge in my sore shoulder as I twitched the bat in the air. "The first pitch comes in, and the batter just stands there. The umpire calls it a strike. The batter gives the ump a dirty look and sets himself again." I twitched the bat. "The second pitch comes in, and once again the guy just stands there. The umpire calls a strike. The guy mutters to himself, some guff about the umpire needing glasses." I kicked the dirt and tightened my stance. "The third pitch comes roaring in and the batter just stands there." I stood still, holding the bat. "The umpire calls it a strike and the batter throws his bat on the ground and confronts the umpire." I threw my bat on the ground. " 'What the hell's the matter with you?' the batter shouts. 'That was a ball all the way.' And the umpire says, *'Son, it was a strike and I called it a strike.'*"

Ike started tapping her foot on the sidewalk. "What's this got to do with philosophy?"

"That umpire was like that priceless Greek fart Plato," I said. "You know, like truth is something that never changes: It was a strike and he called it a strike, as if it couldn't possibly be anything else. He's like you, Ike. That's what I've been trying to tell you. My mistake in Moscow. You called it disloyalty, you called me a cad, you think I'm a monster, and you won't listen to anything else.''

''I thought there were three umpires,'' she said, a wary light in her eyes.

I resumed my crouch and twitched the bat. ''The next day there's a different umpire. The poor slob who's trying to work himself out of the slump gets up to the plate, and once again he's caught looking three times. When the second umpire calls the last pitch a strike, the batter throws his bat into the dirt and turns on the umpire.'' I threw my bat in the dirt. '''What the hell's the matter with you?' the batter shouts. 'That was a ball all the way.' And the umpire just gives him a look and says, *'Son, I've been doing this for twenty years, and I call 'em as I see 'em.'*''

Ike kept tapping her foot.

''Don't you see, Ike? The second umpire is a relativist. It wouldn't matter to him if he was blind in one eye. He thinks he sees the truth just because he's behind the plate.''

''Well?''

''That's my family. They all think I was a bastard to you because I didn't play by the Abagnarro code. That's the way they see things, have always seen things.''

''You *were* a bastard.''

I shook my head. ''You're still umpire number one.''

''What about the third umpire?'' she demanded, sweeping her arm in a large gesture that seemed to take in my length, from the sidewalk up. ''I suppose he's you?''

''Just listen.'' I got into my crouch and lifted the wood over my shoulder. A woman with a couple of shopping bags ducked and scurried around me. ''The last day, there's a third umpire. The player gets up to the plate and, once again, he lets the pitcher whiff him three times. On the last strike call, he tosses his bat into the backstop and goes after the umpire, shoving him and calling him names. The umpire ejects him from the game. Later, a sportswriter asks the umpire what the player's problem was. 'He didn't like that last strike call,' the umpire says, 'and the guy insisted that it was a ball all the way.' The umpire looks at the writer and says, 'But, son, how can that be? *The pitch ain't anything until I call it.'*"

Ike rolled her eyes.

"Don't you get it, Ike? The last umpire is an existentialist. Truth doesn't exist by itself. It's up to him to create it. He's the only umpire that took complete responsibility for the call."

"Like you, I suppose?"

I nodded. "Like me. That's what I've been trying to tell you. I'm responsible for my actions in Moscow. And I'm sorry—not because of what you thought, and not because of what my family thought, but because of what *I* thought. I created that reality, and I create the way I have to live with it. All I want from you is for you to hear me when I say I'm sorry. You never listened to me when I said that. You thought it was just something a guilty person says. But it's not. It's what a responsible person says." I let out a sigh. "I had a right to at least tell you how I felt."

She looked down at the sidewalk and then looked up at my face. "Say it, Abby. I'm listening now."

"I'm sorry."

I felt a hand on my sore shoulder and turned. An extremely tall woman in a severe navy blue business suit was standing there, evidently listening in.

"What do you want?" I asked. "This is a private conversation."

"I was just wondering if you were going to finish the umpires story. I've never heard a man tell it right."

"What do you mean? I *am* finished."

"No, you're not. You left out the best part."

"I did?"

"Yeah." She put her leather briefcase down on the sidewalk and pushed her sleeves up. "At spring training camp the next season, this batter's down in the farm leagues. It's his first at-bat of the year, and as he strides manfully up to the plate, he sees there's a woman wearing the umpire's uniform. He figures his luck can't get any worse, so he gets into his stance." The stranger assumed an elegant batting crouch, perched on her high heels. "The pitcher tosses in three pitches, and once again the batter is caught looking. At the last strike call, the batter turns on the umpire, who happens to be a radical feminist, and starts mouthing off, all about how she can't possibly be qualified to umpire the game because she's a woman. He calls her a dumb broad and starts yelling that the last pitch was a ball. She just gives him an icy look and says, 'Son, you've got an odd impression of this sport. When I call a game, the balls are *behind* the plate.'"

Ike laughed out loud.

The stranger picked up her briefcase, nodded to us, and walked away down Columbus.

"That's not the way I heard it!" I hollered after her.

Ike was still laughing. "Abby, that's what you get for thinking you know everything there is to know about the truth," she crowed.

But she faced me and took my hands in hers. She took a couple of steps toward me, and I could feel her belt buckle against my abdomen.

"No matter how you look at it—from Plato to Sartre to Steinem," she said, inching even closer to me, her silk shirt brushing my thigh and sending sparks of anticipation to whatever organ processes that sort of truth for me, "people need to sleep. There's an absolute for you."

I wrapped my arms around her. The sun had warmed her shoulders and back. "Let's go to my place," I whispered into her hair.

"No, let's go to mine."

"Your place has that obese cat that hates me. Seriously, Ike, The Donald really has it in for me. He'll just stick his whale of a lard-bottom out and—"

She stepped back from me as though she had suddenly detected a strange aroma. "You've got a warped point of view, Abagnarro. The Donald is not obese; he's—"

"Hold on a minute," I interrupted decisively. "That cat's undoubtedly, irrevocably, actually, and in every way, nothing but a two-ton orange hairball, no matter how you look at him."

I released one of her hands and she yanked the other one away. The light changed. She shoved my jacket at me. We crossed and started walking up Columbus. I kept trying to ask her whose place we were going to, but she was yapping about how insensitive I am, as we threaded our way through the crowds, and I knew she wasn't listening.

Oh well, I thought philosophically, as I dodged around a hot dog cart and nearly collided with a fragrant wino. *Maybe something will happen to frighten her. This is New York, after all.*

NIGHT SHADOWS
RON ELY

A Jake Sands Mystery

First Time in Paperback

SHOT IN THE DARK

Posh Santa Barbara offers everything money can buy, including solitude. Here Jake Sands, "recoverer" of missing things, can mourn his tragic past and ignore the future.

When Jake finds a murdered man in his own neighborhood, he covers his tracks and leaves the scene. But the case haunts him, as does a gorgeous woman with a missing husband. Then the two cases merge in deadly and unexpected ways.

In the night shadows, fools are easy to find and dupes are a dime a dozen, but Jake refuses to count himself among them—as long as he can remain alive.

"This first of a projected series of Jake Sands mysteries is simply a dazzler." —*Booklist*

Available in November at your favorite retail stores.

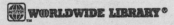

CRIMINALS ALWAYS HAVE SOMETHING TO HIDE—BUT THE ENJOYMENT YOU'LL GET OUT OF A WORLDWIDE MYSTERY NOVEL IS NO SECRET....

With Worldwide Mystery on the case, we've taken the mystery out of finding something good to read every month.

Worldwide Mystery is guaranteed to have suspense buffs and chill seekers of all persuasions in eager pursuit of each new exciting title!

Worldwide Mystery novels—crimes worth investigating...

Ripe for REVENGE

JANIE BOLITHO

An Inspector Ian Roper Mystery

First Time in Paperback

DEAD END

During the hot summer holidays, the quaint village of Little Endesley is rocked to its roots when the body of a young girl is found in the woods. Suspicion immediately falls on Jacko Penhaligon, a family man with an unfortunate history of child molestation.

But Detective Inspector Ian Roper reaches beyond the obvious. The absence of clues seems to indicate a random killing—a passerby who killed for unknown reasons. Some pornographic videos may or may not have any relevance, though they do offer a surprising star.

Ironically, some seemingly unconnected crimes provide Roper with the solution: a vendetta as old as tragedy—and a killer willing to wait until his victims are ripe for revenge.

"Bolitho convincingly demonstrates the far-reaching ramifications of crime and its investigations in a small, close community." —*Publishers Weekly*

Available in November at your favorite retail stores.

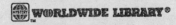

WORLDWIDE LIBRARY®

RIPE

THE IRON GLOVE

RONALD TIERNEY

First Time in Paperback

A Deets Shanahan Mystery

THE NAKED LADY WASN'T YOUR AVERAGE FLOATER

She was, in fact, Sally Holland, wife of Indiana senator David Holland, half of Washington's Golden Couple. Within hours, a suspect is arrested—a young Latino boxer believed to be her lover. Though not at all convinced the police have the wrong suspect, private investigator Deets Shanahan nevertheless agrees to do some digging for the defense.

Another dead body later, along with some answers that just seem too easy and pat for a P.I. who has been around long enough to know the difference, Shanahan dives into the dirty side of politics and the dark side of passion—and the hideous secrets a killer is desperate to hide....

"A series packed with angles and delights."

—*Publishers Weekly*

Available in December at your favorite retail stores.

PAINTED TRUTH

First Time in Paperback

LISE McCLENDON

An Alix Thorssen Mystery

THE ART OF ILLUSION

Art expert/gallery owner Alix Thorssen is called on to appraise the charred remains of a friend's local gallery...a tragedy doubled when the body of artist Ray Thornton is found among the debris.

The death is ruled a suicide, the fire, arson. Case closed. But not for Alix, who believes the body in the fire was not Thornton's.

As her investigation forces her to confront her own foibles and contradictions as an art lover, another murder plot puts her in the hot seat as prime suspect. She must race to find a killer who knows that while life may imitate art...death makes it all the more profitable.

"Will leave you gasping..." —*Kirkus Reviews*

Available in December at your favorite retail stores.